Reader reviews for

The Burnout

'A great mix of comedy, lovable, relatable
characters and a heart-warming story.'

'Exactly what I need when the world seems
upside down.'

'The ultimate in addictive, joyful, and
relatable comfort reading!'

'A great, feel-good Sophie Kinsella knock-out,
made me laugh more than I can remember
in a long time, absolutely loved it.'

'This book is perfect. I couldn't put it down.
The story and characters were brilliant.'

'So many poignant moments that made me feel
a swell of emotion or laugh out loud!'

'I finished this book with an emotional
calmness & 24 hours later I'm still in a cloud
of deliciousness . . . Wonderful book!'

'Sophie Kinsella at her very best.'

www.penguin.co.uk

Also by Sophie Kinsella

The Shopaholic Series

Starring the unforgettable Becky Bloomwood,
shopper extraordinaire . . .

The Secret Dreamworld of a Shopaholic
(also published as *Confessions of a Shopaholic*)

Meet Becky – a journalist who spends all her time
telling people how to manage money, and all her leisure
time spending it. But the letters from her bank manager
are getting harder to ignore. Can she ever escape this
dream world, find true love . . . and regain the use of
her credit card?

Shopaholic Abroad

Becky's life is peachy. Her balance is in the black –
well, nearly – and now her boyfriend has asked her
to move to New York with him. Can Becky keep the
man *and* the clothes when there's so much temptation
around every corner?

Shopaholic Ties the Knot

Becky finally has the perfect job, the perfect man and, at
last, the perfect wedding. Or rather, *weddings* . . . How
has Becky ended up with not one, but two big days?

Shopaholic & Sister

Becky has received some incredible news. She has a
long-lost sister! But how will she cope when she realizes
her sister is not a shopper . . . but a skinflint?

Shopaholic & Baby

Becky is pregnant! But being Becky, she decides to shop around – for a new, more expensive obstetrician – and unwittingly ends up employing Luke's ex-girlfriend! How will Becky make it through the longest nine months of her life?

Mini Shopaholic

Times are hard, so Becky's Cutting Back. She has the perfect idea: throw a budget-busting birthday party. But her daughter Minnie can turn the simplest event into chaos. Whose turn will it be to sit on the naughty step?

Shopaholic to the Stars

Becky is in Hollywood and her heart is set on a new career – she's going to be a stylist to the stars! But in between choosing clutch bags and chasing celebrities, Becky gets caught up in the whirlwind of Tinseltown. Has Becky gone too far this time?

Shopaholic to the Rescue

Becky is on a major rescue mission! Hollywood was full of surprises, and now she's on a road trip to Las Vegas to find out why her dad has mysteriously disappeared, help her best friend Suze and *maybe* even bond with Alicia Bitch Long-legs. She comes up with her biggest, boldest, most brilliant plan yet – can she save the day?

Christmas Shopaholic

Becky is hosting Christmas for the first time. With her sister Jess demanding a vegan turkey, Luke insistent that he just wants aftershave again, and little Minnie insisting on a very specific picnic hamper, will chaos ensue, or will Becky manage to bring comfort and joy at Christmas?

Wedding Night

Lottie is determined to get married. And Ben seems perfect – they'll iron out their little differences later. But their families have different plans . . .

My *Not So* Perfect Life

When Katie's ex-boss from hell books a glamping holiday at her family's farm, Katie plans to get her revenge on the woman with the perfect life. But does Demeter really have it so good? And what's wrong with not-so-perfect anyway?

Surprise Me

Sylvie and Dan have a happy marriage and are totally in sync. But when they introduce surprises into their relationship to keep things fresh, they begin to wonder if they know each other after all . . .

I Owe You *One*

When a handsome stranger asks Fixie to watch his laptop for a moment, she ends up saving it from certain disaster. To thank her, he scribbles her an IOU. Soon, small favours become life-changing.

Love Your Life

Ava falls in love with a handsome stranger on an anonymous writing retreat. But when they return home, it seems they just can't love each other's lives. Can they overcome their differences to find one life, together?

The Party Crasher

Effie isn't invited to the 'house-cooling' party that her dad and his glamorous new girlfriend are throwing, but it's her last chance to retrieve her precious Russian dolls (safely tucked up a chimney). All she'll have to do is sneak in, making sure no one sees her – especially not her ex-boyfriend. It hardly counts as crashing the party if it only takes ten minutes. How wrong can it go?

For Young Adults

FINDING AUDREY

Audrey can't leave the house. She can't even take off her dark glasses inside. But then Linus stumbles into her life. And with him on her side, Audrey can do things she'd thought were too scary. Suddenly, finding her way back to the real world seems achievable . . .

For Younger Readers

The **Mummy Fairy and Me** *Series*

Ella's family have a big secret . . . her mummy is a fairy! She can do amazing spells with her Computawand to make delicious cupcakes, create the perfect birthday party and cause chaos at the supermarket. But sometimes the spells go a bit wrong and that's when Ella comes to the rescue!

Prepare for magic and mayhem in this sweet and funny new series for young readers.

The Burnout
Sophie Kinsella

PENGUIN BOOKS

TRANSWORLD PUBLISHERS
Penguin Random House, One Embassy Gardens,
8 Viaduct Gardens, London SW11 7BW
www.penguin.co.uk

Transworld is part of the Penguin Random House group of companies
whose addresses can be found at global.penguinrandomhouse.com

Penguin
Random House
UK

First published in Great Britain in 2023 by Bantam
an imprint of Transworld Publishers
Penguin paperback edition published 2024

A CIP catalogue record for this book
is available from the British Library.

ISBN
9781804990810

Typeset in Palatino LT Std by Jouve (UK), Milton Keynes.
Printed and bound in Great Britain by Clays Ltd, Elcograf S.p.A.

The authorized representative in the EEA is Penguin Random House Ireland,
Morrison Chambers, 32 Nassau Street, Dublin D02 YH68.

Penguin Random House is committed to a sustainable future
for our business, our readers and our planet. This book is made
from Forest Stewardship Council® certified paper.

For my children:
Freddy, Hugo, Oscar, Rex and Sybella

ONE

It's not the emails that make me panic.

It's not even the 'chasing' emails. (*Just wondering if you got my last email as I have had no reply?*)

It's the 'chasing-the-chasing' emails. The ones with two red exclamation marks. The ones that are either super-pissed off – *As I mentioned in my TWO previous emails* – or else faux-concerned and sarcastic – *I'm starting to wonder whether you have been trapped down a well or suffered some other calamity??*

Those are the ones that make my chest spasm and my left eye start twitching. Especially when I realize I forgot to flag them. My life is governed by the flagged email, my *life*. But I forgot to flag the latest one and that was days ago and now my colleague sounds pretty pissed off, although he's being nice: *Seriously, is everything OK with you, Sasha?* So now I feel even more guilty. He's a nice guy. He's reasonable. It's not his fault I'm doing the work of three people and keep dropping all the plates.

I work for Zoose, the travel app that's everywhere right

now. *You didn't use Zoose?* That's our latest ad campaign, and it's genuinely a good app. Wherever you want to go in the world, Zoose finds you instant itineraries, bargain tickets and a great rewards programme. I'm Director of Special Promotions, covering fourteen territories. The fancy title lured me into the job, I'll be honest. And the fact that Zoose is such a buzzy start-up. When I tell people about my job, they say, 'Oh, that! I've seen it advertised on the Tube!' Then they add, 'Cool job!'

It *is* a cool job. On paper. Zoose is a young company, it's growing fast, there's a living wall of plants in our open-plan workspace, and free herbal tea. When I first started here, a couple of years ago, I did feel lucky. Every day I woke up and thought 'Lucky me!' But at some point that transitioned into waking up and thinking, 'Oh God, oh please, I can't do this, how many emails have I got, how many meetings, what have I missed, how will I cope, what am I going to do?'

I'm not sure when that was. Maybe six months ago? Seven? But it feels as if I've been in this state for ever. Kind of in a tunnel, where the only thing I can do is keep going. Just keep going.

I write myself yet another Post-it reminder – *FLAG EMAILS!!!* – and stick it above my computer screen, next to *APP??*, which has been there for months.

My mum's into apps. She's got a Christmas-planning app and a holiday-planning app and a talking clock from her gadget catalogue, which reminds you to take your vitamins every 7.30 a.m. (It also reminds you to do pelvic-floor exercises every night and calls out 'inspirational quotes' randomly throughout the day. I find it very weird and controlling, although I haven't told her that.)

Anyway, I'm sure she's right – if I could just find the right app, my life would fall into place. But there are too many to choose from and, my God, they all need so much *input.* I have a bullet journal, which came with coloured gel pens. You're supposed to write out all your tasks, colour-code them and tick them off. But who has time for that? Who has time to select a turquoise pen and write 'Answer those thirty-four furious emails in your inbox' and then find an appropriate sad-face sticker? I've got precisely one entry in my bullet journal, which I made a year ago. It reads: 'Task: work'. And it's never ticked off.

I glance at the clock and feel a nasty lurch. How is it 11.27 already? I need to get on. Get on, Sasha.

Dear Rob, I'm so sorry I have not yet got back to you on this, please accept my apologies. I must type those words, what, twenty times a day? *We are looking at 12 April now, and I will be sure to advise you of any change. Meanwhile, on the subject of the roll-out (Netherlands), the decision was made that—*

'Sasha!'

I'm so preoccupied that when a familiar strident voice breaks into my thoughts, I jump right off my office chair.

'Got a sec?'

My whole body stiffens. A sec? A sec? No. I do not have a sec. I'm sweating through my shirt. My fingers are on fire. I have a million other urgent emails after this one, I need to get on, I do not have a sec . . .

But Joanne, our Empowerment and Wellbeing Officer, is heading towards me. Joanne is in her forties, maybe ten years older than me, although she often says 'Women of *our* age' in meetings, with a glance at me. She's dressed in her usual athleisure trousers and expensive, understated T-shirt, and has a disapproving look in her eye that I recognize all too well. I've messed up. But how? Hastily I grope in my mind for crimes I might have committed, but I can't think of any. With a sigh, I stop typing and turn my chair towards her a smidge. Just enough to be polite.

'Sasha,' she says briskly, flicking back her straightened hair. 'I'm a *little* disappointed with your level of engagement in our employee joyfulness programme.'

Shit. Joyfulness. I knew I'd forgotten something. I thought I'd written myself a Post-it – *JOYFULNESS!* – but maybe it fell off my computer? I shift my gaze and, sure enough, there are two Post-its stuck to the radiator: *JOYFULNESS!* and *GAS BILL.*

'Sorry,' I say, trying to sound ingratiating and humble. 'I'm really sorry, Joanne. Sorry.'

Sometimes, if you say 'Sorry' enough times to Joanne, she moves on. But not today. She leans against my desk and my stomach clenches. I'm in for the full lecture.

'Asher has also noticed your lack of participation, Sasha.' She eyes me more closely. 'As you know, Asher is *particularly* committed to the joyfulness of employees.'

Asher is Head of Marketing and therefore my boss. He's also the brother of Lev, the founder of Zoose, the famous one. Lev is the one who came up with the idea of Zoose. He was arriving at an airport when the notion came to him, and he sat in a cafe in the terminal all day, missing six flights to Luxembourg, while he sketched out the first concepts. That's the story, anyway. I've seen him tell it on a TED Talk.

Lev is wiry and charismatic and charming and asks everyone questions all the time. Whenever he's in the office, he walks around, a distinctive figure with his wild hair, asking people 'Why this?', 'Why that?', 'What are you doing?', 'Why not try it this way?' During my interview, he asked me about my coat and my university tutors and what I thought of

4

motorway service stations. It was random and fun and inspiring.

But I never see him now, I only see Asher, who could be from a different planet than Lev. Asher has this thin layer of polished charm, which bowls you over at first. But then you realize he's really self-important and prickly about Lev's fame and very sensitive to anything he sees as criticism. Which is pretty much any response apart from 'That's a ground-breaking idea, Asher, you're a genius!'

(In every meeting, whatever stupid thing he says, Joanne exclaims, 'That's a ground-breaking idea, Asher, you're a genius!')

Anyway. So you have to be careful around Asher, and equally careful around Joanne, who is Asher's old friend from uni and strides around like his henchwoman, looking for heretics.

'I fully support Asher's joyfulness programme,' I say hastily, trying to sound sincere. 'I attended the Zoom lecture by Dr Sussman yesterday. It was inspirational.'

The Zoom lecture by Dr Sussman ('Downwards Can Be Upwards! A Journey to Personal Fulfilment') was compulsory for all employees. It was two hours long and was mostly Dr Sussman talking about her divorce and subsequent sexual awakening in a commune in Croydon. I have *no* idea what it was supposed to teach us, but at least because it was on Zoom I managed to get some work done at the same time.

'I'm talking about the online aspirations mood board, Sasha,' says Joanne, folding her toned arms like a scary gym teacher who's about to make you do twenty press-ups. (*Is* she about to make me do twenty press-ups?) 'You haven't logged in for ten days, we notice. Do you *have* no aspirations?'

Oh God. The online bloody aspirations mood board. I completely forgot about that.

'Sorry,' I say. 'I'll get to it.'

'Asher is a very caring head of department,' Joanne says, her eyes still narrowed. 'He's keen that each employee takes time to reflect on their goals and note their everyday joyful moments. Are you making notes of your everyday joyful moments?'

I'm dumbstruck. An everyday joyful moment? What would one of those look like?

'This is for your own empowerment, Sasha,' continues Joanne. 'We at Zoose *care* about you.' She makes it sound like an accusation. 'But you have to care about yourself, too.'

Out of the corner of my eye I can see that six more urgent emails have arrived in my inbox while we've been talking. I feel nausea rising as I see all the red exclamation marks. How am I supposed to have time to reflect? How can I feel joyful when I'm constantly gripped by panic? How am I supposed to write down my aspirations when my only aspiration is 'stay on top of life' and I'm failing at that?

'Actually, Joanne . . .' I take a deep breath. 'What's most bothering me is, when are Seamus and Chloe going to be replaced? I asked that on the aspirations board, but no one answered.'

This is the biggest issue. This is the killer. We just don't have enough staff. Chloe was a maternity cover who lasted a week, and Seamus stayed for a month, had a flaming row with Asher and walked out. As a result, everyone is overloaded, and there's still no news on any replacements.

'Sasha,' says Joanne condescendingly, 'I'm afraid you've rather misunderstood the function of the aspirations mood

6

board. It isn't about technical HR matters, it's for personal goals and dreams.'

'Well, it's my personal goal and dream to have enough colleagues to do the work!' I retort. 'We're all snowed under, and I've spoken to Asher *so* many times, but he just won't give me a straight answer, you know what he's—'

I cut myself off dead before I can say anything negative about Asher that she'll report back to him and I'll have to retract in a cringy meeting.

'Are you twitching?' says Joanne, peering at me.

'No. What? Twitching?' I put a hand to my face. 'Maybe.'

She's blanked my actual question, I notice. How is it some people can do that? I can't help glancing at my monitor – and Rob Wilson has just emailed yet again, this time with four exclamation marks.

'Joanne, I have to get on,' I say, in desperation. 'But thanks for the empowerment. I feel so much more . . . powered.'

I need to do something, I think frantically, as she finally walks away and I resume typing. *I need to do something*. This job isn't what it was supposed to be. Nothing like. I was so excited when I got it, two years ago. Director of Special Promotions of Zoose! I started off at a sprint, giving it my all, thinking I was on a solid path towards an exciting horizon. But the path isn't solid any more. It's mud. Deep, gloopy mud.

I press Send, breathe out and rub my face. I need a coffee. I stand up, stretch my arms and wander over to the window for a breather. The office is silent and intent; half of my team are working from home today. Lina's in, but she's typing furiously at her workstation, her headphones clamped over her ears and a murderous scowl on her face. No wonder Joanne left her well alone.

Do I leave? Change jobs? But, oh God, it takes so much

energy to change jobs. You have to read recruitment ads and talk to headhunters and decide on a career strategy. You have to dig out your CV and remember what you've achieved and choose outfits for interviews, then somehow secretly fit the interviews into your working day. You have to sound sparky and dynamic while a scary panel quizzes you. Smile brightly when they keep you waiting for forty minutes, while simultaneously stressing out about how behind you're getting with your *actual* job.

And that's just one job application. Then they turn you down and you have to start again. The prospect makes me want to curl up under the duvet. I can't even seem to sort out my passport renewal right now. Let alone my life.

I lean against the glass, my gaze drifting downwards. Our office is situated in a wide, functional street in north London, full of nasty eighties office blocks and a disappointing shopping centre and, totally randomly, a convent, right opposite. It's a Victorian building and you wouldn't know it's a convent if it wasn't for the nuns coming in and out. Modern nuns, who wear jeans with their veil and catch buses to God knows where. Homeless shelters probably, to do good work.

As I'm watching, a couple of nuns emerge, talking animatedly, and sit on the bench at the bus stop. I mean, look at them. They lead a completely different life to mine. Do nuns have emails? I bet they don't. I bet they're not even *allowed* to email. They don't have to reply to 103 WhatsApps a night. They don't have to apologize to angry people all day. They don't have to fill in online aspirations mood boards. All their values are different.

Maybe I could lead a different life, too. Get a different job, move flat, change everything up. It just requires impetus. I need *impetus*. A sign from the universe, maybe.

Sighing, I turn away and head to the coffee machine. Caffeine will have to get me through for now.

I walk out of the building at 6 p.m., breathing in the cold evening air in large gulps, as though I've been suffocating all day. Our company is located above a Pret a Manger and I head there straight away, as I do every night.

The thing about Pret a Manger is, you can buy *all* your meals there, not just lunch. This is allowed. And once you have that revelation, then life becomes manageable. Or at least, more manageable.

I don't know when cooking became so daunting. It kind of crept up on me. But now I just can't face it. I cannot face buying some piece of . . . whatever . . . food, I guess, from the supermarket. And peeling it or whatever, cutting it up, getting out pans and looking for a recipe and then washing up afterwards. Just the thought overwhelms me. How do people do that every night?

Whereas the falafel and halloumi wrap is a nice warm, comforting supper which goes nicely with a glass of wine, and then you just chuck the wrapper in the bin.

I collect my wrap, a choc bar, some kind of 'healthy' drink in a can, and a bircher muesli – which is tomorrow's breakfast – along with an apple. That's my five a day. (OK, one a day, if you're being pedantic.)

As I reach the till, I get out my credit card. And I'm expecting the usual silent electronic transaction, but when I touch my card on the reader, nothing happens. I look up and see the Pret guy smiling at me, his dark eyes warm and friendly.

'You buy the same thing every night,' he says. 'Wrap, bircher muesli, apple, drink, choc bar. Same thing.'

'Yes,' I say, taken aback.

'Don't you ever cook? Go to a restaurant?'

At once, I stiffen. What is this, the food police?

'I usually have work to catch up on.' I smile tightly. 'So.'

'I'm training to be a chef,' he replies easily. 'I'm into food. Seems a shame to eat the same thing every day.'

'Well. It's fine. I like it. Thanks.'

I glance meaningfully at the card reader, but he doesn't seem in any hurry to process the transaction.

'You know what my perfect evening would be?' he says. 'It would involve you, by the way.'

His voice is low and kind of seductive. His eyes haven't left mine, this whole conversation. I blink back at him, disconcerted. What's happening right now? Wait, is he hitting on me? Is he *flirting* with me?

Yes, he is. Shit!

OK. What do I do?

Do I want to flirt back? How *do* I flirt back? How does that go, again? I try to reach inside myself for my flirting moves. For the light, fun version of Sasha Worth who would smile or say something witty. But I've lost it. I feel empty inside. I don't have a line.

'We'd walk round Borough Market,' he continues, undaunted by my lack of response. 'We'd buy vegetables, herbs, cheese. We'd go home, spend a few hours cooking, then eat a beautiful meal . . . and see where that took us. What do you think?'

His eyes are crinkling adorably. I know what he expects me to say. How do I tell him what I'm really thinking?

'Honestly?' I say, playing for time.

'Honestly.' His smile broadens infectiously. 'Be as honest as it gets. I'm not scared.'

'The truth is, it sounds kind of exhausting,' I say bluntly.

'All that cooking. Chopping. Clearing up. Potato peelings everywhere, you know? And some always fall on the floor and you have to sweep them up . . .' I break off. 'It's not really for me.'

I can tell he's taken aback by my answer, but he recovers almost at once. 'We could skip the cooking,' he suggests.

'So, what, straight to sex?'

'Well.' He laughs, his eyes glinting. 'Maybe move in that direction.'

Oh God, he seems a really nice guy. I need to be completely frank.

'OK, so the issue with sex is, I'm not really interested in it at the moment. I can see how *you* would be into it,' I add politely. 'But for me, not so much. Thanks for the approach, though.'

I hear a gasp behind me and turn to see a woman in a purple coat staring at me. 'Are you nuts?' she exclaims. 'I'll come,' she adds huskily. 'I'll come and cook with you. *And* the rest. Any time you like. Say the word.'

'I'll come!' chimes in a good-looking man standing in the other queue. 'You're bi, right?' he adds to the Pret guy, who looks freaked out and ignores both of them.

'You're not into sex?' the Pret guy says, eyeing me curiously. 'You're religious?'

'No, just gone off it. I broke up with someone a year ago and . . .' I shrug. 'Dunno. I find the whole notion unappealing.'

'You find the whole notion of sex *unappealing*?' He gives a loud, incredulous laugh. 'No. I don't believe that.'

I feel a flash of annoyance, because who is this stranger to tell me what I might or might not find appealing?

'It's true!' I retort, more vehemently than I intended. 'What's so great about sex? I mean, when you think about it,

11

what *is* sex? It's . . . it's . . .' I cast wildly around. 'It's genitals rubbing together. I mean, *really*? That's supposed to be enjoyable? Genitals rubbing together?'

The entire shop is silent and I realize that about twenty people are staring at me.

OK, I'm going to need to find a different Pret.

'I think I'll pay now,' I say, my face blazing hot. 'Thanks.'

The Pret guy is silent as he takes my payment, fills my bag and hands it to me. Then he meets my eye again. 'That's just sad,' he says. 'Someone like you. It's sad.'

His words hit a sensitive place, deep inside me. Someone like me. Who is that? I used to be someone who could flirt, have sex, have fun, enjoy life. Whoever I am right now, it's not me. But I don't seem able to be anyone else.

'Yup.' I nod. 'It is.'

Usually I take my Pret supper back up to my desk, but I'm feeling so deflated by now, I decide to go straight home. As soon as I get inside my flat, I sink down on a chair, still in my coat, and close my eyes. Every night, I arrive back here and feel like I've just run a marathon, dragging an elephant behind me.

At length I open my eyes and find myself surveying the array of dead plants on the windowsill that I've been intending to chuck out for about six months.

I will one day. I really will. Just . . . not right this second.

Eventually, I manage to shrug off my coat, pour myself a glass of wine and settle on the sofa with my Pret bag at my feet. My phone is flashing with WhatsApp messages and I log on to see that my old uni friends are all chatting about some new plan where we all hold dinner parties in turn with movie themes, wouldn't that be fun?

There is no way I'm having anyone round for a dinner party. I'd be too embarrassed. My flat is a shambles. Everywhere I look, I see the evidence of some task I've been intending to do – from the unopened tester paint pots, to the exercise bands I was going to use, to the dead plant, to the magazines I haven't read. It was Mum who gave me the subscription to *Women's Health*. Mum, who works at an estate agency and does Pilates and has a full face of make-up on before 7 a.m. every day.

She makes me feel like a complete failure. How does she do it? By my age she was married and making lasagne every night for Dad. I have one job. One flat. No children. But still life feels impossible.

The WhatsApp group has now moved on to the subject of the latest box set and I feel like I should probably join in.

Sounds amazing! I type. *I'll definitely watch that!!*

I'm lying. I won't watch it. I don't know what's happened to me – maybe I have 'box-set fatigue'? Or 'box-set-discussion fatigue'? Conversations light up at work like bushfires taking hold, and it's as if everyone's suddenly in a secret club, outdoing each other with their expert analysis. 'Oh, it's totally underrated. It's *Shakespearean*. You haven't seen it? You *have* to.' Whoever is furthest ahead in the viewing behaves like they're Jed Mercurio, just because they know what happens in episode six. My ex-boyfriend Stuart was like that. 'You wait,' he would say proprietorially, as if he'd invented the whole thing. 'You think it's good so far? You wait.'

I used to watch box sets. I used to enjoy them. But my brain has gone on strike; I can't cope with anything new. Instead, after I've finished eating my wrap, I turn on my TV, scroll down my planner, call up *Legally Blonde* and press 'Play movie again' for maybe the hundredth time.

I watch *Legally Blonde* every night and no one can stop me. As the opening song begins, I sag against my sofa and take a bite of choc bar, watching the familiar scenes in a mesmerized trance. This opening sequence is my downtime. It's a few minutes when I don't do anything, just gaze at a pink, marshmallow world.

Then, as Reese Witherspoon appears onscreen, it's my cue to move. I come to, and reach for my laptop. I open my emails, take a deep breath as though surveying Mount Everest, then click on the first flagged one.

Dear Karina, I'm so sorry I have not yet got back to you on this. I take a swig of wine. *Please accept my apologies.*

TWO

The next morning, I wake up on the sofa. My hair is still in its elastic, the TV is still on and there's a glass of half-drunk red wine on the floor. I can smell its stale aroma, like some kind of noxious air freshener. I must have fallen asleep while I was working.

As I shift uncomfortably and remove my phone from under my left shoulder blade, it lights up with new messages, notifications and emails. But for once, I don't start scrolling, heart thumping in anxiety, wondering what fresh hell is about to greet me. Instead, I roll back on the sofa and stare at the ceiling, feeling a resolution forming in my brain. I'm going to take action today. Big action. Proper action.

As I rub some belated Olay Total Effects Night Cream into my skin, I catch my reflection in the mirror and shudder. My winter-white, freckly skin looks like cardboard. My straight, dark hair is lifeless. My pale-blue eyes are bloodshot. I look *haggard*.

But weirdly, this sight galvanizes me. Maybe I was more stung by the Pret guy's comments than I realized. He's right. It *is* sad. I should *not* be this person. I should *not* be in this situation. I should *not* look so stressed out and haggard. And I should *not* have to leave my job because the department is badly run.

I try to go through my options logically. I've tried talking to Asher. Doesn't achieve anything. I've tried approaching various other senior types – they all said 'talk to Asher'. So I need to try further up. Talk to Lev. I don't have a direct email contact for him, only his assistant. But I'll find him. Yes.

I arrive at the office early, feeling wired, and take the lift straight up to the top floor, where Lev's office is. His assistant, Ruby, is sitting at her glass desk, in front of a massive graphic of the distinctive orange Zoose icon, and my business brain registers that it's a really well-designed and impressive space. This company has so many brilliant aspects. Which is what makes it so frustrating that other parts are so crap.

There's a huge image of Lev, looking as charismatic as ever, with his wild, unbrushed hair and intent gaze. We use his photo a lot in marketing, because he's so distinctive. So cool-looking. He's dating a fashion designer called Damian, and the pair of them look like some sort of *Vogue* shoot.

But cool-looking only takes you so far. I need the real thing. The real man. Some real answers.

'Hi, I'd like to talk to Lev, please,' I say as I approach Ruby, trying to sound matter-of-fact. 'Is he in?'

'Do you have an appointment?' She glances at her screen. 'No.'

Somehow I force myself to leave it at that. This is what you have to do in life: just say 'no', without explaining further. I'm not saying I feel comfortable doing that, but I've seen it on Instagram. It's what successful people do.

'No appointment?' She raises her perfectly tweezed eyebrows.

'No.'

'Well, you should make an appointment.'

'It's urgent.' I try to sound polite. 'So perhaps my appointment could be right now?'

'I'm afraid he's not here.' Ruby lays the information down like a winning card. '*So.*'

Her eyes have a snide glint to them, and I feel a prickle of antagonism. Since when did everyone in this company become such a bitch?

'Well, maybe you could reach him for me,' I say, as pleasantly as I can. 'It's to do with a crisis in his company, so he might want to listen. He might want to know what's going on. Because it's not great, actually. It's not great at all. And if it were *my* company, which I'd started from scratch, you know, I'd want to know. So. Maybe you should give him a call.'

I've lost my pleasant veneer, I realize. In fact, I sound weirdly intense. But that's OK. That's good. It shows I mean business.

Ruby surveys me coolly for a few seconds, then sighs.

'And you are . . .?'

I feel a surge of rage. She knows exactly who I am.

'I'm Sasha Worth,' I say politely. 'Director of Special Promotions.'

'Special Pro-mo-tions.' She draws out the word elaborately, wrinkling her brow and nibbling on a Zoose-branded pen. 'Have you tried discussing this issue with Asher?'

'Yes,' I say shortly. 'Lots of times. That hasn't worked out for me.'

'Have you talked to anyone else?'

'Several people. They all tell me to go to Asher. But you see, talking to Asher doesn't achieve anything. So I want to talk to Lev.'

'Well, I'm afraid he's not available.'

How does she even know that? She's been sitting right here, making no attempt to reach him.

'Well, have you *tried* him? Have you *called* him?'

Ruby rolls her eyes, making no attempt to disguise her contempt.

'There's no point calling him,' she says, in a super-slow, patronizing tone, 'because he's *not available*.'

Something strange is happening to me. All the noises in the surrounding offices are getting louder. My breath is coming faster and faster. I don't feel quite in control of myself.

'Well, there must be someone,' I say, taking a step forward. 'OK? In this entire company, there must be someone. So please find them. Now. Because I have a problem and Asher hasn't fixed it and no one seems able to fix it, and I'm losing the plot. I. Am. Losing. The. Plot. I've gone off sex, do you know that?' My voice is getting shrill. 'That's not normal, is it? To go off sex? I'm thirty-three!'

Ruby opens her eyes wide and I can already see her relaying this whole conversation to her mates over drinks later, but I do not care. I do not care.

'Oooooo-kay,' she says. 'I'll see what I can do.'

She types busily, then pauses, and I see her register some new piece of information on her screen. Then at last she looks up and shoots me a cold smile.

'Someone's coming to talk to you. Would you like to take a seat?'

My head churning, I sit down on the nearby sofa, which is covered in an orange and green retro print. There's a bowl of vegan snacks on the coffee table, several tech magazines and a new brand of filtered water in an eco-paper bag. I remember sitting here when I interviewed for the job. Double-checking my outfit. Running through all the reasons why I would be *thrilled* to join such an exciting, dynamic company.

'Sasha. What's up?'

My chest clenches as I hear the familiar, strident voice. *This* is who Ruby has summoned? *Joanne?* I can hardly bring myself to look at her as she plonks herself down on the sofa in her casual blazer and flared jeans combo, and shakes her head reprovingly.

'Ruby says you've become a little over-emotional?' she says. 'Sharing too much? Losing your temper? As you know, Sasha, I did warn you about the consequences of neglecting your personal reflections. It's up to you to check in with yourself.'

I can't speak for a few seconds. My throat feels choked with rage. Is she saying this is *my* fault?

'It's not a question of personal reflections,' I manage at last, my voice trembling. 'It's a question of staffing, of management failure . . .'

'I suggest you bring any specific problems up with Asher, as your department head,' Joanne cuts me off crisply. 'But in the meantime, I *do* have some news, which Asher will be announcing later: Lina is no longer working for the company.' She shoots me an icy smile. 'So everyone in Marketing will need to pull together! If you could personally take on Lina's projects, just temporarily, that would be helpful. And obviously, any other issues you have may need to wait, as Asher is somewhat stretched as a result.'

I stare at Joanne in disbelief.

'Lina's left?'

'She sent an email this morning indicating that she was not returning.'

'She just *left*?'

'It was quite a shock for Asher.' Joanne lowers her voice. 'Between you and me, I've never known such disrespectful treatment. And quite a rude email, I can tell you!'

I can barely hear Joanne, my thoughts are whirling so fast. Lina got out. She'd had enough and she got out. And now I'm supposed to take on her projects? On top of everything else? I'll collapse. I can't do it. I won't do it. But who do I turn to? Who can I talk to? This place is hell. It's a circular hell with no way out . . .

I need to do the same as Lina, it comes to me in a powerful realization. I need to escape. Right now. This minute. But carefully. Warily. No sudden moves, or else Joanne might tackle me to the floor.

'I'll just pop to the Ladies,' I say in a stilted voice, picking up my bag. 'And then I'll be back. I'll be back in, like, three minutes. I'm just popping to the Ladies.'

Trying to keep a steady pace, I walk self-consciously towards the Ladies. At the door, I pause and look around to see if I'm being observed. Then I dodge into the stairwell and start running like lightning down the stone steps, my heart pumping furiously. I emerge on to the street and stand on the pavement for a few seconds, blinking.

I'm out.

But what do I do now? Where will I work? Will they give me a reference? What if they don't? What if I'm unemployable?

My stomach squeezes in fright. What have I done? Should I go back in? No. I can't, I just can't.

For a few moments, I'm transfixed. I don't feel right. Everything seems blurry. Blood is pumping in my ears. All the cars and buses sound like juggernauts. I should go home, I dimly think. But what's home? A messy, dishevelled, depressing flat. What's my life? A messy, dishevelled, depressing nothing.

I can't do life. The stark truth lands in my brain with a thud. *I can't do life any more.* If I just acknowledged this simple fact, everything would be easier. Life is too hard. I want to give up . . . what, exactly? Working? Being? No, not being. I like being alive. I think. I just can't be alive like this.

My phone buzzes with a message and out of habit I open it, to see a text from Joanne.

Sasha, where have you got to??

In a spasm of panic, I glance up at the office windows and move slightly down the street, out of sight. I should go home, but I don't want to go home. I don't know what I want to do. I *don't know.*

As I'm standing there, coughing on bus fumes, my eyes focus on the convent opposite, and through my brain fog I feel a weird, creeping sensation. A kind of yearning.

What do nuns do all day, anyway? What's the job spec? I bet all they do is pray and knit vests for the poor and go to bed at 6 p.m. every night in their nice basic cells. They have to sing hymns – but I could learn those, couldn't I? And how to put on a wimple.

It would be a modest, healthy life. A manageable life. Why didn't I think of this before? Maybe it was all meant to be.

There's a sudden, blissful release inside my mind, so intense I almost feel giddy. This is my calling. At last!

Feeling more serene and purposeful than I have for years, I cross the road. I head to the big wooden door, ring on the bell marked 'Office' and wait for an answer.

'Hello,' I say simply to the elderly nun who opens the door. 'I'd like to join.'

OK. Not to criticize the convent at all, but I will admit I'm disappointed by my reception. You'd think they'd *want* nuns. You'd think they would have welcomed me in with open arms and a chorus of *Hallelujah!* But instead, a senior sort of nun called Sister Agnes, wearing cords, a sweater and a bright-blue veil, has sat me down in her office, made me an instant coffee (I was expecting a medieval herbal tincture) and has started enquiring about my background. Who I am and where I work and how I found out about the convent.

Why does any of that matter? It should be like the French Foreign Legion. No questions asked, just put on your head-dress and begin.

'So you work for Zoose,' she says now. 'Are you not happy there?'

'I used to work for Zoose,' I correct her. 'Until about half an hour ago.'

'Half an hour ago!' she exclaims. 'What happened half an hour ago?'

'I realized I wanted this life.' I make a simple but telling gesture around the plain little room. 'A pared-back existence. Poverty. Celibacy. No emails, no phones, no sex. *Especially* no sex,' I clarify. 'You don't need to worry about that. I have zero libido right now. I probably have less libido than you do!' I break into a shrill laugh, before realizing that Sister Agnes isn't joining in. Nor does she look amused.

It's probably bad form to refer to a nun's sex drive, I think belatedly. But never mind. I'll learn these things.

'We have emails,' says Sister Agnes, giving me an odd look. 'We have iPhones. Who's your parish priest?'

'You have *iPhones*?' I stare at her, thrown. Nuns have iPhones? That doesn't seem right.

'Who's your parish priest?' she repeats. 'Do you worship nearby?'

'Well.' I clear my throat awkwardly. 'I don't exactly have a parish priest, because I'm not exactly Catholic. As yet. But I totally can be. *Will* be,' I correct myself. 'When I'm a nun. Obviously.'

Sister Agnes stares at me for so long I start to feel uncomfortable.

'So, when can I start?' I try to move the conversation on. 'What's the procedure?'

Sister Agnes sighs and picks up the landline phone on her desk. She dials a number and murmurs something into the handset which sounds like, *We've got another one.* Then she turns to me.

'If you want to explore the religious life, I suggest you start by going to church. You can find your local Catholic church online. Meanwhile, thank you for your interest, and God bless.'

It takes me a moment to realize that this is a dismissal. She's sending me away? Not even 'You can try it out for a day or two'? Not even 'Fill out this application form'?

'Please let me join.' To my horror, I feel a tear trickling down my cheek. 'My life's all gone a bit pear-shaped. I'll knit vests. I'll sing hymns. Sweep the floor.' I swallow hard and rub my face. 'Whatever it takes. Please.'

For a minute, Sister Agnes is silent. Then she sighs again, this time a bit more kindly.

'Perhaps you'd like to sit quietly in the chapel for a while,' she suggests. 'And then perhaps you could ask a friend to come and take you home? You seem a little . . . overwrought.'

'My friends are all at work,' I explain. 'I don't want to bother them. But maybe I will sit in the chapel, just for a little while. Thank you.'

I follow Sister Agnes tamely to the chapel, which is small and dark and silent, with a big silver cross. I sit on one of the benches, looking up at the stained-glass windows, feeling a bit surreal. If I don't become a nun, what will I do with myself?

Apply for another job, obviously, says a lacklustre voice in my head. *Sort my life out*.

But I'm so tired. I'm just so *tired*. I feel like I'm skating over life because I can't get traction. If only I weren't so tired all the time—

'. . . quite bizarre!' A strident voice makes me stiffen and I swivel round on my bench, my skin prickling. No. I'm imagining things. That can't be—

'I *do* appreciate you contacting us, Sister Agnes.'

It is. It's Joanne. Her voice is getting nearer and I can hear the sound of footsteps coming this way.

'At Zoose, I must assure you, we do prioritize wellbeing, so I am rather surprised that *any* of our employees should be distressed . . .'

That nun is a *traitor*. This place was supposed to be a sanctuary! I'm already on my feet, looking desperately for an escape, but there's no way out. In panic, I duck behind a wooden statue of Mary, just as Sister Agnes and Joanne appear at the door to the chapel, like a pair of prison wardens.

The chapel is quite dim. Maybe I'll get away with it. I suck my stomach in, holding my breath.

'Sasha,' says Joanne after a pause. 'We can see you quite clearly. Now, I know you're in a bit of a state. But why don't you come back to the office and we'll have a little talk?'

'Don't think so,' I say curtly, stepping out from behind the statue. 'Thanks a *lot*,' I add sarcastically to Sister Agnes. And I'm striding past them both, out of the chapel, when Joanne grabs my arm.

'Sasha, you really *must* prioritize your own wellbeing,' she says sweetly, her fingers clamped round my flesh so tightly I know I'll bruise. 'You know we all care about you very much, but you need to look after yourself! I suggest you come back with me now and we'll look at your aspirations mood board—'

'Get off!' I wrench my arm out of hers and walk briskly away down the wood-panelled corridor, then break into a run, suddenly desperate to get out of this place.

'Catch her! She's unstable!' exclaims Joanne to a nearby nun, who looks startled, then makes a swipe for my sleeve, but misses.

Seriously? OK, I am never taking refuge in a convent again. With a spurt of adrenaline, I hurtle to the front door, wrench it open and make it out on to the street. I glance back as I run – and to my horror, Sister Agnes is hurrying after me in her cords and trainers, her blue veil fluttering behind her like some sort of miniature superhero cape.

'Stop!' she calls. 'Dear, we only want to help you!'

'No, you don't!' I yell back.

I've reached a group of people clogging up the pavement at the bus stop and frantically I try to push past. 'Sorry,' I say breathlessly, almost tripping on feet and bags. 'Excuse me . . .'

'Stop!' calls Sister Agnes again, her voice like a clarion. 'Come back!'

I look back again and feel a jolt of horror. She's only a few feet behind me now, and gaining on me.

'Please!' I say desperately, trying to dodge through the bus queue. 'Let me through! I need to get away from that nun!'

A burly guy in jeans glances at me, then at Sister Agnes – then he sticks out his arm to block her path.

'Leave her alone!' he bellows at Sister Agnes. 'Maybe she doesn't *want* to be a nun, thought of that? Bloody religious nutters!' Then he turns to me. 'You get away, girl. You run!'

'Run!' chimes in a nearby girl, laughing. 'Run for your life!'

Run for my life. That's what it feels like. My heart pumping, I pick up speed and get through the crowd. Now I'm sprinting along the pavement with only one aim: to escape. Get away from . . . everything. I have no idea where I'm heading, apart from away . . . away . . .

And then, with no warning, everything goes black.

THREE

The *humiliation*. The humiliation of your mum being called away from a viewing of a four-bedroom semi in Bracknell, because you had a flip-out at work and ran straight into a brick wall.

I'll swear that wall came out of nowhere. I'll swear that corner didn't used to be there. One minute I was running as though wildebeest were after me, then the next minute I was on the ground with people staring down at me and blood trickling into my eye.

Now it's five hours later. I've been released from A&E and my forehead is still sore. I've also had a 'chat' with my GP over the phone. I explained the whole story and she listened quietly and asked me a load of questions about my mood and thoughts and sleep patterns. Then she said, 'I think you would do well to have a break,' and signed me off work for three weeks. It turns out I get a week's sick leave at full pay, so that's a silver lining.

'But then what?' I look despairingly at Mum, who came to

the hospital and escorted me back home in an Uber. 'I'm in a lose-lose. If I go back to the office: nightmare. But if I just walk out like Lina, I'll be unemployed. Nightmare.'

'You're burned out, darling.' Mum puts a cool hand on mine. 'You need to think about getting better. For now, don't make any big decisions about your job. Just rest and relax. *Then* worry about everything else.'

She sits down, hitching up her tailored work trousers and glancing at her Apple watch as she does so. Mum became an estate agent after Dad died, and it suits her down to the ground, because it's basically one big authorized gossip. 'The vendors spent a thousand pounds on the kitchen splash-backs alone', 'The couple require a master bedroom with soundproofing capability.' She gets paid to relay nuggets like that. I mean, she'd do it for free.

'I had a little word with that hospital doctor,' Mum continues. 'Very sensible woman. She said she thought you needed a proper, complete rest. It's social media I blame,' she adds darkly.

'Social media?' I peer at her. 'I hardly ever go on social media. I don't have time.'

'Modern pressures,' reiterates Mum firmly. 'Instagram. TikTok.'

'I will just say one word,' says my Aunt Pam, coming in with three cups of tea. She pauses meaningfully. '*Menopause*.'

Oh my God. Save me now. Pam recently became a meno-pause coach and she's obsessed. 'I don't think it's the menopause,' I say politely. 'I'm only thirty-three.'

'Don't suffer through denial, Sasha.' Pam gazes at me earn-estly. 'Maybe you're perimenopausal. Are you having hot flushes?'

'No,' I say patiently. 'But thank you for asking about my body temperature every time we meet.'

'I make your body temperature my business, my love,' Pam says impassionedly, 'because nobody talks about menopause! Nobody *talks* about it!' She looks around the room as though disappointed the sofa hasn't shared its menopause symptoms.

'I don't think the menopause is the point, Pam,' says Mum tactfully. 'Not in Sasha's case.' She turns to me. 'The point is, we must get you some proper R and R. Now, darling, you *can* come home with me, but I'm having the bathroom done and it is a little bit noisy. But Pam says you can go to her house, if you don't mind the parrots. Isn't that right, Pam?'

I don't mind the parrots, but I'm not living with the menopause coaching.

'The parrots might be a bit much,' I say hastily. 'If I'm trying to rest or whatever.'

'I'm sure Kirsten would have you—'

'No.' I cut her off. 'Don't be silly.'

My sister has a baby and a toddler, and her mother-in-law is living in the spare bedroom for a bit while she has her heating repaired. It's chocka there.

'I don't need to go anywhere. It's fine. I can stay here. Chill out. Rest.'

'Hmm.' Mum looks around the flat. 'Is this restful, though?'

We all silently take in my unlovely little sitting room. As though to prove the point, a lorry clatters by outside and a dead leaf falls off a plant. I feel my phone buzzing in my pocket and take it out to see Kirsten is calling.

'Oh hi,' I say, standing up and heading out to the hall. 'How are you?'

'Sasha, what the hell?' she exclaims. 'You ran into a brick *wall*?'

I can tell she's on speaker phone and I picture her in her

bright little kitchen, wearing the cable-knit jumper I gave her for Christmas, holding wriggling baby Ben on her knee while feeding apple slices to Coco.

'It was by mistake,' I explain defensively. 'I didn't line myself up and hurl myself at a brick wall for kicks. It just loomed up.'

'Walls don't just loom up.'

'Well, this one did.'

'Were you *on* something?'

'No!' I retort defensively, because that's what the doctors kept asking, too. 'I was just . . . preoccupied.'

'Mum says the doctor's signed you off for stress. I *thought* you looked stressed out at Christmas, and that's weeks ago,' she adds. 'I said you needed a holiday.'

'I know you did. Anyway, I've got three weeks off. So. How are Ben and Coco?'

'Running into walls isn't ideal, you know,' says Kirsten, ignoring my attempt to deflect the conversation. 'Why were you running, anyway?'

'I was trying to escape from a nun.'

'A *nun*?' She sounds flabbergasted. 'What kind of nun?'

'You know. The nun kind. Veil. Cross. All that. I thought I might join a convent,' I add, 'but it all went a bit wrong.'

The whole thing seems like a dream now.

'You thought you might join a *convent*?' Kirsten's laugh explodes in my ear.

'I know it sounds stupid. It just seemed like . . . the easiest way out. Of everything.'

There's silence, except for the distant sound of Coco singing a tuneless kind of non-song.

'Sasha, you're worrying me now,' says Kirsten more quietly. 'The "easiest way out of everything"?'

'I didn't mean *that*,' I say at once. 'Not *that*.' I pause, because, hand on heart, I'm not sure what I did mean. 'I just felt overwhelmed. Life sometimes feels . . . impossible.'

'Oh, Sasha.' My big sister's voice is suddenly soft and kind, like a hug down the line, and out of nowhere I feel tears gathering.

'Sorry.' I try to pull myself together. 'Look, I know becoming a nun isn't the answer. I'm having three weeks off work.'

'Doing what? Just sitting at home?'

'Unclear. Pam says she'll have me to stay,' I offer quickly, before Kirsten makes some valiant offer to squash me into her house.

'Pam's there? Has she asked you about hot flushes yet?' I can tell Kirsten's trying to cheer me up.

'Of course.'

'She can't leave it, can she? Every time I had morning sickness with Ben she said, "It might be the menopause, Kirsten, don't rule it out."'

I can't help laughing, even as a tear rolls down my face. God, I'm a wreck.

'Sasha! I have the solution!' From the sitting room, Mum's loud, urgent voice summons me. 'The perfect solution!'

'I heard that,' says Kirsten in my ear. 'Text me the perfect solution when Mum's shared it with you. But it's *not* buying a two-bed in Bracknell, if that's what she says.'

I can't help smiling, because Mum's always trying to convince us to snap up bargain properties.

'And listen, Sasha,' Kirsten continues more gently. 'Take this seriously, OK? You need to have a proper break. No emails. No stress. Get yourself back on track. Otherwise . . .'

She trails off into a loaded kind of silence. I can't see exactly

31

where she's heading with *otherwise*, and I'm not sure she knows either. But it doesn't feel like anywhere good.

'I will take it seriously.' I exhale hard. 'Promise.'

'Because I'm not visiting you at the convent. And you won't find Captain von Trapp there either, if that's what you were hoping for.'

'I'm pretty sure he was there,' I counter. 'He was hiding in the cellar.'

'Sasha!' Mum calls again.

'Go on,' says Kirsten. 'Go and hear Mum's plan. And take care of yourself.'

As I head back into the sitting room, Mum is looking at something on her phone with a little smile. Her face has softened and I gaze at her, a bit intrigued. What's she thinking about? What's her perfect solution?

'How much holiday entitlement do you have?' she asks.

'Loads,' I admit. 'I've carried a lot forward from last year.'

I barely took any holiday last year. What's the point? I have finally realized the secret that no one admits: the 'holiday' is a myth. Holidays are *worse* than normal life. You still deal with emails, but on an uncomfortable sunlounger instead of at a desk. You squint at your screen in the sunshine. You're constantly trying to find signal and stay in the shade and talk to the office over a patchy line.

Or the other option is you decide to have a 'proper break'. You put an out-of-office on your computer, enjoy yourself and leave things for when you get back. At which point you're greeted with unfathomable amounts of work that you have to stay up till 2 a.m. for a week to catch up on, cursing yourself for having gone away even for twenty-four hours.

In my experience. Maybe other people do it better.

'Sasha, I have it. I know exactly where you should go.' Mum looks super-pleased with herself.

'Where?'

'I've already phoned up and there's availability,' continues Mum, ignoring me. 'We should have thought of it at once!'

'*Where?*'

Mum raises her head and lets a moment pass before she says simply, 'Rilston Bay.'

The words are like magic.

It's as though the sun has briefly come out and touched my skin. I'm caressed by warmth and light and a kind of euphoria I'd almost forgotten existed. Rilston Bay. The sea. The huge, open sky. The feel of sand under bare feet. That first, magical view of the beach from the train. The piercing sound of the gulls. The foamy surf, flashing and glittering in the baking summer sunshine . . .

Hang on.

'Wait, but it's February,' I say, coming out of my reverie.

Rilston Bay in winter? I can't even imagine it. But at the same time, I can't relinquish the idea, now Mum has mentioned it. Rilston Bay. It's tugging at my heart. Could I really go there?

'There's availability,' repeats Mum. 'You could go by train, just like we always did. Go tomorrow!'

'You mean there's availability at Mrs Heath's?' I say uncertainly.

We stayed at Mrs Heath's guest house every year for thirteen years running. I still remember the smell of the lino on the stairs, the shell pictures in our bedroom, the crochet blankets on the beds. The little outhouse where we left our buckets and spades every evening. The tiny garden with the fairy grotto.

33

'Mrs Heath died a few years ago, love,' says Mum gently. 'I mean at the hotel. The Rilston.'

'The *Rilston*?'

Is she serious? Stay at the Rilston?

We never stayed at the Rilston. We weren't those kind of people. It had a dress code and a weekly dinner dance and its own 'Rilston' taxi for guests that you'd see around town. It was situated grandly, right on the beach. Not like Mrs Heath's place, which was a steep fifteen-minute walk back up the cobbled streets we'd run so merrily down each morning.

But once every holiday, we'd put on smart clothes and go to the Rilston for drinks, feeling delightfully grown up as we stepped into the lobby with its chandeliers and velvet sofas. Mum and Dad would have drinks at the bar, while Kirsten and I sipped Coke with a slice of lemon and giggled over the incredible luxury of crisps served in silver dishes. One time we had dinner there, too, but it was all meat and creamy sauces and 'cost an arm and a leg', as Dad said. So the next year we went back to just having a drink. A drink was enough. More than enough.

So the idea of actually staying there gives me a weird frisson. But Mum's holding out her phone and I can see the words *Rilston Hotel* on it. She's serious.

'Very reasonable rates,' she says. 'Well, it's off-season. And I've heard the Rilston has gone a bit downhill. Bit of a faded glory, these days. So I'll get you a good deal, darling.' I can see the negotiating light in Mum's eyes. 'Take as much time as you can. Get yourself all better. And *then* decide what to do.'

I open my mouth to protest that it's too drastic a step – then close it again. Because the truth is I'm suddenly desperate to go. To see that view again. To feel that sea air. Rilston Bay feels like a closed-up, almost-forgotten part of my soul that I haven't visited for . . . how long? Since Dad was diagnosed, I realize. When that happened, a lot of things changed. And one of them was that we never returned to Rilston Bay. Which means I haven't been there for, what, twenty years?

'The sea air will restore you,' Mum is saying now, as she busily googles something. 'The peaceful atmosphere.'

'The ozone,' puts in Pam knowledgeably. 'The sound of the waves.'

'Long walks, yoga, healthy food . . .'

'Wild swimming!' Pam exclaims. 'Best thing for you, whether you're menopausal *or* premenopausal.'

'Isn't it a bit cold?' I say warily. 'In February?'

'Cold is good,' says Pam with emphasis. 'Shocks the system. The colder the better!'

'There won't be a lifeguard,' objects Mum, glancing up. 'I'm not having you swimming out to the buoy, Sasha.'

'She won't swim out to the buoy!' scoffs Pam. 'She'll just splash about a bit. Have you got a wetsuit, love?'

'*Here* we are,' chimes in Mum. 'This is what you should do. Follow the programme, step by step.'

She shows me an image on her phone and I stare at it, transfixed. A woman in a black wetsuit gazes back at me, her eyes confident, her arms strong, her smile infectious. Her wet hair is lashed across her damp cheeks. Her feet are planted firmly on the sand of a beach which could easily be Rilston Bay. She's holding a bodyboard in one hand and a green smoothie in the other. And below her is a strapline: *20 Steps to a Better You*.

'There's an app!' says Mum triumphantly. 'We just need to download it and get you a few bits and pieces . . . Do you have a yoga mat?'

I can barely hear her. I'm fixated by the girl on the screen. She looks glowing. Happy. Put-together. I want to be her so badly, I feel almost faint. How do I do it? How do I get there? If it takes plunging into the icy sea, I'll do it. Greedily my eyes run down the text beneath, taking in random words here and there.

Noni juice . . . manifest . . . 100 squat challenge . . . grounding . . .

I don't even know what some of those words mean. Noni juice? Grounding? But I can find out, can't I? This list finally feels like the answer. The road map out of who I am right now. I'll go to Rilston Bay. I'll follow the twenty steps. And I'll be a better me.

FOUR

Twenty steps. That's all it takes. And I'm already doing the first one. *Step 1. Have a positive attitude.* The words keep running through my mind and I keep mentally answering. *Yes! I will be positive! Just watch me!*

As I hurry along the platform at Paddington, dragging my suitcase behind me, I'm talking to myself so loudly I'm amazed the people around me can't hear my thoughts. *I can do it. Just follow the steps. I've got this.* Slogans keep popping into my head, each one more inspiring than the last. I feel like a walking Instagram post. I've printed out the photo of the girl in the wetsuit as inspiration, and I've downloaded all the steps from the app and I've brought my bullet journal and gel pens and stickers. I'm *on* this.

It's only two days since I banged my head, but already I feel different. I'm not relaxed, exactly – nothing about preparing for a six-hour train journey is relaxing – but I'm not in the frantic, wired state I was. I feel as though there's an edge of light on the horizon, and if I just keep focusing on it, I'll be OK.

The train is massive – twelve carriages long – and it will take me as far as Campion Sands, where I'll have to change to a smaller, rickety train for the last part of the journey. One of the million things I love about Rilston Bay is the tiny railway station. The little train trundles back and forth to Campion, looking as though it might fall off the cliff at any moment. You can see it from the beach and wave up at the passengers.

At the thought of the beach, I feel a flicker of excitement. I can't believe I'm going to the beach! A cold winter's beach . . . but still!

'Sasha!' Mum's voice greets me and I swivel in surprise to see her rushing along the platform, clutching two carrier bags, a blue foam cylinder and a pink hula hoop. She said she would see me off, but I thought she was joking.

'Mum! You came!'

'Of course I came!' she says. Her voice is brisk, but as she reaches in for a hug, her eyes are anxious. 'Just wanted to make sure you've got everything. Yoga mat? Wetsuit?'

'Yes.' I pat my suitcase.

'Here's your weighted hula hoop . . .' She thrusts the pink plastic hoop at me. 'I know you said you weren't going to bother, but I think you'll regret it if you don't.'

'Mum . . .' I stare dubiously at the hoop. I know 'hula-hooping' is in the twenty-step programme, but I was planning to skip that bit.

'If you're going to do the programme, do it properly, love,' says Mum adamantly. 'And here's your foam roller. Essential.' She presents me with the foam cylinder, and I juggle it awkwardly with the hoop. 'Here's a dryrobe, and some almonds for snacking.' She dumps an enormous carrier bag on to my spare hand. 'Oh, and this!' She adds a paper bag from the National Gallery gift shop. 'Watercolour kit.

Brushes, sketch pad, everything you need. It's on the app, number fifteen. *Find your creative spirit*. I've put in a book of inspirational paintings, too, it's got Rilston on the front cover. You can paint the beach!'

I'm almost overwhelmed by all this stuff. Suddenly, I have an image of myself hula-hooping in a wetsuit whilst simultaneously painting the beach and snacking on almonds.

'Mum ... thanks,' I say feebly. 'This is amazing. You shouldn't have.'

'Of course, darling!' She brushes off my thanks. 'No trouble. Now, I've spoken to the hotel, told them *all* about your situation.'

'You've done what?' I say blankly.

'Don't worry, I was discreet! I didn't say I was your mother, I said I was your PA.'

'My *PA*?' I stare at her.

'Why shouldn't you have a PA?' counters Mum robustly. 'You're a successful woman, Sasha. You should have a PA! We should all have PAs! You had an assistant at Zoose, didn't you?'

My mind flickers back to my 'assistant' at Zoose, a woman called Tania who worked remotely from France for two of us at director level and answered every one of my emails with 'Could you explain this more clearly?' Assistance wasn't really what she gave me.

'I guess,' I say warily. 'So ... what did you tell them?'

'I said you were on a wellness break,' replies Mum crisply. 'I mentioned the healthy food and they said they can make you a green smoothie every day. I gave them the recipe from the app. They said they'd order the kale in especially. And I confirmed your sea-view room,' she adds, before I can remind her how much I hate kale. 'You don't want them

39

putting you on the wrong side of the hotel. You've got a room on the sea-front side and *no* arguments!' Her voice rises as though she's mentally having a fight with the hotel. 'Don't let them mess you around. Oh, I asked about the beach lodges,' she adds. 'But they're not open during winter. Anyway, they're being pulled down.'

'Pulled down?' I stare at her.

'Uninhabitable, apparently. They're building new ones.'

I can hardly believe it. The Rilston lodges were famous. They had their own mystique. Now I look back, the lodges themselves weren't so special – just eight wooden guest houses – but they were right on the beach. That's luxury. And amongst us children, they were the subject of endless rumours: *It costs a fortune to hire one. They're booked up for years. The Prime Minister once stayed in one.*

As children, Kirsten and I would sometimes edge towards the row of lodges and eye up the guests lounging on their expensive decks, enjoying their expensive views of the sea. But there was a kind of protocol. Everyone avoided the sand right in front of the lodges, so it was as though they had their own private stretch of shore. I always used to think, *When I'm a grown-up I'll stay in one of those.* But then of course I forgot all about it.

'Anyway,' Mum is continuing, 'if you need me to phone up as your PA again, just text me. I called myself Erin,' she adds. 'I thought it sounded like a PA's name. Erin St Clair.'

I want to laugh. *Erin?* But instead, I'm blinking away tears, because Mum's been so thoughtful. Even if I do hate kale.

'Thanks,' I gulp. 'Thanks for everything, Mum.'

'Oh, Sasha.' Mum cups my cheek gently with her hand. 'You're not yourself, are you? Will you be all right? Because I *could* come down with you—'

'It's fine,' I say determinedly. 'You've got your conference. You can't miss that.'

Mum goes to the same property conference every year, where she meets up with her old mates and comes home with gossip and fresh fire in her eyes. I'm not asking her to give that up.

'Well.' Mum still seems torn. 'At least you're going to a place we know.'

'Exactly. It's Rilston Bay. It's practically home!'

'I can't believe you're going back.' Mum's face creases into that soft expression she gets when she remembers the past, which isn't often. 'Those holidays were good, weren't they?'

'The best.' I nod fervently.

We did go on holiday eventually, after Dad died. But we never stuck to one place. We tried Norfolk, Spain, even America one year, after Mum became a partner. They were all fine, but nowhere ever replaced Rilston Bay in our hearts.

We didn't want to go back to Rilston Bay without Dad. It was always too soon. Until suddenly it's twenty years later.

'You have a good time, love.' Mum pulls me in for a tight hug. 'No more stressing, Sasha. Enjoy some peace.'

I do enjoy some peace. For about half an hour. The train pulls away on time and I settle back with my coffee and croissant. Somehow I've managed to manhandle my suitcase, the hula hoop, the foam roller and the carrier bags through the carriage – although it took two trips – and thankfully the train is pretty empty. I sit all alone at a four-seater table, watching London ebb away, feeling as though I'm leaving some of my stress behind with it. The pollution, the noise, the busyness . . . that can all stay behind.

I look out of the window and try to focus on my wellness

41

project. But instead, I find myself thinking, *why* did Asher commission that series of 'work language' workshops? It was such a waste of time.

And why do we have to write two different monthly reports in two different formats?

And did anyone follow up on that total fail by Craig's team? Because I can tell you exactly why it happened, it was because—

'Ladies and gentlemen . . .'

The sound of an announcement jolts me from my thoughts and I blink. Shit. This is all wrong. Why am I thinking about work? I need to leave my job *behind*. But it has a big loud voice and it won't shut up, and it seems to be coming with me.

I open up the '20 steps' app and scroll through, looking for advice, till I find the section on meditation.

Try writing troublesome worries down. Don't filter, just write. Then thank your brain for its thoughts, and put them aside for now.

OK. Good idea. I pick up my pens, turn to the back of my bullet journal and start writing furiously.

Half an hour later, I look up blearily and realize I have writer's cramp. What the *hell*? Almost in bewilderment, I leaf back through the pages I've filled. I had no idea I had so many thoughts about Zoose. I had no idea I was so . . . Well. Livid.

I rub my face and breathe out. Maybe that was good. I've emptied my brain of bad stuff and now I can let in the positive stuff.

Thank you, brain, for your thoughts, I say firmly to myself. *But now let's move on, OK?*

I turn to the front of the bullet journal, write a big heading – *Burnout Cure: Twenty Steps* – and then decorate it with my gel pens. I'm just about to add some stickers when we arrive at

Reading and some more passengers come on. Most of them see my pink hula hoop and immediately head the other way (I don't blame them), but an elderly man in a yellow waistcoat seems undaunted and comes to sit right opposite me, even though there's a spare four-seater table across the way.

'Going to join the circus, are you?' he quips, and my heart sinks slightly, because he's clearly a talker. Sure enough, after the inspector's checked our tickets and explained to me about changing at Campion Sands, the elderly man leans across the table, his eyes beady.

'Going all the way to Rilston Bay, are you? You'll need help getting your stuff off and on to the shuttle train at Campion Sands. Luckily for you, I'm going to Campion Sands. I'll help you on to your next train, if you like.'

'Thank you so much.' I shoot him a grateful smile, hoping it also conveys *Let's stop talking now*, but he ignores that bit.

'Live in Rilston, do you?'

'No, I'm just going to stay there.'

'Didn't think I knew you.' He nods, satisfied. 'Been there before?'

'When I was a child we went on holiday every year.'

'Then you'll remember me!' he exclaims, animated. 'I'm Keith Hardy. Or I should use my other name . . . Mr Poppit! HELLO, BOYS AND GIRLS!' he suddenly screeches to my horror, making everyone in the carriage jump. 'It's Mr Poppit! Big red puppet, stripy hat? I have a stand on the beach every year. You must remember Mr Poppit! You must have watched my show!'

This all rings a dim bell. But I find puppets totally creepy, so there's no way I would have watched his show.

'Maybe,' I say cautiously. 'I do remember Terry, who ran the Surf Shack.'

'Well, of course you do,' says Keith, his face falling a bit. 'Everyone remembers Terry. Who doesn't know Terry?'

It's all coming back to me now. There were two surf shops, right next door to each other on the beach. The general assumption was that they were deadly rivals and you had to pick your side, like the Montagues and the Capulets. There was the Surf Shack, run by Terry, and Surftime, run by Pete, but all the regulars went to the Surf Shack, because Terry was the most awesome surf teacher in the world. The most awesome *person* in the world. Some people in life are just head and shoulders above everyone else. They're superior to the rest of us. And everyone recognizes it.

Terry was prematurely grey, but he had a body as tough as a tree and blue, twinkly eyes and he knew us all. Pete was friendly enough – but he wasn't Terry. I can still hear Terry's brusque voice in my head, hoarsened by years of shouting over the wind. In fact, his words of wisdom come back to me quite often at random times. 'Don't worry!' he'd exclaim, if some nervous child was overthinking it. 'Why are you worrying about the sea? The sea sure as hell isn't worrying about you!'

Memories of the Surf Shack are rushing into my head. The dimness as you went in, after the glare of the beach. The smell of neoprene. The grown-up surfers hanging out on the little deck, wearing bright board shorts or wetsuits undone to the waist, exchanging stories. I remember queuing for a body-board, popping with impatience because we were missing the best waves with every second. Rilston is famous for its massive swell in winter – but those smaller summer waves were perfect for us children, still learning how to clamber up on to a board. Terry's wife Sandra would take our names, write down the entries in the book, never hurrying, never

44

skipping a detail. 'Name?' she said every single time. She knew our names, but we still had to spell them out.

'Is Terry still running the shop?' I say with sudden eagerness. 'Is he giving surf lessons?'

Could I get up on a board again? I haven't surfed in years, but maybe this could be Step 21.

'No, no.' Keith shakes his head. 'Terry's retired now. Sold the Surf Shack to a new owner. Down for the surfing, then, are you?' He eyes my hula hoop curiously.

'Not really,' I admit. 'Just having a break. I want some peace and quiet. Yoga. That kind of thing.'

'Peace and quiet!' His face lights up with humour. 'Well, you'll get that, for sure, in February. Not a soul about, in February. Guest houses are shut, beach is empty, whole place is dead.'

'I don't mind a bit of solitude,' I say honestly. 'I've been a bit stressed out recently. I just want a nice, tranquil, feelgood break. Get my head straight.'

'Well, there's nowhere more tranquil than Rilston Bay.' Keith nods wisely. 'Nowhere more feelgood. Scotch egg?' He offers me a paper bag and I shake my head politely. 'So, did you visit often as a child?'

'Every year till I was thirteen. That's twenty years ago.'

It feels impossible when I say it out loud. *Twenty years?*

Keith's face quickens with interest. 'Were you there the year of the kayak accident? That was twenty years ago.'

'Yes,' I say, frowning as I remember. 'Yes, I remember the accident. A boy nearly drowned.'

'*That* was a scandal,' says Keith, taking a bite of Scotch egg. 'Not that there were any deaths, in the event, but there could have been, that's what I say.'

'Right.' I nod. 'Well, it was a long time ago.'

I feel self-conscious about writing any more in my bullet

journal, so I put it away and get out the book of beach paintings Mum gave me. I'm hoping our conversation will end there, but Keith leans forward confidentially.

'You know it was all down to Pete?'

'I hardly remember it,' I admit. 'I just remember being told to get out of the sea. We went bowling.'

'Ah well. Big investigation, they had, and Pete was fined. Ruined him,' Keith adds with relish. 'He shut down, left the area. New couple took over. Never made a go of it, though. The Scullys, remember them?'

'We never went back after that year,' I say shortly.

That kayak accident was the week that Dad was diagnosed. In fact, we were on our way back from holiday when we found out. Mum and Dad got the call and Kirsten overheard them talking, and—

I close my eyes as an old, dull *whoomph* of pain rushes through me. It wasn't anyone's fault. But finding out that our lives had changed for ever at a motorway service station was ... sub-optimal. I've blanked a lot of memories from that week, and this conversation is really not what I need.

'As I say, I just want a nice restful break. You know. Peace and quiet.'

'Of course you do.' Keith nods. 'Peace and quiet. Nowhere like Rilston Bay for peace and quiet.' His face lights up again. 'Were you there the year they got the venomous jellyfish? Now, *that* was a bad business. Three children rushed to hospital. Blamed the coastguards, they did, and to be fair, where were the warnings?'

Venomous jellyfish, now?

'No,' I say a little tightly. 'I don't remember any venomous jellyfish.'

'What about the big food-poisoning scandal?' He looks at

me expectantly. 'You know how many people were taken ill that week? At least twenty-three, and don't you believe any different. They tried to make out it was eleven, hush it up, but you talk to the local doctors.' He wags a finger at me. 'Dodgy prawn sandwiches, it was, though some say it was the mayonnaise. Fresh, you see? Eggs. Lethal.' He points to his Scotch egg and takes another bite.

OK, that's it. I cannot listen to this man any more. He's bad for my health. In fact, he's bad for the whole train carriage. A woman to my right is eavesdropping on us, aghast.

'Actually, I've got to listen to a podcast for work,' I fib, getting out my phone. 'So I'd better do that.'

'You go ahead,' says Keith cheerfully, biting into his Scotch egg again. 'Nice to chat. Oh, young love,' he adds.

'What?' I stare at him, feeling a prickly defensiveness at the mention of love.

'*Young Love*.' He jabs a finger at the cover of my book. 'The painting. The Mavis Adler. That's Rilston Bay, that is.'

'Right.' My eyes run over the painting, which is of a teenage couple kissing on a beach. It's pretty famous – I've seen it on cards and posters. And actually, I think I did know it was of Rilston Bay, but I'd forgotten.

'Maybe you'll find young love!' quips Keith. 'Or are you attached?'

'No,' I say tightly, searching for my earphones. 'I'm not. And I doubt I'll find love on an off-season beach.'

'Never say never! Staying with a friend, are you?' he adds, as I grope with more urgency in my bag.

'No, at the Rilston,' I reply automatically, then instantly wish I'd been more guarded.

'The Rilston!' He whistles with a kind of incredulous humour. 'The Rilston!'

His reaction nettles me. What's that supposed to mean?

'Yes,' I say. 'The Rilston.'

'Didn't know they were taking guests any more. Especially not this time of year. Seen *The Shining*, have you?' He laughs merrily. ' "Here's Johnny!" '

Oh, sod off.

'Well, I like being on my own,' I say politely. 'So that'll work out perfectly.'

There are my earphones. In relief, I shove the buds into my ears, but he carries on talking, undeterred.

'Knocking the whole place down, aren't they? Rebuilding it.'

'I don't know,' I say, searching on Spotify for 'soothing music'.

'Still doing food, are they?'

I lift my head, feeling alarm bells. 'Of course they're doing food. Why wouldn't they be doing food?'

'Because I did hear they had a fire in their kitchen.' He shakes his head, clicking his tongue. 'Nasty business. You hear anything about that?'

'No,' I say firmly. 'Sorry. Well, lovely to chat, but I'd better just—'

To my relief, we've come to a halt at a station, and I pretend to be absorbed in watching the people who board the train. There's a woman and a toddler, in matching pink parkas. There's an elderly gentleman. And then there's a guy with a backpack and a surfboard.

A striking guy.

A good-looking guy, it has to be said. His face looks like maybe he takes it to 'face gym' to sculpt it every week. There are cheekbones and contours going on. There's some stubble. Intense dark eyes.

The train moves off again and I watch surreptitiously as he

takes a seat, hefting his backpack on to the luggage rack with ease and propping his surfboard against the opposite seat. The woman and little girl are in adjacent seats, and the little girl immediately gets out of hers, to have a wander. I'm not usually the broody, maternal type, but *God*, she's sweet, in her padded dungarees and ladybird wellies with her strawberry-blonde hair tied in pigtails. I'm slightly hoping she'll come in my direction, but instead she starts patting the surfboard lovingly with her little dimpled hands and her mother smiles at the guy.

'So inquisitive at this age,' she says. 'They're into every-thing.'

'Agreed,' says the man shortly, which doesn't sound like quite the right answer to me. He should say something nice about the adorable toddler and her delicious, pudgy little fingers.

Nor does he have that *aw, your child is so sweet* expression the mother is clearly hoping for. He looks strained. Pissed off, even.

The toddler's patting turns to vigorous slapping, and with each slap she crows in delight. The woman to my right gives a laugh and catches my eye with a grin.

'Look at that!' exclaims Keith, who has turned his head to watch the toddler's antics. 'She'll make a surfer one day! Where are you headed to?'

'My mum lives near Campion Sands,' says the girl's mother, beaming at Keith. 'It's Bryony's first visit to the seaside, bless her. Bought her a little bucket and spade especially. Not really the time of year for it, but she won't mind.'

Now everyone in the carriage is watching the adorable Bryony with the same indulgent smile – everyone except the guy who owns the surfboard. He looks supremely unamused.

In fact, he's visibly tensed. I can see his hands are clenched. Is he some kind of control freak?

'Does she have to do that?' he erupts at the woman, making me jump. 'Could you stop her? Could you remove her?'

Remove her? Remove an adorable toddler who isn't hurting anyone?

'Remove her?' The woman bristles instantly. '*Remove* her? I do believe this is public transport, or it was last time I checked.'

'Well, I do believe this is my surfboard, or it was last time I checked,' he answers sarcastically, without missing a beat. 'So, could you please control her?'

I look at Bryony slapping the surfboard with innocent, infectious joy. How can he object to that?

'She's not doing it any harm!' I exclaim before I can stop myself. 'It's a surfboard, not the *Mona Lisa*. What the hell is *wrong* with you?'

The man turns to look at me, as though only noticing me for the first time. I don't know if I touched a sore nerve or he just doesn't like being exposed in public – but there's a rawness to his expression that makes me suddenly nervous.

Everyone else in the carriage is suddenly silent. Even Bryony has picked up the vibe and paused in her slapping. Then, abruptly, the man gets to his feet and retrieves his backpack from the luggage rack.

'Excuse me,' he says over-politely to Bryony, and hefts the surfboard under his arm. Bryony instantly wails in protest and tears come to her eyes. But rather than soften, the man flinches, as though with massive repulsion.

'Over to you,' he says to the mother, and strides out of the carriage.

For a moment, no one seems sure how to react – then the mother huffs, her cheeks pink.

'Well!' she exclaims. 'Well, I never! Bryony, come here, love, and have a biscuit. What a rude man!'

She holds her arms out to the wailing toddler, who points miserably at the space where the surfboard was, then utters the single mournful syllable, 'Don!'

'I know it's gone,' says the mother. 'Good riddance. You don't need that toy! Come and play with Ted-ted, sweetheart.'

As Bryony is consoled with a biscuit, I see Keith drawing breath, as though to express his opinion on this little episode. I'm sure whatever he has to say will last for about half an hour, what with the thirty-five accompanying anecdotes.

Hastily I press Play, pointing to my ears in a pantomime of *I can't hear you any more, so sorry*. I lean back and close my eyes tight, letting spa-type music wash over me. Distantly I can hear Keith's voice, muted and muffled, but I don't even open my eyes.

After a few moments, I realize I'm clenching my fists, and I release them, breathing out slowly, trying to relax. Oh my *God*. What was that *like*? My brain feels totally jangled.

And to be honest, it's a good heads-up. I can't cope with random people right now. Especially not talkative people, and *even* more especially, not obnoxious men with surfboards. I'm relieved the hotel will be empty.

In fact, I sincerely hope that in my entire stay at the Rilston, I don't meet anyone at all.

FIVE

Thankfully I avoid Keith's chatter for the rest of the journey by keeping my earphones in. He doesn't seem offended, and leaps into action when it's time to change trains at Campion Sands. By the time he's helped me manhandle my case, bags, foam roller and hula hoop on to the shuttle train, I feel almost friendly towards him.

'I'll look you up!' he says cheerily as he steps off the shuttle train on to the platform. 'I'm always in and out of Rilston. Maybe we can have a drink sometime, I'll tell you some more stories about the place, since you're interested.'

'Great!' I try to sound enthusiastic as I stand there in the train doorway. 'Although I will be quite busy with my . . .' I pat the foam roller. 'So I'm not sure I'll have time.'

'Right you are.' He nods, apparently unoffended. 'Now what are you going to do with your stuff at the other end? Are they sending the car?'

'I don't need a car,' I laugh. 'I'll walk. It's only down the hill.'

'Walk?' he exclaims. 'With that lot?' He runs his eyes over my clobber and I realize he has a point. 'I'll call Herbert,' he adds, dialling on his phone before I can respond. 'Porter at the Rilston. He'll sort you out. I know them at the Rilston . . . Herbert! Keith here. Got a young lady here, coming to stay with you. Needs help with her stuff . . . Yes, that'll be her. Into podcasts. Yoga.' He listens for a few moments, then looks up. 'Herbert says, "Are you the one who wants the kale?"'

Oh *God*.

'Yes,' I say, flushing, 'although it really doesn't matter—'

'That's her!' Keith cuts me off triumphantly. 'So you'll come and meet her, will you? Good man. See you soon, Herbert, we'll have a pint.' He rings off and beams at me. 'Lucky I rang! The hotel's car's out of action, but Herbert's going to meet you personally, help you with your stuff.'

'You're so kind,' I say, feeling a slight wash of shame that I've been avoiding him for the past five hours. 'Thank you very much.'

'Well, you enjoy yourself – wait! I didn't catch your name!' He laughs incredulously, as though this is just happenstance, rather than because I've deliberately kept it from him. But it seems churlish to keep it secret now.

'I'm Sasha.'

'You enjoy yourself, Sasha.'

He walks away down the platform, and after a few moments the doors shut. As the train begins to move, I take a seat, realizing I'm the only passenger in the carriage. The weather has taken a turn, and a fine misty rain is coating the glass, but I still press my forehead against the window, gazing ahead for a glimpse of the bay. It was always a competition between Kirsten and me – who would see the beach first? It was a moment we waited for impatiently, all year round. After all these hours – all these years – I can't believe I'm only minutes away from Rilston Bay. My insides are churning with anticipation and anxiety. What if it lets me down?

It can't let me down. It won't.

'Now approaching Rilston Bay,' says a recorded voice, and I hold my breath, peering through the glass as we round the bend . . .

And there it is. I catch my breath, transfixed, gazing at the happiest view of my childhood. The wide sweep of sand, the rocks, the waves crashing as endlessly as they ever did, it's all the same. The sea might be iron-grey and the sky dull, but I feel the same impatient craving to be down there, at once, now, with sand beneath my feet. The holiday never really began until we were on the beach.

There's a new lightness in my body as we pull into the tiny station and I lug my stuff out. I text Mum and Kristen – Arrived!!! Xxx – then put my phone away and look around for the porter. There doesn't seem to be anyone, so I somehow get everything out to the forecourt, then look around again. The car park is empty. The ticket kiosk is empty. Above me, sea-gulls whirl and shriek and the chilly breeze buffets my face.

There's a single lane that runs down the sweep of hill to the Rilston and as I peer down it I see a figure coming up towards me. It's a thin man with white hair, in a navy over-coat, and he's walking slowly. Really, *really* slowly. At intervals he stops to have a rest, leaning against a lamp post or a wall or whatever's handy, then pushes on. His eyes seem to be focused on me, I realize, and as he gets nearer, he lifts a hand as though in greeting.

Wait. Is this the *porter*?

In slight alarm, I hurry to meet him. He looks about 103. His face is deeply lined, he's puffing hard, and he's so decrepit he can barely even walk – it's more of a totter. My gaze takes in a badge on his coat which reads: *Rilston Hotel. Herbert*. Oh God.

'Are you OK?' I say anxiously.

'Ms Worth?' he greets me in a hoarse, wispy voice, barely audible over the gulls. 'Welcome to the Rilston. My name is Herbert.' There's a pause – during which he seems almost to go to sleep on his feet for a moment – then he comes to. 'I'm here to help you with your bags.'

He's planning to help *me*?

'Would you like a rest?' I say in concern. 'Can I get you . . . a chair? Some brandy?'

'No, no, thank you,' he says in his whisper of a voice. 'Let's just get these bags for you.' He starts to move past me and in slight horror I hurry back to my luggage. No way is he picking up my heavy suitcase. He'd keel over.

'Why don't I take the case and the bags?' I suggest, grabbing their handles. 'And the hoop. Maybe you could take . . . the foam roller?'

The foam roller weighs nothing. He'll be fine.

Herbert peers at it silently, then nods, tucks it under his arm and turns back down the lane. After a few yards he stumbles. I grab his arm to steady him, and we both pause.

'Are you all right, Herbert?' I ask, and he seems to consider the question.

'Do you mind if I rest on your arm for a moment?' he replies at last. 'Just for a moment.'

'Of course,' I say hastily. 'Absolutely.'

I move all my luggage to one arm and extend the other to him, and we proceed together down the hill without any further conversation. As the hotel comes into sight, Herbert's weight gets heavier and heavier on my arm, till I can hardly stagger forward. His head is drooping. His eyes are closed. He's completely silent. Has he fallen asleep? This is surreal. Not only am I carrying my bags, I'm carrying the porter, too.

But never mind! As the familiar white frontage of the Rilston comes into view, I feel a swoop of joy. I remember it all – the pillars and the gravel and the rockery on the front lawn. Soon I'll be in that familiar, grand lobby. Soon I'll be in my room, overlooking the sea. Soon I'll be on the beach. I can't *wait*.

'Herbert!' I exclaim, to wake him back to life. 'We're here!'

Herbert's eyes jolt open and he stands up straight. He totters forward and opens one of the big glass doors. 'Welcome to the Rilston,' he says again.

'Thank you!' I beam at him, somehow manhandle all my stuff into the lobby – then stop dead.

Oh my God.

What—

What's *happened* to this place?

'Welcome to the Rilston!' A pretty receptionist greets me from behind the old-fashioned mahogany reception desk with a vivacious smile. But I can't quite smile back. I'm too shocked by the sight before me.

This lobby used to be a paradise of old-fashioned luxury. Velvet sofas, chintz armchairs, and staff everywhere. Porters in livery, the concierge in a suit, waiters bringing drinks to people, and – I recall – that lady in the pastel-blue suit who was always wandering around, asking everyone if they were quite comfortable. I can see her now, with her pearls and her pleasant smile. *Are you quite comfortable? Can I offer you another drink?* There were always flowers on a big central table, chandeliers glittering, men in smart jackets ordering double gin and tonics. Whereas now . . .

I turn around, taking it all in. The blue patterned carpet is the same, but the central table has disappeared. The chandelier above me looks dusty and half its bulbs have gone. The flowers, the velvet sofas, the armchairs . . . all gone. Instead, there's an assortment of old furniture around the place. Dining chairs, a wardrobe, a mangle. The mangle has a price tag on it, I notice, and there's an ancient grand piano with a label on it: *Free to good home*. There are no bustling staff and certainly no lady in a pastel-blue suit. There's just Herbert, who has collapsed on to a nearby chair and is white as a sheet, and the receptionist, who has her hair in an intricate braid, glittery eyeshadow and looks about twenty-three.

'You all right, Herbert?' she cries brightly as she taps at her computer. 'Herbert gets funny turns when he has to carry luggage,' she adds confidingly to me as I approach the reception desk. 'But he does love doing it.'

'Oh, right,' I say, disconcerted. 'Sorry. I did help him. I carried most of it.'

'Everyone does.' She beams at me and taps at her keyboard again while I look at a wall-mounted plaque reading *Best Luxury Hotel 1973*. 'So!' At last she looks up. 'You're the lady who wants the kale, aren't you? Sasha Worth. It says here, "On a health break." We have a section for notes on the guests, you see,' she adds importantly. 'So that we can help you with your stay. Simon our manager said he spoke to your PA?'

'Er, yes,' I say awkwardly. 'That's right. My PA, Erin.'

'Simon's put five attention stars against your name!' Her eyes widen. 'That's the most in our system! That means "treat guest with special care". Are you a celebrity?'

Oh God. What on *earth* did Mum say?

'No,' I say hastily. 'I'm not a celebrity.'

'Are you a VIP, then?'

'No. And really, I don't need special care.'

'Well, you've got the five attention stars now,' she says, peering blankly at the screen. 'I don't think I can get rid of them. So, enjoy! Here's your key. Room 28, sea-front side.'

She hands me a heavy wooden key fob, with a Yale key dangling from it. 'D'you need help with your luggage? Herbert's having a doze, bless him. Tell you what, you go up the staircase and I'll bring your luggage up in the lift. Can you pick your way past the mangle?' she adds. 'Only we've got a pop-up antiques shop going on. If you've got anything to sell, you're welcome to put it in!'

She looks expectantly at me as though I might say, 'Yes, I brought a sideboard.'

'Um . . . no,' I say. 'I haven't got any antiques with me.'

'Fair enough.' She taps at her computer as though she's writing *No antiques*. 'Most of the guests don't.'

Most of the guests?

'I'm Cassidy, by the way.' She points to her badge, which says *Rilston Hotel. Catherine*. 'I still haven't got a name badge, so I use this one,' she adds cheerfully. 'Starts with the same letter, anyway. See you up at the room, OK? Oh, it's very easy to find,' she adds as an afterthought. 'Up the stairs, take a left along the corridor, through the panelled door, then you need to double back on yourself. You'll see.'

'OK.' I nod, a bit bewildered. 'Thanks.'

'Wait, I haven't finished!' She laughs merrily. 'So then you go down three steps – *don't* take the first door you come to, that's a fake door – take the second door, go right through the library . . . and it's on the left.'

I'm lost. Stairs . . . panelled door . . . go backwards? I have no idea what I'm supposed to do.

'Thank you!' I smile. 'I'm sure I'll find it.'

'See you there!'

As Cassidy hustles my suitcase past the mangle, I don't move for a second. This isn't quite what I imagined. Especially the mangle.

But never mind. I'm here!

Feeling desperate to see the waves, I hurry up the carpeted, creaky staircase and along an endless corridor hung with faded wallpaper and ancient watercolours, each with its own picture light. The royal-blue carpet is worn in places and wrinkled in others, and every floorboard seems to creak as I walk along. There's no sign of any life. No sounds except my own footsteps and the creaking floorboards. As I pace along, I find myself thinking of *The Shining*, which is Keith's fault. It's not at all like *The Shining*, I tell myself firmly. And soon I'll be looking at my own sea view. Everything's worth it for that.

After I've doubled back, gone up and down stairways, tried various doors and walked through the library three times, I eventually find Room 28. The door is open and Cassidy is standing by a double bed covered with a 1970s-style bedspread decorated with orange flowers, matching the curtains, which are drawn shut. The room is massive, but only has two other pieces of furniture. There's a heavy pine wardrobe, varnished to a strange shade of terracotta, and a built-in dressing table. There's vinyl textured wallpaper on the walls. Maybe it was cream once. Now it's an unappealing yellow-beige.

'So, this is your room!' announces Cassidy. 'Deluxe double, sea front, with en suite. Bathroom's through the door. Bath *and* shower.' She hesitates. 'Well, don't use the shower, it plays up.'

I glance through the door to the adjoining bathroom, and see an ancient green bathroom suite. There are brown and green tiles covering both the floor and the walls, and every tile has a woodland animal on it. Badgers, foxes and squirrels all look back at me with beady little eyes, and I turn hastily away.

'Wow.' I swallow. 'Those tiles are . . .'

'Original,' says Cassidy proudly. 'Now, your kettle's here . . .' She points to an elderly beige kettle on the dressing table, next to which are a cup and saucer and a basket of sachets. 'You've got your tea, coffee, creamer, ketchup . . .'

'Ketchup?' I repeat stupidly.

'All the guests love ketchup,' says Cassidy blithely. 'Funny, isn't it? And here's your dressing table . . .' She tries to open the dressing-table drawer, but it sticks – it looks swollen with damp. After a few attempts she gives up.

'You can put your stuff on top,' she says. 'Lots of space. If you want to use a hairdryer, we've got one at reception specifically for guest use. Just call and ask, no problem at all!' she adds encouragingly. 'And have you downloaded our app?'

'App?' I say, still bewildered by the hairdryer situation. 'No.'

'Oh, you must! Simon said I *must* make sure you have the app installed . . . If you give me your phone . . .'

In a slight daze, I hand over my phone. I can't get my head round this place. They have an app, but only one hairdryer?

'Here you go! You're all set. You'll be entered in a prize draw now,' she adds with satisfaction. 'It's every month and the prize is a cream tea, two scones included, raisin *or* plain.'

Cassidy hands me back my phone and I see that I've already received three new text messages from 'Rilston Hotel'.

We see you have arrived at the Rilston. Welcome! We hope you enjoy your stay!

Success! You have been entered in our Cream Tea prize draw!!

A reminder that breakfast is served at 7–10, every morning.

'What else can I tell you?' Cassidy seems to be musing. 'Breakfast is at eight . . . If you'd like a croissant, let us know in advance . . .'

'Hang on.' I frown, puzzled. 'The app says breakfast is at seven.'

'Does it?' Cassidy rolls her eyes good-humouredly. 'Honest to God, that app's always wrong. Let me see?' She peers at my screen, then nods. 'Yeah, don't take any notice of that.'

I look around again, noticing the yellow glow coming from the single pendant light, the worn patch of carpet by the bed, the trouser press in the corner. It's not the most inspiring room in the world.

But I'm not here for the room, I remind myself. I'm here for the sea view.

'Anyway.' I force an upbeat tone. 'Is it possible to open the curtains?'

'Of course!' Cassidy approaches the window, smiles at me, then with a flourish pulls back first one curtain, then the other. 'There you go!'

Whaa-aaat?

I stare at the view, rigid, too shocked to make a sound. The windows are boarded up. Fully boarded. All I can see are planks of wood. I've come six hours on a train for planks of wood?

'That's . . . not a sea view,' I manage at last.

'No, it's scaffolding,' explains Cassidy. 'Didn't you see it when you arrived? Oh no, you came the other way!' She bursts into laughter. 'No wonder you look surprised! You're expecting a sea view, then I pull the curtains back and you see scaffolding!' She seems highly amused. 'Wait till I tell Herbert!'

I'm starting to tremble all over. I think I might lose it in a minute. I've been focusing on this sea view as the answer to everything. I've imagined how it will heal and mend me. The sky. The gulls. The soothing rhythm of the waves. And now I *can't have it*?

'The thing is, my mum – I mean, *PA*,' I correct, 'my PA booked a sea-view room. *Sea view*,' I emphasize. 'And this isn't a sea view.'

'Sea front,' Cassidy corrects me helpfully. 'Not sea view. You *are* on the sea-front side, you just can't see the sea.' She peers at me, slowly starting to realize that all is not well. 'So, were you *expecting* a sea view?'

'Yes!' I sound a bit more shrill than I intended. 'Yes! I was!'

'Right. Got you.' Cassidy chews the side of her mouth, then gets out her phone. 'Bear with me a moment . . .' She dials a number and lowers her voice a smidge. 'Simon? I've got your VIP guest here. The healthy kale lady? Turns out she wanted to see the sea from her room. She's a bit stressed out. So I was wondering, shall I try and take down some of the scaffolding?' She listens a bit longer, then her face clears. 'Oh right. Of course! I clean forgot! Yes, I'll do it straight away. Bye, Simon . . . I'm such an idiot!' she exclaims as she rings off, clapping a hand humorously to her forehead. 'There was a whole thing I was supposed to tell you!' She scrolls through her emails, then draws breath and starts reading aloud in a formal voice. ' "We do apologize for the restricted view at the current time. As recompense, we would like to offer you daytime use of a beach lodge, free of charge, as a means of enjoying the unique and beautiful view of Rilston Bay." '

'Beach lodge?' I stare at her warily. 'I thought the beach lodges were uninhabitable?'

'Well, you couldn't sleep in one any more,' she says, making a face. 'But they're perfectly safe, so we offer them to selected guests as a daytime facility. You can sit in them, stay out of the weather, enjoy the view, whatever you like. "Only eight lodges are available for this exclusive offer," ' she adds importantly, returning to the script, ' "which is offered to a limited number of guests at the discretion of the hotel." '

'Right.' I digest this. 'How many guests are staying at the hotel at the moment?'

'Currently, our numbers are *quite* small,' Cassidy says, looking cagey.

'How many exactly?'

'Well, it's just yourself and the Bergens,' she admits. 'Lovely Swiss couple, but they're not interested in the beach, they only play golf. So the only person using a lodge would be . . . Well, actually . . . ' She shrugs. 'It would be just you.'

Just me.

As I step on to the beach fifteen minutes later, clutching my lodge key, I feel almost unreal. I've made it. The sand of Rilston Bay is finally beneath my feet. After all these hours, all these years . . . I'm back. There's not another soul on the beach, which I suppose is no surprise – the afternoon light is already fading and the weather has definitely taken a turn. The waves are crashing hard, the wind is whipping my hair round my face; the raindrops feel like sharp pins on my skin.

I don't care. I'm here.

I spread my arms wide, feeling the wind buffeting me, then turn around a few times on the sand, relishing my aloneness, the wideness of the sand, the weather, the vastness of the sky, the sound of gulls . . . everything. It's so not London. It's so not the office. It's so not sixty-five emails by tomorrow.

I walk towards the sea, my trainers leaving deep imprints in the sand that become filled with water as I near the surf. My socks are already damp, but so what? I'm here. *I'm here.* I take a few deep, salty breaths, filling my lungs, just letting the sounds and sensations wash over me.

I was expecting to feel instantly euphoric, as soon as I got on to the beach. And I do. Of course I do. It's glorious. It's everything I was hoping for. But quite soon I realize that I also feel a bit strange. A bit tense. There's a disconcerting feeling in my body that I can't quite pin down. The solitude feels liberating – but oppressive. The pounding surf is almost too loud. And now I seem to be breathing faster, which is wrong. I should be breathing slower. For God's *sake*. Can't I even do 'relaxing on the beach'?

I take a few brisk strides along the sand, trying to escape my confusion, but I can't. My head feels alternately exhilarated then tight with trapped tears, elated then panicky. It's as though I'm finally putting down a load I didn't even know I was carrying – but I can't let go so easily. I relax a little, then seize up again. It's as if some part of me keeps grabbing the load back. Maybe for security? Or because I can't remember what it's like not to carry it?

Oh God. Basically, I feel a bit of a mess.

But then, what did I expect?

I turn to scan the terrain, trying to distract myself. The rocks, the cliffs, the lodges, the hotel, and above that, rows of little houses. It all looks almost exactly the same as it did in my memories. That's all there is at this end of the beach. Further down you get the surf shops, cafes, ice creams, all that. But this end is simpler. Sea, sand, rocks, lodges.

I turn towards the lodges, taking in their derelict frontages with tender sadness. The paintwork is peeling, the wood is warped, a few windows are broken. One deck has collapsed completely. The 'millionaires' lodges' now look more like clapped-out beach huts. But who cares? A squall of rain hits me right in the face, and I decide that's enough fresh air. Time to investigate Lodge 1, which is to be mine.

It takes several big hefts to get the door open. I burst through on my fourth attempt, almost falling over, then take a few steps forward on the creaky boards, looking around the space, breathing in the fusty wooden scent.

OK. I see what Cassidy meant. This really isn't habitable. But I can also see that it might once have been a lovely guest house. There are bits of furniture left – a single wooden dining chair, a faded sofa, a pair of lamps. A free-standing heater, which I switch on at once. There's a small fitted kitchen, with all its appliances removed. A staircase leads upwards but has tape fixed over it reading DO NOT ENTER.

Cautiously I approach the sofa and lower myself on to it. I'm expecting clouds of dust, but it seems quite clean. From the sofa, I can see straight through the big picture window to the sea. There's my view.

There's my view.

And suddenly, I feel tears welling up, so hot and strong and powerful that there's no question of blinking them away. No way of resisting. I need to cry. I can't not cry. I have to let go. I feel as if weeks, months, years of strain are pouring out of me. There's no one to see me, no one to hear.

I remember Mum, after Dad died. You'd find her in the kitchen and as she turned around her smile would be bright, but her face wet. 'Leaky eyes,' she'd say. 'Just leaky eyes.'

Well, now I've got leaky eyes. A leaky brain. A leaky body. I brush at my face several times, but the tears just won't stop. My stomach is crunching with every sob, wave after wave.

I don't have any tissues, but I find a packet of loo rolls and rip it open. I wipe my face and blow my nose – five, ten, fifteen times – throwing the screwed-up balls into a cardboard box in lieu of a bin. I'm wondering almost detachedly how long a human can cry for. What if I can't stop? *Freak woman sobs for a year solid; doctors mystified; Kleenex makes compassionate donation.*

But no one cries for ever. At last, my tears ebb away and my chest stops heaving and I lie back, gazing up blankly at the tongue-and-groove ceiling. An overwhelming exhaustion has overtaken me. I feel like I'll never be able to move again. As if my limbs are pinned to the sofa. Or maybe I'm a marble statue in a tomb.

Is this delayed shock? I guess it's been quite a seismic week. One minute I was at work, I was in London, I was functioning. And now I'm here, in a silent, derelict lodge on an empty beach, not quite sure if I'm functioning or not.

I stare at the ceiling, almost in a trance, for a long time. Until at last it goes blurry, and I realize it's dark. Some kind of automated lighting system has come on outside the window, illuminating the deck. OK. Time to move. Experimentally, I try to motivate my legs, which seem reluctant.

Can I move?

Yes. Come on. I can move.

With an almighty effort, I heave myself off the sofa and look around. Already I feel better. Lighter. Clearer. And I've bonded with this lodge, guardian of my secrets. This will be my haven. This is where I will sort myself out. Twenty steps to a new me. I'll begin tomorrow. I already feel resolute. In fact, I can't wait.

SIX

The next day, I wake to a chilly bedroom. I get out of bed, still half asleep, totter to the window, draw back the curtains to see what the weather's like – then flinch. Oh God. I'd forgotten about the wooden boards.

Backing away from the unfriendly window, I head into the bathroom – and give a yelp of horror. I'd forgotten about the beady-eyed woodland creatures, too. That badger looks like it wants to sink its sharp little teeth into my flesh. I'll have to clean my teeth with my eyes shut.

As I get dressed, I firmly avoid looking at either the window *or* the bathroom. Instead, I focus on the photo of the girl in the wetsuit. While unpacking last night, I discovered the screenshot I'd printed out, and I've hung it up on an empty hook on the wall. I'm not saying I'm obsessed . . . but I do look at the girl a lot. I find her inspirational. She looks so strong and energetic. So vibrant. I *will* be her.

I studied the '20 steps' app last night, while I ate my room-service supper, and it recommends aiming for one step per day. But that's for people doing it in their spare time, surely? I'm on the full-immersion programme. So I decided that today I'll accomplish five steps for starters and then see how I go. It's all written out in my bullet journal.

Day One: 1. Wild swimming 2. Grounding 3. Manifesting 4. 100-squat challenge 5. Communion with nature.

My new life starts today! Bring it on!

To be honest, I'm not *quite* as pumped this morning as I thought I'd be. Last night, I imagined waking up full of energy, jumping out of bed and dashing down to the beach. Whereas this morning, when it actually comes to it, I feel a bit more like . . .

Going back to bed, a voice says inside my head, but I ignore it. That won't achieve a better me, will it? I probably just need some breakfast.

My phone pings and I check to see if it's Mum or Kirsten, but it's from the Rilston. *Another* text from the Rilston?

We are proud to announce resident magician Mike Strangeways will be performing tricks in the lobby at lunchtime. Come and join the fun!

I can't help rolling my eyes. Firstly, it doesn't sound like fun. And secondly, this is the fifth message I've received this morning. The others were:

Sex on the Beach, anyone? Remember, cocktails are half price on Wednesdays.

ATTENTION!! There will be a fire alarm practice this
morning at 10 a.m.

Do you have feedback on your hotel experience? Why not
talk to our friendly team?

Woof! Dogs are very welcome at the Rilston. Please dial
067 for details.

As I'm gazing at my phone, it pings again and yet another
text arrives.

Fun fact: The Rilston was the country residence of the
Carroday family until 1895.

I feel a flicker of annoyance. That's not a 'fun fact'. It's just
a fact. A really boring fact, which I didn't need to know and
is now clogging up my phone.

Anyway, never mind. *Think positive.* I thrust my phone in
my pocket, take a deep breath and head downstairs.

Breakfast is served in the dining room, which is massive.
There are vast windows, huge pillars and acres of patterned
carpet, although only about ten tables, oddly spaced here
and there. The waiter who greets me is skinny, with a solemn
face, and seems so young he barely needs to shave. He leads
me to a tiny table in the corner of the room, pours me a glass
of water, then hurriedly disappears. I'm the only person in
the room, I realize, looking around. So why have they put me
here in this dark corner? I could sit wherever I like. I *will* sit
wherever I like.

Picking up my glass of water, I decide on a big table in the
bay window. I take a seat, put my glass of water on the

tablecloth, lean forward to enjoy the view – and the table promptly collapses, me with it.

'Ow!' I cry out before I can stop myself, and the next thing I know, both the waiter and Cassidy are running towards me.

'Nikolai!' Cassidy scolds the waiter as she untangles me from the tablecloth. 'Why did you put her at one of the dodgy tables? It's not really a table,' she adds confidingly to me. 'We're a bit short on furniture so we just whack tablecloths on any old thing. This one's a bit of board balanced on a couple of towel rails,' she adds, quickly reassembling it. 'Clever, isn't it? Looks just like a table.'

'But what if you need to use it?' I say, bewildered.

'We never do,' Cassidy assures me. 'Now, has Simon been to see you? Only he wanted to apologize about the kale . . . Oh look, there he is.'

Approaching us is a man in his forties with a thinning hairline and a harassed expression, wiping his hands down his brown suit.

'Ms Worth, I'm Simon Palmer, the manager. Welcome to the Rilston.' He extends a hand and gingerly I take it, wondering what he was wiping on his suit. 'And before I say anything else, I would like to apologize.' His face becomes stricken. 'Despite our best efforts, we have been unable to source the organic kale that your PA so specifically requested. We hope to receive some today, but I would like to offer you complimentary breakfast this morning as recompense.'

'Don't worry,' I say hastily. 'It's fine.'

'It is not fine.' He shakes his head mournfully. 'It is far from fine. These are not the high standards we expect of ourselves at the Rilston. I made a promise to your PA and I have not fulfilled that promise. We're also having trouble locating goji berries and . . .' He looks at Cassidy. 'What was the other thing?'

'Noni juice,' says Cassidy. 'Sounds rude, doesn't it?' she adds with a giggle, then claps her hand over her mouth. 'Sorry. Unprofessional.'

'Yes. The noni juice.' Simon shakes his head heavily. 'Believe me, Ms Worth, I am mortified by our failure. I will get you that noni juice, if I have to squeeze the noni myself.'

'Well . . . thank you,' I say, feeling embarrassed.

'Other than that, has your stay been comfortable so far? You're here for a health break, I understand? Ah, here's Nikolai with your green smoothie,' he adds. 'In the absence of organic kale, our chef used frozen Birds Eye peas.'

Birds Eye peas?

I stare aghast as the waiter approaches with a glass of green gloop, which is presumably whizzed-up peas. He puts it on the tiny table in the corner as Cassidy watches curiously.

'I don't suppose you want bacon and eggs for breakfast?' she says. 'Or pancakes?'

'Of course she doesn't!' says Simon testily, before I can answer. 'Use your brain, Cassidy! Our guest is here on a wellness break. She will prefer the melon plate. And herbal tea.'

'Yes,' I say reluctantly. 'That sounds . . . great.'

I could *die* for some pancakes, but I can't admit that now.

'One melon plate, one herbal tea,' says Cassidy, as my phone bleeps with another text. I click on it out of habit and see yet another message from the Rilston.

Do you enjoy ballroom dancing? Please accept a complimentary ten-minute ballroom dancing lesson from our resident experts Nigel and Debs!

'Thanks for the dance-lesson offer,' I say to Simon. 'But I don't think I'll have time today.' He looks puzzled, so I peer at my phone again. 'The ballroom dancing?' I clarify. 'I just got a text offering me a complimentary lesson with Nigel and Debs?'

Simon and Cassidy exchange looks of consternation.

'That app!' exclaims Cassidy. 'See, Simon? I told you! It's still inviting the guests to ballroom dancing! We never did have ballroom dancing,' she confides. 'Nigel and Debs don't exist. The tech guy put it on as an example and never got rid of it.'

'Ms Worth, what other messages have you received?' asks Simon, looking beleaguered.

'Er . . .' I scroll down the messages. 'Apparently Mike Strangeways is doing magic tricks in the lobby today?'

Cassidy emits a squeak and claps a hand over her mouth, while Simon's consternation seems to have doubled.

'Mike Strangeways was dismissed a year ago for . . . unsavoury behaviour,' he says, as though speaking with difficulty.

'He got pissed,' puts in Cassidy, winking at me. 'Went a bit too far with his magic wand, know what I mean? He's a one, Mike.'

'Cassidy!' hisses Simon, then he turns to me, breathing hard. 'Ms Worth, I can only apologize that his name has appeared on your phone. These are not the high standards we expect of ourselves at the Rilston. We have let you down and we have let ourselves down. Cassidy, please send Ms Worth some flowers at once, by way of recompense.'

'Of course.' Cassidy busily gets out a notebook and pencil. 'What sort of budget? And what message shall I put? Shall I put "We are devastated and destroyed by our error", like last time?'

Simon swivels his eyes meaningfully towards me several

times and Cassidy seems to notice her faux pas. 'Oh, right,' she says hastily, whipping her notebook away from my view as though it contains state secrets. 'Yes. I'll get on to that, Simon.'

I bite my lip, trying not to laugh.

'You don't need to send me flowers,' I say. 'It's fine. But you might want to fix your app.' As I'm speaking, my phone pings with yet another text and silently I show it to Simon.

Only one week till Christmas! Join us for a festive mince pie at reception!!!

From the appalled expression on his face, I kind of wish I hadn't.

I eat my melon plate all alone, with Nikolai watching me silently from the other side of the room. God knows where the Bergens are; maybe they have breakfast in their room. I'm aware of every clink of my fork and every gulping sound I make as I swallow. Each time I take the slightest sip of water, Nikolai dashes forward to replenish my glass, murmuring 'Madame', until I don't dare have any more. It's a relief to get up, after a final swig of musty mint tea. (How long has that been sitting in the drawer?)

As I trudge upstairs to get my stuff, I don't feel remotely energetic. I sit hunched on my bed for a few minutes, trying to muster some enthusiasm, then gather up my wetsuit, yoga mat, foam roller, hula hoop, iPad and painting stuff. I lug them downstairs, then pause in the lobby, eyeing the sky through the open front door. It's a moody grey, and I can sniff the rain in the air from here.

'Hi!' Cassidy greets me from behind the reception desk,

where she's busily using a sewing machine on a piece of yellow fabric. 'Off to the beach?'

'Yes,' I say. 'I'll probably spend most of the day down there,' I add firmly. If I say it out loud, then I'll *have* to do it.

'Doing yoga?' she enquires, looking at my mat.

'Yoga, meditation, grounding . . .' I try to sound knowledgeable. 'General wellness activities.'

'Wow.' Cassidy looks impressed. 'So you won't want shortbread and coffee in the lounge at eleven?'

Suddenly, all I want in this world is shortbread and coffee in the lounge at eleven. But I can't give up so quickly.

'No, thanks.' I smile briskly. 'I'll be too busy with my schedule.'

'Of course.' She eyes my hula hoop curiously. 'What's that? Looks like a hula hoop!'

'It's . . . exercise equipment.' I hastily nod at the sewing machine, to change the subject. 'What are you doing?'

'Etsy business,' explains Cassidy. 'Bit of cash on the side. I make personalized underwear to order, see?' She holds up the yellow fabric and I see that it's a thong, with pink embroidered words on the front, stating *You'll be lucky*. 'You can have any slogan you want,' she says brightly. 'Up to five words. I'll make you one, if you like! I make quite a lot saying *Happy place* with an arrow downwards, d'you want one of those?'

I try to imagine wearing a thong saying *Happy place* with an arrow downwards. But it just seems like a bad joke. Happy place? Dead and forgotten place, more like. Thrown away the key, more like.

'You seem busy,' I say, avoiding the question.

'I'm doing really well!' she says proudly, holding up a multicoloured handful of thongs. 'Although I don't even want to *tell* you what I've had to embroider for some of the customers.' She lowers her voice. 'I had to look some of it up! I can't do it at home, my gran would have a hissy. She goes to chapel. This one's nice, though.' She sorts through and finds a turquoise thong, with the slogan *F- me*. 'Quite classy, I thought,' she says, admiring it. 'You know, understated. Don't you think?'

'Er . . .' The phone rings before I can answer and she picks up the receiver.

'Hello, the Rilston,' she says cheerily, twirling the *F- me* thong round and round on her forefinger. 'No, that's the other Rilston, in Perthshire. OK. Enjoy your stay!'

As she puts down the phone, I decide to raise something that's crossed my mind a few times since I've arrived.

'Cassidy, is the Rilston . . . all right?' I venture. 'Only, it's quite empty, and half the furniture's gone, and . . .' I look around the faded lobby, wondering how to put this tactfully. 'It's a bit different from how it used to be. It's not going to . . .?'

I can't bear to say *go bust*.

'*Well.*' Cassidy leans across the desk as though for a good gossip. 'Here's what it is. They *are* a bit short of cash. We're what you call a "skeleton staff". Not real skeletons!' she adds, with a sudden laugh. 'We're not ghosts!'

A skeleton staff. OK. That explains quite a lot.

'So anyway, they need to get investors on board for the new lodges,' continues Cassidy. 'They're going to get those done first, then fix up the main hotel. They're going to be called Skyspace Beach Studios,' she adds with relish. 'All glass. Hot tubs on the decks.'

'Wow,' I say, taken aback. 'That sounds . . . different.'

'Oh yeah, you should see the designs.' Cassidy nods.

'They're amazing! Simon's planning a reception for all the investors, actually,' she adds, putting another thong in her sewing machine. 'Or rather, would-be investors. That's why he's a bit stressed out.'

'Right.' I nod, digesting this. 'He does seem quite tense.'

'Simon takes everything so *seriously*.' Cassidy shakes her head sorrowfully. 'Poor love. We had a fire recently. I was like, "Simon, relax, it's only a fire!" But he's all, like, "We shouldn't have fires in the hotel! It's dangerous!" Perfectionist, you see? Oh, you're invited to the reception,' she adds as she starts embroidering again. 'I'm printing out the cards later.'

'*Me?*' I stare at her. 'I'm not an investor.'

'They want some guests along,' she explains. 'Liven it up. Oh, do come! There'll be champagne! Or – wait. You won't want champagne, will you?' She thinks for a moment. 'I'm sure Chef Leslie will make you a lovely kale cocktail.'

'Great.' I gulp. 'Well, maybe. See you later.'

The beach is empty again when I arrive. I stand on the sand for a few moments, taking in the wide open sky – then head to my lodge. I dump my wetsuit, mat, foam roller and ruck-sack on the floor and slump on the sofa. For a while, I just stare out of the window at the sea without even taking off my coat, letting my jangled brain calm down.

Then at last I rouse myself and rub my face. OK. Time to start. I sit up straight, pull my bullet journal out of my ruck-sack and find my list for the day.

Day One: 1. Wild swimming

Wild swimming. Excellent. I can't wait to plunge into the freezing-cold water.

I mean, *bracing* water.

I put down my bullet journal and peer through the window at the heaving sea, trying to imagine getting into the water. Actually into it. In February.

I glance at my new black wetsuit, lying pristine and dry – then look through the window again at the forbidding sea. Waves are lashing the shoreline. The seagulls tumbling in the sky above sound plaintive and warning. It's quite different from the sunshiny blue of my childhood.

My wetsuit's right there, I tell myself firmly. It won't take five minutes to change. I should just do it. Get up. Start.

Proceed.

Minutes pass and I don't appear to be moving. Which is weird, because I *want* to go wild swimming. Very much so. Obviously.

Then a thought occurs to me. I'll need to acclimatize. So maybe I should go and *feel* the water now. Before I put on my wetsuit and get in. Which I am absolutely intending to do.

As I walk down the sand to the surf, a bitter wind catches my cheek and I shiver, pulling my jacket around myself. But as I reach the waves, a shaft of sun comes out from behind a cloud and I feel a sudden burst of optimism. The sea is glittering in places, here and there. There are drifts of blue. The surging waves seem more inviting.

Plus, I'll have a wetsuit on, I remind myself as I reach down to touch the water. So it'll probably be absolutely—

No. *No.*

I grab my hand back out of the water, quelling a shriek. You cannot be serious. That is so cold, it's burning me. It's vicious. It's murderous. There's not a *chance* I'm getting in that, wetsuit or no wetsuit. I back away a few steps and stare at the foaming waves, clutching my icy hand, almost indignant that it could be so treacherously freezing. How am I supposed to 'acclimatize', when three seconds gives me terminal frostbite? How could anyone? How is this a thing?

As the feeling slowly comes back into my hand, I realize that I'm probably not fully equipped. I should have got wetsuit gloves. And wetsuit boots. And a wetsuit hood. And preferably six wetsuits to wear, all layered on top of one another. Or even better, a flight to the Caribbean. I could be somewhere warm, right now. I could be standing in front of a balmy, gentle, caressing sea, not a stroppy, British sea with an attitude problem.

I'm so distracted, I don't notice a stronger wave approaching. I try to jump out of the way, but I'm too late and it washes right over my trainers. I glare at it, outraged. Now my feet are freezing.

'Sod *off*!' I hear myself shouting at the waves. 'You're too bloody *cold*!'

I back away from the waves and stand at a safe distance, watching the water churn itself up endlessly, again and again. There's never any resolution to the sea. There's never any stillness. It's supposed to be soothing, but right now I do not feel soothed. I feel cold and cranky and, underneath it all, like a failure, because I bet Wetsuit Girl would be in those waves now, cavorting with the seals, laughing off the cold like the awesome goddess she is.

I fold my arms, staring morosely at the water. Wild swimming. Huh. When did 'swimming' turn into 'wild swimming', anyway? Why does everything have to be a *thing*? It all seems such a challenge. Such an effort. Slowly I sink on to my haunches, then further down until I'm sitting on the sand. Then I close my eyes and lean back into a lying position.

I'm just so tired. So bone-tired. So heavy and defeated and kind of nothingy. The waves and seagulls are blurring into one mish-mash of sound, which my brain can't unpick. I'm not entirely comfortable, but nor do I quite have the strength to adjust my limbs. They are where they are. If I get cramp, too bad. If I'm washed away to sea, too bad.

I lie there for about an hour, not quite asleep but unable to move. After a while, I notice there are tears running down my face, but I can't even lift a hand to brush them away. I can't do anything. I'm out of energy, out of decision-making. Out of everything.

At last I stir, and move my legs, feeling disoriented. My head is muzzy and I feel a pang of guilt as I realize I've achieved nothing so far except 'lying on the sand'. I rub my face a few times, until I feel a bit more human, then force myself to stand up.

I tramp back up to the lodge and summon up the '20 steps' app on my iPad. Come on, Sasha. I'm not giving up after one failed step. On to 'grounding', whatever the hell that is.

As your soles make direct contact with the earth, you will tap into the earth's natural electrical energy. Your stress levels will lower, your circulation will improve and you will feel more balanced.

OK. Well, that seems simple enough.

I rip off my wet trainers and socks, and cautiously pad out of the lodge. Wincing, I make my way on to a patch of soggy sand and stand there for a bit. I'm trying to channel my thoughts into a positive place. But all my brain seems capable of saying is: *Cold feet. Cold feet. Cold feet.* I can't feel any electrical energy. My stress levels are increasing, not decreasing, and my toes are going to turn blue any moment.

Sod this. So much for grounding. On to the next step.

I hurry back into the lodge, consult my bullet journal, then grab my yoga mat and put on some flip-flops. I need something energetic. The hundred-squat challenge. It's something substantial. Something I can be proud of. And maybe it'll warm me up.

As I place my mat on the beach, I visualize Wetsuit Girl in the app. In the '100 squats' video, she places her mat on a stretch of pristine dry sand. She's wearing a turquoise sports bra and matching sleek leggings. The sun is shining on her ponytailed hair and she looks serene as she bobs up and down.

I, on the other hand, feel drab and windswept. A sharp breeze keeps whipping the ends of the mat up off the sand, which is *really* unhelpful. I do five squats, then have to pause to unpeel the mat from my lower legs. I try to anchor the corners with stones and manage five more squats before the ends have blown up again. This is hopeless – I should never have bothered with the mat. Thoughtlessly I step off it, intending to pick it up – whereupon it blows away down the beach. Shit.

'Come back!' I yell, furiously chasing after it, tripping on my flip-flops. 'Stupid . . . bloody . . .'

At last, with a desperate lunge, I manage to pin the mat down again. Battling as the wind blows it this way and that, I roll it into a sausage, shove it under my arm, then turn to face the sea. Right. Resume.

Hugging the mat, I do three more squats, more slowly this time. Then, after a pause, a fourth. Then I stop. My legs are already aching. My thighs can't do this.

Oh, who am I kidding? I'm not going to do a hundred squats. Nor can I feel the earth's electrical energies through the soles of my feet. And as for wild swimming . . . I shudder at the thought. So that's three fails, already.

Feeling gloomy, I turn, intending to head back to the lodge, whereupon I see a distant figure coming towards me, over the sand. A solitary, indistinct figure, making painfully slow progress, like Lawrence of Arabia approaching through the desert. I squint harder, taking in the shuffling gait, the outline of an overcoat. Is that . . . Herbert?

Yes. It is. And at the rate he's going, it'll take him six weeks to reach me.

Grabbing my mat more tightly, I hurry towards him, breaking into a jog as I see that he's puffing.

'Hi, Herbert!' I greet him as I get near. 'Are you OK?'

There's a pause as Herbert gets his breath. Then he intones in a quavery voice that I can barely hear above the wind, 'The management wish to inform you that unfortunately beach service is not available at the present time.'

'Right,' I say, taken aback. 'I didn't think there was any beach service.'

He's come all the way down here to tell me that?

Herbert is now pulling a piece of paper from his overcoat pocket, and he scrutinizes it for what seems like ten minutes before looking up.

'In addition, unfortunately, the organic kale has not yet arrived. However, Chef Leslie has composed a salad for you which he hopes is to your liking.'

'Oh, right,' I say, taken aback. 'Thanks.'

Herbert nods, then turns, as though to make the long, hard trek back over the sand, and I feel a flicker of alarm. What if he totters and falls? Or the wind blows him over? He's so frail, it probably could. I have a sudden dreadful image of him falling flat on his face on the sand, moving his arms and legs fruitlessly, like a beetle.

'Tell you what, Herbert,' I say quickly. 'Why don't I walk

back with you and have my lunch now? It's a bit early, but I'm quite hungry, so it's no problem.' I hold out an encouraging arm. 'Let's go together!'

'Well, if I could perhaps rest on your arm just for a moment,' Herbert says in his whispery voice. 'Just for a moment.'

By the time we get back to the hotel, I'm pretty much carrying Herbert again. I escort him into the lobby and carefully help him into a big wing chair upholstered in brown fabric and priced at £45. The reception desk is empty, and I wonder briefly whether it's OK leaving him alone – then a gentle snore tells me that he's probably fine.

I can't face my windowless room, and I'm actually quite starving after only having that melon plate for breakfast. So I head straight into the dining room, where a single table is laid.

'Madame.' Nikolai, who was standing by the window like a pillar, springs to life. He pulls back a chair for me, shakes out a starched napkin with lots of elaborate gestures and lays it carefully across my lap. He fills my glass with water, adjusts my knife and tugs at my tablecloth several times. Then he hesitates. 'Madame would prefer a salad,' he ventures.

Oh God. Madame doesn't want a salad, Madame's hungry. But I can't say that, not after they've been to so much trouble.

'Lovely!' I smile brightly at him. 'Thank you.'

Nikolai disappears and then a couple of minutes later returns with a plate adorned with colourful circles. There are slices of roasted carrot and beetroot and tomato, all dotted around randomly. It's actually very pretty. I drizzle my little jug of dressing over the circles, then skewer one with my fork and start to munch. And munch.

Here's the thing: I like salads. I do. But these vegetables are soggy and mushy and turning into a gloop in my mouth, which I can't seem to swallow. I chew and chew and gulp and swig my water. Meanwhile, Nikolai is watching me constantly, ready to leap forward with a deferential 'Madame' if I even meet his eye. He refills my water glass eleven times and each time tugs the tablecloth. It's not the most relaxed meal I've ever had.

At last, I put my knife and fork together and breathe out. Nikolai gives his own relieved sigh, too – I think we both found that a bit of an ordeal.

Also, small point: the whole meal probably contained about twenty calories, tops. I'm still starving.

'How was your salad?' Cassidy's voice greets me as she enters the room with a brisk stride. 'Was it amazing? It was all superfoods,' she adds proudly.

'Delicious, thank you!' I force a smile.

'I'll tell Chef Leslie.' Cassidy beams back. 'He'll be so pleased. His mum just fell over, did her hip in, so he needs a bit of good news. Now, what else can we get you? You won't want pudding, will you? Is there anything else your heart desires?'

I know exactly what my heart desires. I can itemize it. A falafel and halloumi wrap, a choc bar, an apple, a bircher muesli and a canned drink.

'There isn't a Pret a Manger nearby, is there?' I ask casually. 'By any chance?'

'Pret a Manger?' Cassidy looks blank. 'No. Nearest one's in . . . Exeter, maybe? You didn't need one, did you?'

'No! Of course not,' I cover myself quickly. 'I only asked because I hoped there *wasn't* one. I hoped there *wasn't* one,' I emphasize. 'There are too many chains. It's terrible.'

'Agreed.' Cassidy nods earnestly. 'Oh, that reminds me!' She reaches in her bag and whips out a paper flyer. 'Save Our Caves!' She brandishes it. 'Stenbottom Caves are closing, unless we save them, so please go along and support.'

'Stenbottom Caves?' I take the flyer, feeling a wash of nostalgia. We used to go to the caves every year. I remember putting on a hard hat, climbing up and down iron ladders, shining a torch round a series of dark, dank underground spaces, and examining stalagmites. (Stalactites? Whatever.) Every year, Kirsten and I agonized over which semi-precious stone to buy as a souvenir, to add to our 'jewel' collection. I might even still have a couple of them, knocking around.

'They have a Magical Sound and Illumination Experience on at the moment,' says Cassidy. 'Shall I book you in?'

'Yes!' I say. 'Sign me up. Any time.'

'Wonderful!' She claps her hands together. 'I'll tell Neil, he runs it. He'll be chuffed to bits. And how was the lodge today?'

'Tremendous,' I say, smiling back. 'Perfect.'

'Yoga, was it, you were doing out there?'

Oh God. I hope she didn't see me lying on the beach for all that time.

'Yoga, meditation . . .' I wave my hands around vaguely. 'General . . . mindful activities.'

'Amazing! Only I was wondering, will you be out there again this afternoon?' she adds hopefully. 'Because we're having some work done on the floor above your room, and it will be a *tad* noisy between two p.m. and five p.m. There'll be a tiny bit of hammering. And drilling,' she adds, consulting her phone. 'Hammering and drilling and sawing. Just if you were planning on a nap or anything . . .'

Hammering and drilling and sawing.

'It's fine,' I say. 'I'll be on the beach.'

SEVEN

As I head back out to the beach that afternoon, I'm all set for some 'manifesting'. I've read about manifesting before and to be honest it seems like a load of rubbish – but I might as well have a go.

I collect a pen and A4 pad of paper from my rucksack and walk purposefully along the sand. The wind has died down slightly, and the air is feeling a smidgen warmer, which is a plus. I know *exactly* where I'm going to sit, too. There's a big rock to one side of the lodges, which Kirsten and I used to eye up for climbing potential. But whatever time we came along, it was always already commandeered by some posh child or other from the lodges – and in a weird way, we felt like it belonged to them.

But now it's mine. All mine!

I clamber up to the main flat surface – about five feet off the ground – and nestle into a handy hollow, leaning against a solid wall of rock, worn smooth over the years. Very soon I realize something: this rock is awesome! It's like an armchair.

I wriggle luxuriously against the smooth curves, and sigh happily. I could sit here all afternoon. I *will* sit here all afternoon. There's even room to stretch out my legs.

Right. Manifesting.

I search on my phone for the section in the app on 'manifesting' and skim the details. The gist seems to be that you tell the universe what you want, whereupon the universe will give it to you. Which seems like a pretty good deal. *Be specific in your desires*, the app urges. *Be clear and detailed. Write down a description of what you want to bring into your life, then visualize it.*

What do I want to bring into my life?

Oh God. My mind roams around my life, sheering away from one painful, embarrassing area after another. Could I write *A different life*?

No. Too vague. What if they gave me an even crappier life instead? I have a vision of myself stuck on a desert island, yelling at the universe, 'I didn't want *this* life!'

Manifesting is risky, I realize. No wonder you have to be specific. What if you asked for riches and the universe misheard and gave you bitches? Note to self: write clearly. I look down at my phone again to see if there's any more help, and see a section on inspiration.

If you are stuck, just allow your soul to speak. Let your pen sit on the page, then write the first words that come to you.

I rest my pen on the page, gaze out to sea, and find myself writing *A halloumi and falafel wrap.*

No. Don't be stupid. That's not manifesting, that's a lunch order. I rip out the page, feeling embarrassed and hoping that the universe didn't see it. Right. Try again. Proper manifesting.

I set my pen on the page again and look steadily out to sea, trying to empty my mind of visions of choc bars and think of something that I actually want, deep down.

Sex, I write, then stare at the page, taken aback. I didn't intend to write that. Why has my mind gone there? Do I even want sex?

No. I don't. I don't want sex, and *that's* the problem. It stings me, this lack I have. What's happened to me? I enjoyed sex with Stuart. Well, I did for a while. But then, gradually, I didn't. We kept arguing anyway, which isn't exactly conducive. Or did we argue *because* of the sex? It's all a confused jumble of memories now, and all I know is that I'm hollow. My body feels numb. I don't react to anything any more. Hot guy on the Tube: numb. Get chatted up in Pret: numb. Sex scene on TV: numb. The whole activity seems kind of awkward and pointless, even though I can remember once thinking it was the best thing in the world.

So it's not that I want to have sex. I want to *want* sex. I want to *crave* sex. I want to wake up that appetite.

It's all very well, Kirsten saying I should see a doctor. As if I'm really going to walk into an overstretched GP's office and say, 'I'd like a pill to make me fancy people again, please.' Anyway, I've been so busy with meetings and emails, it's almost been a relief not to be juggling work with dating. So I've just parked the problem, thinking 'It'll pass.'

But what if it doesn't? What if the universe could help me? Put it like this, what have I got to lose?

I change *Sex* into *Sexual desire*. Then, to clarify, I add *libido*.

How else can I put it to the universe? Because now I'm actually doing this, I really want to state my case. In fact, I want to jump to the head of the queue, if possible. After some thought, I add a few more words of clarification:

Sexual hunger. Sexual fantasies. Craving for sex.

Then it occurs to me that it's no good having a craving for sex if there's no one there to sate it with. I'd better make that plain to the universe, too.

A man.

No. I must be more precise.

A man with a cock.

I stare at my words, chewing my pen, yet again wondering if that's specific enough for the universe. I feel no detail is so small that it can be safely omitted. Surely the universe is just waiting to crow, 'Ha ha, you didn't say what *sort* of man, did you? You didn't say what *sort* of cock.'

A sexy man with a working cock, I write, with more conviction. *Big, preferably.*

No, wait. Is that greedy? Will the universe punish me? Also, am I phrasing my requests politely enough? I hastily cross out *Big, preferably* and replace it with *Any size, thank you.*

Then I feel a wave of guilt. Is this really all I'm wishing for? I'm a terrible, selfish person. I should want to manifest something more noble, like world peace. Hastily I add it.

World peace.

I stare at my words, then feel a wave of embarrassment. This is stupid. I fold the paper up and tuck it into the pocket of my hoodie. OK, I've manifested. Maybe I'll meditate now. I focus on the shoreline, watching the ebb and suck of the waves, and try to contemplate the beauties of the world.

God, I'm hungry. I'm *so* hungry. How can I exist on melon and salad? My stomach is rumbling so hard it's practically drowning out the sound of the sea.

I consider going back to the hotel, ordering a cream tea for four and scoffing the lot. But, no. I'd have to eat it with Nikolai watching my every bite. And put up with Cassidy exclaiming, 'A cream tea? But we thought you were healthy!'

Plus there's the hammering and drilling, not to mention the sawing . . .

OK. New plan.

Filled with determination, I heave myself off the rock and tramp over the sand to the lodge, where I grab my rucksack. I've been meaning to look round the town anyway, and I've got two twenty-pound notes in here. I'm going to buy myself a feast.

Walking into town is weird. It's the same place I remember, with its narrow streets, cute cottages with pitched roofs, shops and cafes . . . but dead. It looks so sad and empty. During my childhood summer holidays, it used to teem with life and music and people. There would be tourists in every street. Bright inflatable toys and fishing nets for sale on every corner. Surfers carrying boards back to their lodgings, children dropping ice creams and wailing, and dads drinking beers in the pub gardens. The narrow streets would be so full of pedestrians that cars would have to nudge through slowly, the hot sun gleaming off their roofs.

Today, there's no hot sun, no people, no nothing. The shops are silent and the air is full of drizzle. I pass a row of guest houses and shudder at the net curtains in the windows. They look so dreary in the winter light, and one is drooping half off its rail.

The White Hart pub is closed, otherwise I might have popped in there for some crisps. It's an old coaching inn that Dad used to visit every time we came, and I slow down as I approach, remembering him standing at the bar, sipping his beer in that deliberate way he had. I stand motionless for a moment, full of memories, then give a kind of little shudder. Come on. Food.

The old-fashioned fudge shop is still here, but to my disappointment has a sign across the door: CLOSED FOR THE SEASON. The Tea Shoppe is also closed for the season. This is ridiculous. Where am I going to get my feast?

The place has become more chi-chi, I realize as I turn into a street full of galleries. One contains watercolours of the sea, another has glass sculptures . . . and oh my God! There's an open cafe! I quicken my pace and almost burst through the door into a warm, fuggy space smelling of cinnamon. It's a bakery too! Greedily, I scan the display of cakes in a glass case. There's a Bakewell tart, fat iced buns, cheese scones, doughnuts, brownies . . . *everything*.

'Excuse me?' It takes me a moment to realize that the girl behind the counter is addressing me.

'Oh.' I look up. 'Hi.'

'Sorry, but I've got to ask. Are you the lady staying at the Rilston?' She peers at me avidly. 'The kale lady?'

The kale lady?

'I'm Bea, Cassidy's my friend and she's told me all about you,' she continues in an enthusiastic rush. 'How healthy you are. Salads and kale and yoga on the beach all day long. Noni juice – that's a new one. Cassidy called me, asked if we had any. I said, never heard of it! What's it do, then, noni juice?'

Oh God. This bloody noni juice. I have no idea what it does.

'It benefits you,' I say vaguely. 'It has various . . . benefits.'

'Benefits your noni?' She giggles and bites her lip. 'Sorry. It's just that's what Cassidy and I used to call . . . you know.' She glances down at her crotch. 'Those bits,' she adds, in case I haven't understood. 'Down below. Privates.'

'Right. Yes. Got it.'

'Anyway, how can I help?' she asks, as the door *tings* and

another girl comes in, wearing an anorak. 'Paula, it's the kale lady!' Bea points at me excitedly, then adds, 'We're not the healthiest shop in the world . . .' She looks around doubtfully. 'I don't know what you'll have.'

'The spelt scones are gluten-free,' offers Paula as she takes off her anorak.

'No, they're not,' contradicts Bea.

'Well, they're something-free. Are you vegan?' Paula peers at me.

'She's *healthy*,' Bea answers, before I can reply. 'It's different. Ooh, I know!' Her face brightens. 'We do salad garnishes. You could have a couple of those. I'll put them on a plate, give you a doily. Two pounds fifty, that all right?'

Oh *God*. How do I order six doughnuts and a Bakewell slice now?

No. I can't. I can't face the kerfuffle.

'I'll just have some mineral water, please,' I say after a pause, and Bea nods respectfully.

'Of course. Didn't think of that. Mineral water.' She hands me a bottle and takes my money and as I'm leaving calls out, 'Hope you get your noni juice!'

Back outside, I breathe out hard. Enough messing about. I need *food*. From some nice anonymous outlet. Hunching my shoulders, I start marching through the streets, right to the other end of town, where the cute cottages merge into less cute breeze-block buildings and garages and run-down flats. I dimly recall a tiny supermarket at this end of town, and . . . Yes! It's still here.

It's the tiniest, grimmest shop, staffed by a silent guy in a brown T-shirt. There's nothing fresh, only packets and jars, but that suits me fine. I collect three bags of crisps, some chocolate biscuits, a bag of salted peanuts, a bottle of wine and a tub of ice cream. I throw in *Heat*, *Grazia* and *Best Dressed Celebrities* and finally a Mars bar, then head to the till. The guy in the brown T-shirt looks at me hard for a moment, surveys my items, raises his eyebrows, then shrugs and starts to scan them. I stash what I can in my rucksack and put the rest in a plastic bag. As long as I don't get spotted on the way back, I'll be fine.

I pay with cash and as the guy gives me my change, he touches his nose briefly.

'I don't see nothing,' he says in sepulchral tones and nods at my bag. 'I don't say nothing. More to life than kale.'

Oh my God.

Everyone knows?

Feeling totally conspicuous, I hurry back through the drizzly streets, my bag of treats tucked under my arm, where I hope no one can see them. As soon as I can, I turn through the car park and make for the sand dunes which run between here and the beach. They're huge sandy hills with grasses sprouting on top and steep-sided paths winding between them. They'll shield me from view.

As I approach the dunes, I'm suddenly flooded with childhood memories. We spent hours here, playing hide-and-seek, sliding down them, lying on the tops of them, plucking at the vegetation and talking about life. I choose a path I remember well and as I make my way up a familiar sandy incline, I feel the same anticipation I always did, knowing that any minute I'll emerge on to the beach and see the sea . . .

Then a deep male voice stops me in my tracks.

'Dear Sir Edwin, I would like to apologize for my behaviour last week.'

Hang on. I know that voice, don't I? A dry voice with an edge of impatience. I've heard it before.

I think intently for a moment – then realize. It's that guy from the train, the one with the surfboard. And he sounds just as tense and sarcastic as he did then. He may be saying sorry, but he doesn't sound sorry.

The voice continues: 'I should not have raised my voice to you in the departmental meeting, even though you're a complacent, smug, *total* bloody—'

He stops mid-stream and sighs deeply, while I roll my eyes. Obviously apologizing doesn't come naturally to this guy.

'I should not have raised my voice to you in the departmental meeting,' he resumes. 'Nor should I have slammed my coffee cup down on the boardroom table, causing spillage and damage to papers. I respect you highly and can only express my dismay at my actions. I am taking some time out from work to consider my behaviour. I look forward to seeing you again at the office and may I apologize again. Best, Finn Birchall.'

There's silence. I don't know what to do. I'm breathing hard, I realize, clutching my bag of goodies tightly against me, leaning against the sandy slope as though it will hide me. I don't want to confront anyone right now, least of all some man with a temper issue. And I'm just debating whether to back away when the voice starts up again.

'Dear Alan, I would like to apologize for my behaviour last week. I should not have punched the coffee vending machine in your presence, nor threatened to dismantle it with a sledgehammer.'

He did *what*? I stifle a giggle.

'I'm sorry that you were unnerved by my actions and can only apologize. I am taking some time out from work to consider my behaviour. I look forward to seeing you again at the office and may I apologize again. Best, Finn Birchall.'

This is excruciating. I shouldn't be hearing this, but I'm riveted.

Slowly, silently, I creep forward, keeping to the side of the sandy path. I know this path. There's a bend ahead and a little hollow where we used to sit as kids – I bet he's there.

Sure enough, a moment later I glimpse him – and I was right. It's the man from the train. Tall, dark-haired, leaning against the side of the hollow, dictating into a phone. He's angled away, so all I can make out is broad shoulders in a North Face jacket, a glimpse of ear, his hands holding his phone, and that firm, stubbly jaw. As I'm watching, he edits his text, then starts a new dictation, and I freeze.

'Dear Marjorie, I would like to apologize for my behaviour last week. I should not have exhibited frustration with the office ficus plant for dropping leaves into my lunch, nor threatened to chainsaw it into bits.'

I give another stifled giggle, clapping a hand over my mouth.

The man runs his own hand roughly through his hair, as though marshalling his thoughts. It's a strong hand, which I now imagine crashing a coffee cup down on a boardroom table or chainsawing a ficus plant. I wonder what he does. Something involving clients. And colleagues. God help them.

'I understand that you are fond of the ficus plant and were upset by my intemperate language,' he continues. 'Again, I apologize. I am taking some time out from work to consider my behaviour. I look forward to seeing you again at the office and may I apologize again. Best, Finn Birchall.'

He breaks off, looks at his phone for a moment, then thrusts it into his pocket, exhaling hard. From my partial view, I can detect that his face is creased in a deep frown. There's a silent beat during which I don't even breathe. Then he stands up straight from his leaning position, as if to go, and I feel a spike of panic. Shit. Shit! What am I doing, watching him like this? What if he catches me? He'll do more than slam down a coffee cup. Does he have a chainsaw about his person?

On lightning-fast, silent feet, I sprint back down the slope, along the edge of the dunes and into the next sandy hollow. Soon I'm out of sight, concealed between two high dunes and hardly breathing. I have no idea where the guy is, but it doesn't matter. The point is, he didn't catch me listening.

I wait a few seconds, safe in my hiding place, then put on my best 'natural' air as I proceed down a steep bank and then out on to the beach. The tide is out; the shore is vast and empty. The lodges are way over at the other end, and I turn my steps that way, forcing myself not to look around for the guy. It would be a complete giveaway.

In any case, it's fine. He must have gone in some other direction, because there's no sign of him or anyone as I tramp over the sand.

I reach the lodge without any other encounters, shut the door firmly, sink down on the sofa and tear open a bag of crisps. And oh my God. That first salty, crispy, oily crunch is heaven. *Heaven.* I tear through the first packet, savouring every mouthful, then start cramming peanuts into my mouth. They feel solid. They feel like food. I was starving, I realize, starving.

After a while, my mouth starts to feel too salty and I realize I could have done with an apple or something.

But I've got something even better. Wine.

I slosh some into a Rilston Hotel mug, sit back on the sofa, open *Heat* magazine, take a deep slug and breathe out. OK, now you're talking. *Now* you're talking.

It's sharp wine, I realize after a second slug. It's almost vicious. The label on the bottle says *White Wine* with no other information. But I don't care. Who needs extraneous, pointless facts? It's wine. The end.

And now I have my steps for the rest of the afternoon all planned out. *1. Drink wine. 2. Eat crisps. 3. Consume ice cream. 4. Read about celebrities until my brain addles. 5. Repeat.*

I'm not sure these steps will lead to a 'better me', but they will lead to a 'happy me'. 'Better me' can just wait for a bit. In fact, I'm tempted to tell 'better me' to sod right off.

By 5 p.m., I've consumed the entire tub of ice cream, half the wine and all the magazines. My teeth are coated with sugar, my brain is dazzled by celebrity boob jobs, my thoughts are fuzzy with wine and I feel a kind of general wellbeing, just tinged vaguely with the sense that I've polluted my body with a year's supply of crap.

Well. Whatever.

It's getting dark, and I don't fancy dozing off on the sofa and waking up at 3 a.m., so reluctantly I rouse myself. I'll go back on the programme tomorrow, I resolve. I'll do some squats and eat some bean sprouts. But now, what I most feel like doing is sleeping for about seventy-two hours.

As I get back to the hotel, the lobby is full of commotion. Nikolai is moving antique chairs around while Cassidy bossily directs, and Herbert is holding a French horn which looks like it dates from 1843.

'We're going to have a little concert!' Cassidy announces, as she spots me. 'Perk up the guests. Next week, we thought, only we're going to rehearse tonight. Herbert can play the horn and Nikolai says he can recite poetry in Polish and he'll tell us what it means, after. Did you have a lovely day?' she adds to me. 'And were you wanting to eat in the dining room, later?'

'I'll have room service tonight,' I say. 'Thanks.'

'Well, Chef Leslie has created a special dish just for you,' she adds proudly. 'Plain poached chicken breast, steamed spinach and crispbread. No butter, of course.'

'Wonderful,' I say sincerely. After scoffing sugar all afternoon, plain chicken and spinach sounds about right.

'And could we tempt you to some ice cream?' Cassidy suggests. 'As a one-off treat, maybe?'

My mind flashes back to the whole tub of Cookies 'n' Cream I've just demolished. I feel a bit sick at the thought. 'No, thanks,' I say. 'No ice cream.'

'Not even one tiny scoop?'

'Not even one tiny scoop,' I say firmly.

'Aren't you disciplined?' Cassidy exclaims admiringly. 'You put us all to shame with your healthy regime. Oh, hello, Mr Birchall,' she adds, looking up.

Mr Birchall? Wait. I know that name. Oh God, please don't say . . .

As I follow her gaze, I stiffen in horror. Coming down the stairs into the lobby is the guy who punches vending machines and wants to chainsaw ficus plants and reduces toddlers to tears. Here, in the same hotel. He looks as super-relaxed and approachable as he did before, i.e. not at all.

'Ms Worth.' Simon comes hurrying into the lobby, looking as harassed as ever. 'A *thousand* apologies. I am mortified. I am distraught.'

'What's wrong?' I say, taken aback.

'We have still not been able to source your organic kale.' Simon shakes his head dismally. 'A supply arrived today but was unfortunately damaged. Chef Leslie has used spinach instead, but I will naturally waive the entire charge on your dinner bill tonight.'

I'm not sure if I want to laugh or tell him 'Get a grip!' How does he expect to make any money if he keeps giving me free meals?

'You don't have to give me a free dinner,' I say firmly. 'Spinach is fine.'

'I appreciate your kind words, Ms Worth,' says Simon, lifting his chin nobly. 'However, we at the Rilston have certain standards and we have not lived up to those standards. Your PA was adamant that you had certain specific, tailored requirements. Organic kale. Goji berries. Noni juice.'

'Wow,' says Finn Birchall. 'Sounds a bunch of fun.'

He's standing at the base of the stairs, waiting for Nikolai to move out of his way, his fingers drumming on the banister. What's it got to do with him, anyway?

'Oh, Ms Worth doesn't eat anything fun,' Cassidy assures him. 'Not even a biscuit! She's so virtuous! My friend Bea said you went to the bakery today and all you bought was a mineral water? Nikolai, get out of Mr Birchall's way!' she adds to Nikolai, who is hovering uncertainly with a chair. 'Just put it down anywhere. Can I help, Mr Birchall?'

'I have a specific, tailored requirement,' says Finn Birchall. 'I don't know if you can help. It's for a double whisky on the rocks.'

Is he making a dig at me? I glare at him, and he looks back impassively.

'Of course!' says Cassidy, oblivious to any subtext. 'Please take a seat at the bar.'

'I will attend to this myself,' says Simon, practically leaping forward. 'I will pour the whisky myself. I hope all is satisfactory with your stay, Mr Birchall, and please may I apologize yet again that your room was being used for cheese storage when you arrived. These are not the high standards we expect of ourselves at the Rilston.'

I suppress a smile as I glance over at Finn Birchall. Did his face just give the tiniest of amused flickers?

No, I must have imagined it.

'Now, I *must* introduce you two,' says Cassidy, as Simon hurries off towards the bar. 'Sasha Worth, meet Finn Birchall. You're both using lodges on the beach.'

I blink at her in shock. What?

'You're the only two guests using them,' Cassidy continues chattily. 'Nice for you both to have some company.'

Nice? I feel growing dismay as I digest this appalling news. I had the place to myself. It was all perfect. And now Mr Angry has to barge in. I can tell my face is crestfallen – and he doesn't look exactly thrilled, either.

'Shall I put you next door to each other?' Cassidy suggests brightly. 'You could be neighbours!'

'No!' I exclaim fervently, before I can stop myself.

'No!' Finn Birchall says simultaneously, and our eyes meet as though at least we agree on this.

'If that's OK,' I add awkwardly. 'I think it would be better if . . .'

'Far better.' He nods.

'I suppose you'll be doing your yoga and all that,' says Cassidy, as though the reason is dawning on her. 'Ms Worth is here for a wellness break,' she informs Finn Birchall. 'She's our healthiest-ever guest! Only eats salad, and does mindful activities all day on the beach!'

Finn Birchall looks totally repulsed. 'Sounds tremendous,' he says, barely hiding his contempt.

'It is,' I shoot back. 'Very.'

God, this man is obnoxious.

'So maybe it does make sense for you to have some space . . .' Cassidy pauses thoughtfully. 'I'll put you in Lodge Eight then, Mr Birchall. Right at the other end from Ms Worth, with six empty lodges in between.'

'Thanks,' says Finn Birchall curtly. 'I appreciate it.'

I feel nettled by his tone. His whole demeanour, in fact. It's not like I want him next to me, either.

'I appreciate it, too,' I put in sharply. 'Even more so, I should think.'

Cassidy has been following our exchange in slight bemusement, and now she hands Finn Birchall a lodge key.

'Here you are, then,' she says. 'Key to Lodge 8. And you know what?' she adds reassuringly, looking from him to me and back again. 'It's a big old beach. I expect you won't even notice each other.'

EIGHT

I wake up the next morning with my head teeming. Not with good stuff. Not with forward-looking, mindful thoughts. But work stress. Round and round. It won't let me alone.

The more I've stepped away from Zoose, the more I can see how badly run the marketing department is. Asher is like some child letting off fireworks. He likes short-term, flashy stuff. But where's the long-term strategy? Where's the consistency? Where are the values?

And where the hell is Lev? You can't just keep on sending your apologies and expect your company to flourish. You need to have a vision, you need leadership, you need a presence . . .

I'm breathing hard, I realize. My heart is thumping. I'm already imagining going back to the office in three weeks; feeling a curdling mixture of dread and frustration. I'm doing the opposite of relaxing and recuperating.

Honestly.

I grab my bullet journal, turn to the back and start

adding to the notes I made on the train. It's quite cathartic. It's like writing down all the reasons you hate your ex-boyfriend and then throwing the list in the bin. After I've drawn a diagram of the way I think the marketing department should be structured, I find myself adding more and more notes.

The staff are so stretched that nothing works as it should. Departments seem in denial that they are working for the same organization. Support staff do not support. Helplines do not help.

Still breathing hard, I look at my words. OK. I need to calm down. *Thank you, brain, for your thoughts. That's enough now.*

But my brain is still whirling. It doesn't want to stop. I still have about a thousand words I could write. What do I do?

I look up at Wetsuit Girl, trying to find inspiration. Does she have a job? Is she seething because of her boss? Does she have similar struggles? Maybe holding a surfboard on a beach and looking fab *is* her job. Maybe her only struggle is, 'Which wetsuit shall I insert my spectacular body into today?' Pah, it's all right for some . . .

No. Stop. Abruptly I realize I'm in danger of sitting here all day thinking curmudgeonly, negative thoughts. Bitching about Wetsuit Girl in my head is not going to help anyone. It's not her fault she's shiny and happy. Resolutely I flip to the front pages of my bullet journal, turning away from all my stressy work notes to the positive part, with the stickers and the resolutions.

I'll write down five steps for today. Come on. Go.

1. Meditation.

Yes. Good way to start. I'll sit on the rock and gaze out to sea and let the sound of the sea calm my brain.

2. 100-squat challenge.

I'm not giving up on that. I can do some squats.

3. Communing with nature.

Apparently this boosts the immune system.

4. Dance like no one is watching.

Apparently, this also boosts the immune system. (What doesn't boost the immune system? Answer: half a bottle of White Wine and a tub of Cookies 'n' Cream.)

5. Sea-shore walk.

Strictly speaking, I did a walk yesterday, but I'm not sure 'Walk to the shop to buy sugar-filled crap' is what Wetsuit Girl had in mind. So let's try that again.

I underline each entry firmly and I'm just trying to find some stickers to plonk next to each step when my phone rings. It's Mum.

'Hi, Mum,' I greet her. 'Just doing my bullet journal.'

'Well done, darling!' she enthuses. 'And are you feeling any better? Less stressed?'

I think back to my frantic scribblings about Zoose, my

pounding heart, my feeling that I want to yell at someone. Hmm. Not really.

'Yes,' I say firmly. 'Definitely.'

'Oh good! Have you been in the sea? Are you following the app?'

'Kind of.' I cross my fingers. 'In my own way.'

'Because I read a piece today in my health magazine,' says Mum in the urgent voice she uses for imparting nuggets of information. 'Do you know what the most important thing for your wellbeing is? Your gut!' She delivers the punchline with aplomb. 'They think ninety per cent of burnout cases are due to poor gut health!'

I stare at my phone dubiously. What per cent? Who did they study? That seems very unlikely. But before I can dispute this statistic, Mum's off again. 'Anyway, don't worry, it's all in hand. I've phoned Reception and told them you urgently need some kefir and fermented cabbage.'

My face drops. Fermented cabbage?

'I spoke to a very helpful girl,' Mum powers on. 'Said I was your PA again, and she assured me she'd get right on to it. I mentioned reflexology, too, and she's making enquiries. They do seem good at the Rilston,' she adds approvingly. 'Nothing too much trouble. Are they looking after you? Oh, and I didn't even ask, they did put you on the sea-front side, didn't they?'

'Yes,' I say, glancing at the boarded-up window and away again. 'Yes, they did. All good. They even sent me flowers,' I add, looking at the bouquet which arrived last night. The message says *A thousand apologies for your substandard treatment, for which we are deeply mortified.*

'Wonderful!' says Mum. 'Well, I'd better go, darling. Oh, I spoke to Dinah.'

'*Dinah?*' I peer at the phone.

Dinah is my friend, my oldest friend. But I haven't talked to her in what feels like for ever. She's a cheerful, competent lawyer-turned-doula and I love her to bits, but I guess I've been avoiding her. I haven't had the energy to be 'on' and cheerful; nor do I want to dissolve into sobs. I guess this is how people slowly turn into recluses.

'I was wanting to send you a little surprise,' explains Mum, 'and I thought she'd know what to get. We settled on laven-der bath oil. There now, it's not a surprise any more. But love, Dinah didn't have any idea! I had to put her in the picture.'

'I know,' I manage. 'I was getting round to contacting her.'

'Darling, there's no need to hide this all away. Your friends want to help!'

'I know,' I say. 'Bye, Mum.'

As I ring off, tears prick my eyes. I don't know why I haven't reached out to Dinah. Or any of my friends. Because . . . I'm embarrassed, I guess. They can cope with life. And I can't.

Anyway. That's a goal I can work towards. Right now, I need food.

As I reach the dining-room door, I tense up at the sight of Finn Birchall sitting at a table.

'Morning,' he says curtly.

'Morning,' I reply, equally shortly.

'Good morning!' Cassidy bustles up to me. 'I do hope you slept well! Now, I heard what you said about wanting your own space. So we've seated you two right away from each other. Ms Worth, you're over here.'

She ushers me to the other end of the dining room, and into a chair. To be fair to her, I'm about as far away from Finn

106

Birchall as I could possibly be. In fact, we make quite a ludi-crous sight.

'Thanks.' I smile at her. 'I appreciate it.'

'I had your PA Erin on the phone this morning,' Cassidy says in tones of slight awe. 'She starts early, doesn't she? You do work her hard!'

'She's . . . full of energy,' I manage.

'I've noted down all the requests she mentioned . . .' Cassidy consults a list, her brow wrinkled anxiously. 'Only I wanted to ask, what kind of kefir did you require?'

Oh God. I know Mum means well, but I'm totally embar-rassed. I have nothing to say about kefir. Isn't it just liquidy yogurt?

'Any kind,' I say, trying to appear knowledgeable. 'Although preferably organic, obviously. For the organic benefits.'

'Obviously,' says Cassidy reverently. 'Now, the fermented cabbage may take a *little* time. But the good news is, your organic kale's been delivered! Chef Leslie's making your smoothie as we speak! It looks so healthy,' she adds encour-agingly. 'Really green and sludgy.'

'Great!' I try to sound enthusiastic. 'Can't wait!'

'Your PA also said you need a reflexologist,' adds Cassidy, consulting her notebook, 'and I'm working on that. We *do* have a reflexologist in the summer, lovely lady, very holistic, but unfortunately she works at Burger King in Exeter during the winter, so she's not presently available . . .' Cassidy sees that Finn Birchall's hand is raised and turns to him. 'Mr Birchall!' she calls across the room. 'How can I help?'

'Am I able to make a request directly?' he enquires, dead-pan. 'Or should I ask my PA to phone the reception desk? Is that how it works here?'

In spite of myself, I flush. OK. I can see what I look like. Just for a nano-second I consider saying, 'It wasn't my PA phoning, it was my mum.' But then, almost instantly I feel nettled at the idea. Why should I explain myself? It's a free country. I can have a PA if I want to.

'Oh no!' says Cassidy earnestly, missing his point completely. 'You can ask me anything, Mr Birchall.'

'I'd like a black coffee, please.' He glances briefly my way. 'But if I need to ask my people to email your people about it, then let's make that happen and circle back. Maybe I'll loop in my chief of staff.'

Ha ha. Hilarious.

'Oh no!' says Cassidy, wide-eyed. 'Just ask me.' She beams at him. 'One black coffee coming up – and Nikolai will be out for your food orders directly.'

I lift my chin, ignoring Finn Birchall as pointedly as I can, and sip my water. A moment later, Nikolai arrives at my side, holding the breakfast menu and a glass on a silver tray. It contains some sort of livid-green substance and smells of algae.

'Kale smoothie,' he says with an air of pride.

My stomach clenches. It looks undrinkable. Unspeakable.

'Thank you!' I say, as brightly as I can, whereupon Nikolai proffers the menu, pointing helpfully at 'melon plate'.

'Madame would prefer melon plate,' he says confidently. 'Melon plate as yesterday.'

Oh God. It's easier just to say yes.

'Yes, please.' I force a smile. 'One melon plate. Thank you.'

'How is the kale smoothie?' Nikolai gestures eagerly at the green slime and my heart sinks. I can't dodge it. I'll have to try it.

I take a sip and try not to heave. It tastes of swamp. I've

never drunk a swamp, but somehow I know instinctively that this smoothie is exactly what they taste like.

'Lovely.' I force another smile. 'Perfect! Please thank the chef.'

Nikolai looks satisfied, then approaches Finn Birchall at the other end of the room.

'Sir. Some breakfast?'

'Yes, please.' He nods. 'Two eggs over easy, bacon, sourdough toast, butter, marmalade, orange juice and a stack of pancakes.' He pauses, noticing that Nikolai is scribbling frantically, then adds, 'And maple syrup. And another black coffee.'

My stomach is growling desperately as I listen to this list, but I try to keep my expression pleasant.

'Kale smoothie, Sir?' Nikolai gestures over at my glass. 'Organic kale, very healthy?'

Finn Birchall looks nauseated. 'No. Thank you.'

Defensively I take another sip of the kale smoothie and nearly gag. What is in this?

Nikolai scurries off and there's silence while we wait for our food. I try to relax, but somehow I can't. There's something about Finn Birchall's presence that makes me prickle. Is it because his fingers keep drumming the table? Is it because he looks so murderous? *It's breakfast!* I feel like exclaiming. *What's the problem?*

He's tense, I realize. He's tense, and he's making me tense, too. I preferred it when it was just me and Nikolai anxiously saying 'Madame' every three seconds.

At last, Nikolai reappears and I breathe a sigh of relief. First he sets down a plate of melon in front of me. Then he returns to the kitchen and brings out the epic feast that is Finn Birchall's breakfast.

I want to swoon. The sight of it. The *smell* of it. Bacon. Eggs. Pancakes. A pile of toast. Solid, warm, delicious food with maple syrup sploshed all over it.

I can't watch him eat all that, I'll collapse with hunger. Hastily I consume my insubstantial melon slices, sip my herbal tea, then survey the kale smoothie with childlike dread. Could I get up and just leave it? No. Not after they've gone to such trouble.

Could I throw it in a plant pot? No. There isn't a plant pot.

Then, with a sudden idea, I call Nikolai over.

'Hi,' I say. 'I need to get going, I'm afraid. Could I have my smoothie to go, please?'

Back upstairs in my room, I sit on the bed and stare at the wallpaper until I feel calmer. Then I pack up my stuff and walk through the lawned garden to the beach, clutching my smoothie in its paper cup. The air is cold but there's a hint of blue in the sky and crocuses peeping out on the lawn. It's a good day, I tell myself. Let's begin like I mean to go on, with positive thoughts.

As I walk, I visualize a successful meditation. I'll sit cross-legged on the rock. Yes. I'll gaze out to sea. Yes. I'll listen to the waves and be inspired. *Yes.* I have such a clear image of myself that when I finally catch sight of the rock, I stop dead in shock.

Finn Birchall is on the rock. *My* rock.

Picking up my pace, I stride over the beach and head towards my lodge, which is the lodge closest to the rock. Just saying. I know rocks don't belong to anyone, but if that rock did belong to anyone, it would be me. How did he get down here so quickly, anyway?

He doesn't even turn his head as I draw near. He's lounging

in the hollow of the rock, just like all those entitled posh lodge kids used to, and I can't help it, I feel a flare of indignation.

A voice inside me is saying, *It's just a rock*. And *Chill out, Sasha*. But another, less rational voice is saying, *It's so unfair. The beach was MINE.*

I approach the rock from the side, and look up at him. He's staring ahead at the sea, his face in a glower, his fingers relentlessly drumming. Is he meditating? He doesn't look like it, unless his mantra is *Sod the world and everyone in it*.

Isn't he even going to greet me?

'Hello,' I say, my polite manner masking a subtle passive aggression.

(OK, maybe it's not that subtle. Also, maybe I'm not masking it.)

For a moment, he doesn't even respond. Then at last he turns his head to regard me with dark, impassive eyes.

'I thought we were going to ignore each other?'

'We are.' I give him an even more polite, loathing smile. 'Absolutely. Just being a civil human being. Forget I said anything.'

'Apologies if I don't leap down, shake your hand and ask you in for tea,' he says, the sarcasm clear in his voice. 'But I didn't come here to be sociable.'

'Nor did I.' I fold my arms. 'I came here for solitude. That's why I was so pleased to see that the beach was empty. Until now, obviously.' I flick my eyes over him, and momentarily his face alters as he comprehends. Then he resumes his murderous stare.

'Well, sorry to ruin your party,' he says, with a shrug that clearly reads *not-sorry*.

'No problem. Nice rock.' I nod at it.

'Yup.'

'I used that rock yesterday to meditate.'

'Good for you.'

He turns back to gaze at the sea again; clearly our conversation is over. Well, sod him. I don't need the rock, anyway. I'll just get on with my wellness programme and ignore him.

Except, he's there. He's just *there*, and somehow I can't ignore him.

From his vantage point on the rock, he has a view of the whole beach, I realize, as I walk along the sand with my exercise mat and hula hoop. Trying to stay aloof, I stride straight down to the waves, plonk my exercise mat on the sand and sit cross-legged, facing the sea, to meditate. *Calm thoughts*, I tell myself firmly as I watch the waves whooshing in. *Calm thoughts. Focus on the sound of the—*

Is he watching me?

Casually, I glance round, catch his eye by mistake and flush, instantly swivelling back to face the sea again. Damn.

Why do I care if he's watching me?

I don't. Obviously I don't. But it's an unwelcome distraction, having another presence on the beach. I can feel his gaze boring into my back. Or I imagine I can. Either way, I am not lost in a trance of relaxation and this is not working.

I do a few desultory stretches, then wonder if I should move on to the hundred-squat challenge instead. But that'll be even worse. I really don't need an audience for that. And which way do I face? Either I'll have to do them facing away, in which case he sees my bum bobbing up and down. Or I turn around, in which case I look like I'm curtseying to him.

Casually I glance round to see if he's left – but no. He's still on the rock. Damn him.

Feeling self-conscious, I stand up, roll up my mat, shove my hula hoop over my shoulder and decide to move on to *Step 3. Communing with nature.* To remind myself of my task, I open the app on my phone and find the advice, which is illustrated by two photos of Wetsuit Girl. In one, she's cavorting with a dolphin, which seems to be smiling joyfully back at her. In the other, she seems to be in a rainforest, touching the bark of a massive tree, an expression of awe on her face.

The ancient natural world can soothe any troubled spirit. Animals instinctively want to help and nurture. Plants want to heal. Harness their power. Reach out to them and feel your mind and body respond.

I'm not wildly optimistic, but let's give it a try. I shove my phone back in the pocket of my anorak and cast around the beach for some nature. There are seagulls shrieking above me, and I peer up at them, but they're too far off to make a connection. Also: do seagulls instinctively want to help and nurture? In my experience, they instinctively want to pinch your food and make messes on your shoulder.

I glance at the waves – but I've already tried looking at the waves. OK. What else is there?

Seaweed? Dubiously I walk over to a patch of seaweed and stare down at it. It's brown and gloopy and kind of unattractive. I'm not sure it's doing anything for me. There's a tiny crab walking over the top of it though, and I crouch down to look at it more closely. *Hi, crab,* I say silently, but the crab doesn't seem to respond. *Hi, crab,* I try again, but it disappears between two strands of seaweed.

I turn my attention to a whelk and stare at it for a bit, wondering if I could commune with that. *Hi, whelk,* I try experimentally. Then it occurs to me to turn it over – and it's not even alive. It's an empty shell.

This is stupid. It's *embarrassing*. What do I think I'm doing? I'm not swimming with a dolphin in turquoise waters, I'm on a chilly English beach, crouching over seaweed, trying to 'reach out' to a dead whelk. Forget it. What's next on the list?

I get up, shaking out my legs, and before I can stop myself I glance over at the rock yet again. Argh. Stop it. Don't *look* at him, Sasha, I instruct myself sternly. What is wrong with me? I'm not here to look at a boy on a rock. I'm not thirteen years old. I have a wellness programme to follow. Briskly I pull out my phone and consult the next step on the app: *Dance like no one's watching.*

This is a big section, with lots of resources. There are guides to dance moves like the twist and the floss. There's a film of Wetsuit Girl dancing joyfully in an empty wood. And there's some helpful advice:

Be the star of your own rock video. If you're in a crowded area, just tune out! Mix it up with hula-hooping and skipping. Don't worry about all the people around, just enjoy yourself. Be Beyoncé! Be Shakira! The euphoria will soon be addictive.

There's even a playlist, so I call it up and shove my earphones into my ears. I listen to the pounding beat for a moment, trying to get into the zone. Then I try shimmying across the sand, swaying my hips, waiting for the euphoria to kick in.

When it doesn't kick in, I shimmy back again, waving my arms. But I still can't feel any euphoria, just acute embarrassment. My toes keep catching on the sand in my bulky trainers and I don't feel anything like Beyoncé or Shakira. (I'm wearing an anorak. How can I feel like Shakira?) Maybe freestyle dancing is a mistake, I think after a bit. Should I try something specific like the floss? I begin some awkward floss-like movements – then instantly regret it. I could never do the floss and anyway, it's the stupidest dance in the world.

My eyes drift towards the rock – and he's watching me. Oh *God*.

Maybe I'll switch to hula-hooping. Studiously ignoring him, I step into the pink hoop, place it round my waist and give it a twist, jerking my hips back and forth. The hoop falls straight down to the sand. I try again. The hoop clatters down again.

I glance at the rock and he's still watching. Wait, is he *laughing*?

OK. Here's the thing. I wouldn't worry if there were loads of people. If there were crowds on this beach, I would meditate, do my squats, dance, talk to the seagulls, do it all. I would feel anonymous and unselfconscious.

But there aren't crowds. There's just one guy, sitting on a rock, watching me. I can't 'dance like no one's watching' because they are. He is.

In a burst of frustration, I march up the beach to the rock. He's now leaning back, staring up at the sky, and doesn't move an inch as I approach.

'Hi,' I say. 'I have a question. How long are you planning on being here?'

'This beach not big enough for you?' he says, without even turning his head.

'I didn't say that. I asked you a question.'

'Don't know.' He shrugs. 'How long are you planning on being down here?'

'Don't know,' I say, before I have time to think.

Damn. That wasn't exactly a brilliant, killer reply. Which is obvious from the fact that he doesn't even bother to respond.

Stalemate.

'Well, enjoy,' I say in pleasant-not-pleasant tones, and stomp off to my lodge.

Once the door is closed, I flop on the sofa, rip open a bag of crisps and devour them all in a haze of comforting bliss, interrupted only occasionally by minuscule stabs of guilt. I know exercising on the beach should fill me with euphoria. But frankly I'm getting more euphoria from these salt 'n' vinegar crisps. They should be on the list. Maybe Wetsuit Girl just hasn't ever tried them.

When I've finished the crisps and licked every salty mouthful of crumbs off my fingers, I read all the horoscopes in my celebrity magazines, because I missed those out yesterday. My undrunk kale smoothie is sitting in its cup on the floor, and I eye it with revulsion. Maybe I should dispose of it. But it's so thick, it'll clog up the sink if I pour it down there. On the other hand, if I venture outside, Mr Obnoxious might spot that I haven't drunk it and make some sarcastic comment.

I'll just leave it for now, I decide. No one will see. This lodge is my safe space. So safe that I find myself opening the last bag of crisps and stuffing them in. Maybe I can't commune with nature. But I sure as hell can commune with carbs.

After I've finished them, I sit for a while doing nothing, just blankly watching dust motes float through the air – but then at long last I rouse myself. Come on, I can't sit here all day. I poke my head cautiously out of my lodge door and see that the rock is still occupied. He's still sitting there, staring out to sea, and now he's drinking . . . Is that *whisky*?

I creep cautiously on to the deck, ready to dart back into my lodge at any moment if he turns round. Yes. It's whisky. He's got a bottle and a glass and . . . are those peanuts? I feel slightly indignant that he's basically set himself up with a bar. Where did he get that whisky? He must have climbed down, fetched the bottle from somewhere, then reclaimed his position on the rock. If I'd been paying attention, I could have nabbed his place.

As though he can feel my gaze on his back, he turns and catches me staring. Drat. Hastily I pretend I'm doing a calf stretch on the deck. And now a quad stretch. Lots of stretches, la la la, pretend I can't see him . . .

'Is there a problem?' he calls.

'No, not at all,' I call back. 'Enjoy the view. Enjoy your whisky.' I give the word 'whisky' a pointed edge, I'm not even sure why. I'm not anti-whisky. So why did I say it like that? I don't quite understand the way I'm behaving around this guy.

'I will, thanks.' He takes a slug. 'Want some?'

'No, thanks,' I say politely.

'I assumed you didn't.' He gives me a level gaze. 'That was a joke.'

Oh. Ha ha. I'm just searching around for some devastating put-down when a roaring sound makes me jump. Is that a motorbike? On the beach?

I watch in disbelief as a bike races towards us over the sands. Is that a *pizza delivery bike*? It draws up beside the rock and a guy gets a pizza out of his pannier, then looks up at Finn.

'Finn Birchall, Rock by the lodges, Rilston Bay beach?'

'That's me.' Finn nods.

My jaw is on the floor as I watch Finn take his pizza and pay for it. That's genius. Pizza delivery. Why didn't I think of that? The bike roars away again and Finn glances down to see me still staring at him, agog.

'Sorry, does pizza offend you?' he says shortly. 'I'm not

sure if it's organic, let me check what toppings I ordered . . .' He pretends to consult the box. 'Oh yes, pepperoni with extra toxins. Guess not.'

'Pizza doesn't offend me,' I say frostily. 'In fact, I'm really not interested in what you eat.'

'Oh really?' he shoots back. 'Could have fooled me. Every time I look up, you're giving me a sanctimonious look or asking how long I'll be or giving me a hard time for sitting on your rock.' He gives me a steady stare. 'Which it's not. Can't a guy just sit on a bloody beach?'

Sanctimonious? I feel a surge of rage. I'm not sanctimonious!

'On the contrary, I'm just getting on with my wellness project,' I say in distant tones. 'Obviously I was hoping to use that rock for my meditation this morning, but you go ahead. Have it all day.'

'Thanks. I will. You don't mind if I listen to the cricket, do you?' He gestures to the speaker beside him.

'Of course not.' I smile sweetly. 'You don't mind if I do some primal screaming, do you?'

'Be my guest.'

He pulls out a slice of pizza and the waft of pepperoni makes my stomach crunch up with envy. It smells like really good pizza. I want to ask where he got it from. It's crisp, well-cooked, covered in onions and herbs . . .

'Shit!' Finn shouts in shock, as I simultaneously gasp. A huge seagull just dived down and stole his pizza out of his hand with no warning. 'You shitting bird!' Finn yells. 'Give me back my food!' He looks up furiously at the offending seagull, a hand shading his eyes. 'Come back, you bloody vermin!' I can't help snorting with laughter and he turns his murderous glare on me. 'Wait. You think that's funny?'

'Quite funny.' I nod. 'Because I have a sense of humour.'

Finn looks momentarily discomfited and I take the opportunity to make an exit while I have the advantage. Also because I can see three more seagulls heading towards him with purpose. This may not be pretty.

'Lovely place for a picnic,' I say lightly and turn on my heel.

It's not pretty. Soon Finn is batting away seagulls with both hands as they circle his head, shrieking and dive-bombing and basically attacking him. He's swearing and shouting to no avail, but there are too many of them.

Thank you, seagulls, I say silently as I watch from behind the lodge window. They did commune with me, after all! They heard my needs and they responded.

As I watch, Finn finally caves in. He clambers down from the rock, holding the remains of his pizza and whisky protectively away from the marauding seagulls while cursing them vigorously. A few moments later, I hear footsteps on the boardwalk that runs along the front of the lodges, followed by the slam of a door. He's gone. Ha!

It wouldn't do to grab his spot immediately. It might look as though I were crowing over him in some triumphalist, unseemly way. So I leave it a full, tactful ten seconds before I emerge from my lodge, make my way nonchalantly to the rock and climb up. I settle back in the hollow and breathe out in satisfaction. At last. Peace. The seagulls have flown away. It's calm. It's perfect. Totally tranquil. Just the sound of the waves, and a pleasant little breeze in the air, and—

Hang on. Was that a spot of rain?

I peer up at the sky and feel a splash in my eye. No way. No *way*. Stupid bloody nature. It was supposed to be on *my* side.

Well, who cares? I'm not giving in. I'm tougher than that. I pull my anorak hood over my head and try to hunker more deeply into the hollow of the rock as the rain starts properly falling. It's all good, I tell myself firmly as the downpour drums on my hood. It doesn't matter that my jeans are damp and my hands are freezing. I'm being mindful. Exactly. Mindful rock, mindful rain, mindful—

As I hear a sound, my head whips round before I can stop it, and rain pours off the edge of my hood into my face. As I'm spluttering water out of my mouth, I see Finn standing in the doorway of his lodge, perfectly dry, with an umbrella in one hand and his whisky bottle in the other. For a few beats there's silence between us. I'm glaring grimly at him through the rain and I can tell he's trying not to laugh.

'What happened to the primal screaming?' he says.

'I'm meditating,' I reply stiffly.

'Ah. Well, enjoy.'

He heads along the boardwalk and I watch resentfully until he's gone, then turn back to face the sea. Come on, Sasha. *Meditate*.

I focus on the waves and take a deep breath of damp, rainy air, trying to be present and mindful and grateful for the things in my life.

Rain is in my life. And I'm grateful for rain, because . . .

A sharp breeze makes me shiver and I look around the deserted beach. Oh, who am I kidding? I want a cup of tea. I'm done.

NINE

By afternoon I've had a cup of tea, a long hot bath and an even longer nap, and I'm feeling a lot more human. The rain has been pounding down relentlessly, which I know because I've heard it on the other side of my boarded-up window. But around three o'clock the drumming noise dies down and according to my weather app it's now fair, with a chance of sunshine.

I dress in dry clothes, put on my spare anorak, and venture out through the empty hotel lobby into a lovely, clear afternoon. The rain has stopped and there's a pale, watery sunshine reflecting off puddles everywhere, which makes me squint after the darkness of my room.

Without pausing to consider, I walk briskly through the town towards the same goal as yesterday. Inside the dingy supermarket, I stock up on biscuits, peanuts and a cherry Genoa cake. The same guy is sitting behind the till, and as I pay he gives me a knowing nod, as though we're old friends.

'Going to the Cash and Carry soon,' he says in a low voice,

as I stash the packets in my inside pocket. 'Get you anything you like. Say the word.'

'Thanks.' I match his low tone. 'Maybe.'

He leans across the counter and lowers his voice still further. 'Get you a box of Club biscuits, twenty quid.'

Club biscuits! I haven't eaten a Club biscuit since . . . when? Probably since I was on holiday here. Terry used to hand them out after surf lessons, and just at the memory my mouth is watering.

'Yes, please,' I say, instinctively glancing around to see if anyone can hear. 'Orange, if they're available.'

'Orange Club biscuits.' The guy nods, and taps the side of his nose. 'Got it. Drop them up at the hotel, shall I?'

'No,' I say quickly. 'I'll collect.'

'You're the boss. Any time after five.' I hand him a twenty-pound note and his eyes swivel to the door, where a pair of women have come in. 'Mum's the word.'

As I walk out, my phone buzzes and I pull it out to see a name flashing. At once I feel a leap of joy.

'Hi!' I answer. 'Hi! Dinah. How are you?'

'How am I?' Her Irish brogue nearly knocks me off my feet. 'I'm grand. It's you I'm concerned about, Sasha. Running into walls now, is it?'

I laugh, instantly relaxing. God, it's nice to hear her voice. Why haven't I called her before?

'I don't know what happened,' I admit. 'I flipped out. It was the Wellness Officer did it. She wanted me to answer three hundred and seventy-five emails *and* be joyful.'

'Joyful!' snorts Dinah. 'When you're at work you're a labouring woman. You're concentrating on the job. You need sensitive support and peace to get on with the demands being made of your body and mind. Sod the doctors! I mean, the wellness officers.'

Since Dinah became a doula, she sees everything in terms of childbirth, and occasionally slips into 'labour' pep talks. Which are actually quite instructive.

'So, what are you up to?' she demands now. 'I heard you went to the seaside.'

'Trying to be restful. And healthy.' I look at my shopping bag of crisps and cake. 'Let's say it's a work in progress.'

'You'll get there,' says Dinah firmly. 'You're stronger than you realize. You have to believe it. How's the old libido doing?'

Dinah knows full well about my missing libido, and she even once gave me a leaflet 'Getting back into sex' for post-natal women, which had lots of advice about sore nipples. (So not *that* helpful.)

'Still can't get excited about it,' I admit. 'It's like looking at a plate of chicken drumsticks when you're not hungry.'

'Chicken drumsticks!' Dinah collapses into laughter, and I can't help sniggering myself. 'Well, if you're burned out, it's no surprise. You've got sexual burnout, that's what it is. So, no holiday romance then?'

'There is a guy here,' I admit. 'Quite hot-looking. But *probably* wouldn't want to hook up with a woman who's repelled by the idea of sex.'

'Probably not ideal,' agrees Dinah.

'Also, he's awful. He was mean to a toddler.'

'No!' exclaims Dinah in outrage. 'OK. Well, leave him out of it. And don't despair, it'll all come back. You can do miracles with that body of yours, Sasha. Your body is designed to succeed, you know that? Designed to succeed.'

'Dinah, I'm not giving birth,' I remind her, laughing.

'Well, maybe you should!' she answers promptly. 'Give birth to a whole new Sasha.'

We chat on about this and that – but for the rest of our conversation, that phrase keeps coming back to me. *Give birth to a whole new Sasha.* Maybe I could. Maybe I will.

As I ring off, half an hour later, I feel transformed. Just one easy, gossipy conversation with a friend has done wonders for me. I feel light. Energized. Confident. Strong. I need to find some grit, I find myself thinking. *Grit.*

On impulse, I walk into the small, empty car park next to the supermarket, put my shopping bag on the floor and jut out my chin, remembering Dinah's advice. *You're stronger than you realize. You can do miracles with that body of yours. Your body is designed to succeed.*

I'm feeling a doggedness I haven't had before. Mind over matter. I *can* be strong. I *won't* be defeated by this. If the setting for my transformation isn't a glorious beach but instead a grotty car park, then so be it. We can't all have picturesque epiphanies. Sometimes we just have epiphanies. And my epiphany is that I'm going to do this bloody hundred-squat challenge. Right here, right now.

I take a deep breath and start doing squats. Come on, Sasha, come *on*. I do ten. I pause. I do another ten. I have a longer pause – then do ten more. After fifty, I have a motivational snack and let my muscles have a short rest – then I resume. I'm panting and my legs are burning, but I've never felt better. It wasn't that my thighs couldn't do squats – it was that my head couldn't.

It takes me an embarrassingly long time to reach a hundred, a few at a time with lots of breaks. But at last, puffing and hot in the face, I get there. I did it! I did the squat challenge!

I sink on to the ground and just pant for a bit, trying to

avoid the curious gaze of a delivery driver. Then, on trembling legs, I head out of the car park and wander down to the beach. Talking about Club biscuits earlier filled me with nostalgia. I want to check out the Surf Shack again.

As I see the wooden structure, my heart skips a beat. There was always a party feel around the Surf Shack. It was the centre of the beach, the place to be. It was where you met friends and hung out. And Terry was the king.

Every day, groups of kids would eagerly line up on the sand, ready to learn. I can still remember the warm-up routine – the running on the spot, the lunges, the arm whirls. Experienced surfers – all old pupils of Terry's – would often join in the warm-up routine, laughing and bantering with Terry while he pretended to get cross and called them 'freeloaders'.

The grown-up surfers were always a chilled bunch, endlessly generous to the kids. They'd applaud a success, or commiserate after a disastrous wipeout. Dad never surfed, but he watched and applauded us, too. And he always had a chat with Terry. They got on well, Dad and Terry. Maybe that's another reason why I remember this place so fondly.

As I draw near, though, I realize it's not the same building. It's a similar wooden structure, but more sturdy, with different signage. Well, what was I expecting? I guess whoever bought the business from Terry rebuilt it. There's a sign on the door: *Closed. For surfboard hire call number below*. And then a mobile number.

Instinctively, I turn to check the swell. The sea's pretty flat this afternoon. Maybe when it rises, the new owner will come along and open up shop. But for now, it's just a silent, lifeless building on an empty beach.

Except . . .

Oh, *great*. The beach isn't empty. Finn is approaching over the sand in his padded jacket and shades. And he's seen me notice him now, so I can't turn away, it would seem too weird. Maybe he'll walk straight past.

But he doesn't. He comes to a halt about a metre away from me, pushes his shades up and stares at the building for a few silent seconds. Just like I did a moment ago.

'Sorry to disturb your solitude *yet again*,' he says at last, with an exaggerated politeness that makes my hackles rise. 'I used to have surf lessons here when I was a kid. Just wanted to have a look.'

'Really?' I say before I can stop myself. 'Me too.'

'You had surf lessons with Terry?' He sounds sceptical and I prickle at his tone. What's he implying? That he's surprised I've had surf lessons at all, or that he's surprised I had surf lessons with Terry?

'Well, I didn't have them with Pete Huston,' I say tartly, and get a small, appreciative smile out of him.

'Glad to hear it. Or else we could never have spoken again.'

I want to retort, *That wouldn't exactly be a hardship*, or something equally snippy, but something stops me. He had surf lessons with Terry. He's Team Terry. Which means I can't help softening towards him, just a smidgen.

Now he's surveying me as though for the first time. 'I don't recognize you,' he says at last, flatly. 'Were you a regular?'

'Yes!' I reply, stiffening at the implied insult. 'And I don't recognize you either.'

'I'm thirty-six.' He peers at me as though trying to gauge my age from my freckles. 'I'm guessing you're, what, thirty?'

'I'm thirty-three.'

'Did you come here every year?'

'We stopped coming when I was thirteen. But every year before then. We probably just stayed here on different weeks.'

'Must have done.' He shifts his gaze back to the Surf Shack. 'Terry Connolly,' he says at last. 'What a man. Pretty much everything I've learned in life, I learned from Terry.'

'I know what you mean,' I say, slightly stunned that we're in agreement about something. 'I asked if Terry still does surf lessons, but apparently he's retired. He sold this place to someone else.'

'I know.' Finn nods. 'And they told me at the hotel that Sandra died three years ago.' He grimaces. 'Wasn't expecting to hear that.'

'Everything moves on, I suppose. Pete's place doesn't even exist any more.' I look at where the Surftime shack used to be, five metres away.

'He left after there was an accident,' says Finn. 'There was a problem with a dodgy kayak. A boy nearly drowned and they found out Pete was to blame.'

'I know,' I say. 'I was on the beach when it happened.'

'So was I.' Finn frowns as though putting this together. 'So . . . we did overlap.'

There's a pause, while I reassess things slightly. We were both here on this same beach, all those years ago. Do I remember him? Mentally I scan my memories of all Terry's pupils for a boy like Finn. But there's nothing.

'We left Rilston the next day,' I say at last and he nods.

'We'd just arrived. First day of the holidays, and the lifeguards order everyone out of the water. I was in another kayak at the time, actually. I tried to swim over and help, but they yelled at me, told me to get back to shore.' He rolls his eyes. 'Great start to the week.'

'We went bowling,' I volunteer. 'Did you hang around?'

He nods. 'It was a pretty big deal.'

'I know it was,' I say pointedly. 'I remember.'

I'm trying to sound as authoritative as he does. But truthfully, I don't remember much about that day, except a kind of mayhem, screaming, people clustering on the sand, pointing out to sea, and lifeguards running. I'm not even sure how accurate my memories are. Maybe I've invented seeing the lifeguards running. When Dad was diagnosed, our life was thrown into such turmoil that everything else slid into unimportance.

'Maybe we overlapped in other years, too,' Finn suggests and I nod again.

'Probably did, we just didn't know it.'

There's a different energy between us. We're looking at each other with a tad more interest.

'So you still surf?' I say.

'Now and again. You?'

'I have done, once or twice.' I shrug. 'So, did you use to stay at the Rilston when you were a child? Did you take a lodge?'

I'm so prepared to hear that he was one of those annoying entitled lodge kids that it's a surprise when he shakes his head.

'My aunt lived here and the whole family congregated every summer. But then she moved to Cornwall and we started going there instead. My cousin moved back to Devon, though, lives the other side of Campion Sands. I went to visit her before I came here to Rilston.' His eyes narrow with interest. 'Why, did *you* take a lodge?'

'No!' I give a sharp laugh. 'We were very definitely not the Rilston Hotel types. We stayed in a guest house.'

'So, what are you doing here, off-season?' He gestures

128

around at the empty beach. 'Strange time to choose if you're not a big surfer.'

The question catches me off-guard, and it takes me a few moments to decide on my answer.

'I just wanted a holiday,' I say at last. 'You?'

'Same.' His gaze is distant. 'Just wanted a holiday.'

Liar. He's such a liar! This isn't a holiday, he's been told to have time off work to 'consider his behaviour'.

But then, I'm a liar, too. This isn't exactly a standard-issue holiday for me, either.

There's silence, as though neither of us quite wants to carry on that line of conversation.

'Well . . . have a good walk,' I say at last.

'You too.'

I turn on my heel and start stomping away over the sand, feeling a bit discombobulated by the exchange. Random memories of Terry, of our holidays here and even of my dad's illness are all resurfacing. Combined with a notion that maybe this guy isn't quite the monster I imagined.

I need chocolate, I decide, and reach into my pocket to get a Galaxy. As I pull it out, a paper comes fluttering out with it, and I make a half-hearted swipe at it before it's lost on a gust of wind. It's only three seconds later that I realize, with a jerk of horror, that it's my manifestation. My manifestation about sex. In black and white. And now it's blowing over the sand towards Finn. The most embarrassing document I have ever written in my *life*, dancing around freely on the breeze.

As it flutters in his direction, my heart spasms. What if he picks it up and reads it? No. He won't do that. Don't be ridiculous, Sasha.

But what if he does?

What if he thinks it's litter and he's the type to pick it up?

He'll reach for it, he'll see the words, he'll know I wrote them . . .

OK, this cannot happen. I need to get it back. Frantically, I hurl myself back along the sand, my eyes fixed on the paper scrap. But almost at once I realize my mistake, because Finn picks up on my urgency. He spots the paper and calls, 'I'll get it!' Then he launches himself at it as though it's a lost Lottery ticket, pins it down with his foot, then reaches to retrieve it before I can utter a syllable.

'No! Don't . . . That's confidential!' I yell in a strangled voice. *'Confidential!'* But he can't hear me over the wind. Already it's open in his hand, there's a faint frown on his face . . .

And . . . it's happened. The worst has happened. He's read it. I can tell from his face. The widening of his eyes; the tilt of his mouth. He's just read my innermost thoughts about sex.

Thanks a *lot*, Wetsuit Girl.

As I reach him, I'm desperately trying to put together some coherent words.

'That's just something . . .' I clear my throat. 'It's not . . . Anyway. Thanks.'

Finn hands me the paper silently. His eyes are scrupulously turned away, but he doesn't fool me. I know he saw it. The words are large and they would have taken about five seconds to read. As my eyes scan my own writing, I feel such a wash of embarrassment, I want to sink down into the sand.

Sexual hunger. Sexual fantasies. Craving for sex.
A man with a cock. A sexy man with a working cock. Big, preferably. Any size, thank you.

World peace.

Should I explain? No. I can't. There is no explanation.

'Thanks,' I manage again, my face prickling.

'No problem,' he says politely.

The fact that he hasn't made a single sarcastic comment – or even met my eye – is almost the worst aspect of all. It shows he's tactfully avoiding the subject. Oh God, I can't bear this, I have to say *something* . . .

'I was writing a song,' I blurt out. 'It's . . . lyrics.'

Finn raises an eyebrow and I watch him mentally running over the words again.

'Catchy,' he says at last, then lifts a hand in farewell and heads away towards the dunes. And I stand stock-still, my heart thumping, unable to move for mortification.

Did he buy the lyrics thing? No. Of course he didn't.

Oh God, why did I have to drop the note? And why does he have to be here? This last thought gathers steam in my head until I emit an exasperated scream. I'd be having a completely different experience if it weren't for him, constantly popping up and rubbing me up the wrong way. I'd be relaxed. I'd be enjoying myself. *Why* does he have to be here?

As I walk back, dragging my feet, I'm prickly and embarrassed and bad-tempered. I'm also pondering on the conversation that Finn and I had about the past. I can't stop wondering, did I know him, back then when we were kids? By sight, at least?

On impulse, I dial Kirsten's number. She'll know.

'Sasha!' Her voice greets me against a background noise of kids' TV. 'How's it going? Mum told me about the kefir and reflexology. Sounds like you're busy!'

'Well,' I say. 'Kind of.'

'How are you feeling?' Her voice softens. 'Are you recovering? Breathing the sea air, all that?'

'I'm doing OK,' I say. 'Actually, I slept most of today. Didn't do a stroke of wild swimming. Don't tell Mum or Pam.'

'Circle of trust,' says Kirsten. 'Although I *will* just mention that sleeping is a symptom of the menopause. You might want to check that out.'

'Hilarious.' I roll my eyes. 'Anyway, I'm getting lots of sea air. All good. And here's a weird one – d'you remember a guy called Finn Birchall?'

'Yes.'

Her simple answer takes me aback. I wasn't expecting a plain 'yes'.

'Well, he's here. I don't remember him at all.'

'He was there a few years running. I think I had surf lessons with him, maybe? Does he live in Rilston?'

'No, he's at the hotel. We're practically the only two guests.'

'Oh, right.' She hesitates. 'Oh, *right*. Is he kind?'

'Kirsten!' I exclaim.

I know exactly what she means by 'Is he kind?' She means, 'Are you planning to sleep with him?' Kirsten and I have a long-developed theory that the only important attribute of any man is that he is kind. In fact, to sleep with a man who is *not* kind is a form of self-harm. We even made up a slogan: *If you're not kind, never mind*.

'First of all, I'm totally off sex, as you well know.'

'Which you should see a doctor about,' puts in Kirsten. 'As *you* well know.'

'Whatever.' I brush her off. 'And second of all, this guy and I are pretty much arch enemies. He's totally arrogant and obnoxious and I have actually *witnessed* him making a toddler cry. He wasn't even ashamed of himself.'

'OK.' Kirsten laughs. 'Well, it sounds like I don't need to worry. *Except*.' She suddenly puts on a Grand Inquisitor air. 'Is he hot?'

'He's . . . not unpleasant to look at,' I admit.

'Built?'

'Pretty built.' I recall his tall, firm torso. 'Quite hot. As obnoxious, arrogant men go.'

'Well, don't get carried away and sleep with him by mistake,' instructs Kirsten. 'You do not need an unkind man in your life right now. Or ever,' she amends. '*Ever*.'

Honestly. *Sleep with him by mistake?* Who does Kirsten think I am?

'I think I can avoid sleeping with him by mistake,' I say, rolling my eyes. 'I'm going to be polite to him and nothing more, the end.'

TEN

Polite. I can do polite.

The next morning I head downstairs to breakfast with some bland conversational openers prepared. Like, 'Have you done the coastal walk?' and 'Do you know the weather forecast?'

But as soon as I enter the dining room, I sense something is wrong. Finn is sitting at his table with the most thunderous look on his face, while Nikolai is hovering nearby, looking close to tears. His face is pale and his hands are trembling, I notice.

'Good morning,' I say warily, and Finn just gives a kind of grunt.

What's been going on?

As I slip into my chair, Nikolai gingerly places a rack of toast on Finn's table.

'Sourdough toast,' he says in a quavering voice. 'Sir, I apologize for the error. I apologize for the white toast.' He bows his head abjectly. 'It was error.'

I'm watching him, aghast. What the hell has brought about this pitiful confession?

'It's fine,' says Finn shortly, and I swivel my gaze suspiciously towards him. His face is set. His jaw is super-tight. Poor Nikolai is backing away now, almost genuflecting.

Has Finn somehow turned Nikolai into a gibbering wreck?

Of course he has. It's obvious. He's given that poor, sweet Nikolai the special Finn Birchall angry treatment, hasn't he? He's yelled or slammed his fist down or whatever it is that gives him kicks. Over toast!

I shake out my napkin, buzzing with outrage. I was right first time, he *is* a monster. Who the hell does he think he is, that he can lash out at people? Do the normal rules not apply to him?

Forget 'polite'. Polite is *off*.

And another thing: he was told to consider his behaviour! Does snapping at Nikolai count as 'considering his behaviour'? I don't think so. In fact, I haven't seen any signs of any 'considering', unless you count drinking whisky, which I do not.

I shoot a scathing glance at Finn, but he's scrolling on his phone now, oblivious. Pah. As Nikolai approaches my table, I smile at him charmingly to make up for Finn's horrible behaviour.

'Good morning, Nikolai! How are you?'

'Good morning, Madame,' he says, his voice still wobbly. 'Madame would prefer a melon plate?' he continues and I smile back sympathetically, even though the thought of yet more melon makes my heart plummet.

'I would absolutely love a melon plate, thank you. And some toast, please. *Any* kind of toast,' I add, with a meaningful edge to my voice. 'Some details aren't worth troubling about.' I glare at Finn, who seems bemused. Does he really think I haven't put together what happened? 'Toast is toast,' I continue. 'It really doesn't matter which kind, does it? Unless you're some sort of mean-spirited obsessive. Thank you so much, Nikolai. I greatly appreciate all your help.'

'Madame would enjoy a kale smoothie?' ventures Nikolai, and I nod enthusiastically.

'Of course! I'd love a kale smoothie! Although, in a take-away cup,' I add as an afterthought. 'If that's OK.'

After a few minutes, Finn gets up to leave, nodding at me brusquely, and I eat my breakfast in silence, feverishly planning all the things I'm going to say to him. If he thinks he's unaccountable, then he's going to learn a lesson. I'm actually quite looking forward to having a bona fide excuse to let off steam at him.

After breakfast, I get ready for the day briskly. I head downstairs with my rucksack ready-stuffed with snacks, and march straight down to the lodges. As I arrive, I see that Finn is already on the beach, gazing at something on the sand. Perfect. No time like the present.

'I'd like to have a word with you, if that's OK?' I greet him crisply as I approach. But he doesn't move. He seems trans-fixed by whatever it is he's staring at. 'Hello?' I try again. 'I just wanted to talk about this morning. I have a couple of questions.'

At last, he moves his head.

'Look at this,' he says.

Deflection. Typical.

'I don't want to, thanks,' I say. 'I want to talk about what-ever happened at breakfast.'

'No, seriously,' he says. 'Look at this.'

For God's sake.

Impatiently, I dump my rucksack on the deck and go to join him on the beach. I'm expecting a washed-up piece of flotsam or maybe a weird-looking dead fish, but when I see what he's looking at, my jaw falls open. It's a bottle of champagne in a rubber chiller, weighed down with heavy-duty plastic sheeting and a couple of rocks. But it's not just the champagne that's making me stare – it's the message written in the sand. It's gouged out in huge letters and lined with stones and is clearly legible:

To the couple on the beach. Thank you.

'Wow,' I say at last. 'That's weird.'

'I know, right?' Finn seems perplexed.

'Is that real champagne?' I take a step forward. 'Should we touch it?'

'It's not a crime scene!' Finn laughs – then stops. 'Maybe it is.'

'It's a glass bottle.' My mind is already on the practical issues. 'It might break and cut someone's foot. It's dangerous.' I look at the message again. 'What does it mean?'

'Means something to the couple on the beach, I guess,' says Finn.

I swivel around sharply, as though hoping to spot the elusive couple, but the endless stretch of sand is as empty as ever.

'Well, what do we do?'

'I'll talk to Cassidy,' says Finn. 'Find out if they know what it is.'

'*I'll* talk to her,' I contradict him, getting out my phone and taking a photo of the message. 'I think I'll probably handle it better, wouldn't you agree?' I glance up at Finn, expecting him to look abashed, or maybe even give some explanation for this morning, but he frowns.

'What's that supposed to mean?'

God, he really *is* in denial.

'I just think maybe I'm better at communicating with the staff than you are?' I say pointedly. 'Just my opinion.'

'Your opinion?' he echoes incredulously.

'Yes. My opinion.'

'Well, *my* opinion is that if I deal with this, we won't need to wait until your PA's made a call and your team's confirmed the details. We can just talk directly. You know? Like normal, down-to-earth people?'

I do not believe this. Is he having a dig at me?

'At least I know how to talk to the staff in a civilized manner,' I say icily. 'Unlike *some*.'

'Civilized?' He gives a shout of laughter. 'The woman who gets her PA to issue high-handed commands every morning? Kefir! Kale! Reflexology! At seven a.m.! Whatever you pay that PA of yours, believe me, it is *not* enough.'

I feel a jolt of shock. Is that how he sees me?

Well, OK. So what if he does? I don't have to explain myself to him. Even so, I can't help retorting, 'You don't know anything about me.'

'Oh, really?' he shoots back. 'I know you're a princess who's got everyone running after you. And a health freak who blanches at the sight of sugar. Let alone booze. Let alone anything fun whatsoever. Sorry we can't all live up to your high standards of nutrition and exercise and general perfection,' he adds sarcastically. 'It must be very distressing for you to have to witness a real, flawed human being.'

Whatever irritation I felt towards this man is turning to rage. Princess? *Health freak?*

'What, I'm a health freak because I don't sit on the beach drinking whisky and ordering pizza all day?'

'I'd take whisky and pizza over frog vomit,' he instantly replies, nodding at the kale smoothie in my hand.

Frog vomit is such an apt description of the smoothie that I'm momentarily halted.

'Well, at least I don't yell at the staff!' I snap, changing tack, and Finn's face jolts defensively.

'Yell at the staff? What are you talking about?'

'This morning,' I say. 'You nearly gave poor Nikolai a nervous breakdown.'

I'm expecting Finn to look guilty, but he stares at me, his expression unchanging.

'What are you talking about?' he repeats.

'Come on!' I exclaim in frustration. 'I know you yelled at him, or swore, or . . . I don't know. Punched the wall? Threw a chair? Got out your chainsaw? I just know you scared him somehow. Maybe I drink frog vomit, but at least I'm not a sociopath with anger issues.'

A tiny pulse is beating in Finn's forehead. For a few moments he says nothing, but I notice his fists have clenched. When he does speak, it's in an unnaturally calm yet tense voice.

'Do you make a habit of hurling unfounded accusations at people? Or is it just a fun holiday pursuit?'

'Don't deny it,' I say indignantly. 'Nikolai was a wreck. He could barely speak!'

'Maybe he couldn't.' Finn's face is resolute. 'But what has that got to do with me?'

Seriously? Does this guy think he's kidding anyone? I can see he's trying to rein in his anger right now. Look at his stance. Look at the way he's breathing through his nostrils, as though trying to contain his emotions.

'Look, I *know*, OK?' I say impatiently, before I can think whether this is a good idea or not. 'I know what happened in your workplace. I heard you dictating letters in the dunes.' Finn's face blanches in shock and I feel momentarily bad – but too late. He should have thought of that before he was mean to Nikolai. 'I know you're not just on holiday. I know you're here to "consider your behaviour".' I fold my arms disapprovingly. 'But you're not considering anything! You're just drinking whisky and lashing out at some poor blameless waiter who wouldn't harm a fly!'

With a flourish, I turn and stalk off towards my lodge, but to my dismay, Finn follows. As I reach my door he's still behind me and I wheel round to kindly tell him to leave me alone. But my words shrivel on my lips. He looks livid. And somehow several feet taller. More intimidating. My eyes run over his body as though for the first time. Powerful chest. Powerful arms. Powerful jaw, even tighter than before. Despite myself, I feel a tremor of nerves.

'OK, Ms Health Nut of the Year,' he says evenly. 'I have just about had it.'

'Are you *threatening* me?' I swallow.

'No, I am not threatening you!' he erupts hotly. 'I'm telling you a few home truths. Maybe you're so used to bossing your PA about you've forgotten the rules of decency. Or maybe it's your low-calorie diet. It's messed with your head.'

'*I've* forgotten the rules of decency?' I echo in disbelief. '*I* have? You have to be joking! You're the guy who made a toddler cry on the train!'

A look of utter shock passes over his face, as though I've caught him out.

'I was stressed,' he says defensively.

'Stressed?' I retort. 'We're all stressed!'

Quickly I step into my lodge and shut the door with a bang, feeling slightly relieved to have escaped. But at once he raps on the door, so hard that I jump.

'That's right, hide from reality!' His voice resounds through the wooden door, only slightly muffled. 'You think you know everything, but you don't! And by the way, the reason I'm here is *none* of your business.'

I feel a pang of guilt, because he's right – but I can't bear to give up my moral high ground now.

'This conversation is over!' I shout back through the door. 'Over!'

'It is not over! You don't malign me and then just do a runner!'

'I did not malign you!' I yell back. 'I never malign people! I just report what I see!'

'Well, you didn't see this, did you?'

I shriek in terror as the door bursts open and take a step back, my heart pumping. Is he going to yell at me? Throw something at me? Hit me? There he is, framed in the doorway, his face glowering, one arm raised, his sleeve rolled up to the elbow and . . . Hang on.

What's that?

There's a red weal on his wrist which makes me flinch to look at it. It looks fresh and raw and really painful. That's what he's showing me, I realize. An injury.

'What *happened*?' I ask, shocked – but Finn doesn't seem to notice that I've spoken. He's silent and motionless, except for his eyes, which are widening. For a moment I don't understand – then my insides plunge as I realize what he's looking at. I turn to follow his gaze – and swallow hard as I see it all through his eyes.

The magazines. The chocolate wrappers. The crisp bags.

The empty ice-cream tub. The wine bottle. The tissues from my crying jag, still spilling out of the cardboard box. And, like an exhibit in a court room, my two undrunk kale smoothies.

I'm trying to think of some witty remark, some way to style it out . . . But I can't. I have no style. No veneer. Nothing to hide behind.

This is me.

'I'm sorry,' Finn says at last, in a different, awkward voice. 'I shouldn't have intruded. I apologize.'

I open my mouth to tell him it's fine, but before I can make a noise, he's gone, the door has closed, and I'm standing there, breathing out, hard. Slowly I bring my fists to my forehead. I can't even utter a sound. Any sound would be inadequate.

It seems like an eternity that I stand there, reeling from the entire exchange. The shouting. The sight of that red weal on his flesh. And the mortification. For a moment I feel like leaving. Just packing up, checking out, going back to London. Anything, rather than face him again.

But that would be pathetic. And there's a more pressing matter. Why wasn't there a dressing on that wound?

At last I take a deep breath and stride out. Finn is sitting on the deck outside his lodge and he starts as he sees me, shooting me a wary look.

'How did you injure your arm?' I ask bluntly.

'Nikolai spilled coffee on it.'

'Oh God!' I bring a hand to my mouth. 'No!'

'He's a jittery guy,' says Finn with a wry half-smile. 'Shaky hands. Not a good fit for serving hot beverages.'

'So that's why you sounded so curt. When you were talking about the toast.' I exhale sharply as it all falls into place, and a look of comprehension comes over Finn's face, too.

'Right. OK. Now I get what you meant earlier. The reason

I spoke to him the way I did is, I was in quite a lot of pain. For me at that precise moment, that was top-level charming. Bearing in mind he messed up the breakfast order, too. Guess he was unnerved.'

I'm replaying the entire breakfast scene with this new knowledge, I have to say, it all makes sense. No wonder Nikolai looked so abject.

'As for the incident on the train . . .' Finn looks strained. 'I know. It was bad. I was just very, *very* sensitive to noise at that moment, and the sound that child was making was intolerable. It was hurting my brain and I just flipped. Guilty.'

I let this all sink in for a moment. I kind of understand now. I've had a few frayed moments when every noise in the world seemed unbearable, and I sympathize. *Not* that he should have been so curt and rude – but it's an explanation.

Then suddenly I come to.

'But wait. Why are you still sitting here? Why aren't you having your arm seen to? You haven't even got a bandage on it!'

'I ran some cold water on it. It's fine.' Finn waves his arm impatiently and I roll my eyes.

'It's not fine. You need to get that dressed. It might get infected. Are you aware of the risks of infection?'

I know I sound like Mum. But I can't help it. The sight of his raw skin is making me all itchy round my spine.

'We're going up to the hotel right now,' I continue firmly, 'and we're getting you some first aid. Actually, I might have a plaster . . .' I reach into my pocket and bring something out, but it's not a plaster. It's a chocolate wrapper.

Finn's eyes fall on the wrapper and meet mine, then hastily look away again. For a moment we're both silent.

'You're right,' I say at last, trying to sound light. 'Appearances can be deceiving.'

143

'I made . . . assumptions about you,' says Finn heavily, his gaze averted. 'I would like to apologize for doing that. I'm also very sorry that I raised my voice. And that I swore.'

'You didn't swear,' I point out.

'Didn't I?' Finn's brow flickers. 'Well, that was a mistake. I intended to.'

I can't help laughing, but Finn doesn't relax. He looks stricken. Anxious, even.

'I can only apologize for my behaviour,' he says, clearly following the official script, and I sigh, feeling a sudden wave of compassion for him. It can't be easy, issuing apologies all day.

Well, I should know.

'It's OK,' I say, softening. 'You don't have to give me the official apology. But thank you. And I apologize, too. I over-stepped the mark. I shouldn't have called you a . . .'

I trail off. I can't believe I called him a sociopath with anger issues.

'I overstepped the mark, too,' he replies quickly. 'I made inappropriate comments, which I now deeply regret. I'm sure you have a very good relationship with your PA and her remuneration is no concern of mine.'

Oh God, I have to put this myth to rest.

'Look, you should know something,' I say. 'The person calling the desk every morning isn't my PA. It's my mum.'

'Your *mum*?' He looks briefly staggered. 'Right. OK. Why . . .?'

'No.' I shake my head. 'Let's . . . let's not. Not now.' As he meets my eyes, I see a mirror image of my own compassion and quickly turn away. He sees me. He sees the real, messed-up, struggling me. And I'm not sure I'm ready for that.

'Come on.' I find refuge in brisk practical tones. 'Let's sort you out. And no arguing,' I add, as he opens his mouth. 'You're not getting an infection on my watch.' As I turn, I hear Finn's phone buzz, and as he checks it he emits a sound of frustration.

'Did you download the hotel app?' he asks. 'Because it's driving me *insane*. "We see that you are on the beach,"' he reads aloud. ' "Fun fact: Did you know Queen Victoria once visited this beach? Why not take a moment to imagine her on the sand?" I mean, seriously?' He looks up. 'Do they need to bother us with this garbage?'

'I've muted their notifications,' I confess. 'I did it yesterday after they invited me to celebrate the Fourth of July.'

'The Fourth of July barbecue invite! I got that, too. In February! What the hell?'

He sounds so indignant, I can't help giving a snort of laughter, and after a moment he's grinning, too.

'Notifications muted,' he says firmly, jabbing at his phone screen.

As we arrive in the lobby, Cassidy is tapping busily at her computer, and when she sees Finn's scalded arm she breaks off with a dismayed shriek.

'Mr Birchall! How did you manage that?'

'Just one of those things,' says Finn casually, and I shoot him a tiny smile, appreciating his tact. 'Got some hot water on it. No big deal. But I wondered, you don't have a Band-Aid, do you?'

'I'm the First Aid Officer!' Cassidy beams triumphantly. She bends down and produces a plastic box from under the desk. 'Oh, look!' she exclaims as she opens it. 'There's the key to Room 54. We searched everywhere for that.'

As she dresses Finn's arm, I decide to broach the message on the beach.

'Cassidy, we found a bottle of champagne on the sand,' I begin. 'Right in front of the lodges.'

'Champagne?' she echoes absently.

'On the beach,' affirms Finn.

'Did someone leave it behind?' she asks, cutting a length of Elastoplast.

'No, it's like a present. At least, we think it is. We can't tell.'

'For who? Was there a note? Just too late for a Valentine!'

'There was a message on the sand,' I explain, almost reluctantly. It said, "To the couple on the beach. Thank you."'

'The couple on the beach,' echoes Cassidy thoughtfully. 'The couple on the beach . . .' Then her head pops up and she looks first at me then at Finn, her finger pointing triumphantly.

'You're the couple on the beach! It's for you!'

'But we're not a couple,' I say.

'Very much not a couple,' agrees Finn.

'*Not* a couple,' I reiterate. 'At all. So it can't be us.'

Cassidy looks blank. 'Well, there's two of you,' she explains helpfully. 'And you're on the beach all day. I'm sure it's for you.'

'But it can't be,' I object. 'Who would give us champagne? And it said, "Thank you." There's no reason to thank us for anything.' I summon up the photo of the message on my phone, and as I show her, her expression changes.

'Oh, right!' she says. 'One of those. It's like the Mavis Adler messages,' she adds, as though this will explain everything.

'The what?'

'The local artist? You know, she painted *Young Love*? The couple kissing? There's a copy in the library. I'm sick of the sight of it, to be honest.' She rolls her eyes. 'We get fans coming here every summer, pretending to be the couple. There's a local photographer called Gill, she makes her whole living taking photos of tourists kissing in that spot. It's mad.'

'Right,' I say, bewildered. 'I know the painting. What's that got to do with anything?'

'Well.' Cassidy leans forward as though for a cosy gossip. 'About five years ago, Mavis Adler did an exhibition, only it wasn't paintings, it was messages on the beach. Protesting about the environment. Look.' Cassidy summons up a photo on her own phone, then turns it around for me to see. It shows two messages just like the one we saw this morning. Deeply gouged letters lined with stones read NO OIL and POLLUTION IS HELL.

'Wow,' says Finn, looking over my shoulder. 'Punchy.'

'Yeah,' says Cassidy. 'She wrote about ten of them and then took photos and put them in an exhibition. I think she wanted her messages to become as famous as *Young Love*? Only they never did. Awkward.' Cassidy makes a comical face. 'Everyone was like, "Paint another couple kissing"! But she didn't want to.'

'I guess artists have to follow their hearts,' says Finn, shrugging.

'I suppose.' She puts her phone away. 'Anyway, then people started copying her and writing their own messages on the beach, only they got a bit rude.' She snorts with laughter. 'My friend wrote a really funny thing about our old headteacher, only he didn't find it funny.' She gives another giggle, then bites her lip. 'Yeah, that didn't go down well. Anyway, the council said we had to stop and they put signs on the beach and then it all died down.'

'Right,' I say. 'So someone's copying those again?'

'Looks like it.' She nods. 'And handing out champagne.

Only I wonder who? Ooh, I wonder if it's from Herbert?' Her face brightens. 'He thinks you're both lovely guests, don't you, Herbert?' She raises her voice, but Herbert, who is slumped, apparently comatose, in a nearby armchair does not respond. 'Oh, he didn't hear, bless him. He's not asleep, he's just having some Herbert-time,' she assures us. 'He's been busy today! First he had to help the Bergens check out with their golf clubs, and now he's just carried two massive suitcases in for some new guests. Leather ones, proper heavy.'

'From the station?' I ask, in slight shock.

'From their car,' explains Cassidy. 'Tired him out, poor love. I'll go and ask him about the champagne.' She finishes off Finn's dressing, then puts down her scissors and heads across the lobby.

'Herbert!' she cries, straight into his face. 'Did you give this lovely couple some champagne?'

'We're not a couple,' says Finn, sounding a bit tense, but Cassidy seems oblivious. Herbert has lifted his head about an inch off the chair back, as though to impart his last words to the world, and she bends down to hear his papery whisper of a voice.

'He says it wasn't him,' she announces, standing up. 'Funny, isn't it? Mystery bottle of champagne on the beach. Ooh, maybe it's for our new guests. You're a couple, aren't you?' she adds blithely, as a middle-aged man and woman walk into the lobby from the dining room. The woman, who has long, straight hair and glasses, tenses up.

'A couple?' she echoes, sounding on the brink of tears, and glances at the man, who shifts uncomfortably, his hands stuffed in his jeans pockets. The pair of them look pretty miserable for a couple who have just started a holiday.

'Mr and Mrs West, isn't it?' adds Cassidy.

'For now,' says Mrs West, after a pause. She glances at her husband, who instantly swivels his head away, as though he wants to avoid not only Cassidy's friendly gaze and the sight of his partner, but basically the whole conversation. Mrs West's face jolts as though he's dealt her a blow, and then she nods, her lips tightening, as though this confirms everything she thought about life, and then some.

'It's just, we were wondering if you were expecting a bottle of champagne?' Cassidy presses on.

'Champagne!' Mrs West sounds on the edge. She eyes Cassidy as though suspecting she's being mocked. 'Champagne? Why would we expect champagne?'

'Maybe not,' Cassidy backtracks hurriedly. 'Only there was a bottle addressed to "The couple on the beach", and—'

'The couple on the beach?' Mrs West cuts her off. 'You want to know the truth? We don't *know* if we're still a couple.'

Yowser. My eyes flit to Mr West, who is standing motionless, his face granite, as though his worst nightmare is being played out. Which maybe it is.

'Maybe we'll find out the answer on this holiday,' adds Mrs West, wrapping her thin arms miserably around her torso. 'Or maybe not.'

She's wearing her wedding ring, I notice. But she's also clenching her hands pretty tightly.

'Of course,' says Cassidy, looking flummoxed. 'Well, it takes all sorts, doesn't it? Here's hoping that . . .' She stops, as though not sure how to proceed. 'Although, may I say, if you did want to move into . . . perhaps adjoining single rooms, I'm sure we could waive the surcharge . . .'

'I don't *believe* this!' Mr West rounds on his wife. 'What have you been saying about our sex life?'

'I didn't need to say anything, it's obvious to everybody!' she snaps back, her voice high with distress. '*Everybody!*'

I glance at Finn, who pulls an awkward face back.

Actually, it wasn't obvious to everybody. Or indeed anybody. But I'm not sure this is the moment to tell Mrs West that. There's an embarrassed, prickly silence, broken only by Herbert snoring gently.

'So!' Cassidy clears her throat. 'Well. That's ... I hope you're enjoying your stay, apart from the ... Obviously ...' She clears her throat. 'Did you still want dinner at eight?'

'Eight will be fine,' says Mrs West, over-politely. 'Thank you.'

We all watch, silent and riveted, as they walk up the stairs, and it's only when they disappear from view that I exhale. I hadn't realized I was holding my breath.

'Lovely couple,' says Cassidy, then she seems to reconsider. 'Or ... whatever. I probably shouldn't have mentioned their sleeping arrangements.' She makes a regretful face. 'Only, you want people to be as comfortable as possible, you know?'

'I think that guy would be most comfortable in a different hotel from his wife,' says Finn. 'Or maybe a different country.'

'Poor loves. Shame our reflexologist isn't here,' adds Cassidy pensively. 'She does couples therapy as well. Got the Walkers back together again after he slept with that jet-ski girl. But as I say, she's working at Burger King at present ... *Anyway.*' Her face brightens. 'While I've got you both, can I mention a couple of upcoming events in our entertainments calendar? You'll already have seen the invitation to our lobby concert. On the app!' she adds, noting my blank look. 'I've just sent it out. Check your phone!'

Finn and I exchange shifty glances.

'I'm trying not to use my phone,' I say. 'Digital detox. Maybe you could just . . . tell me?'

'Of course,' says Cassidy unsuspectingly. 'Here you are.' She hands me an A4 printed sheet inviting me to a *Special Lobby Concert, featuring Herbert Wainwright on French Horn and Other Acts.*

'Great!' I try to sound enthusiastic. 'I'll do my best to make it.'

'Marvellous! And now, the caves. You're all booked for this afternoon, two p.m. Both of you,' she adds to Finn. 'Enjoy!'

'Both of us?' I echo, taken aback.

'Yes, you both expressed interest and that's the only available slot. In fact, you're the only takers.' Cassidy lowers her voice. 'They're opening up just for you.'

I glance awkwardly at Finn.

'Is that a problem?' he says at once. 'Because I'm happy to bow out if you'd rather tour the caves alone.'

'No, no,' I say a bit stiffly. 'You go and enjoy the caves. I'll bow out.'

'Aren't you polite?' cries Cassidy in admiration. 'Why don't you both go? They're big caves, you know. You can easily avoid each other. I know that's your thing,' she adds knowledgeably. 'Avoiding each other. I've marked it on your notes.'

'Yes, I guess that is our thing,' says Finn, his mouth twitching as he meets my eye.

'We try our best.' I nod.

'That's settled, then,' says Cassidy. 'And I'll order you a taxi there, if you like. If you don't mind sharing?' she adds warily. 'Because if you do, I could always order two taxis.'

Oh my God. What would we look like, arriving there in convoy?

'No, it's fine,' I say, glancing at Finn for confirmation. 'We can share a taxi, I'm sure?'

'We'll stare out of opposite windows,' agrees Finn, deadpan. 'I won't speak or move a muscle and maybe you could do the same.'

He's quite funny, I'm realizing. Underneath his frowny, bad-tempered demeanour.

'Well, if that's all, I must just pop to the kitchen,' says Cassidy, coming out from behind the desk. 'Nice to see you both. You know, you do *look* like a couple,' she adds musingly. 'Funny that you're not, isn't it?'

'Well,' I say, feeling my face heat up. 'It's . . .'

I'm not sure how to finish that sentence.

'Hilarious,' says Finn.

As Cassidy starts walking across the lobby, I call out quickly, 'Wait, before you go, what about the champagne on the beach? You're sure it's nothing to do with the hotel? Because it's glass. We shouldn't leave it there. What do you think we should do?'

Cassidy turns back and looks at me, apparently nonplussed, then shrugs. 'Drink it?'

ELEVEN

True to his promise, Finn sits in total silence all the way to the caves, and if he's breathing, I can't hear it. I sit facing the other way, equally silent and rigid, determined to match his implacability. But as we get near, my calmness starts to slip. These are roads I haven't seen for years and they remind me so strongly of Dad that I feel a physical ache.

The caves were his thing. Whenever we visited them, Mum would stay behind and have a little nap, whereas Dad would leap at the chance to clamber about the caverns and give us talks on rock formation. 'Look,' he'd say every year, his glasses gleaming with enthusiasm in the dim subterranean light. 'This rock is a thousand years old. Nearly as old as me!'

Every year we took the same cheesy picture of ourselves grinning self-consciously in the Rainbow Cave, our favourite of the caverns. I searched out those photos last night and scrolled through, watching the gradual unfolding of time. Dad looks the same enthusiastic, slightly goofy Dad every year, barely aging beyond a thinning of the hair. But Kirsten and I transform, year by year. In the first photo, I'm a toddler; I only reach Dad's knees. By the age of twelve, I'm up to his shoulder.

I'd be up to his ears now, almost eye-to-eye. And he'd be grey. He never went grey. He's eternally forty-six.

A tear runs down my cheek and in embarrassment I wipe it away. I'm hoping Finn won't notice, but he must be more aware than he lets on, because he asks quietly, 'Are you OK?'

'It's just my dad used to bring us here every year. When he was alive. I was remembering.' I force a smile. 'It's fine.'

The taxi pulls up and I busy myself with finding cash – we're going strictly half-and-half on the fare. By the time we're both standing on the street, I've got my composure back, but Finn is surveying me in consternation.

'Have you just been through—' He stops himself. 'I don't want to pry, but are you here because you're grieving?'

'No, Dad died years ago. I'm here because of . . . something else.' There's a long beat of silence and for a moment I consider leaving it there. But I have a weird compulsion to confide in him. Finn's seen my messed-up lodge; he knows something's up – he might as well know the whole story. 'I had a flip-out at work,' I explain, avoiding his eye. 'I was quite stressed. It all got a bit much, and . . . Anyway. The doctor signed me off. I needed some time out. So . . .' I spread my arms around. 'Came here.'

'Huh,' says Finn after a pause. 'Me too. I had a kind of meltdown at the office—' He stops dead. 'Oh right, you heard.'

'Look, I want to say sorry about that,' I say guiltily. 'I didn't mean to eavesdrop. I came across you in the dunes and I . . . I heard you before I could help myself.'

It's a white lie. I could have crept away the minute I realized I was hearing something confidential, and he must know that. But he doesn't call me out on it.

'The sand dunes were a pretty stupid place to dictate emails,' he says with a wry smile.

'I don't know anyone else who dictates emails,' I say honestly, and his smile broadens.

'I do it when I'm stuck for words. I was particularly stuck for words right then.' He shrugs. 'Anyway, what I did at work is no secret. If you embarrass yourself at the office, everyone's going to know about it in a heartbeat.'

'*God*, yes. I'm sure everyone's talking about me at my company. What I did was . . .' I lift my hands to my face. 'Mortifying.'

'I'm sure you didn't embarrass yourself as much as I did,' Finn counters.

'Believe me, I did, a million times more.' I half smile, half wince. The memory of running down the street, away from Joanne, drenches my whole body with embarrassment. What was I thinking? Why didn't I just stop and talk calmly? Already I feel like I have more perspective. 'Anyway.' I draw breath. 'We should go in. They'll be waiting for us.'

We both turn to survey the entrance to the caves, which is marked by a big faded wooden sign reading, *Stenbottom Caves, Cafe and Gift Shop, Ice creams, Treats!* It's the same sign they had when I was a child.

'Have you been here recently?' I ask Finn.

'Not for years.'

'Me neither. I'm sure it's different now.'

But as soon as we get inside, I realize it's not different. It's exactly the same as it ever was. The same wooden ticket booth, the same stone floor, the same chilly air. Behind the ticket booth is a guy with red hair and an eager expression, who springs to life as he sees Finn and me entering.

'Welcome to Stenbottom Caves!' he exclaims. 'Save our caves!'

'Save our caves!' echoes a tiny voice beside him, and I blink as I notice a second figure – a woman with a thin face and a mass of dark curly hair, lurking shyly behind him.

'I'm Neil Reeves, Manager of the caves,' carries on the man, 'and this is Tessa Connolly, Assistant Manager, and we would like to welcome you warmly to your Magical Sound and Illumination Experience, which we hope will be a transcendent experience for you both.'

'Thank you!' I say, slightly bowled over by his enthusiasm.

'Connolly,' says Finn, frowning thoughtfully. 'Any relation to Terry Connolly?'

'Tessa is Terry's daughter,' says Neil. 'Aren't you, Tessa? She's shy,' he adds. 'Needs to come out of herself. Tessa, step out of the shadows! Say hello!'

I feel a pang of sympathy for Tessa, who reluctantly shuffles sideways, into the light, and pushes some hair off her face.

'Terry's my dad,' she allows.

'We were wondering, is he still around?' asks Finn. 'He taught us both surfing. I'm Finn Birchall and this is Sasha Worth, and we both have really fond memories of your dad.' He glances at me and I nod.

'Really fond,' I say. 'He was such an inspiring teacher.'

'Terry was the best,' chimes in Neil. 'Taught me to surf, too. Taught us all to surf.'

'Dad's doing well,' says Tessa, in such a timid voice that I can barely make out the words. 'Considering.'

'Considering what?' asks Finn.

'He's not himself,' says Tessa, looking anxious. 'He's not . . . how you would remember him.'

'Hasn't been well, Terry hasn't,' puts in Neil soberly. 'Not these last . . . three years, is it?' He glances at Tessa, who nods, her face tight, as though this whole conversation is a misery for her.

'I'm so sorry to hear that.' Finn looks dismayed. 'Please send him our love. We were saying earlier what an awesome teacher he was. Awesome person.'

'Thank you.' Tessa nods. 'I'll tell him. Thank you.' Her face has become rigid as we've been talking, and her hands are twisting together, I notice.

'Tessa love, why not get us both a coffee?' says Neil, and Tessa disappears at once into the back room.

'Sorry,' I say. 'Did we upset her? We had no idea about Terry being ill.'

'Don't worry. She just gets a bit shy, Tessa does,' says Neil confidingly. 'Freezes up. She wants to take a management qualification, but whenever she sees the customers she goes silent or hides. It's a bit of a challenge . . .' He looks momentarily troubled, then brightens. 'Anyway, we'll get there! And luckily, I don't mind chatting to the punters. In fact, you can't shut me up!' He passes two tickets across the wooden booth. 'You'll want to get going on your tour. Two Magical Sound and Illumination Experiences coming up. Hard hats to your left, earphones included.'

'Earphones!' I say, impressed. 'There never used to be earphones.'

'Ah, well, that's the upgrade, isn't it?' says Neil proudly. 'That's the "sound".'

'What about the "magical illumination"?' asks Finn.

'Is there a light show?' I ask, starting to feel excited.

'Very much so!' Neil nods. 'Self-automated light show. Pick up a torch from the basket and shine it around the ancient rocky caverns for a magical spectacle!'

Finn and I exchange glances.

'Is that an upgrade?' asks Finn. 'Didn't you always used to get a torch?'

'The torches have been upgraded,' says Neil without flickering. 'Long-life batteries. Hardly ever run out any more.'

'Gotcha,' says Finn, his mouth twitching. 'Sounds excellent.' He glances at me. 'Shall we?'

Two minutes later, Finn and I are descending the steep stone steps into the caverns, both in hard hats and carrying torches. My earphones are playing a kind of eighties synthesizer music, and as we reach the bottom of the staircase, a voice intones in my ears.

'Welcome to the ancient, mysterious world that is . . . Stenbottom Caves!'

It's Neil's voice, I realize at once. He sounds like someone playing a wizard in Dungeons and Dragons and has obviously turned up the Reverb button to the max. There's a series of plinky-plonky electronic notes, then he declaims, 'I am the Cavemaster!' and I giggle before I can stop myself.

I glance at Finn, who mouths 'Cavemaster?' with such a funny expression that I giggle again.

I press Stop and say, 'I'm not sure I need the sound experience.'

'Ditto.' Finn presses Stop too, then sweeps his torch around the rocky space. 'Quite cool, though, isn't it? I'd forgotten.'

I'd forgotten, too. As we make our way along the narrow paths into the first big cavern, I feel a kind of awe that I never did as a child. It's so old. It's so spectacular. It's so *huge*. There are rock formations on either side of me, jutting up in weird and wonderful shapes. Above us, the pale limestone is iridescent, and as I flash my torchlight over it, the surface glitters.

I mean, fair enough. This *is* a magical illumination experience.

Finn is silent, just looking around, and I'm grateful. I was nervous he might turn out to be the type that lectures, but he hasn't said a word. For what seems like ages, we just stand there, taking in the view. After a while, I can feel my breathing slow down. My brain seems to be clearing. I'm too busy looking at the weird and wonderful rocky shapes to think about anything else. Maybe, finally, I'm communing with nature.

After a long while, as though we're psychic, we both move forward, picking our way along another narrow path into the Rainbow Cave. This is the best cavern of all, no question. The rock is pink and yellow and forms little basins, into which flows spring water. It's like a mermaid's grotto. As I look around the colourful, shining space, I can't help emitting a happy sigh, and Finn grins.

'It's quite something,' he says.

'I came here every year,' I say. 'But I don't think I ever realized how special it was.'

'Same. You don't, when you're a kid.'

'And no one else here!' I spread my arms around the echoing cave. 'This always used to be chocka during the summer. Everyone taking photos.'

'Off-season.' Finn shrugs.

'I like off-season.'

I perch on a metal bench and lean back, watching a stream of rose-tinted water trickle endlessly into a rocky pool. After a moment, Finn sits down too, on the only other bench, on the opposite side of the cave. Again we're both silent for a while and I gradually realize that it feels comfortable. We couldn't share the beach, but we can share this cave.

'I took that bottle of champagne from the beach,' Finn says after a while. 'Just so no one cuts themselves.'

'Really?' I sit up.

'Health and safety.' His eyes gleam. 'Or maybe I didn't want anyone else pinching it.'

'So *you* pinched it.'

'No one else has claimed it.' He shrugs. 'So I reckon it's ours.'

'It's not ours!' I try to sound indignant, but I can't help smiling and he grins back.

'I think we should drink it. I'm just putting it out there. We should drink it tonight.'

I don't reply at once, because I don't want to capitulate. But maybe he has a point. If we don't drink it, who else is going to?

After a while, as though by mutual agreement, we move on again, winding our way through the Cave of Statues, the Waterfall Cave, and at last, back up the five thousand steps, or whatever it is, to the surface.

'I'm so unfit!' I gasp, as I emerge at the top of the staircase.

'That's what they all say!' Neil's cheerful voice hails me. 'Enjoy it, did you? Mention us on Tripadvisor, won't you?'

'I loved it,' I say sincerely. 'I'll give you a five-star review.'

'It was great,' says Finn, arriving at the top of the stone steps behind me. 'Tremendous sound. Very atmospheric.'

'Ah, well.' Neil looks delighted. 'Got to be creative, haven't you? Now, before you leave, have you seen our new Mystery Grotto?' He ushers us towards a small stone wishing well. 'Tessa, why don't you introduce the Mystery Grotto? It's a fundraising venture, really,' he adds confidingly. 'Save our caves!'

A moment later, Tessa lets herself out of the wooden booth and approaches us, looking awkward.

'Welcome to the Mystery Grotto,' she says in a tiny voice, staring at the ground. 'Simply throw a donation into the grotto, write down a question you want answered, and the Grotto Spirit will inspire you with the answer.' She hands each of us a slip of paper and nods at a nearby pot of pencils.

'Here's some cash.' I put a fiver in the grotto. 'But I don't know what to write.'

'Just a bit of fun!' Neil calls over from the booth. 'Write anything! I wrote, "Why do I always lose my socks in the machine?" Still haven't had the answer, though!'

As I stare at the slip of paper, a series of questions runs through my mind, none of which I can possibly write down. I glance over at Finn, and he seems equally perplexed by the task. But then suddenly his face clears.

'I have it!' he says, and grabs a pencil. 'I have the perfect question. In fact, the only question. *Who does the champagne really belong to?*' he reads aloud as he carefully prints. He drops the slip of paper in the wishing well, then winks at me. 'If we get an answer by five p.m., we pass the bottle to its rightful owner. If not, we drink it.'

At five p.m., I receive a text from Finn, the first since we exchanged numbers at the caves.

No answer to the riddle. Champagne on the beach? I even have glasses. (Plastic.)

I find myself smiling as I read the words, and quickly pull on my anorak. I hesitate, wondering if I should put on some lipstick or something – then abandon the idea. There's no one to see me except Finn. And I'll only have to take it off again when I go to bed.

He's already down on the sand when I arrive. The sea is a shimmering navy and the sun is glowing pinkly behind a bank of clouds on the horizon. Above us, the sky is deepening in colour, minute by minute.

'Wow,' I say, as I take a seat beside him. 'Sunset.'

'Nice one,' says Finn, nodding, and pours me a glass of champagne. 'Cheers.'

'Cheers.' I lift my glass to him. 'Here's to stolen goods.'

'If the rightful owners come along, we'll buy them a replacement,' he says, looking unmoved. 'Meanwhile, we have champagne and a sunset and I'm taking that as a win.'

'Fair enough.' I take a gulp and close my eyes as the delicious bubbles hit my throat. This is quite superior to White Wine, no vintage.

For a while, neither of us speaks, we just sip our champagne and watch the waves. This is a real plus point of Finn, I'm realizing. He doesn't feel the need to speak, but nor does the silence feel uncomfortable. The sky grows darker and darker until little pinpricks of light begin to appear, and I tilt my head backwards to take in the whole, star-speckled sky.

'Top-up?' says Finn, and I extend my glass.

'Do you know anything about constellations?' I ask, as he pours. 'I have no idea.'

Finn tops up his own glass, then considers the starry sky for a while. 'That one's called the Gherkin,' he says at last, pointing with his champagne flute. 'And there's the Lawnmower.'

I laugh, and lift my own glass, gesturing at a random cluster. 'Look, there's the Surfboard.'

'Huh.' Finn gives an appreciative smile, only just visible in the dimming light. 'Weird meeting Terry's daughter,' he adds. 'I never met her before.'

'She lived with her mum most of the time, that's why,' I tell him.

I was curious about Tessa myself, so I texted Kirsten earlier, and she filled me in with what she knew.

'Apparently Terry and his first wife Anne were divorced and Tessa only came to Rilston for part of the summer,' I explain. 'My sister told me. They're about the same age.' I find the text on my phone and read out what Kirsten put. *'She was really shy, though. She wouldn't join in the surf lessons, she just helped behind the scenes.'*

'Well, she hasn't changed, has she?' says Finn, swigging his champagne. 'Funny for Terry to have such a timid daughter, when he was such a big personality.'

'Maybe that's why. Maybe she reacted against him being so out there. I keep remembering those lessons with him – although all my memories are jumbled up. I can't remember which year was which.'

'Same,' says Finn, nodding vigorously. 'I have a million great memories. The first time I caught a wave . . .' He grins widely. 'It was the best feeling. Like flying. Or like when you discover sex. You're like, "No way! How can anything feel this good? Has everyone known about this, the whole time?"'

'It's the biggest-kept secret,' I say, laughing.

'Yes.' He nods, deadpan. 'Only surfers know.'

I laugh again. 'The first time I caught a wave, I was just convinced I was going to fall.'

'But you didn't,' says Finn. 'And I bet Terry was there on the beach to high-five you.'

'Of course he was.' I smile, recalling those days, hugging my knees. 'D'you remember how he used to finish every warm-up session? He used to point out to the ocean and say, "Go get it."'

'Of course I remember,' says Finn. 'It was like his blessing. "Go get it."'

'"Infinite waves, infinite chances,"' I say, remembering another of Terry's sayings, and Finn nods.

'"You don't catch a wave by staring at the sky."'

'"No one remembers the wipeouts."'

'"Don't doubt around all day."' Finn imitates Terry's hoarse voice. '"Seize that wave."'

'"Why are you worrying about the sea?"' I do my own imitation of Terry. '"The sea sure as hell isn't worrying about you."'

'The sea sure as hell isn't worrying about you.' Finn laughs.

'And "The ride is it."' I turn my head towards Finn. 'Remember that? "Kids, you *have* to enjoy the ride. The ride is it."'

'The ride is it.'

'The ride is *it*.'

I lift my glass to Finn, who smiles back and raises his own. As we both sip, with the dark waves crashing on to the sand in front of us, it's like a little tribute to Terry.

'So, tell me,' says Finn, as we both lower our glasses. 'How did you mortify yourself at work?'

'Oh no!' I give a defensive laugh. 'You're not getting me to reveal that.'

'Fair enough.' He pauses, then adds, 'But I still can't believe it was worse than what I did.'

I hear again some of the words he dictated in the dunes. *I should not have raised my voice in the meeting . . . slammed my*

coffee cup down on the boardroom table, causing spillage and dam-
age to papers . . . punched the coffee vending machine . . . exhibited
frustration with the office ficus plant . . .

'Can I be honest?' I say.

'Go ahead.'

'You don't seem like the kind of guy who would slam his coffee cup down, causing spillage and damage to papers. Or threaten to massacre a ficus.'

'Oh, I am,' says Finn, a bit grimly. 'I have. I did.'

'You haven't slammed down a single cup since you've been here.'

'That's because I haven't been angry. I haven't been stressed. When I get in a certain state . . . It's like a fog comes over my brain.' He exhales deeply, almost despairingly. 'I'm not proud. I used to be in control of myself.'

'What happened?'

'I was . . . in a . . .' He pauses, his eyes flickering darkly. 'I found myself in a difficult situation. I was overdoing it. Not sleeping. I guess I wasn't the invincible guy I'd kidded myself I was. You know you're in trouble when your secretary stages an intervention.' He shuts his eyes and rubs his forehead with his fist. 'And you start punching vending machines. Not my finest moment.'

'I have always *wanted* to punch a vending machine,' I say, and he laughs.

'Believe me, it's not all that.'

'So, what do you do?'

'Management consultant. You?'

'I do marketing for Zoose.'

'I've heard of it.' He nods. 'I work at Forpower Consulting, which you definitely won't have heard of. We're niche. We pretty much just advise green energy companies.'

'And why did you . . . What happened to tip you over the edge?'

There's silence, and something bleak ripples across his face.

'Hard to say,' he says at last, as though speaking with difficulty. 'I guess it was a bunch of stuff.' He doesn't elaborate and I realize that's where he's drawing his line.

'Well, at least you didn't run away from your office and try to join a convent,' I say, trying to cheer him up.

'A *convent*?' He looks truly astonished.

'I know!' I bury my face in my hands briefly. 'I lost my mind for a moment. My workload got to me and I couldn't see a way out. Becoming a nun seemed the obvious solution.'

'Becoming a nun.' He gives a short, sharp laugh. 'Interesting choice. What about . . .?' From the upswing in his voice I know exactly what he's referring to.

'Sex?' I turn my head briefly. 'I'm off sex. Not a problem.'

'Right,' he says after a longish pause. 'Got it.'

Of course he's got it. He read my 'song lyrics'.

There's another weird-feeling pause, in which I digest the fact that I have revealed to this guy the most intimate details of my life. On a beach. When I hardly know him.

But somehow I'm not freaked out. Finn feels safe and trustworthy. And most importantly, he gets it. He knows how I feel. Just to meet someone who's been through something similar is such a *relief*.

'So the nun thing didn't work out?' he enquires.

'They wouldn't have me.' Suddenly I see the funny side of it, and start laughing. 'Our Empowerment and Wellbeing Officer came to fetch me and I was running away from her when I bumped my head on a brick wall and ended up in hospital.'

'She did her job properly, then,' says Finn, 'the Wellbeing Officer.'

'You should have seen her chasing me down the street.' I collapse into fresh paroxysms. 'She thought I was losing it. I mean, she was right.' I shrug, wiping my eyes. 'I *was* losing it. So anyway, I'm in disgrace.'

'Same,' he says with feeling. 'Definitely in disgrace.'

'The two disgraces.' I clink my champagne flute against his and we both sip again.

'I thought maybe you'd had a bad breakup,' says Finn.

'I suppose I broke up with my work.' I consider. 'No, it wasn't a breakup. It was a big row. We're still not speaking.'

'Huh.' Finn nods. 'But at least you managed not to slam down your coffee cup and alienate all your colleagues.' He looks bleak again. 'I think back to how I behaved and I just . . . I'm like, *Was that me?*'

'Maybe I didn't shout, but I bought the same supper from Pret a Manger for five months straight,' I confess. 'Every single night. I couldn't even deal with choosing food, let alone cooking it.'

'Really?' He looks amused. 'What did you buy? Wait, I'll guess. Something hot. A panini.'

'Close. Halloumi wrap, choc bar, apple, bircher muesli, drink.' I reel off my order. 'Every night.'

'Nice.' He pauses a beat. 'No kale smoothie?'

'Stop it!' I laugh. 'I told you, that's my mum. She thinks I can transform myself with an app.'

Finn raises his eyebrows. 'Some app.'

'I'll show you,' I say, getting out my phone. I find the picture of Wetsuit Girl and the banner *20 Steps to a Better You*. 'My aim is to be her,' I explain.

Finn surveys Wetsuit Girl for a while, then frowns. 'Why do you want to be her?'

'Because, look at her!'

'I'm looking at her.' Finn shrugs. 'Still don't get it.'

'I'm fixated by her,' I admit, taking the phone back from him. 'I want to be her, but I slightly hate her, too. I bet she doesn't have a single unanswered email in her inbox. I bet she wakes up with a calm smile on her face and thinks, "Which dolphin shall I swim with today?"' Abruptly I realize how negative I'm sounding. 'I shouldn't bitch about her,' I add apologetically.

'Why not?' says Finn. 'Bitch away. I'll start. I think she looks like a nightmare. She looks like the kind of woman I thought you were when I first saw you. Sanctimonious and kind of glib. I mean, twenty steps. Really? Why twenty, for a start, why not nineteen?' He nods at the app. 'Is any of this stuff working?'

'Some,' I say, a bit defensively. 'I did some squats. Is drinking six bottles of whisky a day working?'

'Touché,' says Finn, after a pause. 'Give me time, I'll let you know.'

'Well, I'll let you know about the kale smoothie. If I manage to drink any of it.' I raise my eyes heavenwards. 'It's vile.'

'Knew it!' says Finn triumphantly. 'What else is on the list?'

I hand him my phone and he reads through the twenty steps.

'I mean, you *could* do all this,' he says as he reaches the end. 'Or you could, you know, enjoy yourself. You're on holiday, right? Here to have fun?'

'I guess so.' I look around the darkening beach and laugh. 'Maybe I should make a sandcastle.'

'Now you're talking.' Finn sits up with enthusiasm. 'That's what beaches are for. Building sandcastles.'

'And rock castles,' I say, remembering. 'We always used to make rock castles at Kettle Cove, have you ever been?'

'Went every year.' He nods. 'We had a checklist of things to do.'

'Same!' I say eagerly. 'Caves, surfing, cream tea . . . fish and chips?' I look at him.

'Of course, fish and chips! Who doesn't have fish and chips on holiday?'

My mind is suddenly filled with a memory of eating fish and chips, sitting on the wall outside the fish shop, swinging my legs and looking down proudly at my new red sandals. I must have been, what, ten? I was with my family, I had saltwater in my hair, the sun was warm, and there were chips. Life was bliss. It was actual bliss.

Was that being here, or was it just being ten years old?

'Can you ever get childhood levels of happiness back?' I say, staring out at the water. 'Could we ever be as happy as we were here, as kids?'

'Good question,' says Finn, after a long pause. 'I hope so. Maybe not exactly the same kind of happiness, but . . .' He shrugs. 'I would hope so.'

'I hope so, too.'

It's so dark now I can only just catch the gleam of his eyes, the pale line of his teeth in the moonlight. It's getting cold, too, and I shiver. For a moment I wonder whether to suggest we go and eat supper together in the dining room . . . but no. Too much.

'This has been lovely, but I'm going to go now,' I say instead. 'I have an appointment with room service and a long bath.'

'Fair enough. I'll stay out here a while.' He flashes me a grin. 'But don't worry, I won't drink any more of the champagne. I'll stick a spoon in it, keep it fizzy for tomorrow evening.'

'OK.' I get to my feet, feeling ungainly as my trainers catch on the sand, and quite glad that it's dark. 'Well, have a good evening.'

'You too. See you tomorrow.'

I'm looking forward to seeing him, I realize. I'm actually looking forward to having company on the beach.

'Great.' I smile. 'See you then.'

TWELVE

The next morning, Finn is already in the dining room when I arrive for breakfast and I give him a friendly wave as I take my seat on the opposite side of the room. Within about ten seconds, Nikolai is by my side, proffering a kale smoothie on a silver tray, and I arrange my features into an expression of delight.

'Wow! Nikolai. A kale smoothie, already. That was ... quick.'

Nikolai looks delighted, and draws breath. 'Madame would prefer—'

'Eggs,' I cut him off.

'One boiled egg?' ventures Nikolai. 'And melon plate?'

'No, two scrambled eggs, please.' I smile charmingly. 'Also bacon, sausages, pancakes with maple syrup and a cappuccino, please. Don't bother with the melon plate. That's all,' I add, since Nikolai seems too confused to move. 'Thanks!'

Looking a bit shellshocked, he writes down the order, then heads towards Finn's table.

'Nikolai!' exclaims Finn with gusto as Nikolai approaches his table. 'Good to see you this morning. I hope you're well. I'd like the melon plate this morning. That's all.'

'One . . . melon plate?' echoes Nikolai, his eyes swivelling to me and back to Finn, as though suspecting a trick.

'Exactly.' Finn nods. 'And black coffee. Thanks. Detox,' he adds to me as Nikolai heads away, whereupon I raise my eyebrows sardonically.

'Detox? Or hangover cure?'

'What's the difference?' He shoots me a wicked grin. 'Enjoy your kale smoothie. It looks very . . . amphibian.'

'Thanks.' I smile sweetly back. 'I will. So tell me something. Are you using the rock today?'

'Hmm.' Finn's expression flickers briefly. 'Depends if I get there first.'

His challenge is obvious, and I feel a little spike of adrenaline, mixed with an urge to giggle. I'm so getting to that rock first. The race is *on*.

The minute I've finished eating, I hurry upstairs to get ready. Finn was lingering over yet another coffee when I left the dining room, so I'm sure I'll make it down to the beach before he does. I scrub my teeth, grab my iPad and shove on my anorak as I'm hurrying down the corridor.

But as I reach the beach, I see that Finn is already on the deck outside his lodge. Nooo! How did he do that? Trying to be stealthy, I creep over the sand, then break into a run. At once Finn's head jerks up – and the next moment, he's vaulting over the railing from the deck, down on to the sand and making for the rock.

'Mine!' I cry, sprinting towards the rock, laughing helplessly. '*My* rock! Get away!'

'Mine!' he exclaims with equal determination. 'I got here first!'

I feel like I'm an eight-year-old playing forty-forty as I hurl myself at the rock. I fling out a hand, trying to bar Finn and simultaneously scramble to the top. Bashing my knee, I haul myself up into the hollow, crashing into it with an inelegant flop.

'Got it,' I pant. 'It's mine! I claim it!'

'Look at that!' exclaims Finn, still stuck on a lower jutting level.

'Nice try.' I narrow my eyes, not yielding an inch. 'But you don't distract me that easily. *My* rock.'

I'm waiting for him to launch another attack, but he seems to have given up.

'Look,' he insists. 'Another message.'

'*What?*'

I raise my head and find myself reading a new set of words carved out on the sand and lined with stones. Next to it is a bouquet of flowers.

To the couple on the beach. Thank you. 18/8

'What the hell?' I say feebly, and move aside so Finn can join me in the hollow of the rock. 'Flowers?'

'I know, right? And what does that date mean?'

'Is it art?' I say, remembering what Cassidy told us. 'Is it for a new exhibition?'

'Maybe.' Finn shrugs. 'But why wouldn't we see the artist? I haven't noticed anyone taking photos, have you?'

My leg is feeling squashed against the rock and I shift slightly, trying to think this all through. At once I notice Finn adjusting his own position so that we're not touching, which is considerate of him.

'OK, the eighteenth of August. That's a way off.' I screw up my face, thinking. 'Is this about redeveloping the lodges? They're going to be called Skyspace Beach Studios. Maybe it's a message thanking the first customers. Or the investors? Maybe a couple on the beach put in some money?'

'You wouldn't thank them like this,' asserts Finn, typing something on his phone.

'You might,' I object, more for the sake of objecting than because I'm particularly convinced. 'Maybe the eighteenth of August is when they're going to open up again. Or maybe the eighteenth of August next year,' I amend, thinking through how long it will take to knock down the lodges, build new ones and open them up. 'Anyway, whichever year, this is for publicity—'

'It's the accident,' Finn interrupts and I stiffen.

'What?'

'The kayak accident. I've just googled the date and "Rilston Bay" and I got a series of news reports.' He looks up, meeting my gaze. 'It's the accident. It happened on the eighteenth of August.'

I feel a tingle down my spine. This is all getting a bit weird.

'Is it a shrine?' I peer again at the message. 'A memorial? But no one died. No one was even hurt, were they?'

'Not as far as I know.'

'I mean, the boy who came off the kayak, he was OK, wasn't he?'

'I thought so. I mean, I guess he was a bit freaked out and chilled after being in the water, but . . .' Finn shrugs, looking baffled.

We both survey the message again. I've never been more mystified by anything in my life.

'Who saved him?' I ask in sudden inspiration. 'Is that what this is? Was it a couple on the beach?'

'It was a dad, wasn't it?' Finn scrolls down his phone. 'Yes. "Quick-thinking father-of-three Andrew Ilston pulled James Reynolds to safety." '

'James Reynolds.' I nod. 'That's right. I'd forgotten what he was called. Do you know him? Was he a pupil of Terry's?'

Finn shakes his head. 'I think he was only there for the day. There was a stack of day trippers that day and they all wanted to go on the water. That's why they ran out of kayaks and James Reynolds ended up with a damaged one which should never have been hired out.'

'Right.' I digest this. 'I don't think I ever knew the details.'

'Well.' Finn shrugs. 'Long time ago.'

On impulse, I jump down off the rock to examine the message more closely and Finn follows me.

' "To the couple on the beach," ' I read again. '*What* couple on the beach?'

I swivel round as though some random couple will come walking up and say, *Ah, this must be directed at us*. But the beach is as windswept and desolate as ever. There isn't anyone in sight, let alone a likely couple.

'I think this is somehow for you.' I pivot back to face Finn. 'You said you were out on another kayak. You said you swam over to help. It can't be coincidence. Maybe James Reynolds thinks you saved his life.'

'But I didn't save him!' retorts Finn. 'I didn't get anywhere near. And I'm not a couple. Maybe the date is just a coincidence.'

'It can't be. Come on, look at the facts.' I tick off on my fingers. 'You were on the beach that day and you tried to save him and now there are flowers on the beach saying thank you. They *have* to be for you.'

'As I said, I'm not a couple,' repeats Finn, rolling his eyes. 'Anyway, if he was going to thank anyone, he would thank Andrew Ilston. I don't think the jigsaw fits together. Give it up.' He bends down, picks up one of the pebbles, examines it, then replaces it. 'If it's anything, it's art. It's probably worth five million pounds.'

'Art.' I roll my eyes disparagingly. 'That is not art!'

'Well, shall we agree we'll never know?' suggests Finn.

'No,' I reply stubbornly. 'I'm convinced this is to do with the accident. Maybe James Reynolds knows you're staying here. He knows you tried to save him, and . . . Yes! He thinks you made the attempt with someone else.'

'Who?' demands Finn at once.

'Unspecified. But he thinks the two of you tried to save him.' I point at the message. 'Hence "the couple on the beach".'

I knew I would come up with a theory if I thought about it hard enough.

'That's bollocks,' says Finn forthrightly. 'How would he even know I was here?'

'Because . . . he saw you.' I whip round, scrutinizing the surrounding area. 'He recognized you. Maybe he's here!'

'You think he's hiding behind the lodges?'

'Maybe!' I peer at the derelict lodges for a moment, then get out my phone. 'I'm going to track him down and ask him. He'll be on Facebook.'

Finn stares at me for a moment. 'What, you're just going to contact him, out of the blue?'

'Why not?' I say, summoning up Facebook. 'That's what social media is for. Cracking mysteries.'

'Didn't know you were such a detective,' says Finn, sounding amused. 'Is this your hobby?'

'It's my last case,' I say, typing busily. 'I was looking forward to a nice easy retirement, but now this comes along, so . . .'

'Got it.' Finn nods. 'Drawn back in.'

'Exactly.'

'And I'm what, your sidekick?'

'Not sure,' I say absently, scrolling through profiles of people called James Reynolds. 'Maybe you're the cop at the precinct saying, "Why are we opening this cold case? Don't we have more important things to do?"' I look up, my eyes narrowed, and jab a finger at Finn. 'Which probably means you wrote the message yourself and there's a body underneath it.'

'Excellent!' says Finn appreciatively. 'Good to know I'm the killer. Although, I'm just wondering, who did I murder? Also, why did I draw attention to it?' He gestures at the message. 'Seems a strange move. I probably could have got away with, you know, burying the body and *not* writing a message on the beach.'

'Fair point,' I agree. 'Luckily, I don't need to know how it all works out. You'll tell me yourself in a big monologue at the denouement.' I flash him a smile. 'Can't wait. It'd better be exciting. And make sure you wrap up all the loose ends.'

'Of course.' He nods, deadpan. 'Although, surely leave one for the internet to keep guessing at?'

I can't help laughing. 'You're good.'

Finn shrugs. 'I watch TV too.'

I wait for him to tell me which box set he's watching and

how I must watch it and how he predicted three of the twists, which he will now explain to me in great detail then add, 'That's not a spoiler,' when it totally is. But he's silent, which is a relief. Finn really is much less annoying than a lot of men, I find myself thinking. Which I appreciate doesn't sound like much of a compliment – but it is.

I scroll down a bit more, but Facebook is buffering and I click my tongue in frustration.

'Found James Reynolds?' Finn asks, and I shake my head.

'Signal's gone. I'll find him later. Oh, look.' I point at a big white ship that has appeared, some way out to sea, and instinctively we both move forward over the sand to have a look.

'Obviously I'm the killer,' adds Finn, as we walk along, naturally matching each other's stride. 'So I *would* say this, to throw you off the scent. But I do have another theory.'

'Oh yes?' I look up with interest.

'Your mum's behind all of this.' He gestures back at the message. 'She's created it to keep your mind distracted.'

'Oh my God.' I burst into laughter. 'Have you met my mum? That is *exactly* what she would do.'

'If she can ring up the hotel with orders for kale smoothies at seven a.m., I'm thinking a couple of messages on the beach wouldn't be beyond her.'

'I'm fairly sure she's at a conference in Leicester,' I say regretfully, 'otherwise I would a hundred per cent say you're right.'

Just for a moment, I think, *Is it Mum?* But mystery messages aren't Mum's style, nor presents on the beach where anyone could come across them. She's not really whimsical, Mum – she's all about being practical.

We reach the water's edge and stand there for a while,

watching the ship move almost imperceptibly across the bay. I feel a bit like that ship myself, I realize. Moving slowly in the right direction. I'm in a better place today than I was yesterday. Yesterday, I was in a better place than when I ran down the street from Joanne. I just have to keep going.

Wondering if Finn feels the same, I shoot a sidelong glance at him. His dark hair is being blown about by the wind; his gaze is fixed intently on the horizon; his expression is unreadable. I notice small creases at his eyes that look like smile lines. He looks like he has a face that's meant to smile. Although maybe he hasn't had many reasons to, lately.

Sensing my gaze on him, Finn turns – and I quickly clear my throat.

'I was just thinking how each day I feel better. How about you?'

'For sure.' He nods. 'And I don't even have twenty steps to help me.' His eyes crinkle. 'What's on the agenda for today?'

'Yoga on the beach,' I reply. 'And before you ask, I don't know how to do yoga. I feel like everyone else got the yoga memo and I missed it. Overnight, everyone in the world could do yoga except me.'

'Yes!' Finn nods emphatically. 'Agreed! At my workplace, no one did yoga – and then suddenly everyone did yoga. They were all like, "Don't you do yoga?"' He waggles his eyebrows in a pantomime of shock. '"You don't do *yoga*?"'

'Exactly!' I laugh. 'Anyway, I missed out on the worldwide yoga orientation session. I must have been answering emails at the time. But it's on my list. So I will be standing on one leg any minute. Don't laugh.'

'I wasn't going to laugh,' says Finn mildly. 'I was going to say, "Do you want company?"'

'Company?' I stare at him suspiciously. 'You mean . . . you want to do yoga?'

Mr whisky-and-pizza wants to do *yoga*?

'Why not?' He shrugs. 'Let's see what all the fuss is about.'

I have never laughed so much in my life. We prop my iPad up on the big rock, put down my yoga mat and a towel for Finn on the sand and follow Wetsuit Girl through a series of moves. Or at least, we don't exactly follow her so much as marvel at her, ignore her, insult her and swear at her.

'I'm not doing that,' Finn says, about every ten seconds. 'I'm not doing that. Sod off.' He peers at the screen and makes an incredulous noise. 'OK, Sasha, you try that one. If you don't break your leg, I'll have a go.'

'I don't know how she isn't falling over,' I gasp, as I plant my hands on my mat. 'This is like playing Twister.'

'She has secret superglue on her hands,' says Finn. 'Also, she's not real. She's a yoga bot.'

Eventually we reach the cooldown. We listen, cross-legged, while Wetsuit Girl tells us what a good job we did and how it's time to lie down and relax.

'OK, this I can do,' says Finn, lying down on his towel. 'They should have cut straight to this bit.'

'Shh,' I say. 'You're disturbing my chakras.'

To be fair, it is quite relaxing, lying on the beach, staring up at the pale sky, listening to tinkly music. In fact, I'm quite sorry when the video ends.

'Thank you for the fun yoga party,' says Finn, as we both struggle up to sitting positions. 'In return, may I invite you to a spot of whisky later on?'

'I'm not wild about whisky.' I make an apologetic face. 'But I'll have some more of our stolen champagne?'

'Great!' says Finn, looking pleased. 'It's a date— Wait.' He catches himself. 'Sorry. An appointment.'

He looks awkward and my stomach twinges. I don't want anything to feel awkward between us. What does he think – that I find him deeply unattractive? It's not him, it's me, and I honestly mean that. *I'm* the one with a problem.

So why don't I tell him? He knows everything else. He's seen my crumpled tissues, my chocolate wrappers, my distraught mess, and he hasn't judged or laughed. Maybe telling him would be *good*.

'So . . .' I pause, my heart beating a little faster, because this is pretty embarrassing. 'So, I told you I've gone off sex.'

'Right,' says Finn, looking shocked. 'Yes. I mean . . . I wasn't . . .'

'I know you weren't. But I wanted to explain a bit more.'

He seems flabbergasted by my candour. And I'm pretty flabbergasted myself. Except that out here, under the endless gaping sky, every secret, every problem, every embarrassment seems somehow smaller, flimsier. It feels safe to blab on the beach, I realize. It's as if all your words get swept away by the wind, out to sea, gone.

'It's really disconcerting.' I flop back down on my yoga mat, so I can talk without seeing his face. 'It's as if my body's checked out. That's why I wrote . . . what I wrote on that piece of paper. It wasn't really lyrics. It was a manifestation. You're supposed to make stuff happen in your life by writing it down. And that's what I wanted to happen. I want to . . . to come alive.'

There's a long silence. I gaze directly upward, into the pale, cloudy sky, feeling the breeze on my cheeks. I can't believe I've just revealed so much about myself to a relative stranger. But I don't feel embarrassed. I feel calm.

'Maybe you will come alive,' says Finn, after a long pause. 'If you don't worry about it.'

'Maybe.' I nod, thinking about this. 'I mean, I used to be normal. I used to have a love life. But now . . .'

'Not so much?'

'A few days ago, a guy in Pret chatted me up and I told him I couldn't see the point of sex, because it's just genitals rubbing together.'

The memory is so horrifying that tears are springing to my eyes as I talk. Or maybe they're tears of mirth. Or relief, that I'm confiding in someone. I have no idea.

'Genitals rubbing together,' echoes Finn, sounding dumbfounded.

'I know.' My voice starts shaking, but again I'm not sure if I'm laughing or crying. 'And I said it loudly, in front of all the customers.' I clap a hand over my face. 'Genitals rubbing together.' Now I'm laughing properly, almost hysterically, tears are pouring down my face and suddenly I break into a coughing fit.

'Are you OK?' asks Finn in alarm.

'Well, clearly not,' I manage. I sit back up and cough a few times more, emptying my lungs, before I get control of myself. 'Clearly I'm a bit of a mess. Sorry for dumping on you. You didn't want to hear that. Now you're thinking, "How do I get away from this weirdo?" If you like, we can blank each other for the rest of the trip.'

'I don't want to blank you!' He laughs. 'Seriously. Who am I to judge? I'm a mess myself.'

'You're a mess?' I turn to survey him sceptically. 'How are you a mess? I mean, I know you're here, and I know what happened at your office . . . but you look pretty put-together to me. No quirks. No strange behaviour.'

There's a pause and Finn's jaw tightens a little. I'm starting to recognize his facial moves and this one is a defence mechanism. It's the way he looks whenever I venture on to tricky territory. I resign myself to another five-minute silence, followed by an abrupt change of subject.

But then, to my surprise, he says, in a low voice, 'I wake up at three every night. I'm stressed out at—' He breaks off and his eyes flicker as though with some painful thought or memory. 'I'm stressed out at some stuff that happened. And I'm angry at myself.' He breaks off, shaking his head, looking despairing. 'It's corrosive, that kind of feeling.'

'Do you ever manage to get back to sleep?' I ask cautiously.

'Haven't slept a full night for a long time.' He flashes me a rueful glance and I notice again the shadows under his eyes. They've been so permanent I'd thought of them as just part of his face – but now I see them as fatigue. Deep, engrained fatigue.

'Have you tried any . . . remedies?' I say, aware that this sounds totally feeble.

'A few.' He nods.

'Have you tried seeing anyone?'

Finn doesn't reply, just makes an indeterminate noise. After a while, I sense he's not going to divulge any more than that. To be fair, by his standards, he's been forthcoming.

'The pair of us!' I try to sound light-hearted and almost succeed.

'I know, right?'

'But luckily, we have yoga.' I flop down on to my mat again and stare at the sky. 'Yoga solves everything.'

'Amen to that.' Finn lies back on his towel and we both lie in quietness.

After a while, I glance over at him and see that he's closed his eyes and is breathing evenly. I hope he's fallen asleep. He must be exhausted if he's up at 3 a.m. every night.

I stretch my legs out silently, gazing up at a bank of clouds, feeling a kind of lightness, almost optimism. I've just covered Step 18 on my programme, I realize. *Confide in someone you can trust.* And it made me feel better, just like Wetsuit Girl promised. I can still remember the advice on the app: *Protect yourself and think carefully who to talk to. If you're going to open up, you need to be secure. If in doubt, call one of the helplines listed below, or visit our online forum.*

But I don't need a helpline or a forum. I have someone I trust, right here.

THIRTEEN

That afternoon, I go for another stroll through the town. I've got used to my little routine of striding briskly along the beach, then winding round the narrow streets and lanes, peering into shop windows. Although I am not going to buy crisps today, I tell myself. I am *not*.

I head along the beach towards the Surf Shack and then beyond it, to the place where Surftime used to stand. Maybe the building doesn't exist any more, but this is where the accident began. This is where James Reynolds rented out his damaged kayak. Maybe I can find a clue here.

As I gaze at the empty patch of ground where Surftime used to stand, I find myself remembering Pete, who ran it. Now I think back, with an adult's perspective, I can appreciate that he was good looking. Tall and strapping with a dark beard and loads of earrings. Kirsten and I sometimes hired bodyboards from him when Terry had run out and you'd think we might have had a crush on him. But we didn't. No one did. There was something off about him, for all that he had a wide smile. It didn't seem real.

I guess it couldn't have been easy, being in competition with Terry, I think, trying to be fair. Pete tried to copy Terry, but he just couldn't quite manage it. He was impatient, I remember that. He didn't like answering questions. He would snap at children who couldn't manage their wetsuits. You'd see his classes doing their warm-up routines on the beach, and it all looked quite cursory. I'm not surprised he cut corners with safety, to be honest.

I perch on a wooden post, get out my phone and dial Mum, then Kirsten, but neither of them answers. I'm not surprised; they're both so busy. So I WhatsApp them a photo of the second message, then type:

Hi both! Just wondering, does this mean anything to you? It appeared on the sand. It's the date of that kayak accident. What do you remember about that? Was there a couple involved in some way??

As soon as I've sent it I realize I should also have given them an update, so I add another message:

All good here. Feeling really great, so much better. Did yoga on the beach today!!! Xxx

I wander through the dunes, across the big car park and into the town, meandering aimlessly here and there, looking for possible gifts to take back. Every gallery seems to be selling pictures made out of driftwood. Would Kirsten like one of those? Or are they in the category of 'It looked fab when we were by the sea but not so much in Hackney?'

As I'm dawdling along, a massive copy of *Young Love* draws my attention, and I cross the road to look at it. Beside it is a sign: *Authorized signed print. We are proud to be the exclusive stockist of Mavis Adler in Rilston.* Underneath the picture is a display of mugs, purses, tote bags and calendars, all plastered with images of *Young Love*, and I can't help feeling they detract from the main picture. But I guess it's the merch that sells.

What with the messages on the beach, I feel a bit connected to Mavis Adler, and I peer at *Young Love*, looking at it closely for maybe the first time ever. I know nothing about painting, but it uses quite vivid colours. The sand, the rocks, the shadows, are all in rich ochres and cobalts and . . . whatever the posh name is for red. There's even red in the shadows and the clouds. The whole picture has a glow. It's an intense piece of artwork. It's arresting. I guess that's why it's so popular. And the young couple kissing have a kind of body language that makes you envy them. His arm is wrapped around her waist. Her head is thrown back slightly. You can't see their faces, but you can see her young, coltish legs dressed in shorts; you can tell he's a teenager from the back of his head.

I think I've always dismissed this painting as being just 'that picture on postcards', but now I'm looking at it properly, I rather love it. Maybe I'll buy a tote bag.

As I push open the door to the gallery, there's a *ting* and a woman comes forward to greet me. She has greying hair, a blue printed smock stuffed into ballooning linen trousers and what seems like three pairs of socks on, stuffed into clogs. On her chest is a wooden badge carved with the name *Jana*.

'I saw you looking at *Young Love*,' she says with a friendly smile. 'If you're interested, Mavis Adler has a new exhibition beginning here a week on Saturday. A very exciting new collection.'

I can't say, 'No thanks, I was just interested in that one painting,' so I take the leaflet and eye it. Then a moment later, my mind starts turning.

'All new art?' I look up.

'All new art.' Jana nods.

Oh my God! I am officially top detective and I win. The messages on the beach *are* some kind of art and we're the only witnesses because we're in the lodges.

'Tell me something,' I say, in my best, swaggering, slam-dunk, TV-detective manner. 'Is Mavis Adler's new exhibition by any chance a series of messages on the beach?'

'No,' says Jana.

I frown, put out. 'No?'

'No,' she repeats. 'You're thinking of a previous collection, *Land Conversations*, which made use of Rilston Bay beach.'

'Well, what's this new exhibition?'

'It's a series of sculptures using natural and man-made materials. Here, have a look.' She opens a catalogue on a nearby display case. 'If you'd like to buy an exhibition cata-logue, they're twenty pounds,' she adds.

'Right,' I say, trying not to sound like a philistine cheap-skate. 'Well . . . maybe.'

I flip over the pages to see photographs of huge metal gir-ders welded together into weird shapes. Some of them have bits of driftwood incorporated, and one is nestling in a mas-sive coil of rope, only I can't tell if that's part of the art or not. I glance at the title to see if that helps, but it's called *Untitled*.

'Amazing!' I say as I get to the end of the catalogue. Jana seems to be expecting me to say more, so I grope for some more phrases. 'Very powerful. Visceral. I loved the . . . the . . .

structural . . . forms. Quite different from *Young Love*. And *Land Conversations*.'

'Yes.' Jana smiles. 'Her new work is possibly more challenging than anything she has done previously. But very rewarding.' She juts out her chin as though she's daring me to disagree.

'Definitely!' I say hastily. 'Very rewarding. So, has she ever painted any more pictures like *Young Love*?'

'No.' Jana's smile becomes more fixed. 'No, she hasn't. But she is working on a new secret project called *Titan*. We're all waiting to see what that is.'

I wander over to a display board entitled *The Story Behind Young Love* and see a collage of newspaper articles about 'the real teenage couple who took the art world by storm'.

'I never knew they were real!' I exclaim, and scan a few paragraphs about the couple, who are called Gabrielle and Patrick. 'Wait, they got married in real life? That's so romantic!'

'It was all quite widely reported,' says Jana, as though I'm a bit dim. 'There was a TV documentary.'

'Oh. Well, I missed that.'

I survey the picture from a *Daily Mail* piece, showing the couple in their wedding finery, and suddenly an idea occurs to me.

'She could paint an update!' I swing round to Jana. 'She could paint them in their wedding gear and call it *Wedding Love*. Or if they have kids, she could paint *Family Love*. Everyone would love it! You'd sell loads of mugs.'

I'm already creating a marketing campaign in my head. Hashtags, images, partnerships, events, the biggest digital presence you've ever seen . . .

Then I blink and come to, almost in surprise at myself. I never expected my brain to come alive like that. I thought

I was off marketing, off work, off all of it. It just shows. Something.

'Yes,' says Jana, her smile growing still more rigid. 'Various people have suggested updates over the years. However, Ms Adler has chosen not to re-engage with *Young Love*. Obviously we support her artistic integrity and are very excited about her new direction.'

I bite my lip, feeling a bit sorry for Jana. Obviously she'd *die* for a lovely new romantic painting from Mavis Adler, but instead she has to be super-excited about metal girders. I'm sure the metal girders are very powerful, only I can't see anyone putting them on a pencil case.

'And you're positive she isn't doing any messages on the beach at the moment?' I return to my original enquiry.

'I don't know.' Jana spreads her hands. 'It's possible. She's currently in Copenhagen, of course.'

'*Copenhagen?*' This ruins my theory. She can't be simultaneously in Copenhagen and planting messages on the beach.

Although now I think about it, it was always more Finn's theory than mine. So I still win.

'She's back in two days and we're running a special event at the Rilston ballroom. Ms Adler will be unveiling *Titan*,' she adds momentously.

'Wow!' I say, feeling that some response is required. '*Titan!*'

'Exactly. It will be a big moment. There's a drinks reception, if you're interested? The details are in there.' She nods at the leaflet in my hand. 'Now I'll let you browse.'

I drift around the gallery, looking at watercolours and oversized pottery vases, then return to the gift-shop area, which is about ninety per cent *Young Love* merchandise, mixed with a few postcards of the messages on the beach. I pick up a *Young Love* tote bag and approach the till.

'Lovely choice,' says Jana, as she scans it. 'And would you like the catalogue for the new exhibition?' She's already reaching for one, as though it's a foregone conclusion that I'll buy it, and I quail inwardly. Oh *God*. I'm going to have to admit that I *am* a philistine cheapskate.

'Um, just the tote bag, thanks.' I clear my throat. 'I'll ... think about the catalogue.'

'Of course!' she says, replacing the catalogue with over-deliberate movements. 'No problem.'

There's a massive pile of catalogues on the floor behind her, I notice. Clearly everyone thinks like me. Which makes me feel bad. But not quite bad enough to spend twenty quid on photographs of metal girders I'll never look at.

When I get back out on the street, I reach for my phone to see if Mum or Kirsten has replied to my WhatsApps, but there's nothing. So I turn my steps towards the beach.

As I'm striding along the sand, the wind kicks up, and soon it's blowing gusts of top sand across the beach. I stop to watch for a bit, because it's kind of eerie. Swathes of sand are travelling in whorls and patterns, all streaming in the same direction. It looks as though the ground is moving beneath my feet.

I film a bit on my phone to show Finn, then resume marching on, my eyes fixed on the Surf Shack, which is the natural focus of this part of the beach. As I get nearer, a few raindrops hit my face and I roll my eyes. Honestly, the weather. Just as you think you've got it tamed, it rains on you again. But even so, I'm enjoying this stride, this fresh, bracing air, this eerie whirling sand, the gulls circling overhead. I'm communing with my surroundings again, I realize. Go, me! I knew I could crack it—

Then, midway through my train of thought, I freeze. Everything else vanishes from my mind. *What* am I seeing?

There, on the deck of the Surf Shack, is a figure I didn't notice before, but now I can see him clearly. It's Terry. Terry, back in his spot, standing on the deck, arms outstretched, for all the world as though he's about to assemble a surf class.

What the . . .?

I pick up my pace, walking faster, then almost running to get to the Surf Shack.

'Hi!' My voice tumbles out eagerly as I approach. 'Hi, Terry! It's Sasha, d'you remember me?'

He's dressed in loose corduroy trousers and a fleece, rather than the wetsuit or board shorts I remember, but I guess I never saw him in winter, or even off-duty. He was only ever on the beach, tanned, dressed for surf lessons and ready to command the action.

As I get closer, my stomach flips over as I realize that his clothes aren't the only thing that's different about him. His face is thinner, his hair whiter and more tufty. His legs are scrawnier, I can tell from the way his trousers fall. His hands are bony. And they're trembling slightly, I notice. He looks frail. Terry Connolly looks frail.

Of course he's older, I tell myself, willing myself not to be shocked by his appearance. Of *course* he is. Twenty years have gone by since I last saw him. What did I expect? But there's a secret dismay inside me, a sadness, a kind of longing for Terry as he was. Strong and barrel-chested and master of the waves. Master of the beach. Master of life.

'Hi, Terry!' I say again, and he turns his head as though only just noticing me. His face looks kind of caved in, with deep-etched grooves running down each cheek. He doesn't have his stubble any more, but is clean-shaven, and it makes his face look soft and vulnerable. His blue eyes are vague for a moment, then they light up as though he's worked out who I am.

'Have you come for a lesson?' he asks, his voice feebler than I remember but with a shade of his old gusto. 'First class is at ten o'clock. Have you surfed before?'

'It's me, Sasha.' I step up on to the deck, trying to catch his wandering gaze. 'I used to learn surfing from you!'

'Ten o'clock,' repeats Terry, nodding. 'Do you need a board? Speak to Sandra, my wife, she'll sort you out.' He glances behind him as though expecting the door to be open, Sandra standing at her table, children in wetsuits spilling in and out.

But Sandra died three years ago.

'OK,' I say, swallowing. 'OK, I'll do that.'

Terry's gaze travels over the empty beach as though puzzled. 'Not many here yet.'

'No,' I manage. 'No, there aren't.'

My heart is crunching. I don't know what to say. I don't know how to react.

'You'll have to take that off!' He gestures at my anorak in amusement. 'Can't surf in a coat!'

'I'll . . . I'll take it off for the lesson,' I say.

'That's good. That's good.' He nods vaguely. 'Beginner group, are you?'

'I . . . yes. I'm a beginner.'

'You'll make a fine surfer!' he says encouragingly. 'You'll do well.' Then his eyes roam over the beach again in confusion. 'But where are the others? They're all late! Go and tell them, will you?'

'I . . . um . . .'

'Sandra, how many in the first class?' he calls, then seems to wait for an answer. He heads across the deck to the closed

193

door, surveys it for a full minute, then shakes his head as though in bemusement. 'Don't know where she's got to,' he mutters after a bit. 'Ah well . . .' He looks at me and his faded gaze refocuses. 'Oh, it's *you*!' he exclaims in sudden animation.

'Yes!' I say, feeling a clutch of relief. 'It's me, Sasha! Remember my sister Kirsten? We used to—'

'Now, I've had to put you in the first class,' says Terry, without appearing to hear me. 'The ten o'clock class. I know you've surfed before, but . . .' He pauses, looking surprised. 'Love, where's your board? You'll need a board!'

I can't find a reply. I'm gripped by sadness, by shock. As I gaze at Terry's kindly, enquiring face, I feel two tears trickle down my face. When Tessa said her father wasn't himself, I thought . . .

The truth is, I didn't think. I didn't imagine. I wanted Terry to be like he was in my memory, for ever.

By now, Terry has spotted my tears and he shakes his head sorrowfully.

'Oh dear! You're in the wars, my dear, aren't you? Now, look,' he says, stepping towards me. 'Look, look, look.'

I wait breathlessly. This is how he began every pep talk. 'Look, look, look,' he'd say, before dispensing some nugget of wisdom. But how's he going to give me a pep talk about this? How can he?

For a few seconds, Terry also seems nonplussed as to how to continue. But then his brain seems to click into gear, and he smiles kindly at me.

'You took a tumble. The sea had some fun with you, that's all. But remember this.' He turns and points out to the grey sea. 'You're never failing, you're learning. Learning how to manage the sea and how to manage yourself. Everything

194

you did today, right or wrong, was experience. Experience! Can't beat it. And you'll learn from it, just you wait. Now, did you get any injuries? Any cuts, bruises?' His gaze roams over the vestiges of the bruise I got from running into the brick wall, and he clicks his tongue. 'Does that hurt?'

'No, it doesn't hurt,' I tell him quickly. 'It's better now.'

'Good!' He looks pleased. 'So it's just inside here we have to fix.' He taps his head.

'I'd love that,' I say. 'Believe me.'

'You know what you've got to do?' He leans forward, his blue eyes suddenly cogent and intent. 'Trust yourself. Believe in yourself. Will you do that?'

'I . . . OK.' My voice is choked. 'I'll try.'

'Oh, my dear.' Terry's eyes cast around the beach again, as though he's trying to work out the reason for my distress. 'Look, look, look,' he resumes eventually. 'I know your friends laughed at you. And I'm going to have a word. But what you must remember is this. No one remembers the wipeouts. They don't! People remember the triumphs!' His blue eyes give a hint of the old twinkle. 'They'll remember all the times you caught that wave and you rode it into shore. I've seen you do it,' he adds encouragingly. 'I know you can do it.'

I can't move. I can't reply. His words are hitting me, deep inside.

'Now,' adds Terry knowledgeably. 'You want to know why you wiped out?'

'Yes,' I say, desperate to hear his answer. 'Tell me. Why did I wipe out?'

'Because you tried,' says Terry simply. 'You tried, my dear. And that puts you above most people.' He lifts his hand for a high-five, and as I gently slap his hand, he clasps mine, his fingers dry and papery. 'Believe in yourself. You'll do well.'

'Thanks, Terry.' Two more tears spill down my face and I wipe them away. 'For . . . everything. Everything.'

'It's my pleasure!' Terry looks pleased, and a little confused. 'Always a pleasure. You did well today!' His eyes dim, as though he's losing his train of thought, then he adds, more decisively, 'Now, you can leave your board on the beach or take it away for the day. But let Sandra know, won't you? Oh, hello!'

A broad, bulky woman with a kind smile is approaching us over the sand.

'Time to go, Terry,' she calls, and greets me with a friendly wave. 'Hello, there. I'm Deirdre.'

'Hi,' I say, hoping my face isn't too tear-stained. 'I'm Sasha. I'm . . . I used to know Terry.'

'Teach you surfing, did he?' she says.

'Yes. I hadn't seen him for twenty years. Till now.'

'Ah.' She meets my eyes with a smile of sad understanding. 'Well, he's changed. But still Terry inside, aren't you, my love? Ready for some tea? And Tessa'll be round later!'

Terry gives her a docile nod and takes the arm she holds out.

'He's often here on the beach, if you want to say hello again,' she adds, as she leads him off.

'Thanks,' I say eagerly. 'I will. I do. Bye, Terry. It was lovely to see you.'

'The thing you *must* remember is . . .' Terry replies intently, as though we're mid-conversation. 'The thing is . . .' He trails off and blows out, as though in frustration at himself.

'Don't worry, Terry,' says Deirdre reassuringly. 'No rush. Take your time.'

For a moment there's silence except for the waves and the wind – then Terry seems to recall what he was going to say.

'The thing you *must* remember is to enjoy the ride.' He looks at me with a sharp blue gaze and just for an instant I'm looking at the old Terry. 'Enjoy every moment. Because if you don't, what's the point? The ride is *it*.'

'I know.' I nod, smiling, even though my eyes are wet. 'The ride is *it*.'

'Exactly.' He nods, looking satisfied, then points at the forbidding grey surf. 'All right. Enough talk. Go get it!'

'That's right,' says Deirdre comfortably. 'She'll go and get that sea. And we'll go and have some cake. Bye, love.' She smiles at me. 'Nice to meet another pupil of Terry's. There are so many of you, turning up here and there! He must have taught a lot of lessons.'

'Yes,' I say simply. 'He did.'

Terry gives me a sweet smile over his shoulder, then walks away with Deirdre, and I sink down on to the deck of the Surf Shack, lost in a mish-mash of thoughts and memories.

FOURTEEN

As I meet Finn that evening for drinks on the beach, I'm brimming over with all my news.

'I saw Terry,' I blurt out as soon as I catch sight of him, sitting on the deck with the champagne bottle and glasses ready.

'*Terry?*' Finn's face lights up, just as mine did, and I already know he'll take the news about him as hard as I did, too. Sure enough, he listens in sombre silence as I describe Terry's frail appearance and confused mind.

'I guess we had to expect . . .' he says at last. 'Terry's had some wipeouts of his own. We didn't think he ever would, but he did.'

'You know what he said to me this afternoon?' I raise a flicker of a smile. 'No one remembers the wipeouts. Everyone remembers the triumphs.'

'Well, that sounds like the old Terry.' Finn grins. 'Did he end with "Go get it"?'

'Yes!' I sit down next to him. 'That's the weird thing! He was the old Terry, some of the time. He was saying all the old

Terry stuff, he was practically giving me a surfing lesson, only . . . it wasn't real.'

'I guess that's his happy place.' Finn's eyes soften. 'On the beach, teaching kids the thing he loves best.'

'I guess.' I nod. 'And lucky us, that we got to have him as our teacher.'

'Amen to that.' Finn's face creases in a smile. 'I remember there was a kid in my group one year. After the first day of lessons, his mum decides he's going to pull out and do crazy golf instead.' Finn suddenly starts laughing. 'Terry went ballistic. Not because he couldn't fill the spot, but because he thought it was morally wrong. As if the first commandment was, *Thou shalt surf.*'

'I'm sure I heard him say that.' I grin at Finn.

'I was signing my board back into the shop at the time,' continues Finn, 'so I was inside the Surf Shack and I could hear Terry having a go at this woman in the back office. He was saying, "I am offering your child *heaven*. Learning to ride these waves is getting the gates to *heaven*. Do you understand me? Literally *heaven*. And you're choosing *crazy golf*?"'

'What did the kid say?' I ask, agog.

'Just stood there, embarrassed. Probably had a wipeout, got water up his nose and didn't like it. Probably never wanted to surf in the first place.'

'He's probably winning the Masters now,' I say, and Finn laughs.

'Fair enough.' He sips his drink, then stands up. 'Oh, I forgot! Wait there.'

He heads along the deck to his own lodge, then returns with something crinkling in his hands. 'I bought snacks.'

'Beetroot crisps?' I read the label wonderingly.

'Healthy!' says Finn, sounding pleased with himself. 'Possibly also inedible,' he adds as an afterthought. 'But it's a start, right?' He opens the packet and offers me one, then takes one himself.

We both chew silently, eyeing each other.

'Not bad,' I say, after a bit.

'Not great,' says Finn.

'Well, no. Not great either.'

'Life's too short for beetroot-flavoured cardboard,' says Finn decisively. 'If you're going to eat crisps, eat crisps.'

'You sound like Terry,' I say, laughing.

'Excellent,' says Finn. 'If in doubt, think, "What would Terry say?" He'd say, "Eat the damn crisps and enjoy them."' Finn folds over the beetroot crisp packet and puts it aside, then adds, 'As I said before, pretty much everything I've learned about life, I learned from Terry Connolly.'

I gaze curiously at Finn over my glass. At first, I thought this guy was the most obnoxious monster in the world. But the more we talk, the more we chime. The more I relate to him. The more I recognize. I want to know his opinion on things, I realize. I feel like they might be wise opinions. There aren't too many people I can say that about. We're both quiet for a bit, and I stare up into the dark, star-speckled sky. Maybe all this time I just needed a friend.

An hour later, the champagne bottle is empty and I'm shivering. It's time to go inside.

'I can't face room service again,' I say as we walk back up to the hotel. 'I'm going to eat in the dining room.'

'Me too,' says Finn. 'I actually booked a table.'

'You booked a table?' I can't help giggling. 'What, to beat the crowds?'

'Habit,' admits Finn. 'I rang down and said, "Do you have availability for dinner tonight?" Whereupon Cassidy spent about half an hour trying to access the system, and then do you know what she said? "I think we can fit you in, Mr Birchall."'

'Fit you in?' I collapse into fresh laughter. 'Fit you into the empty dining room?'

'Maybe they've got hordes of people arriving tonight,' says Finn with a shrug. 'Anything's possible. Do you have plans tomorrow?' he adds casually.

'I haven't thought. More of the same, I suppose.'

'Only, I was wondering,' he says, pushing open the back door of the hotel. 'D'you fancy going to Kettle Cove? We could walk along the cliff path.'

'I'd love to,' I beam at him. 'Brilliant idea.'

By now we've arrived at the door to the dining room and I blink in surprise. It's even more cavernous than before, because some of the tables and chairs have vanished, leaving only dints in the carpet in their place. Other than the fake, table-like contraption in the bay window, there are now only three dining tables in the entire vast space. There's my little table on one side of the room. There's Finn's table on the other side. And there's a table for two, right in the centre of the room, at which the Wests are seated, looking supremely uncomfortable.

'Wow.' I gape at the new arrangement. 'What happened?'

'We sold some furniture!' says Cassidy brightly, coming up behind me in a bright-red jacket which looks like part of an air hostess uniform. 'On eBay! Got three hundred quid, not bad! Were you wanting to eat in the dining room tonight, Ms Worth?'

'If there's . . . space?' I say, darting a look at Finn. 'I haven't booked, I'm afraid.'

'Hmmm . . .' Cassidy looks thoughtfully around the empty dining room. 'Yes, I believe we *can* seat you. Table for one, was it? And Mr Birchall, you've already reserved a table.'

'I thought it wise to book,' says Finn gravely, and I bite my lip.

'Excellent!' says Cassidy earnestly. 'Now, I know you'll want to be as far away from Ms Worth as possible,' she adds to Finn. 'Indeed, this is a priority for you both. So I will just point out that our new improved seating arrangement creates even more space between the two of you than before. There are ten metres between your tables!' She smiles proudly at us both. 'Ten full metres! And hopefully your dining experience will be all the more agreeable for this adjustment. It was Simon's idea.'

I shoot an awkward glance at Finn, who looks equally nonplussed. It seems like ages ago that we were so prickly at having to share the beach.

'It's not the *hugest* priority to be apart . . .' I begin tentatively, just as Finn says, 'I wouldn't say it's essential . . .'

'It's no trouble!' Cassidy sweeps away our protestations. 'We pride ourselves on the personal touch at the Rilston. We want to make our guests as happy as we can, and obviously for you two that means being as separate as possible!' She beams at me. 'If you'll follow me, Ms Worth? Nikolai will be here presently, he's just assisting Simon with a very small emergency relating to a fox discovered living in one of the bedrooms.'

Immediately I glance at Finn and have to clamp my lips shut, trying not to laugh.

'I can see how that might not be optimal,' says Finn gravely. '*Bon appetit,*' he adds to me.

I follow Cassidy over the creaking, carpeted floor to my

usual table, which now seems several miles away from Finn's. As I pass the Wests, I smile at them, and Mrs West nods once, then looks away, her jaw tight. Mr West doesn't seem able to move at all. He looks rigid with wretchedness. Feeling awkward at witnessing such misery, I sit down at my marooned little table, then wave at Finn, who is sitting down at his own little table. A thought occurs to me and I get out my phone to text him.

I feel like we're doing an exam!!!

Almost at once his response comes back:

IKR? Though if they didn't want us cheating they should have taken our phones, suckers.

I grin appreciatively, then open the menu, which is familiar to me from room service. There doesn't seem to be anything extra available except 'Chef's Special: saddle of lamb for two people'.

That actually sounds pretty good. After a moment's thought, I get out my phone and text Finn again:

You want to go halves on the saddle of lamb?

It doesn't take long for his answer to arrive:

Excellent idea.

I give him a thumbs-up, and he lifts his glass to me in reply. No sign of Nikolai yet. I guess the fox is resisting its eviction.

At the table in the centre, the Wests are conversing in curt, hostile whispers. Occasionally, they break off to sweep a glance round the room as though checking whether they're being overheard, and I studiously start looking at my phone, just to indicate that I'm not interested. I search for 'Kettle Cove', just to check they haven't closed it or anything, then click on 'surrounding attractions'.

'It's not just the sex!' Mrs West's voice rises in distress and I feel a wave of embarrassment. Okaaay. Do *not* look their way. I tilt my head even more ostensibly towards my phone screen, trying to indicate *I am far too engrossed in my googling to hear your marital dispute.*

And actually, this page I'm on is quite engrossing. It turns out there's a new zip wire near Kettle Cove, and I read the description feeling a sudden yearning to try it out. *Experience the exhilarating ride of your life as you fly over Kettle Cove, with stunning speed and spectacular views.*

I watch the video on mute, feeling a vicarious thrill as a woman in a harness whizzes along a high wire, above a stretch of sparkling water. Not only does this sound amazing, it's also on my Twenty Steps list. *No. 11. Seek adventure. Jolt your body with a blast of adrenaline. Bungee jump, zip wire or just go see a scary movie. Anything to blast your senses alive.*

I could do with blasting my senses alive. On impulse, I get to my feet and head across the dining room to Finn's table, smiling awkwardly at the Wests as I pass their table. They've lapsed into silence now. Mrs West is folding and refolding her napkin, her thin hands trembling, while Mr West is gazing resolutely upwards, as though fascinated by the ceiling mouldings.

'You came to visit!' Finn exclaims as I approach. 'Welcome to this side of the room.'

'Very nice,' I say, gazing around as though in admiration. 'Now, look at this zip wire I've found. It's right by Kettle Cove.'

Finn studies the page, his eyes widening as he plays the video.

'Awesome!' he says at last. 'Is it open?'

'I'll check. If it is, shall I get tickets?'

'Yes! Let's do it.'

I head back to my table, trying to tiptoe over the creaky floor as I go past the Wests' silent table.

'Sorry,' I murmur, although I'm not sure what I'm apologizing for, and Mrs West gives me a tight, half-smile.

A few moments later, Finn gets up from his table and comes over to mine. Unlike me, he doesn't seem remotely concerned about the Wests, who are still in their stony, wretched silence. He strides confidently across the floor, making a thunderous series of creaking sounds, and greets me in a resounding voice.

'OK, additional plan. What about cream tea afterwards? Or are you too health-conscious for a cream tea?'

'No!' I say, laughing. 'I *have* to have a cream tea at least once while I'm in Devon. It's the law.'

'Well, exactly,' says Finn. 'It's compulsory. I'll see if there's anywhere near Kettle Cove, shall I?'

'I think we went a few times to somewhere called The Tea Kettle?'

'Yes. I know that place. I'll see if they're still open. And when Nikolai shows up, I'll order the saddle of lamb for us both.' He salutes me, then strides back to his place.

A moment later, it occurs to me that we should order some side dishes. I leap up, and I'm trying to make my way unobtrusively across the room, picking my way over the creaky floorboards, when Mrs West gives such an obvious huff of annoyance that I pause.

'Sorry if I'm disturbing you,' I say humbly. 'I just wanted to ask my friend something else.'

'I have an idea: why don't you have our table and we'll go and sit at yours?' says Mrs West in short, brittle tones. 'It's not as if we've got anything to say to each other and it'll save you two getting up and down all the time.' She starts to gather her bag and scarf, while I watch in consternation.

'Hayley!' exclaims Mr West.

'Well, it's true,' she says, her eyes suddenly glittering with tears. 'What have we got to talk about?'

'You're being ridiculous,' he mutters.

'We came here to rescue things. How is sitting in silence rescuing things?'

'Well, what am I *meant* to say?' Mr West bursts out miserably. 'Sorry for everything I've ever done, since before I knew you? I've said I'm sorry, Hayley. I can't say it any more.'

'You say it, but you don't mean it!' she answers shrilly, then claps a tissue over her face.

'I don't know what I mean any more,' says Mr West in heavy tones. 'I've lost the will to live.' He gestures roughly at Finn and me. 'I don't care if they hear it.'

He strides out of the room and Hayley stares after him, her face getting pinker and pinker – then she gives a gasp, and follows him. A moment later, I hear her calling, 'Ade! Adrian!'

For a few moments, neither Finn nor I move. Eventually, cautiously, I turn to face him.

'Yikes,' I say quietly.

'That was . . .' He shakes his head, looking thunderstruck.

'I wonder what happened?' I wince. 'They both looked so miserable.'

I feel quite shaken by seeing such raw distress. I have a ridiculous urge to run after them both and give them a hug – but I'm not sure that's very sensible. Nor will I share this urge with Finn, who will probably laugh at me.

'Should we take their table?' says Finn, pivoting straight on to the practical. 'She's right, it makes sense.'

'No!' I shake my head. 'What if they reconcile and come back and we're sitting at their table?'

'*Reconcile?*' Finn gives a short, incredulous laugh.

'They might! I reckon Hayley wants to reconcile. She ran after Ade. If she really didn't want to reconcile, she would have sat back and let him go.'

'Interesting,' says Finn. 'But does he want to reconcile?'

'Unsure,' I admit. 'But we should leave their table free, just in case.' I hesitate, looking at Finn's table, then at mine. 'Even so, it might be more fun to . . .'

'Sit together?' says Finn lightly. 'Easier than texting. Shall we pull our tables together?'

'Let's do it.' I nod. 'I'll do mine, you do yours.'

Slowly and carefully, we both start dragging our tables away from the outskirts of the room, towards the centre. My wine glass and cutlery are jiggling as I go, but I'm determined to manage it without knocking them over or removing them. Finn is making a similar journey from his side of the room, but as I look up, he removes his wine glass and dumps it on the carpet.

'Cheat!' I say.

'Just being practical.'

Eventually we meet at a central point, about three metres away from the Wests' table. We fit our tables together, rearrange the cutlery, get rid of a spare flower vase, then Finn retrieves his wine glass and ushers me into my chair.

'Milady.'

'Thank you!'

He takes his own seat opposite me, and I'm just about to look around for Nikolai when a cry of dismay rings through the air.

'Mr Birchall!' I turn round to see Simon standing in the doorway, staring at Finn and me, his eyes round with horror. 'Mr Birchall, Ms Worth, I am mortified. I am appalled. I cannot think what has brought about this catastrophic error. All the staff are *fully* aware of your desire to be seated as far apart as possible—'

'It's fine!' I interject quickly, but he doesn't seem to hear.

'We at the Rilston pride ourselves on—' He breaks off. 'Cassidy! What is this?' He gestures wildly at us. 'What is this I'm seeing?'

As Cassidy spots us sitting together, she nearly drops the water jug she's carrying.

'I don't know!' she says defensively. 'But it's not my fault! I seated them miles apart from each other! *Miles* apart!' At this moment, Nikolai joins the group, and she rounds on him. 'Nikolai, did *you* move the tables?'

'No!' Nikolai seems horrified at the sight of us. 'No, no, no!'

'Well, separate them, *quick*!' hisses Simon in a savage undertone. 'Mr Birchall, Ms Worth,' he says more loudly, stepping forward, 'my apologies for this unfortunate oversight. If you would like to enjoy a complimentary drink in the bar, we will rearrange your seating to a more conducive—'

'We'd rather stay like this,' Finn cuts him off mildly. 'At the same table. If we may?'

'It was us,' I add, gesturing at the furniture. 'We pulled the tables together.'

208

'It was . . .' Simon looks utterly bewildered, his head swivelling from me to Finn and back again. 'It was *you*?'

'I hope that's OK,' adds Finn. 'There was no one around to consult, so we took matters into our own hands.'

'But why do you want to sit together?' blurts out Cassidy. 'You're not a couple. You can't stand each other!' Her gaze narrows. '*Are* you a couple?'

Just for a microsecond, my stomach flutters at the word *couple*, and I blink. Wait. Why did that happen? Why the flutter?

Oh my God.

Am I . . . could I be . . . is it at all possible I'm interested in sex, suddenly? Am I finally coming alive again? Am I waking up?

Quickly I try to imagine a sex scene, to tease myself – to test myself. Come on. What's sexy? *Two naked bodies. Copulating.*

Argh. No. Bad word.

Having intercourse.

Argh. Also a bad word.

Every vision of sex I conjure up seems distant and irrelevant. So maybe I'm not fully back to life. But I definitely felt *something*. Will it come back? Maybe?

'No, we're not a couple,' Finn is saying patiently. 'We're just two guests hanging out together who wanted to chat. Right, Sasha?'

'Right!' I give a super-bright smile. 'Just that.'

'I see!' says Simon at last, in the tones of someone who totally doesn't see. 'Well. Enjoy your dinner.'

FIFTEEN

God, the sea air smells good. Everything feels and smells and tastes good at the moment, I realize. From the breeze to my new organic shower gel. My senses are coming alive, my energy levels are up, everything's feeling good. No libido as yet, but I don't even care about that, as I am a healthy, balanced person with many facets in my life, from exercise to fun to friendship. I've been in text contact with Dinah every day, and after each conversation, I'm smiling.

Best of all, I've stopped waking up every morning obsessing about Zoose and writing a thousand words of raging, frustrated notes. I'm not planning what to say to Joanne. I'm not re-running all my most miserable moments at the company. I've let it go. Finally. When I get back to the office, *that's* when I'll start thinking about it again. Not till then.

I don't know what's helped most – the squats, the sleep, the sea air, or just Finn's company. It's a week since we dragged the tables together at dinner – and since then we've done something together every single day. I've screamed myself hoarse, flying over the trees on the zip wire. We've walked the cliff path. We've looked round the tiny Museum of Seashore Oddities at Campion Sands and tried to hide our giggles from the elderly curator. We've eaten delicious picnics made for us by Chef Leslie and even shared a tub of fermented cabbage (which tasted surprisingly OK).

Today, we've clambered over rocks, I've ripped my jeans, Finn has drenched his trainers in a shallow pool and we've both eaten our second massive cream tea. And now we're idly walking around Kettle Cove, our steps crunching on the pebbles. The late-afternoon air is mild; there's even a hint of spring in the air.

'Chocolate?' says Finn, producing a box from his pocket, and I laugh.

'I'm too full. And I can't *believe* you brought them.'

The chocolates were on the beach outside the lodges this morning, along with a message much the same as the previous ones: *To the couple on the beach. With appreciation. 18/8.* They've been coming every day and I've almost given up trying to guess what they mean. Except I know it's not art, I just *know* it.

'We should probably start walking back soon,' I say, glancing at my watch. 'If we're aiming to get back for supper.'

'Unless . . .' Finn shoots me a wicked glance. 'Fish and chips on the beach and then a cab back to Rilston?'

'Yes!' I say. 'Except I'm too full for fish and chips.'

'You won't be,' says Finn with assurance. 'Not once you get to the chip shop. Not once you smell the vinegar.'

'Fish and chips on the beach,' I say fondly. 'Beats the office any time.'

'Certainly beats the office,' agrees Finn, with a firm nod. He pauses, then adds, 'So, since you've brought up the subject of work, there's a question I've been wanting to ask.'

'Oh yes?' I look up. 'What?'

'You sound like you were so miserable at Zoose. Why didn't you change job a long time ago? Why stick it out till you were at such a desperate point you ran away?'

'Because changing job is exhausting,' I point out. 'It's a job in itself. You have to find new opportunities, go to interviews, sparkle . . .'

'You sparkle,' says Finn at once.

'I do not.' I give a wry laugh.

'Didn't you ever get calls from headhunters?'

'Yes, but I didn't take them.'

'Why not?'

'Didn't have the time. Or energy.'

'Hmm.' Finn thinks for a moment. 'Do you want to leave marketing? Do something else?'

'No!' I say, surprising myself with my conviction. 'Marketing is great. It's creative. It's finding solutions. It's fun. Or, you know, it can be. It's what I *do*,' I finish emphatically.

'Got it.' Finn chuckles.

'My previous job, that was in marketing, too. I loved it. But Zoose . . . Zoose was a game-changer.'

'OK then, another question,' persists Finn mildly. 'Why did you let yourself get so exhausted that you couldn't even muster the inner resources to change jobs? Why did you keep saying "yes"?'

'Because . . .' I exhale, thinking back. 'Because the work needed to be done and no one else was there to do it. That's what Zoose is like. It's chaotic.'

'So you refuse. You say "no".'

'"No" doesn't work. They just pile on more tasks.'

'So you threaten to move on. You leave jobs undone and

explain why you didn't have time to complete them. You create boundaries and stick to them.'

As I gaze at him, I feel like he's speaking a foreign language. 'That's not really me,' I say at last.

'It has to be you.' He meets my gaze resolutely. 'You're talking as if you have no value, no leverage. If it came to it, couldn't you just leave your job and get by for a while till you found a better one?'

I feel a spasm of panic, which I swallow down. 'Don't know. I'm pretty risk-averse. I really, *really* don't want to fail.'

'So you think it's better to be half-living than risk failure?'

I feel a visceral shock at Finn's words. 'Half-living' is a pretty brutal assessment of what I've been doing. Although possibly accurate.

'I've never wanted to be caught out,' I say, staring rigidly ahead. 'Financially.'

'So your bank balance is healthy.'

The way he leans on the phrase *bank balance*, I know exactly what he means. My bank balance might be healthy, but every other bit of my life: not so much.

'I know I should leave my job,' I hear myself say. 'I will leave it. I really will. I'll leave it.'

Again, words are slipping out of me that I didn't intend. I stare up at the darkening sky in a state of slight shock. I'm going to leave my job? Leave my job? Actually leave my job?

A weird, heady feeling is rising up inside me, very slowly. It feels like ... happiness. Bright, golden happiness. It's euphoria, joy, freedom.

Is this what I've been chasing?

'I can just leave my job if I want to.' I give a strange, almost hysterical laugh. 'I can resign.'

'Yes. You can.' Finn nods. 'You have that power. *Power*.' He leans forward and squeezes my hand. 'You're valuable, Sasha. You're in demand. Believe it.'

'And Zoose is . . .' I pause, trying to think of another way to describe it. 'Zoose is *dysfunctional*.'

'Tell me more about Zoose,' says Finn, and I laugh.

'I'm serious,' he persists. 'I'm a consultant. I like to hear about dysfunctional companies. Helps me sleep at night.'

So I tell him. I describe the lack of staff, the wrong priorities, the in-fighting . . . everything. I describe Asher. I describe Lev. I describe Joanne. I find myself analysing everything differently, now I've had some time away.

'Sounds messy,' says Finn as I come to a finish. 'Start-ups often go through a tricky stage, especially if they grow too quickly. It's great to be successful, but be careful what you wish for. And the incompetent-brother thing . . .' He shakes his head wryly. 'Your founder will end up paying off his brother to get rid of him, but he needs to do it soon. Tell him that.'

'I will.' I laugh. 'Next time I'm in conversation with him.'

'Great.' Finn nods as though I'm perfectly serious. 'Now, fish and chips?'

Finn volunteers to go into the fish and chip shop, which is crowded with a bunch of kids, so I give him a tenner, then wait outside, sitting on the exact same wall I sat on when I was ten years old. I was filled with good feelings then, and I'm filled with good feelings now. Good, jittery, surreal feelings. But still good.

I could leave my job. No, I'm more certain than that: I *am* going to leave my job. When shall I do it? How shall I do it? Do I need to think about this more?

For a few seconds I sit, with my eyes closed, processing everything – then I open them.

No. I don't need to think any more. Enough thinking, waiting, stagnating. I know Mum said, 'Don't make any big decisions,' but I have to. I need action. Right now.

Trembling, I take out my phone, find the email address of the Head of Human Resources at Zoose, Tina Jeffrey, and begin typing.

Dear Tina

I would like to resign from my post as Director of Special Promotions. I believe my current holiday entitlement is sufficient to cover my notice period, therefore I will not be returning to the office.

Sincerely

Sasha Worth

Without pausing to consider, I lift my thumb and press Send. Then, as Finn appears, holding fish and chips and two Cokes, I look up, forcing my mouth into a smile.

'I just left my job.'

'What?' He stops dead and stares at me. 'You what?'

'I left. While you were getting the fish and chips. I emailed the Head of Human Resources.'

'Wow!' His eyes widen. 'That was quick.'

'I know!' I try to sound extra-positive, because beneath my smile I'm already feeling the swell of panic. It didn't take long. Questions are bombarding my mind: should I have waited? Do I need to tell Mum? What will everyone say?

And a larger, more terrifying question: have I just made the most dreadful error, which I will regret for the rest of my life?

But I'm not going to sink into terror. I'm determined to shut down the fear, the catastrophizing, the self-doubt. I have savings. I have experience. I have a CV. I will find another job.

'You OK?' says Finn.

'Yes!' I say, trying to sound confident. 'Yes.' I pause, then add more honestly, 'I will be.'

'Leaving a job isn't nothing.' He sits beside me. 'That took guts.'

'I had to go.' Putting it in the past tense is already more relaxing, I realize. 'I had no choice.'

Finn hands me my fish and chips and I reach for a chip to stuff instantly into my mouth. 'I think you did the right thing to leave. And for what it's worth, I don't think you should be rushing into any new job. If your finances can bear it,' he adds carefully.

'They can bear it.' I nod, still chewing. 'For a while.'

'Good. And when you do decide to take the plunge, if you ever want any headhunting contacts, ask me. Or a sounding board. Whatever. You'll get a job,' he adds assuredly, perhaps noticing my wavering doubt. 'You'll get a great job.' He gestures at the dark sea. 'Remember what Terry says? Infinite waves. Infinite chances.'

'I remember.' I laugh. 'And thanks for the support. I couldn't have done that without talking to you. You helped me understand myself.'

'OK, now you're flattering me,' says Finn, his eyes crinkling. 'You would have worked it out. But I'm glad.'

He's a good person, I find myself thinking. He's wise. He doesn't have an agenda. As we sit there, peacefully munching our fish and chips and swigging our Cokes, I feel an overwhelming affection towards this strong, kind man who sees what I can't see, but doesn't feel the need to boast or brag or even share his thoughts unless you ask him.

'What about you?' I ask, determined that our little support network of two should be fair. 'What about your work? What's the situation there?'

'Oh.' Finn shrugs, and his face closes up like it always does. As if he's not interested and I can't possibly be, either.

'Are you going back?' I persist. 'Is your company dysfunctional, too?'

'Not like yours.' He shakes his head. 'Where I work, it's not perfect, but . . . No. The company was not the problem. I'll be going back to work there. But I had . . .' He pauses for so long I hold my breath. 'I had other issues,' he finishes at last. 'There was other stuff.'

Something has changed in his face as he's been speaking. There's a downward, weary cast to his forehead, to his eyebrows, to his eyes. Just for a moment, he looks as though he can't endure the world.

I gaze at Finn in dismay, feeling that whatever I say will be inadequate. I have no idea what he's been dealing with; I can only see how much of a strain it's been. But unless he gives me any kind of detail, how can I help?

'I'm a good listener,' I venture. 'You can tell me. Tell me anything.'

'Thanks.' He flashes me a semi-smile. 'But I don't think it helps me to . . . But thanks.'

I feel ridiculously hurt that he won't confide in me. But at the same time, I know what it's like when the timing is wrong. Maybe he's just too exhausted to share.

'You should see someone, maybe?' I suggest. 'A therapist.'

'That's what they want me to do at work.' Finn rolls his eyes.

'How do you mean?'

'They sent me off to do two things. Have time away and

start therapy. They actually made it a condition of my coming back.'

I sit up straighter and stare at him. 'You have a therapist?'

'Haven't started yet,' says Finn, looking evasive. 'There's a woman. She's called a couple of times, left messages.'

'Have you called her back?'

Finn is suspiciously silent and my eyes narrow as I begin to work out what's going on.

'You *haven't* called her back?'

'I will,' says Finn defensively.

'When?'

'Don't know. I will.'

'Are you avoiding this?' I say incredulously. 'Are you avoiding professional help?'

'No!' exclaims Finn. 'I just . . .' He breaks off and rubs his face. 'I'll get to it.'

He is avoiding it. He's hiding here in Rilston Bay, instead of doing the therapy he needs to get his life back on track.

'What's so scary about therapy?' I say, and Finn makes an expression of such horror that I start laughing. 'OK. Even so. You need to call her.'

'I know.' Finn gets out the box of chocolates. 'I plan to. Have a chocolate.'

'You can't bribe me with chocolates,' I say, taking one at random. 'I'll bug you about this. I won't let it go. Because that's what you do when—'

I stop awkwardly and stuff the chocolate in my mouth, wondering: where was I going with that, exactly?

That's what you do when you care about someone.

I was about to tell Finn I care about him.

Which is fine, I argue in my mind. It's true. I don't need to be embarrassed. I do care about Finn. I mean, not like that, obviously . . . Not like that . . .

Then . . . like what?

What *are* we like, exactly?

I glance at his strong, stubbled jaw and feel a rush of self-conscious heat, combined with . . .

Hang on.

Just . . . hang on.

What is this flicker inside me? What is this rippling and tingling that I thought I'd never feel again? This sensation is like the flutter before – but tenfold. I can't quite believe it. Things are revving up inside me at last, at last! It feels as if the pilot light to some ancient stove is dimly coming alive, right at my core. Nothing's on fire, exactly, but nor is it cold and dead.

My whole body feels alert. My breathing is more shallow. I'm super-aware of Finn's thighs resting on the wall next to mine. I can smell a faint scent of aftershave. I can imagine what his skin feels like; how it would feel to kiss him. As I glance at him again, my stomach flips over and I blink in disbelief. Do I want sex?

No. Noooo. Easy there, tiger. I'm still at base camp; I don't know what I want, exactly.

But, still. Still. Oh my God. I have a sex drive. What now?

Later that evening, we travel back to the Rilston in a cab and I can tell from Finn's easy-going manner that he's oblivious to my new sexual *frissons*. He can't feel the prickliness between us, only I can. He's not darting constant sidelong glances, only I am. Everything has changed for me – but not for him.

It's around ten o'clock when we arrive back. The lobby is empty when we enter the hotel and we walk up the creaky stairs together, for all the world like a couple going up to bed.

'Where's your room?' I ask at the top of the stairs. It seems odd that I don't know this, but it hasn't seemed relevant. And still isn't, I tell myself firmly. Still isn't.

'Up another flight,' says Finn. 'Then along about six corridors. It's a maze.'

'I know, right?' I laugh. Then my phone buzzes, and I take it out to have a quick glance. Kirsten has sent me some photos of the children which I'll look at properly later and I have an email from the Zoose Human Resources department, with an attachment. My heart thuds and I glance instinctively up at Finn.

'Everything OK?' he asks.

'Email from Zoose.' I open it, my mind speculating wildly. Maybe the attachment is a letter from Joanne . . . or Asher?

But no.

'It's a standard-issue letter acknowledging my resignation,' I say, skimming the words. 'Someone's got it and just pressed Send.'

'Working late.' Finn raises his eyebrows.

'Everyone works late at Zoose, I thought I mentioned that . . . Oh my *God*,' I add, as I see the last paragraph. 'Listen to this. *We're so sad to hear you'll be moving on, but we're a company who cares. So we'd love to hear in this form if there's anything we could have done better. Because it's those little tweaks that make all the difference.*' I raise my head, my blood boiling. 'Little tweaks? *Little tweaks?*'

'Sounds like you need to let them know about the "little tweaks" they could make,' says Finn, looking amused.

'Seriously, tell them everything you told me. Sock it to 'em between the eyes. Why not? Might make you feel better.'

'OK.' I nod slowly, already composing my email. 'OK. I will. And again . . . thanks. Big day. Good day.'

'Good day.' Finn nods.

The hotel is silent around us; the lamps are casting shadows; it's kind of magical. Before I can stop myself, I lean slightly forward, as though we're going to kiss – then, just in time, my brain shrieks, *What are you doing?* Hastily, I pivot into bending down and adjusting my shoelace, which doesn't need adjusting.

'So!' I pop up again, 'So. Goodnight. Sleep well.'

'Night. You too.'

And then he's heading up the stairs and I'm gazing after him, wondering what he's thinking; what he noticed; what he's feeling about us – then realizing the answer is probably *nothing*.

SIXTEEN

In the morning, my new sexual desires are still there, and then some. Finn is hot, I keep thinking, as I lie in bed, staring at the ceiling. He's hot. He's *super-hot*. I imagine him kissing me, and a tingle runs over my body, as though someone nudged me. As though someone whispered, 'This will be fun' in my ear.

But Finn never *will* kiss me, obviously, because I could not have done more to put him off if I tried. I've displayed no romantic interest in him. I've told him I've gone off sex. I have even illustrated this fact by using the phrase 'genitals rubbing together'.

Good move, Sasha. Excellent decision.

So, what should I do now? Now that I'm plagued by these brand-new feelings?

Dear Agony Aunt, I have this really lovely platonic friend and all of a sudden I discover I would really like to kiss him, only I previously told him 'Sex is basically genitals rubbing together'.

Dear Reader, you have no chance, if I were you I would join a convent.

I can't stop cursing myself for being so thoughtless. I should have been serene and mysterious and kept all possibilities open. *Why* did I have to over-share? *Why* did I use the word 'genitals'? And what do I do about it now? Because Finn is hot. He is hot. *How* did I not see this before?

Do I make a move?

No. I do not make a move, because what if it made things awkward? Argh. I can't bear to ruin this lovely, supportive friendship we have with some clumsy kiss.

But he's so hot.

Anyway, would I kiss him? Or just slide an arm casually across his gorgeous, muscled back?

I can't believe I'm thinking like this. I can't believe I've woken up. I was the numb girl. The sexless girl. The girl who wasn't interested. But now . . .

I wriggle in my bed, trying to remember how sex goes. It's been so long. So, so long.

Would I be interested in the Pret guy now? I find myself wondering. I think back experimentally, but . . . no. He doesn't do it for me. Only Finn. Finn, with all his contradictions that I've got to know. His scowling face and his infectious laugh. His powerful body and his tender voice. His wisdom and his blind spots. His mouth, which is generous but manly, smiling but strong.

He has good teeth, I think fondly, lying back on my pillows. Then I see the clock and hastily jump up. It's getting on. I need to have breakfast. And see if there's another message on the beach. And say hello to Finn. And, above all, *act normal*.

He isn't at breakfast, so I quickly munch some cereal, drain a cappuccino, then saunter down to the beach, with my hair in a ponytail like Wetsuit Girl and wearing only a smidgen more make-up than usual. (Which would be 'some' make-up.)

'It's here!' Finn's voice hails me as I arrive. I hurry on to the sand to see him staring down at a new message, written in pebbles.

To the couple on the beach. Thank you again. 18/8.

This time, there's a fruit cake in a tin, packaged up in plastic.

'Who is it?' demands Finn, looking around. '*What* is it? There has to be an answer. This is driving me mad.'

'Me too!' I swivel in turn, surveying the empty sea, the desolate beach. There's no sign of life, but even so I feel convinced that someone must be watching us.

'So, did you send your email to Zoose?' asks Finn.

'Oh. Yes, I did. I spent about three hours on it last night,' I admit. 'I didn't get enough sleep.'

'Say what you wanted to say?'

'Yes.' I roll my eyes. 'And some.'

'Excellent!' He gives me an appreciative grin, and I search his face for any sign of . . . something else. Anything else. A sign. A hint. A sexy glint in his eye. But there's nothing. His expression is wide and friendly and platonic. It could not be more platonic.

But! Is this because I told him I'm off sex? Is he deliberately not allowing himself to 'go there', even though he maybe – just maybe – could find me attractive? I curse myself furiously for dropping that bit of paper, and wonder how I might remedy my error. I could do another manifestation, maybe. I could write:

Dear universe, thank you for the returned libido, much appreciated. All working! Now, as previously mentioned, if it's not too much to ask, I just need a man. Named Finn.

Then I'd let it flutter away in the wind and Finn would pick it up . . . he'd read it . . . look up at me, his eyes burning with a new desire . . . we'd move towards each other . . . his lips would . . .

I cringe. No. No. None of this would happen. Terrible idea.

'So!' I say quickly, trying to gather my wits. 'Do you have any plans for today?'

'Not a one.' Finn raises his eyebrows. 'How are you going on with the twenty steps?'

'Haven't had any noni juice yet. And I don't know when I'll get on to the two-day fast, if you wanted to join me on that?'

'Hard pass,' says Finn, making an appalled face. 'How about skimming stones on the sea?'

We head down to the sea together and skim a few stones, but the waves are getting raucous in the wind and it's hard to make the stones bounce. I'm about to suggest we call it a day when the Wests come into sight.

'Hello!' I say in my most friendly voice, and Finn lifts a hand in greeting.

'Hi,' mumbles Adrian, and Hayley just gives us a tight smile. They walk down to the edge of the waves and stare out silently, while I exchange glances with Finn. For a few minutes, we stand awkwardly, all four of us, then Hayley murmurs something to Adrian. She gives me a nod, then they turn and start walking away along the beach.

'Jeez.' Finn breathes out, when they're out of earshot. 'The friction between those two.'

'It's awful.' I watch them walking, their misery apparent in their stiff backs. 'I wonder what happened? Did one of them have an affair? Did they just fall out of love with each other?'

'I think he still loves her,' says Finn slowly. 'He has a way of looking at her when she's not paying attention. I noticed it at dinner.'

'I think she still loves him,' I reply, slightly fixated by her birdlike steps along the beach. 'It's the way she runs after him. If she didn't care, she'd just let him go.'

'They're walking together,' adds Finn, following my gaze. 'Look, he keeps slowing down to wait for her.'

'Together but apart. They're not touching.'

We watch, mesmerized, for a minute longer, then turn back to look at the sea. The waves are swelling up on the horizon, one after another, without pause. I can hear Terry's voice in my head: *Infinite waves. Infinite chances.* And then Finn's voice from last night: *You'll get a great job.*

A job will rise up on the horizon. I have to believe this. I have to make it happen. I gaze at the infinite waves, trying to tap into their strength, trying to visualize the job that's out there for me, if I only believe in it. Then an idea comes to me and I swivel to Finn, just as he turns, too.

'We could surf!'

'Surf's up!' he says simultaneously. 'And guess what? The Surf Shack is open. The owner's in there, I saw him earlier when I went for a walk. There are boards for rent, if you need one. I brought mine.'

'I *know* you did,' I say, and he has the decency to look abashed. He seems much more relaxed than that moody guy on the train, snapping at a toddler. 'Bit early for a walk, wasn't it?' I add, letting him off the hook.

'Before breakfast.' He nods. 'Saw the dawn.'

'Don't you sleep?' I joke – then realize it isn't a joke. He doesn't. 'Anyway, thanks for the tip, I'll rent a board.'

'You've got a wetsuit, right?'

'Er . . . yes,' I say, wondering for the first time whether this is a good idea. 'I mean, I haven't tried it on. And I haven't surfed for years. Maybe you should surf and I'll have a coffee and watch.'

'You're kidding, right?' Finn stares at me. 'Look at this sea. Look at it!' He gestures at the waves, and as though to bolster his argument, a shaft of sunshine appears from behind the clouds, making the surf twinkle and look almost blue. 'We have the beach to ourselves, practically. We have waves. We have sunshine. We have boards. You are being offered the keys to heaven, literally *heaven*, and you're considering having a coffee?' He sounds so like Terry that I laugh.

'Fair enough. I'll surf.'

OK. Reasons I should not be attempting to surf in front of the guy I have belatedly realized I have a crush on:

1. I'm in a wetsuit, which makes me look not like Wetsuit Girl but like 'Sasha squashed into a wetsuit'.
2. I've forgotten how to surf.
3. Every time I wipe out, my hair gets plastered all over my face.
4. Every time I try to stand up, I wipe out.
5. Finn can surf.
6. Really well.

But on the other side of the argument:

1. Terry was right. Nothing beats this.

I'm out at sea, beyond where the waves break, sitting on my board, feeling the familiar motion of the sea rising and falling beneath me, staring at the horizon. Everything else in

227

the world has stopped existing. All I'm focused on is the waves. That's all there is. Waves, only waves.

Finn can surf better than me. A lot better. A few times we've gone for the same wave, and he's ridden smoothly on to the beach, whereas I've timed it badly or didn't manage to get up on my board. Or rolled over and over in the kind of unstoppable wipeout that leaves you spreadeagled and gasping in the shallows.

But I'm not giving up. I keep hearing Terry's voice: *Infinite waves. Infinite chances.* You can't dwell or think about what might have been. There's always another wave. Although you have to be looking the right way to see it.

'Look for the waves!' he used to bellow at us, when we were too busy chatting or moaning about the water up our noses to focus on the horizon. 'Look the right way! Look for the waves or you won't catch them!'

That's what I wasn't doing in my life. I needed to look the right way, away from my screens, my emails, my narrow life, my limitations. I need to look to the horizon, to see the opportunities rising and paddle towards them. And again I hear Terry's voice, hoarse with exasperation, *Don't just sit there, paddle! Paddle hard! Harder!*

Finn is up on his board again, and I watch him ride into shore, feet firmly planted, legs powerful and secure. He's finding waves I'm completely missing. Just for a moment I feel a kind of crushing failure, but then I give myself a Terry-like pep talk. Finn last surfed two years ago in the Canaries, he told me as I got my board. Whereas I haven't surfed for, what, a decade?

There's a tell-tale bump looming on the horizon, and I squint at it, trying to assess it. So much of surfing is judgement. It's experience. It's reading the waves. I haven't sat on a board scanning the horizon for years. But there must be a residual muscle memory in my brain, because it's slowly coming back to me. The way the waves break and fall. Bits of surf slang I once knew. Above all, I'm remembering the tricks the sea plays. The phony, deceptive non-waves which seem to build, then disappear. As opposed to the strong, powerful, genuine swells that seem to come from nothing, but were there all along.

Because that's the other thing: it's not enough to be able to read the waves, you have to have courage and timing. The courage to go for a wave. The timing to know *when* to go for it.

The distant bump I was tracking has died away, but now I can see a new one rising. A real possibility. There's always hope out there on the horizon. Which is why surfing is obsessive. It's addictive. I'd forgotten. I've lost track of time; I've forgotten every other thing in my life. I have to catch a wave and nothing else matters. I already know that when I go to bed tonight, when I close my eyes, all I'll see is endless waves.

OK. The second bump on the horizon was real. It's coming, it's a wave, it's moving fast, and without even knowing I'm going to react, I start paddling. My entire body is focused on the task. My muscles are already burning but they need to work faster, and now the water is rising beneath me and I'm pushing with all my might, cursing myself for not visiting the gym every morning, but . . . I'm there. Yes! Somehow I'm on my feet, my back protesting, then I'm straightening up and it's happening! I caught it!

Oh my God, I'm flying. I'm in heaven. My board is skimming so fast over the water, I can't breathe. My feet are planted skew-whiff and I wouldn't get any points for style, but I'm doing it, I'm riding the wave . . . And now I'm reaching the shore, still upright, breathless, an ecstatic smile plastered across my face.

I hop off my board and pick it up, then beam at Finn, who is whooping on the sand.

'High-five!' He slaps my hand, then grasps it, just like Terry. 'I did it!'

I'm floating with elation. I flew over the sea. I defied gravity, the elements and my own muscles. All of them. Right now, I feel like all I ever want to do in life is fly over the sea, again and again and again.

I *totally* get why people give up their regular lives to do this.

'Have you ever thought of dropping out of your job to surf all day?' I say impulsively to Finn. 'Because . . .' I spread my arms around at the waves, the beach, the view. 'I mean . . .'

'Every time I surf.' He grins back. 'I have a short but perfectly formed fantasy in which surfing is my life. Then reality hits.'

'Reality.' I roll my eyes.

'But it doesn't need to hit yet. We can be surf dudes all afternoon. Bro.' He high-fives me again and I laugh.

'Bro.'

'The ride is it.'

'The ride is it!'

And then we both head back into the foaming, thrilling water with our boards. Right now, I never, ever want to stop.

At last, I'm too exhausted to carry on. I stand on the sand, panting after my last thrilling ride, watching as Finn hoists his board under his arm and comes over to me. Water is dripping from his hair on to his face, and his grin is infectious.

'I'm done,' I say.

'Me too.' He nods. 'We can come out again tomorrow, maybe. Look, this place is popular.' He jerks his head towards the other surfers who have appeared, further down the beach from us. There are two teenage boys, a woman of indeterminate age and a wizened-looking guy who's probably far younger than he seems. The woman lifts a hand in greeting as she sees us looking over, and I wave back.

'Honestly,' I say to Finn, deadpan. 'They've *ruined* the place.'

'Totally.' Finn nods. 'I remember when you could come to this beach and there'd be two people. Max.'

'I remember when you could come here and there'd be one person,' I counter. '*Those* were the days.'

'Touché.' He laughs and dumps his board on the sand, next to mine.

The sun is dancing on the turquoise water of the shallows; it feels almost summery. Finn glances down, then exchanges incredulous looks with me.

'Sorry, are we in the Caribbean, all of a sudden?'

'Must be.' I reply, smiling.

I sink down to sit in the shallows, stretching my legs out in the glassy, translucent water. I don't have the energy to surf any more, but I don't want to leave the magic of the sea. As the water foams over my legs, I feel such lightness rising through me, I think I might float up off the sand with happiness. I don't know if it's the surfing or the sun or the sea or Finn beside me, but life doesn't get any better than this. My muscles feel burned out – but my brain feels exhilarated. I was doing it the wrong way round before.

And now my exhilaration is turning to something different. A desire for Finn that I can barely control. I remember this now, I *remember* it.

I want him right now, I think, and blink in such astonishment I nearly giggle out loud. I'm normal! It's back! I crave the whole, entire deal. Full, proper sex, genitals included.

Finn comes to sit beside me and I immediately redden. Oh *God*. First, he has to look like a surfing god in his black wetsuit, riding waves I can't manage, hefting his board with ease, high-fiving me. And now he has to come and sit right by me, with his *muscles* and his *chest* and his *smile*. Does he know what he's doing to me?

My arms are desperate to wrap around him. My lips are desperate to kiss him. My . . . my *everything* wants him. Just look at his hands. Just imagine what they could do.

Oh God, stop staring at him, Sasha.

But what do I do? The fire inside me is a forest fire. It's engulfing me. I feel hot and impatient and almost demented with urgency. My body has well and truly come alive, that's for sure.

I stare straight out to sea, flaming inside, clueless how to proceed. In my current fevered state, everything seems suggestive. Casually I lean back on the sand on my elbows, then sit up again before he can think . . .

What?

Sasha clearly wants sex, just look how she's lying back on the sand on her elbows.

He will not think that. I'm an idiot. But, oh God, if he did . . .

And now I've opened the door in my brain, the fantasies start flooding in. Finn gently cupping my chin. Finn kissing me with that strong, generous mouth. Finn and me tumbling together in the waves, the water foaming and rippling around our naked bodies . . .

No, wait. Too fast. Rewind.

Finn slowly unzipping my wetsuit, kissing my skin as he goes. Oh God. Just the idea is making me feel heady. A tremor rises through me and I adjust my position on the sand.

'OK?' says Finn.

'Fine!' I squeak, convinced he can read my thoughts. 'Fine.' Somehow I muster a normal, cheerful smile. The smile of a woman *not* consumed by crazed sex fantasies about her platonic male friend who is sitting right beside her. 'It's amazing,' I add inanely. 'The sea. The blueness.'

The blueness? Is that even a word?

But luckily Finn doesn't pick me up on it. He seems to have his own thoughts going on. They're pretty deep thoughts, from the furrow in his brow. *Maybe he's going to confide in me at last*, I think. Oh God. Maybe this is where it all comes together, the shared emotions and the momentous sea and the epic sex, in one big raging . . . furnace.

Do I mean raging wave?

One big something, anyway.

'Just looking at the sea is a cure for . . . whatever.' His voice sounds a little gravelly, either from whisky or shouting over the roar of the sea.

'Agreed.' I nod as a wave crashes over my legs, then recedes, dragging pebbles with it. 'It's amazing. Like being hypnotized.'

'Heartache. Burnout. Breakup. Fuckwit bosses. Whatever the trouble is. Come and sit here and look at the sea for a while, and just . . .' He exhales. 'Breathe.'

'I thought you were going to say, "Just drink whisky,"' I say, and Finn gives a shout of laughter. He's silent for a moment, as though piecing something together in his mind. Then he adds, more slowly, 'I was trying to numb myself. But maybe I needed to feel myself instead. Feel myself. Remember myself.'

I'm silent, motionless, hardly daring to breathe, hoping he'll say more. Reveal more. And after a minute or two, he speaks again.

'I think I've been avoiding therapy because I'm afraid of what I'll find. I'm a pretty standard-issue guy, but everyone's got something, right?'

'Yes,' I say softly. 'Yes, everyone's got something.'

'And the idea of breaking down in front of some counsellor . . .' He shudders. 'Crying. Not being able to control myself. What if I got furious with him or her? What if I lash out, like I did at work?' His forehead crumples. 'I'm a liability.'

That's his worry? Oh, dear, sweet, vulnerable Finn. He's so much more anxious than he gives away. And he *is* kind, I mentally tell Kirsten. He *is*.

'You'll be fine,' I say sincerely, and risk putting a tentative hand on his arm. 'You won't get angry. And if you do, you're with a skilled professional. What, they've never seen a stressed-out guy destroy a ficus plant before? They probably have extra ficus plants just *so* you can destroy them. They keep them in the Ficus Plant Room. Bring your own chainsaw. All included.'

Finn throws back his head and roars with laughter, putting his own hand over mine. 'Oh, Sasha,' he says affectionately. 'Thanks for being here. I don't think I'd be in such a good place, if you hadn't been keeping me company. Burnout buddy.'

Burnout buddy. Can burnout buddy turn to sex buddy?

Yes. Yes, I think it can.

'Oh God!' I retort, my voice a bit shrill and squeaky. 'No. I need to thank *you*.'

My breath keeps catching as I speak. My limbs are trembling. Am I actually in the right state for sex? Because I feel all over the shop.

'If you stare out to sea for long enough, you could almost

believe in manifesting,' I say, playing for time. 'It feels like this huge . . . I don't know. Presence.' I spread my arms, taking in the whole ocean. 'Like it wants to solve our problems.'

'I know what you mean.' Finn nods. 'Terry believed in the sea. He thought it had all the answers. Maybe it does.'

Solve my problem, I silently entreat the sea. *Go on. Solve it. Send a massive wave on to the beach that knocks Finn and me together so hard that our faces are smooshed together and we have no choice but to kiss. Go on . . . go on . . .*

But the next wave that washes on to the beach is, if anything, on the gentle side. It doesn't knock Finn and me into a clinch. It doesn't even try. It rolls calmly over my legs and I know what it's saying to me. It's saying, *You need to take ownership of this yourself, lovey.*

The sea is wise.

'So, one good thing has . . . er . . . happened.' I swallow hard, forcing myself to speak. 'I've woken up. My . . . Um. My . . . libido.' I whisper the last word, but I can tell Finn registers it from the way he shoots me a startled look, then hastily looks away again, a muscle working in his cheek.

There's a long pause. Quite an embarrassingly long pause. So long, in fact, that I consider burying myself in the sand and never speaking to Finn or anyone ever again. My body is consumed with mortification. If he'd been hoping for this, waiting for a sign, like some lovelorn suitor, he would have reacted by now. But he hasn't moved.

'Excellent,' he says at last, and I feel the blood sink from my face to my feet.

Bad, bad response. He sounds like he's pleased my broken-down car now starts. That's his level of engagement.

Unless . . . Unless! Hope rises again in my chest. He *is*

235

interested, he *does* find me attractive, but he's worried about coming across as a sexual predator. This could easily be the case. He's just got in trouble for behaving badly at work. Of course he's going to be super-careful. Of course he's going to hang back. I need to make it subtly clear that I am up for a hot, fun encounter, and give him consent and establish that everything's OK. Subtly. But clearly. The crucial thing is to be unambiguous. Yes. Subtle, clear and unambiguous.

But not clingy or needy.

Or desperate.

'So!' My voice swoops up uncertainly. 'Now I just need to . . .' I cough a few times. 'I guess I need a casual . . . get back into the saddle. Nothing serious. Just a, you know, fling.' I give the most hideous little laugh. 'One of these days.'

'Good idea,' says Finn after a pause, without moving his head.

Good idea? What does that mean?

'Well, you know.' I give another strange laugh. 'Just a . . . It's a thought.'

'Uh-huh.' Finn nods.

'Right. So. Um.'

I rub my nose. This is the most surreal conversation of my life. I think I'm going to stop talking now. And possibly emigrate.

For a while I'm silent, my face tingling, wondering how long the pair of us will sit here on the sand, not looking at each other and also not addressing what just happened. Until Finn takes a deep breath.

'I've sworn off casual sex,' he says, in a manner which is so studiedly relaxed that I know he was rehearsing it in his mind. I look at him before I can stop myself, and catch his eye by mistake, then hastily turn away, my cheeks burning.

He looks supremely uncomfortable, and frankly, I want to evaporate.

'Good for you,' I say, my voice a bit crunchy. 'Good move. Makes sense. Makes a lot of sense.'

Why do I feel there's a massive great story behind that one statement? A story he's not planning to share with me?

'Yes,' says Finn. 'Well.'

I open my mouth to make another meaningless remark, then catch sight of his awkward face and abandon the idea. Enough. A wave runs over my feet and I shiver. We've been sitting here in the sea too long. Hope and sexual fantasy were keeping me warm, but now I feel cold and embarrassed and stiff and as if I'll never get my wetsuit off.

'I think I'll take my surfboard back,' I say, trying to sound relaxed. 'I've had enough. It was fun, though.'

'Let me,' says Finn at once, leaping to his feet.

'Don't be silly!' I protest, but he's already hefting my board under his arm.

'OK, well, thanks,' I say, realizing I can't exactly wrestle it off him.

'No problem.' He flashes me a brief smile, then heads off down the beach. He's striding. Quickly. Almost as if he wants to get away from me.

No. Scratch that. Exactly as though he wants to get away from me.

I watch him for a few moments, feeling a creeping hollowness. Well, there we are. I've messed up. I've made things awkward. We were friends. I had a burnout buddy. I had a good person in my life. But now he can't even look at me. Great, Sasha. Just great.

SEVENTEEN

Two hours later, my spirits have plummeted still lower. Sure enough, it took me ages to peel my wetsuit off my clammy, shivering body, while I hopped around my lodge, yanking at the neoprene. By the time I finally emerged, Finn had disappeared, so I hurried back up to the hotel, hoping for a long, hot bath and room service. But in the lobby, there was Cassidy, setting out chipped gilt chairs and concert programmes, and she greeted me by crying, 'I've saved you a place at the front! And a grape juice, because you won't want cava, will you? You are coming, aren't you?'

I was too slow to think of an excuse, so I promised to come. And now I find myself sitting in a gilt chair, clutching a glass of grape juice, listening to Nikolai recite poetry in Polish. Finn is nowhere to be seen. He must have been cleverer than me and dodged the lobby. The audience is mostly elderly people who must live locally and the only person I recognize is Terry's daughter, Tessa, who is sitting in the same row. She seemed to be peering over at me earlier, almost as if she wanted to talk. But when I smiled, she bit her lip and looked away. She really *is* shy.

I glance at the programme and try not to sigh. After Nikolai, it's Herbert on the French horn, and then 'Esteemed local raconteur, Dickie Rathbone, who will entertain us with stories of his time in the Merchant Navy'. I take a sip of grape juice, then look up as someone takes the seat next to me.

Oh my God, it's Hayley. She's being ushered to her chair by Cassidy, and looks about as thrilled to be here as I am.

'I saved you a seat!' Cassidy is whispering breathily to her. 'Hotel guests get the premium seats. All complimentary!'

Meanwhile, Nikolai is still holding forth in Polish. He gives a sudden dramatic sob and I squirm uncomfortably. They really should have provided a translation. I glance at Hayley, who is sitting rigidly, and notice that her eyes are a little glassy, too. She sees me looking and bristles, so I hastily turn back and fix my eyes on Nikolai, who finishes with a flourish, then bows to the ragged smattering of applause.

'Nikolai, that was wonderful!' says Cassidy, leaping up in her role as MC. 'And now, maybe you could tell us what the poem was about?' She beams encouragingly at Nikolai, who is mopping his face with a hanky. He nods, then clears his throat, as though for a speech.

'The gentleman, he love her,' he proclaims, his voice still throbbing with emotion. 'But she not love him.'

There's silence, as we all wait for more – then realize that's it.

'Well!' exclaims Cassidy. 'I think we all really picked up on the drama there, Nikolai, thank you very much. And now a small interval, while Herbert prepares his French horn. Please enjoy your drinks.' She leads a further round of applause, and Nikolai bows several times, looking spent and exhausted, as if he's just played Hamlet.

I sip my juice – then see Finn coming into the lobby, accompanied by Adrian. They're both holding glasses of what looks like whisky, and from their flushed faces I'd guess this isn't their first drink.

'Mr Birchall!' Cassidy salutes him loudly. 'And Mr West! Just in time! There are seats in the front row for you. Or—' She stops dead as the two guys plonk themselves down in the back row, well away from Hayley and me. 'That's also fine.'

I can't meet Finn's eye. I can't even look in his direction. I expect he went straight to the bar to get over the embarrassment of having a fellow guest throw herself at him.

'Pleasant concert,' says Hayley, making me jump.

'Yes.' I nod.

'Although I didn't understand a word of that poem.'

'Me neither,' I admit. 'It sounded very passionate, though.'

'Yes,' says Hayley tightly. 'Well. Passion.' She leaves a pause before adding, 'I'm Hayley, by the way. My husband's Adrian. You probably heard that the other night.'

'I'm Sasha,' I volunteer. 'Nice to meet you properly.'

Hayley's hand is clenching her glass and she's quivering all over. She seems brimming over with misery. I feel as if with one little tap it would all come spilling out.

'I've got the hairdryer, by the way,' I venture warily. 'In case you need it.'

'I travel with my Dyson, thank you,' says Hayley, and swigs her drink, blinking hard.

Oh God. I can't bear it. She looks so unhappy. Should I venture on to personal ground? Should I encourage her to talk? What if she snaps at me? She's pretty scary when she's in full flow.

Well, if she snaps, she snaps. I can at least have a go.

'I'm sorry if things are hard,' I say in a low, soft voice.

Hayley's head whips round as if suspecting a trick – but when she sees my sincere face, something seems to break inside her.

'Yes. They are hard.' She nods several times, her eyes fixed on her glass. 'Very hard.' She pauses, and I'm scrambling for something anodyne to say when she speaks again. 'You don't get married and expect that twelve years later you'll be texting your friends, asking for divorce lawyers, do you? Are you married?' she adds, without giving me time to answer.

'No.'

'Wise,' she murmurs, her face taut. 'Wise girl.'

'Well, it hasn't really come up as an option,' I start to explain – but I can tell Hayley is lost in her own thoughts.

'What would we do with the *sofa*?' she says in sudden anguish, and two tears fall on her lap. 'Because we both chose that sofa and they don't make them any more.' She swigs her cava, her eyes bright with more tears. 'You don't expect either, when your bridesmaid's blow-drying your hair, to be wondering who'll get the sofa in twelve years' time. Do you?'

'I don't suppose you do,' I say feebly.

'No. You don't.' She pauses, then adds, 'My bridesmaid was a professional hairdresser. In case you were wondering. She got me the Dyson cheap, too.'

'Right.' I nod. 'Makes sense.'

Hayley's gaze has moved to the back row, where Adrian is deep in conversation with Finn.

'I don't know how he can look so calm,' she says bitterly. 'But that's always him. Just shrugs or says "Sorry". But does he explain?'

'Explain what?' I can't help asking.

'Everything. *Everything!* I have no idea *how* he thinks!' Fresh tears start falling on her lap. 'Now, you tell me. You ask your husband – who's a qualified carpenter, mind – you ask him nicely to put up some shelves and he says he will – but then he doesn't. You ask him constantly for a year. He just says he'll get to it. At last, you hire a handyman to do it. Three simple shelves with brackets, takes no time. What do you expect your husband to say?'

'Um . . .' I'm trying to unpick this story. 'I'm not quite sure . . .'

'Nothing! That's what he said. Came in, saw the shelves, sat down, had a beer, said nothing. They were to display my grandmother's antique plates, came to me in her will. He didn't say anything about the plates either. Royal Doulton.' She's speaking in an undertone, but her eyes are wild with emotion. 'I wait. And I wait. At last I say, "So I got the shelves done, Adrian, see?" He just shrugs. Won't talk about it. The only word he'll say is "Sorry". I want to know *why*! Was he too tired to build shelves? Then tell me! I'd understand. But blanking me! It's so hurtful! It sums up everything that's wrong! Why would he treat me like that?' She blinks furiously, as though holding back tears.

'I . . . I don't know,' I say helplessly.

'And then there's our intimate life,' she adds, shooting another glance at the back row. 'Sorry for being so frank, but you are a woman and I can't tell my girlfriends.' She takes a deep gulp of cava. 'Whereas I don't know you from Adam, so why should I be embarrassed if my husband doesn't know one end of an orgasm from another?'

'No problem!' I try to sound unfazed. 'Here to help.'

The irony.

Shall I give her my award-winning advice on sex? That it's merely a matter of rubbing genitals together, so why does anyone bother?

'Do *you* have sex in front of the football?' Immediately she checks herself. 'Sorry. I say too much when I've had a drink.' She puts a hand on my arm. 'You're very understanding. You're a lovely girl.'

Now I'm wondering how many drinks Hayley had before she got on to the cava. Her cheeks are blotchy, I notice, and her eyeliner has streaked underneath her eyes.

'It's no problem,' I say, searching for something bland to say. 'I hope things get easier for you.'

'Still in the honeymoon period, you two, are you?' Her eyes swivel towards the back row. 'Looks like it. Why isn't your chap sitting with you? Don't you mind Adrian monopolizing him?'

'Actually,' I say, trying to get a word in, 'we're not a couple.'

'Not a couple?' She peers at me blankly, as though not following. 'Of course you are.'

Something is squeezing my chest. My cheeks are hot. Damn it.

'We're not,' I say, with a resolutely cheerful smile. 'So.'

'But . . .' She glances again at Finn, as though we've got crossed wires. 'You're with him. You pulled your tables together in the restaurant, I saw you.'

'I know. But we're not together.'

'You're not?' She turns to survey Finn, frowning. 'Well.

That's just . . .' She gulps her cava. 'That's just bizarre. You should be.'

We should be? *We should be?*

I want to grab her sleeve and ask her, 'What do you mean? Why do you say that? Tell me everything you think about Finn and me.'

But instead, I sip my drink in silence, congratulating myself on my self-control. And the next moment, Herbert walks out, wearing a maroon velvet suit and carrying an ancient-looking French horn. He bows deeply, his expression grave, and announces, 'Minuet.'

He then puts the mouthpiece to his thin, papery lips. As he puffs on his French horn, a feeble farting noise fills the air, and I sense everyone in the audience quell a giggle.

Undeterred by the sounds he's making, Herbert carries on puffing on the horn, producing fart after fart. As the noises continue, there's a general snuffling sound of people holding in laughter, and I'm suddenly desperate to meet eyes with Finn. Even if things were awkward between us earlier, we can still share a joke as friends, can't we? Nonchalantly, I lean back on my chair and turn my head, telling myself I'll catch his eye, just once.

But the back row is empty. He's gone.

EIGHTEEN

He's sworn off casual sex. Is that like going vegan? Is it a thing? It's bugging me as I lie in bed the next morning, staring up at the peeling ceiling. How casual is 'casual', anyway? And why didn't I have a better reply? Why was I so dumbstruck?

But what could I have said?

And anyway, was he actually saying something else? Of course he was.

I shut my eyes, letting the painful truth assail me once more. He was being tactful. Letting me down gently. Letting us both save face. He just doesn't see me that way.

At least he didn't begin, *Sasha, I really like you, you're a lovely girl, but* . . .

My already-cringing insides cringe still harder. My stomach feels like one big stew of embarrassment, and now I have to *see* him. Maybe. If he hasn't already checked out and deleted my contact from his phone.

I'm so dreading our encounter that I almost decide to skip

breakfast. Except that I'm also starving hungry. So eventually I sidle into the dining room, trying to blend in with the wallpaper – and breathe out in relief when I see that I'm the only guest.

I intersperse eating my scrambled eggs with telling Nikolai how brilliant he was last night, and glossing over any mention of esteemed raconteur Dickie Rathbone, who spoke for half an hour and laughed so hard at his own jokes that I couldn't understand anything he said.

When I've finished my breakfast, I take my kale smoothie in its paper cup – tomorrow I *must* try to head that off in time – and walk out of the dining room. The lobby is empty and for a few seconds I pause, my heart thudding. Shall I dodge the whole situation? Go off somewhere for the day and avoid Finn completely?

No. That would be lame. Come on, Sasha. Bite the bullet.

Holding my head up high, I walk straight out of the hotel, through the garden and down to the beach. As I get near, I can see he's there, on the sand.

My stomach is churning with nerves; I'm not sure I can speak. But I don't have to, because as I approach, Finn turns to greet me, with such a warm, glowing expression that I feel a clench of disbelieving hope. Is he pleased to see me? Thrilled to see me, even? I find myself hurrying forward with an eager smile, thinking: did I miss something?

'At last!' he says. 'Sasha! I've been waiting for you!'

'Have you?' I give a tremulous laugh, my heart galloping.

'Of course!' He points at the sand where he's standing. 'New message,' he adds and I stop dead in my tracks.

The messages. That's why he's excited.

I mean, of *course* it's the bloody messages.

'Amazing!' I manage, my smile still bright. 'What did they say? Let me see!'

As I hurry forward, I try to refocus my mind. The message will be a good distraction, I decide, so let's take it seriously. It's written on the sand in exactly the same way as the other messages – letters lined with pebbles – and next to it is a fruit cake in a tin.

YOU DID EVERYTHING. 18/8

'We did everything,' announces Finn proudly, as though I can't read. 'Apparently.'

'Except we did nothing,' I object, almost out of habit. 'And it's not us.'

'Well, who else is it?'

OK. I'm going to really think about this. Distraction, distraction, distraction.

'What else happened that day of the accident?' I crinkle my brow. 'What did you do?'

Finn shrugs. 'Hung around. Watched the coastguards. Talked to the police.'

'Talked to the police?' I look up at him sharply. 'About what?'

'Everything.' He rolls his eyes. 'First, they gave me a lecture about not trying to be a hero. Then they wanted to know where I got my kayak from, who signed it out, was there a safety protocol, blah blah.'

'You didn't tell me that before,' I say, my brain starting to turn. 'That you talked to the police, I mean.'

'Thought it was obvious.' He shrugs. 'Nothing happened. They talked to me, said thanks very much, gave me a sweet, off I went.'

His words are sparking a memory in my head. *A sweet*.

'A humbug.' The words come out before I know I'm going to say them. 'They gave out stripy mint humbugs.'

'Yes.' Finn looks surprised. 'You're right.'

I can see them now. The basket they were in. I can see it all: the room, the people, everything.

'I talked to the police, too.' I rub my face, feeling discombobulated. 'I'd forgotten. Was it in the Seashore Cafe?'

'Yes, upstairs. They talked to loads of people. Lots of kids. Everyone.'

I remember sitting on a plastic chair. Hot and sweaty and uncomfortable because everyone was waiting. I held the whole family up. We couldn't leave for home till I'd seen the police. *How* could I have forgotten that?

'I saw them the day after the accident,' I say slowly. 'One of the policemen had a red beard. And there was a really annoying electric fan in the waiting area. It kept stopping.'

'Yes.' Finn stares at me. 'But why did you have to see the police? You weren't even in the sea.'

'I don't know.' I shake my head helplessly. 'Don't remember.' I glance down at the message. 'Could it be related to this?'

'Who knows?' Finn is silent for a moment, his face screwed up in thought, then he makes a frustrated exclamation. 'Nothing makes sense! The accident wasn't even a big deal. James Reynolds was fine. Everyone was fine.'

'Apart from Pete,' I point out. 'He lost his business.'

'Well, OK, Pete,' concedes Finn. 'But he shouldn't have loaned out a dodgy kayak. And aside from that, it was basically a non-event. Lot of excitement over nothing.'

'James Reynolds nearly *drowned*,' I point out reprovingly.

'Yes, but he *didn't* drown,' retorts Finn, mimicking my tone.

'I'm going to ask my mum why I saw the police,' I say with sudden determination. 'She must remember.'

I open my phone and type a WhatsApp to Mum and Kirsten.

Hi both. Hope all is well. I am still trying to gather info about that kayak accident. Did I speak to the police? What about? All good here. Surfed yesterday!! xxx

I press Send, but there's no signal. Still, they'll get it later.

'So, what shall we do?' I look at the message again, then take a photo of it.

'Let's leave it for now.' Finn shrugs. 'Get on to . . . what's on our wellness agenda for the day? More yoga? Seaweed-eating? Stone-hopping?'

Our wellness agenda. He wants to be friends. It's quite clear. He wants to be platonic, burnout-buddy friends, and that makes me feel all churned up with conflict, because of course I want him as my friend, of *course* I do. It's a dream come true, to have a strong, loyal, wise friend like Finn.

It's just, I had other dreams. Which I will now put away in my dreams cupboard.

'Hula-hooping?' I suggest, just to wind him up, and he laughs.

'What happens when you've done all twenty steps? Do you get a medal?'

'I turn into Wetsuit Girl, of course.'

'Don't do that.' Finn's voice deepens a smidgen – and something about his expression makes me catch my breath. 'Don't change into Wetsuit Girl.'

I reach for some light, jokey retort . . . but I don't have one. For a weird, tense beat we're silent, our eyes locked, and I'm just feeling as if we might stand here for ever when Finn's gaze shifts to something over my shoulder. I breathe out, almost in relief, then turn to see what he's looking at. Adrian is picking his way down to the sea, his face as dejected as ever, and I feel a wave of pity for him. He lifts a hand to greet us, and we both wave back.

'His wife confided in me last night,' I murmur under my breath to Finn. 'She was crying. She's finding a divorce lawyer. It's so sad. What did he tell you? He must have said something. You seemed like best friends at the concert.'

'He latched on to me at the bar.' Finn lowers his voice further as Adrian approaches. 'Started on a bit of a rant. All she does is find fault. At least, that's what he says.'

'Did he mention a set of shelves?' I can't help asking.

'Yes!' Finn turns to face me, looking surprised. 'She's obsessed by some shelves he didn't build. Can't leave it alone, even though he says he keeps apologizing.'

'That's the problem!' I explain eagerly. 'He just says "Sorry". But he doesn't ever say *why* he wouldn't build them. Like, was he too tired? In which case, why didn't he just say, "I'm too tired" instead of saying he'd do it, then blanking her for a year?'

I look expectantly at Finn and he laughs.

'I guess he had his reasons. Is it a big deal?'

'Of course!' I retort. 'She felt hurt! You know he's a qualified carpenter? And he said he would do it. But she had to hire a handyman in the end, and when they were done, Adrian didn't say a word. Just ignored them. They were for her grandmother's antique plates,' I add. 'Royal Doulton.'

Finn seems taken aback by my level of knowledge, and I clear my throat, suddenly feeling embarrassed. I may possibly have over-invested in this relationship. I may also have taken Hayley's part without hearing Adrian's point of view.

'I mean, I only heard her side of the story,' I backtrack. 'But you have to admit, it's weird. If he's a carpenter and he'd said he would do them.'

'Bit strange,' agrees Finn.

He shrugs and stretches out his arms, as though the conversation is over and that's the limit of his interest. But I'm just getting going. I survey Adrian's stiff, wretched back as he kicks a stone into the waves. He's miserable. She's miserable. They're both going on about the shelves. If they could just sort that one issue, then maybe it would help everything.

'Ask him!' I say impulsively. 'Straight out. Ask, "Why didn't you just build the shelves?" Man to man. He'll tell you.'

'Are you insane?' Finn stares at me incredulously.

'No, but I'm *dying* of curiosity,' I confess. 'And he'll tell you! Look, he's all alone.' I nudge Finn, nodding my head at Adrian, who is standing moodily at the water's edge. 'He wants some company. You're his guy. You can find out.'

'What, just ask him, "Why didn't you make your wife's shelves?" '

'Get on to the subject gradually,' I suggest. 'Talk about DIY projects. See if he takes the bait.'

'OK,' says Finn at last. 'I'll try. But you come, too. Otherwise you'll only decide you want to know something else and send me back on another fact-finding mission.'

'I wouldn't!' I grin at him and he rolls his eyes wryly.

'Are you always this curious?' he adds, as we start walking together down the beach towards Adrian. 'Curious-slash-interfering?'

'No,' I say after a bit of thought. 'Not recently. In fact, the opposite. I've been living with tunnel vision. Maybe that's why I'm waking up now. I'm realizing there's *life*.' I spread my arms around, savouring the crisp, energizing sea air. 'There are *people*. There's stuff going on. And it's not interfering just to have a conversation,' I add, a bit defiantly.

'If you say so.' Finn rolls his eyes again, but he's smiling.

'Oh, they also have problems with sex,' I murmur as we draw near to Adrian. 'But maybe don't go there . . . Hi!' I raise my voice, grinning inwardly at Finn's aghast expression. 'How's it going?'

'Hi.' Adrian looks catatonic with despair. 'Cold, isn't it?'

'Pretty cold.' I nod, and shoot a meaningful glance at Finn.

'I was just thinking about all the DIY projects I've got waiting for me at home,' says Finn gamely, and I give him a little appreciative grin.

'I hear you, mate,' says Adrian gloomily, then lapses into silence, shoving his hands in his pockets and staring out at the waves. Finn shoots me a look which clearly says *What now?* so I draw breath.

'I love Royal Doulton,' I venture brightly. 'China. All that. I like . . . um . . . displaying it.'

Do I dare add *on shelves*?

No.

Adrian has stiffened, but he hasn't looked at me or even replied.

OK, the subtle approach isn't working. Time to be direct.

'Forgive me, Adrian.' I wait until he looks round, his gaze suspicious. 'I'm really sorry to do this, but can I ask you a question? I'm not selling anything,' I add hastily.

'What question?' Adrian's brow lowers ferociously.

'Well . . . I was talking to your wife last night.'

'Huh,' says Adrian at once. 'Bitching about me, was she?'

'No!' I say, swiftly deciding that what Hayley said was not bitching, it was a valid expression of sadness. 'Not at all! But she's just so hurt, and I think . . . you know, as an onlooker . . . if you could explain *why* you never built those shelves—'

'Not the bloody shelves!' erupts Adrian, and I clap a hand over my mouth. Oops. 'She goes on and on . . .'

'So tell her,' suggests Finn. 'Tell her you're not a shelf-builder and she'll have to take it or leave it.'

'I *am* a shelf-builder!' Adrian roars. 'I'm a bloody *excellent* . . .' He breaks off, shaking, and I glance at Finn, unnerved. I never knew shelves could be such an emotional subject. For a few moments, no one says anything. I don't even dare move, in case Adrian lashes out at me.

'You want to know the truth?' he mutters at last, staring down at the foaming water. 'Truth is, I didn't know what she meant. She kept saying she wanted to show off each plate to its best advantage. Fourteen plates. Somehow I got the wrong idea stuck in my head. I was thinking, fourteen shelves – how do I make that look good? But I didn't want to say I couldn't do it. So I stalled. I thought maybe she'd forget.'

'Forget?' I say incredulously. 'Forget displaying her grandmother's antique plates?'

'Or change her mind,' says Adrian defensively. 'Whatever. But she didn't. Then some bloke she hired came and did it in one morning, three shelves, boom, and I thought . . . oh shit. That's what she meant.'

I have a vision of him sitting at a kitchen table with a beer, ignoring Hayley's new shelves, and feel a swell of frustration.

'Did you think of *saying* that to her?' I blurt out.

'Say what?'

' "Oh, wow, great shelves. I feel bad now, I didn't understand exactly what you meant." '

Adrian's face closes up sulkily. 'I would've looked like a total numpty.'

'So you'd rather she thinks you're a horrible, uncaring husband than look like a numpty?'

'It was too late, anyway.' Adrian looks still more sulky. 'They were built, weren't they?'

'It's never too late,' puts in Finn, and I shoot him an appreciative look. I don't know why Adrian and Hayley have got under my skin so much, but I want to help them. Or at least try.

'It's never too late,' I say robustly, echoing Finn, and Adrian shoots me a resentful glance.

'Are you a pair of bloody counsellors?'

'No.' Finn meets my eyes, looking amused. 'Very much not.'

At that moment, Hayley's figure comes into my line of sight. She's walking down the beach, wearing a navy cagoule, about twenty metres away. I lift a hand, wondering what she makes of the sight of Finn and me talking to her husband. Then I glance at Adrian – and that familiar, grumpy attitude has already come over him.

'Are you telling me you'd rather Hayley leaves you than confess one embarrassing misunderstanding?' I say, a bit impatiently. 'Really?'

'She won't *leave* me,' says Adrian, as though this idea is ludicrous.

'But in the lobby she said, "We don't know if we're still a couple",' I point out.

'She says stuff like that.' Adrian brushes it off. 'She just likes having a go. Wanted a minibreak, needed to find a reason. I'll get her a present. She'll calm down.'

Oh my God. Is he dense or in denial or both? For a few

moments I agonize about breaking Hayley's confidence. But then, did she say 'this is in strict confidence'? No. She didn't know anything about me and she was blabbing her whole life story.

'Adrian,' I say gently, 'she's phoning her friends for numbers of divorce lawyers.'

The effect on Adrian is staggering. He goes pale. He looks from Finn back to me. His prickly air has disappeared.

'Divorce lawyers?' he stammers at last.

'Look,' says Finn. 'For what it's worth, here's my advice. You fix this right now. You go over there.' He points at Hayley, who is now standing at the water's edge, some distance from us. You say, "I'm so sorry I never did the shelves. I didn't understand what you meant, and I was too embarrassed to admit it. My bad. I want to make this work. I care about you so much."'

' "So deeply",' I suggest.

'Yes.' Finn nods. 'Better. "Deeply. I'll go to counselling if you like, but now . . ."' He pauses to think. ' "Now, could we walk along the waves while I tell you why I fell in love with you in the first place?"'

I stare at Finn, transfixed. His voice is ringing through my soul. I want him to say more. I want him to speak like that to me. I want to pull him down on to the sand and watch the sun dipping below the horizon while he talks to me like that for ever.

'You have to be bloody joking.' Adrian's mutinous voice pulls me out of my reverie. 'I'm not saying that.'

'Why not?' Finn retorts.

'Exactly!' I force myself to join in the conversation. 'What's the worst that can happen?'

'Practise it,' instructs Finn.

'You're a pair of nutters,' says Adrian – but after a moment, he takes a deep breath. 'Sorry I never did the shelves,' he mutters, looking at Hayley's distant figure. 'I didn't understand what you meant, and I was too embarrassed to admit it.' He pauses, and I see something shift in his face. 'My bad. I want to make this work. I care about you so much.' Again he pauses, for longer this time. There's a kind of agitation in his face. A silent maelstrom. He swallows hard a few times, his eyes locked on Hayley's unwitting back. 'Can we walk along the beach?' he continues, his voice suddenly husky. 'Can I tell you why I love you? Because I always have. Since we were eighteen years old and you pranged my bloody car in Morrisons car park. Ever since then.' He breaks off, breathing hard, and I glance at Finn, my eyes hot.

'Go,' says Finn. 'Go.'

Without pausing, Adrian heads across the sand to Hayley, his shoulders set and determined. I watch, breathless, as she turns her head, her body language wretched and defensive. I see her face jolt as he starts speaking. Her eyes widen. Then I turn away, because they should have privacy right now. All my fingers are crossed. Maybe that'll help things along.

Finn has turned away too, and we begin walking back to the hotel.

'As it turns out, I think he loves her,' says Finn after a few steps.

'Yup.' I nod. 'I think he does.'

'You were right,' adds Finn thoughtfully. 'You saw it before I did. I just saw fighting, but you picked up on their love.' He shoots me a smile, his voice warm. 'You saw love.'

Stop saying 'love' out loud, I tell him silently and furiously. *Stop saying 'love'. Because every time I hear you say it, I melt, and I mustn't melt.*

'So, what now?' Finn continues in the same warm voice, and just for one stupid, mad moment, I think he's talking about us.

Oh God, I've lost all sense of reality. I need to get my head straight.

'Actually,' I say, 'I need to make some calls. So I'll head back to my room.'

'Oh, OK.' Finn nods. 'Well, I'll catch you later.'

'Sure!' I try to sound casual. 'See you then.' I shoot him my best effort at an easy-breezy smile, then quickly turn my steps towards the hotel, almost stumbling in my hurry.

Here's the problem. Here's the issue. I'm falling in love with this man. Properly, hopelessly in love. And I need to get away, while I still have a chance of un-falling in love.

NINETEEN

By that evening, I feel more level-headed. An invitation was
shoved under my door mid-afternoon, inviting me to a *Reception and Presentation of Skyspace Beach Studios, 6 p.m., Smart
Casual*. I'm actually quite intrigued to hear about these new
buildings and the invitation promises champagne. So I've put
on the only outfit I have here that might fit the bill of 'smart
casual': a clingy black dress that packs easily and a pair of
heels, which I only brought because I thought the Rilston
might still be all liveried porters and a dress code in the lobby.

I'm dressing to impress Finn, I realize. I'm seeing myself
through his eyes. But I have to be realistic: it's not a goer. He
sounded *so* awkward when he told me he'd sworn off casual
sex. It was *so* obvious, what his actual message was. And if
I'm anything, I'm someone who can take a hint. We're supportive friends, is all – and that's *good*.

Anyway, maybe I'll meet someone else tonight, I think,
giving myself a little pep talk. Yes. Finn is not the only man
on the planet. I will meet a brand-new man, who will sweep

away all thoughts of Finn, and who is actually romantically interested in me.

I spend a few moments conjuring up this new man in my mind – maybe really tall and thin, maybe very shy and reserved . . . anyway, nothing like Finn – and as I head down the staircase, I'm almost imagining he'll be at the bottom, ready to greet me. But instead, I come across Simon, man-handling a big display of flowers.

Oh God. Is the universe trying to offer up Simon Palmer to me?

No way. *La la la, I can't hear you, universe . . .*

'Miss Worth, I must apologize,' Simon begins, in his usual abject manner. 'I have been shamefully absent, these last few days, distracted as I have been with tonight's investors' reception.'

'Don't worry!' I say, but Simon doesn't seem to hear me.

'I am devastated to have been unavailable to guests,' he continues mournfully. 'In acknowledgement of this, I have arranged for a small gift of a bottle of vintage champagne to be delivered to your room. To each of the resident guests. A very meagre recompense.'

'Really, it's fine,' I try to say again, but Simon is on a roll now.

'Your stay is satisfactory?' he enquires anxiously. 'Your wellness break is progressing to your liking? Chef Leslie tells me he has found a very reputable source of organic kale, would you concur?'

'Yes, the kale's great,' I assure him. 'It's so . . . green.'

'Indeed. And I believe that, as of this afternoon . . .' His eyes swivel to behind my shoulder and he emits a small gasp. 'Yes! Perfectly on time! Ms Worth, I'm pleased to announce that at last we have sourced you some noni juice!'

I turn to see Nikolai approaching, holding a silver salver with a glass of brown fluid sitting on top. Nikolai's face is wreathed in smiles, and as he proffers me the salver, Simon clasps his hands together as though overcome with emotion.

'Noni juice for Madame,' says Nikolai, grinning even more widely. 'Please enjoy.'

'Thank you!' I say, feeling self-conscious, and take the glass. 'How ... wonderful.'

I peer at the glass, repulsed. What *is* this stuff? Why is it so brown and manky-looking? Do I actually want to drink this?

'Enjoy!' repeats Nikolai, gesturing encouragingly at it. 'Please enjoy your noni juice!'

OK. Here goes. Nikolai and Simon watch in fascination as I take a cautious sip and try not to retch. Good God, what *is* this? It tastes as though someone collected together some putrefying body parts, liquefied them and called it 'juice'. My mouth feels polluted. My body feels polluted. *How* can this be good for you?

'Is it good-quality noni juice?' asks Simon, already looking worried. 'Is it of the highest standards?'

'Madame is feeling the health benefits?' enquires Nikolai eagerly.

'Definitely!' I manage, trying to swallow down the revolting aftertaste. 'It's ... it's very good noni juice. Very pure. Very filtered. Thank you so much.'

'I don't mind saying, you've inspired us all, Ms Worth,' says Simon admiringly. 'With your kale and your noni juice and your yoga ... We're considering launching a little wellness-break programme, on the strength of what we've seen you doing. Maybe you could be our health and diet consultant!'

'Oh, right. Well, I'm not sure . . .'

'Madame is strong,' Nikolai asserts encouragingly. 'The healthy drink always. The healthy walk on the beach. The salad. The zero alcohol. All the other guests, alcohol. Madame, no alcohol.'

'Well.' I swallow, my mind flitting guiltily to the empty wine bottle in my lodge. 'I suppose it's just a matter of . . . you know, self-control . . .' I turn as something catches my attention, and freeze.

Coming through the hall towards us is the guy from the supermarket. He has a large cardboard box in his arms, emblazoned with *CLUB BISCUITS* and *Orange Flavour*. And he's heading straight for me.

No. Noooo. Frantically I try to think of a way out of this, but it's too late to head him off.

'Got your you-know-whats,' he addresses me in his usual sepulchral tones, then seems to realize his lack of discretion. He places a hand over *CLUB BISCUITS* – only hiding three letters – then winks at me and resumes. 'Didn't see you in the shop and I was coming up here anyway, so I brought them. There's ninety-eight in there,' he adds, nodding at the box. 'That enough to keep you going?'

My face is blazing. I can't look at anyone. Club biscuits. Not even oatcakes. Club bloody biscuits. The guy thrusts the box at me, but I don't take it. I *can't* admit I ordered ninety-eight Club biscuits for my own private consumption. What do I do?

And then the solution suddenly comes to me.

'Actually . . .' I turn to Simon, trying to sound convincing. 'These are for you! For all the staff. As a . . . um . . . present. For all your hard work.'

There's a slightly flabbergasted silence. The guy from the

shop looks puzzled. Simon and Nikolai are peering uncertainly at the box. Nikolai seems particularly flummoxed, as though he's never seen a cardboard box before.

It's Simon who regains his cool first.

'Club biscuits!' he exclaims. '*Club biscuits!* Ms Worth, you are too good. Too kind. Nikolai, look at this generous present of Club biscuits. Let us open it.'

'No,' I say hastily. 'Honestly . . .'

But it's too late. The guy in the brown T-shirt dumps the box on a table and tears off the tape, then opens the flaps, revealing a pile of seven-packs, encased in plastic.

'Look at this.' Simon surveys the packs reverently. 'Orange Club biscuits. We will distribute these among all our hard-working staff. Cassidy!' He summons her from across the lobby. 'Come and see Ms Worth's wonderful gift of confectionery! Tonight, we will feast on Club biscuits!'

My face is puce. This is *hideous*. I should have just taken them.

'You're . . . very welcome,' I say feebly. 'Enjoy.'

'Club biscuits?' says Cassidy brightly, as she approaches. 'Nice!'

'Well.' I swallow. 'I just thought you might like them.'

'Ooh, the noni juice!' says Cassidy, as she sees it in my hand. 'I tried some of that, thought it was rank. But guess what? Chef Leslie's made you a special cocktail with it for tonight. It's called the Noni-jito. Clever, isn't it? It's got kale in it, too,' she adds triumphantly. 'Alcohol-free, of course, we know you love your alcohol-free.'

I stare at her, blinking hard. I am *not* drinking noni juice with kale, when everyone else is on champagne.

'Actually . . .' I hear myself improvising, 'a vital part of my health regime is Kickback Night. It's important to relax your rules every so often. So I'll probably have champagne tonight, for wellbeing, and maybe the noni thing tomorrow.'

'Kickback Night!' Cassidy's face gleams. 'I *love* that! We should put that in our wellness regime, too.' She turns to Simon. 'Let's have Kickback Night every night. We'll serve tequila shots and we'll tell the guests it's for their own wellbeing! Win-win!'

As though on cue, a girl bearing a tray of champagne flutes arrives in the lobby. I recognize her as Cassidy's friend Bea from the bakery. The next moment, the front door opens, revealing a pair of men in suits, and at once Simon bristles with tension.

'Investors!' he hisses at Nikolai and Cassidy. 'The investors have started arriving! Cassidy, coats. Nikolai, canapés! *Canapés!* Good evening!' He hurries forward, smoothing his hand down on his trouser leg. 'And welcome to the Rilston Hotel.'

I grab a glass from Bea, shake back my hair and stride confidently into the dining room. *Eligible men, here I come.*

The only trouble is, there aren't any. Unless the term 'eligible' is stretched waaay beyond where I am prepared to stretch it.

It's nearly an hour later and the dining room is humming with guests. I've drunk two glasses of champagne and done the rounds. I've chatted. I've smiled. And the results have been terrible.

I've talked to a property developer with a paunch from Exeter who has told me four times that his ex-wife got the convertible. (No.) And to his friend with halitosis. (*No.*) I've also met a gay local historian called Bernard, who is here to tell investors about the area, and a woman called Diane who represents the Garthwick family that own the hotel.

Finn isn't here. I'm super-aware of that. (I thought that might be him, just now, but it's a guy with dark hair I don't recognize.)

The Wests aren't here either, and I find myself hoping that they're in bed, all loved up again, maybe on position 15 of the 'reconciliation-sex handbook'. (Lucky them.) In fact, I'm the only mug of a guest who has actually showed up, I realize.

'Sasha!' A booming voice greets me and I turn to see Keith from the train, wearing a bright-blue jacket and holding a garish puppet with a seriously creepy face. 'Remember me? Keith? Mr Poppit?'

'Hi!' I say, trying not to look at the puppet. 'Lovely to see you again. Are you performing?'

'Doing a set after the speeches,' says Keith, nodding. 'Bit of an "adult" theme. Mr Poppit in the Red Light District, nudge, nudge.' He gives me an elaborate wink and I make a firm resolve to leave straight after the speeches. 'So, having a nice time, are you?'

'Great, thanks. I saw Terry the other day,' I add, remembering our conversation on the train. 'I was quite shocked at how different he is now.'

'Ah, Terry.' Keith winces. 'Yes, he's in a bit of a state. Poor man, been through a lot, he has. By the surf school, was he?'

'Yes.' I nod.

'That's his haven.' Keith nods. 'That's his safe place. He always goes back there, everyone looks out for him.'

It suddenly occurs to me that Keith might know something relevant about the kayak accident, although I'm not sure how to frame the question.

'I was talking to a fellow guest about that kayak accident,' I begin. 'And I remembered that I spoke to the police. It was a big deal, wasn't it?'

I'm hoping this might trigger a gush of gossip, and sure enough, Keith's face lights up.

'Now that was a scandal. If they hadn't uncovered the truth, think where Terry would have been!' He stares at me with bulgy eyes and so does the puppet.

'What do you mean, "uncovered the truth"?' I ask. 'What truth?'

'That it was Pete's kayak, not Terry's,' says Keith, as though it's obvious. 'The police thought it was Terry at first. They were investigating him. Could have been his business that shut down.'

'Why would they think it was Terry's kayak?' I say, confused, and Keith frowns.

'I don't remember the details now, but there was a reason. Did Terry lend out the kayak? Or had they got mixed up? Anyway, it was looking bad for Terry at one point. He was beside himself, poor man.'

'It could never have been Terry,' I say hotly. 'Terry would never lend out a damaged kayak!'

'Well, the police seemed fixed on him, only something changed their minds ... Ah, yes!' He's distracted by an approaching man in a T-shirt and black jeans, holding a microphone. 'Sound-check time, is it? No rest for the performers, is there, Mr Poppit?'

'No rest for the performers!' echoes the puppet, moving its painted mouth, and I hide a shudder.

'Well, good luck,' I reply, backing away, and bump into someone. 'Sorry!' I say, wheeling round – then catch my breath. It's Finn. He's here. He's in a well-cut jacket and looks kind of ... What's the word?

Handsome, says my brain. *Gorgeous. Delicious. Sexy*.

No. Enough. Don't start down that path. He looks *well*

groomed. Exactly. Smart shirt. Aftershave. Nice shoes, I notice, glancing downwards.

'Hi,' he says. 'Wondered if you'd be here.'

'Couldn't resist the free drinks,' I say, sipping my champagne. There's something new about his expression. A different light in his eyes. Or am I imagining it?

'Good,' says Finn. 'Because I wanted to talk to you.'

He pauses, and I feel my heart skip. Then my brain kicks in, chiding my heart for skipping. Now my chest feels tight. My fingers are damp, round the stem of my glass. God, my body is so *unruly*.

And still Finn is looking at me, his face alive with some thought or feeling, but silent, as though he doesn't know where to begin. Or perhaps he does know where to begin, but he's apprehensive about beginning.

'I've been meaning to ask you,' I say, to fill the gap. 'Did you get through to your therapist?'

'Oh, yes,' he says, frowning, as though confused by the question. 'Yes. I . . . yes.' He pauses and looks around the room, which has become more raucous. 'It's noisy in here. Could we go somewhere?'

My heart skips again. *Go somewhere?*

But I'm not making the mistake of listening to my skippy, romantic heart. I'm listening to my solid, somewhat jaded brain instead. He probably means, *Go somewhere to talk about the hotel's billing policy*. Or, *Go somewhere, so I can update you on the cricket score.*

'Um, sure,' I say, gulping my champagne. 'Sure.'

However, at that very moment, Simon taps on a glass, shushing everyone. Nikolai starts threading through the guests, topping up the champagne as though it's a wedding, and Cassidy arrives at our side.

'Simon's going to give a speech,' she says chattily. 'He's dead nervous. I said, "Simon, just imagine the audience all wearing one of my Etsy thongs," and he was like, "What Etsy thongs?" He didn't know! So I showed him and he got all stressed again, poor love! He thinks I should do them "in my own time".' She laughs merrily. 'I was like, "Simon, sitting at that desk *is* my own time, nothing ever happens!" But he was all like . . .' She breaks off and applauds vigorously as Simon steps on to a small podium and taps the microphone. 'Woooh! Go, Simon!'

'Ladies and gentlemen,' says Simon, as the chatter dies to a hush. 'Welcome to the Rilston Hotel . . . and an exciting new chapter.'

A screen behind Simon fills with an artist's rendition of six sun-drenched glass buildings on Rilston beach, with a vivid blue sky emblazoned with the words *Skyspace Beach Studios at the Rilston.*

'Wow,' I breathe. 'That's . . . different.'

'Today, the Rilston steps into the next millennium,' Simon continues, reading off a card. 'With style, substance and, of course, sea views. I bring you Skyspace Beach Studios!'

The next moment, funky music is crashing through the room, and a video is showing a series of photos of the beach, the town, the hotel, a close-up of *Young Love*, and then the design of the studios.

'The Skyspace Beach Studios project brings together the majesty and tradition of the Rilston Hotel,' a female voiceover breathily declaims, 'the talent of architects Fitts Warrender, the artworks of renowned local artist Mavis Adler, and interior design by a top designer, unconfirmed. The latest in stylish beachside accommodation. For holidays. For living. For you.'

As the video finishes, there's an uncertain spattering of applause, and Simon lifts his arms theatrically as though he's holding back the roar at Wembley Stadium.

'Save your applause,' he says, his face glowing. 'Architect Jonathan Fitts will speak to us in a moment. But first, I would like to pay tribute to *heritage*. I speak, of course, of the original beach lodges, still standing on Rilston beach.' Now he begins a round of applause and soon everyone in the room is clapping.

'Have they *seen* the beach lodges?' Finn says in my ear, and I bite my lip.

'And to celebrate this rich heritage, I would like to invite two guests, Sasha Worth and Finn Birchall, to join me here. Come on, Sasha and Finn!' He beckons us as though he's a quiz-show host. 'Don't be shy!'

'*What?*' exclaims Finn, bemused, and I shrug.

'No idea.'

Shooting each other wary glances, we wend our way to the stage and stand awkwardly, side by side.

'Sasha and Finn first visited this resort as children, ladies and gentlemen, and now they're here again, faithful to Rilston,' begins Simon. 'They're the kind of guests that bring the heart to Rilston. The kind of guests that turn a resort . . . into a *family* resort. Sasha and Finn are the last guests ever who will occupy the original historic beach lodges, and we at the Rilston would like to thank these two honoured guests for keeping the tradition alive.'

I can't quite believe it, but I'm getting misty-eyed. I guess the lodges have always been part of the Rilston Bay scenery. I'm glad I got to have one, just in time.

'To the lodges!' exclaims Simon. We all raise our glasses

and then a photographer dashes forward, a massive camera round his neck.

'Quick photo, if you don't mind?' he says to Finn and me. 'If I could move the happy couple a *leetle* to the left . . .' He quickly changes the lens on his camera. 'Not the happy couple, but you know what I mean . . .'

'Oh, they're not a couple,' says Cassidy importantly, coming forward. 'I know they *look* like a couple, but they're not. Funny, isn't it? We call them the not-couple.'

The not-couple?

I don't dare look at Finn. I'm standing facing the camera, my dress brushing against his shirt, feeling the touch of his jacket against my arm.

'Little closer?' The photographer motions for us to shuffle together. 'That's it, lovely.' The camera flashes and he squints at his screen, then looks up again. 'You mind putting an arm round her, Mr Not-Couple? Haven't got a wife to complain?'

Finn says nothing, just places an arm around my shoulders, and it feels like lightning through me.

My body is burning to touch him. Kiss him. Pull him closer. But my brain keeps remembering his uncomfortable expression yesterday. And those killer words: *I've sworn off casual sex. AKA I don't fancy you.*

'Nice shots,' says the photographer, scrolling through his screen. 'You *do* look good together.' He looks up with a cheerful wink. 'You should think about it.'

'Hahaha!' I laugh so shrilly I nearly choke, and clear my throat.

'I'm done,' the photographer adds, and Finn glances at me.

'Shall we?' He nods to the door. 'Unless you want to listen to the architect?'

'No.' I shake my head. 'Lovely speech, Simon,' I add to him. 'Hope you get lots of investment.'

As a young guy in specs comes on to the podium and the screen lights up again, Finn and I slip out of the room. Without saying anything, Finn leads us into the bar, which is quiet and empty, then stops. He's breathing harder than usual, and for a moment he stares beyond my shoulder. Then he looks straight into my face.

'I want to—' He stops. 'No, start again.' There's silence, and I see his eyes flicker a few times. 'Sorry. Mind's blank. OK, I'll take my inspiration from Terry.'

'Always a good idea,' I say, a bit nervously.

'"Don't doubt around all day." Remember that?'

'Yes!' I nod. 'Don't doubt around all day. Seize the wave.'

'Exactly. Seize the moment, I guess. Don't screw yourself up in a ball, thinking . . . hesitating . . .' He breaks off, his gaze directly on mine, then continues in a lower tone. 'I know what you were saying, on the beach yesterday. But I dodged it. I avoided replying. Because . . . Anyway.' He draws breath. 'Sasha, you're beautiful.'

The compliment comes out of nowhere, *woomph*, like a tidal wave.

'I . . . thank you,' I manage. 'You're—'

'No.' He lifts a hand. 'Let me finish. Beautiful inside and out. So strong. So inspirational. So funny. Such a good person. And so hot.' He pauses for a while, his eyes darkening, while I gaze back, transfixed. 'I missed the wave yesterday. I doubted around. Terry would give me hell.'

'Right.' I can barely speak. 'Well. Sometimes it's hard to judge the wave.'

'Am I judging this one right?' He gently touches my chin, and the world swirls around me.

'Yes,' I whisper, my whole face tingling. 'Although I took on board what you said on the beach. And I was wondering what the opposite of "casual sex" is. So I looked it up.'

'You looked it up.' Finn's face creases. 'Of course you did. What did it say?'

'I found "platonic love" and "dream crush" and "love without sexual desire".'

Finn's hand moves to my neck, finding the nape, caressing my skin. The sensation is so intense I close my eyes. My body cannot believe this. My body is *yearning* for this.

'None of those,' I hear him say, and I force myself to open my eyes.

'Then I found a different site and it said, "intimate sex".'

'Intimate sex.' Finn gazes at me a moment. 'Oh yes.' And then he lowers his lips to mine.

Oh my God. Stars are alive in my brain. I'm overwhelmed. I'm nothing but one hundred per cent sexual craving. His mouth, his skin, the smell of him, the touch of him ... I needed this. I need him, I want all of him.

Finn breaks away from me, heads to the door and closes it, then jams a chair under the handle.

'Here?' I say.

'Here.' I can see him eyeing up a velvet sofa and feel a squirm of anticipation. 'Now.'

'But what if someone comes in?' I can't help an incredulous laugh.

'Then we jammed the door by mistake. We're the not-couple, remember?'

He turns to face me and I can see he's hard (*thank you, universe*), and for a few moments we just stare at each other.

I get to have him. A disbelieving, giddy voice is singing in my head. *I get to have this man. This body. This experience.*

He takes me by the waist and presses his body into mine and at the feel of him I make a noise I don't even quite recognize. This is a kind of exquisite agony. I'm on the brink and we haven't even begun.

'A bar isn't intimate,' I say, as his mouth runs down my neck. My dress buttons are already slipping out of their buttonholes, the silky fabric is falling open and Finn makes a kind of guttural sound, his mouth finding my skin instantly. Then his hands are inside my underwear and I'm already riding the first wave, the waves I'd forgotten existed, but now I'm catching, again and again, shuddering against his chest.

At last I open my eyes and draw back to see Finn watching me, a tiny half-smile on his face. His shirt is damp and I peel it off him.

'That intimate enough for you?' he says.

'Not nearly.' I reach down for him and at my touch he inhales sharply, his eyes briefly closing.

'Me neither.' His face has a kind of distorted, almost drunk expression.

Applause breaks out from the adjoining dining room and we meet eyes with silent smiles as we peel off our remaining clothes and head to the sofa. As I see the full glory of him I send another message to the universe. (*Thank you. You have gone above and beyond.*)

He's brought protection and as he's sorting himself out, I wonder if he had it all along, or if he didn't because of the casual-sex thing? But then, what is this? Casual? Not casual?

It's sex! my brain screams. *Shut up with the over-thinking! It's sex!*

Meanwhile I've draped a tablecloth over the sofa, for the

full wedding-night look, and I arrange myself on it in what might possibly be an alluring position. Or not. But who cares? I'm just desperate for the real deal, now.

'Come.' I reach out my hands as he turns. 'Come.'

The sofa creaks under Finn's weight, and I pull him to me, breathing in the heady scent of him, nuzzling his chest, listening to his breathing intensify as his hands run down my body.

'Sasha . . . this *is* OK?' He says the words as though with monumental effort, and I pull him in for a kiss, cupping his face, running my fingers through his hair, loving him.

No. Wait. *Not* loving him.

Oh God. Loving him. That's the truth.

Tears suddenly edge my closed eyes. I love him. The universe sent him to me and thought, *Let's give her one she'll fall desperately in love with.*

Deal with that tomorrow. Finn's still waiting for my answer, beloved Finn.

'Yes,' I whisper. 'Yes. Yes.'

And then my mind is a blur and we're everything. All of it. Together.

TWENTY

When Nikolai sees us in bed together the next morning, he nearly collapses. His face drains of colour, he staggers, and the tray he's carrying wobbles precariously.

'Hi, Nikolai,' says Finn in an unconcerned voice. 'Put the coffee on the bedside table, thanks. And I forgot to mention, could you bring another cup for my guest? You know Sasha, don't you?'

'Morning, Nikolai,' I say, from the comfortable depths of Finn's bed.

Nikolai seems unable to reply. He opens his mouth three times, then appears to give up. Eyeing me warily, he makes his way to the bedside table, places the tray on it, then retreats.

'I can't believe you've been having room-service coffee all this time,' I say, as the door shuts. 'It never even *occurred* to me.'

'Live a little,' says Finn, grinning. 'This is the Rilston Hotel, don't you know?'

He pours a cup of coffee and hands it to me.

'That's yours,' I protest.

'Yours now.' He grins again. 'Maybe we'll have to share. I'm not sure Nikolai can face us a second time.'

Sure enough, when there's a knock at the door a few minutes later and Finn calls, 'Come in,' it's Herbert who totters in, bearing a single cup and saucer on a tarnished salver with a price tag dangling from it.

'Herbert!' exclaims Finn. 'Good to see you. Shall I take that?'

Herbert is silent for a few moments, his eyes shifting constantly between Finn and me, then he offers the salver to Finn, who removes the cup.

'Good morning.' Herbert finally speaks. 'Sir. Madam.'

'Good morning,' I reply, trying to smile at him, but Herbert dodges my gaze and hastily turns round. He heads to the door and as he exits the room I hear him saying, 'It's true, all right.'

'It can't be true!' Cassidy's muffled voice penetrates the door. 'What, just like that?'

'They are couple!' Nikolai's voice sounds impassioned, even through the door. 'I tell you, they have coupled!'

For a few minutes the conversation in the corridor dies down to the level of mumbles. Then there's a brisk knocking and the door begins to open.

'Good morning, Mr Birchall,' Cassidy's self-conscious voice greets us. 'I just wanted to check . . .' She rounds the doorframe, sees me in bed and stops dead, her eyes huge. 'I just wanted to . . . um . . .' She stops again, her gaze moving avidly from Finn's naked chest to my bare shoulders. 'To . . . um . . .'

'Check . . .' prompts Finn politely.

'Yes! Check the . . . um . . .' I can see her casting around. 'That the heating is satisfactory.'

'The heat situation is great,' Finn says, deadpan, squeezing my thigh under the duvet. 'Would you agree, Sasha? How's the heat for you?'

'Hot,' I say, swallowing down a laugh.

'It can always be hotter.' Finn's fingers are moving upward and I feel a blush come to my face.

'It's good.' I try to address Cassidy naturally. 'Thanks.'

'You two!' Cassidy's professional demeanour completely collapses into unvarnished glee. 'You two!' She points a finger at me, then Finn. 'I knew it! We should have had bets on it. I *wanted* to have bets on it,' she adds confidentially, 'but Simon was all like, "It's unprofessional to bet on whether the guests will shag or not."' She rolls her eyes. 'He's such a spoilsport.'

'Spoilsport.' Finn nods. 'I would have placed a bet. I wouldn't have given myself good odds.'

'Aww.' Cassidy's eyes soften, and for a moment I think she's going to sit on the edge of the bed and ask us how it was. But then she seems to remember where she is. 'Can I offer you breakfast in bed?'

'I'd love that.' Finn nods and turns to me. 'Would you love that, Sasha?'

'I'd love that.'

'We'd love that,' he says, looking back at Cassidy, and she gives another delighted beam.

'You see? You're "we" already. I knew, I *knew* it . . .'

She heads out of the room and as the door closes, Finn says, 'She didn't ask us what we want for breakfast.'

'Whatever.' I laugh. 'This *place*.'

'We're going to miss it when we're gone.'

'Don't say that! I've been institutionalized. This is home now.'

'You're never going to leave?' Finn looks amused. 'You'll have to get a job here, then.'

'I'll be the wellbeing consultant,' I say, remembering my conversation last night. 'No! I'll carry luggage. In fifty years I'll be the new Herbert. They'll call me Herbetta.'

'Herbetta.' Finn grins, then kisses my neck and I reach to pull him closer. The scent of him is intoxicating, and I rub my face against his skin. *Breathe in the scent of a hot man* should be on the list of twenty steps to wellbeing. In fact, after last night, I can think of a few other ideas. I could write my own '20 steps' and they could go in Mr Poppit's adult show.

'You're delicious,' I murmur, and Finn gives a rumble of a laugh.

'Never been called that before.'

'What have you been called?'

'Oh, workaholic, self-centred, nightmare.' He speaks lightly, but I draw back to stare at him, because that's quite a list. Who called him that?

But before I can ask, there's a knock on the door and Nikolai enters, bearing a tray. It holds a kale smoothie, an orange juice, a small posy in a vase and a sprinkling of red rose petals. It looks like something for Valentine's Day.

'Smoothie, juice for the happy couple,' he says, grinning widely. 'Enjoy. May I take your order?'

After we've ordered breakfast and Nikolai has retreated again, we exchange looks, then I burst into giggles. I lie back against Finn's chest, nestling into the crook of his shoulder, and gaze at the peeling ceiling.

'This hotel room is *really* manky,' I say, noticing a patch of damp.

'Thanks!' says Finn. 'Let's remember we agreed that my room was marginally better than the woodland creatures from hell.'

'That's not my point,' I say, smiling. 'My point is, this hotel room is really manky. I don't have a job. I don't know what's in the future. But I'm happy. Right now. In this moment.'

'Here's to that.' Finn kisses my head.

'What about you, burnout buddy?' I ask, so directly that he can't avoid the subject. 'What about your job? What about the anger and the sleep and the wanting to destroy vending machines? Where are you at?'

I also want to ask, *Who called you a workaholic, self-centred, or a nightmare?* Because I can believe the first one, but not the second two. But it seems tactless to mention it. I'll leave it for now.

'Work in progress,' says Finn, after a pause.

'What about sleep? You slept last night. A bit, at least,' I add with a smile.

'I slept pretty good.' Finn kisses me. 'Can't think why.'

'When are you having your first therapy?'

'Oh, that,' says Finn. 'I'm actually going up to London this afternoon, to see this therapist. Just overnight. I'll be back here tomorrow.'

'Wow.' I widen my eyes.

'She said we should have our first session in person. After that, we can Zoom or whatever.'

His mood seems to have plummeted. He's deeply apprehensive, I can tell.

'She'll only find good things, Finn,' I say, putting my hands either side of his face so he looks at me full-on. 'You're the kindest person I know. The wisest. The best.'

'You can't know many people, then,' says Finn with a

laugh. But I can see he's relaxed a smidge, and I pull him in for a hug. I'm manifesting the best possible therapist for him. Not just any old random person, the *best*. You hear that, universe?

'Are you decent?' Cassidy's voice comes through the door. 'Are you at it? Carry on, don't mind me, I won't look, just pull the duvet over!'

'Come in!' calls Finn, and I giggle.

'You two!' Cassidy exclaims as she wheels in a trolley full of food. 'Now, I've got your breakfasts and a little extra Buck's Fizz, compliments of the management, get you in the mood, *not* that you need it . . .' She beams at me. 'And I couldn't resist . . .'

She hands me a champagne flute stuffed with some sort of shocking-pink silky fabric. Taken aback, I pull it out and unfurl a thong. It's trimmed with black lace, and has *Loved Up* embroidered on it in turquoise.

'Cassidy.' My eyes fill with silly, sentimental tears. 'I love it. Thank you!'

'Aww.' Cassidy tilts her head on one side and surveys us fondly. 'We're all so thrilled for you! You didn't even want to be on the beach together! And Simon said he never thought you would, because—' She stops, as though realizing she's about to cross a line. 'But *I* always thought you would. I said, "*Look* at them!" And now, look at you! Well, enjoy!'

As the door closes behind her, I catch Finn's eye.

'*Look* at us,' I say, copying Cassidy's inflection.

'*Look* at us,' he echoes, smiling.

'Still wish I had the beach to myself, though,' I say teasingly.

'I hear you.' He nods. 'And just so you know, I have dibs on the rock today.'

'In your dreams!' I shoot back. 'You snooze, you lose.'

I watch as he gets out of bed and starts investigating the breakfast trolley, idly observing the movement of his back muscles and wishing my hands were on them.

'They forgot your eggs,' he says, turning round. 'But you could have a croissant, some melon and a random slice of black pudding?'

'Bliss,' I say. And I mean it.

TWENTY-ONE

It's mid-morning when I emerge from Finn's room, wrapped in a towel and sated in every possible way. My clothes are all in my room, so I saunter along there to get dressed, then stroll down to meet Finn in the lobby. As I descend the stairs, he greets me with a wink and a *you and me* smile that brings back every exquisite moment of last night. Not to mention this morning.

'Shall we see if the sand fairy sent us a message?' he says, and I laugh a bit nervously.

Last night, on impulse, we went out to the beach in the dark, lay on the sand for a bit and talked nonsense about the stars. Then, just as we were about to retreat inside out of the cold air, I said, 'Wait!' and found a stick. I gouged out *The couple on the beach* in letters in the sand, then drew a love heart around it. It was so dark, I'm not sure Finn realized what I was doing.

Now I feel embarrassed at having drawn a love heart. An actual *love heart*. I mean, Finn won't think ... ? Oh God. Maybe I can scrub it out with my foot.

But as we near the beach, I realize I'm too late. There's a woman I don't recognize on the beach, and she's staring down at the sand.

'Look,' I say to Finn. 'Someone's on our beach.'

'Someone's on *our beach*?' Finn adopts an expression of mock outrage. 'That won't do!'

'I know!' I join in. 'Don't they realize it's our private, very exclusive beach?'

'Hi!' he greets the woman, who is now in earshot. She turns to stare at us, and I smile.

'Hi,' I say, but the woman barely registers me. She seems riveted by the sight of Finn.

A possessive, prickly feeling is already rising in me and I tell myself off. It's very uncool to be possessive. It's also uncool to notice that she's very pretty, with her sleek black Puffa jacket, cropped jeans exposing a hint of ankle, and bouncy ponytail.

But does she *have* to keep staring at him like that? Even Finn seems to have noticed.

Also – hang on. Isn't she familiar? Now it's my turn to stare. I've definitely seen her somewhere. But where?

'Finn?' For the first time she speaks, in a husky, sexy voice. 'Finn Birchall?'

'Yes.' Finn looks confused. 'Sorry. Do we . . .?'

'Gabrielle. Gabrielle McLean. Used to be Gabrielle Withers. You don't remember. Well, why should you?' She gives a kind of incredulous laugh. 'This is so weird.'

'Remember what?'

'This.' She points to the message on the beach, and for the first time I look down. It's the same as when I wrote it last night. *The couple on the beach*, with a love heart around it. But

282

it's blurred now, and our mystery beach fairy has added another bouquet of flowers.

'What about it?' says Finn, and Gabrielle laughs.

'It's us!' she says, gesturing at him, then herself. 'It's for us. It's about us. We're the couple.'

What?

I'm sorry . . . *what*?

I want to say, 'Actually, I wrote that message,' but my face feels oddly paralysed. She seems so convinced. So confident. Who *is* she?

Finn looks dumbstruck, and Gabrielle seems to realize she needs to elaborate.

'Do you know a painting by Mavis Adler?' she says. 'It's called *Young Love*. Quite famous.'

'Ye-es,' says Finn warily.

And suddenly I know exactly who she is.

'You're the girl from *Young Love*!' I exclaim. 'I saw the newspaper cuttings. You got married to the guy you were kissing.'

'That's the story,' she replies slowly, her eyes constantly on Finn. 'That's the story.'

There's a silent, breathless beat – and then, in a heart-rushing swoop, everything falls into place. I *know*. I can see it. I can see him. His back. His head. *How* could I not have seen it before?

But incredibly, Finn still looks flummoxed.

'D'you remember the summer when you were fifteen?' Gabrielle addresses Finn directly. 'D'you remember a beach party here? We kissed behind the rocks. Quick teenage snog.'

'Right.' Finn's brow is crumpled, and I can tell he's trying to recall. 'Sorry, I don't—'

'Mavis Adler was here that day,' says Gabrielle. 'Painting.' She leans on the last word meaningfully and finally I see comprehension flash into Finn's eyes.

'It's *us*?' he says, looking stunned.

'It's us.' She nods. 'We're *Young Love*.'

'Jesus.' Finn breathes out. 'You're kidding. I've looked at that painting, what, a thousand times?' He seems dazed. 'It was me all the time?'

'So why does the world think it was you and your husband?' I can't help asking, and Gabrielle instantly looks chastened.

'That's my fault.' She breathes out and takes a few paces away. 'I was already going out with Patrick that summer.' She makes a face at Finn. 'Sorry. Didn't mention that. Anyway, Patrick and I were always snogging on the beach and he looked pretty similar to you from the back. When the painting was launched and everyone assumed it was Patrick, I just went along with it. Mavis had no idea who we were.'

'Pretty risky gamble,' says Finn, raising his eyebrows.

'I didn't realize the painting would end up so famous!' exclaims Gabrielle defensively. 'It was only after the Tate put it in a big exhibition that it all kicked off. Patrick and I were engaged by then! I'd already said it was us, I couldn't back down. So we ended up in the *Daily Mail*. Sorry,' she says to Finn again, biting her lip. 'It's been a bit of a money spinner. Personal appearances, videos, all sorts. I guess that would have been you, if I'd been honest.'

'Really.' Finn lifts his hand, looking faintly repulsed at the idea. 'That's fine. Carry on.'

'But you're telling Finn now,' I say curiously. 'Why?'

'Patrick and I are getting divorced.' Gabrielle juts out her chin. 'It's over. There's no reason to lie any more. That's why

I came to tell you,' she addresses Finn. 'I've had enough of lying.'

'So does Patrick know it's not him in the painting?' I can't help asking.

'He does now.' She looks shamefaced. 'I told him a couple of years ago, actually. He was pretty shocked. I don't know if that's what started our problems. Or did I tell him because I secretly knew it was over?' For a moment she's silent, and I see a mix of emotions pass across her face. 'Anyway, that's what this is.' She points at the message in the sand. 'It's fans. I'll show you. Mavis's assistant takes photos every year. She calls it Fan Activity.' Gabrielle takes out her phone and starts searching. 'You know there are *Young Love* tours to Rilston?'

'I heard,' I say.

'Well, they do beach messages, too. They do all sorts.'

She hands me her phone and wordlessly I scroll through a series of images. Couples re-creating the kiss in *Young Love*. Names written on the sand. I see *Young Love* written on the sand again and again, sometimes decorated with flowers.

'The messages started after Mavis did an exhibition of slogans on the beach,' explains Gabrielle. 'The super-fans follow her like a guru. It's nuts.'

'It's incredible,' I say at last, and hand the phone to Finn. 'It's a whole world.'

'Guess that painting speaks to a lot of people,' says Gabrielle, as Finn starts scrolling.

'Guess it does.' I nod.

'It spoke to me, when I first saw it,' she adds ruefully. 'I thought, "Shit! Busted." I was in the gallery with Patrick. He was like, "Oh my God, look, babe, that's us!" I panicked. I said, "Yes, it's us!" and that was it. Sorry,' she adds to Finn, biting her lip.

'Believe me,' says Finn, looking up from the images. 'I feel as though I've had a lucky escape. And I would be very happy if we keep this revelation to ourselves.'

'Fair enough.' Gabrielle shrugs. 'I'll keep schtum.'

'So how on earth did you know I'd be here?' asks Finn in sudden curiosity. 'You haven't been stalking me, have you?'

'No!' She laughs wryly. 'The truth is, I've been planning to find you for ages now, but I never did anything about it. Life gets in the way, you know? Then I saw your name on the guest list for the Mavis Adler event and I thought, no way! It said you were staying at the Rilston, so I went and asked and they said you'd probably be on the beach. I couldn't believe it would be so easy. If I hadn't found you this morning, I was planning to tell you at the event.' Her eyes drift down again to the message on the sand. '*The couple on the beach*,' she reads aloud, curiously. 'That's different. Normally they write *The young lovers*.'

'Actually . . .' I swallow, feeling embarrassed. 'Actually, I wrote that message.'

'*You* wrote it?' Gabrielle stares at me. 'But you're not a fan.'

'It wasn't . . .' I rub my nose awkwardly. 'It was a different thing.'

'But the flowers just appeared,' puts in Finn.

'Fans,' says Gabrielle. 'They do that.'

I can't explain my own reaction to all of Gabrielle's answers. Why am I so prickly? I should be thrilled. We've cracked the mystery.

But I secretly think she's wrong.

'We've been getting messages on the sand almost since we arrived here,' explains Finn. 'We thought it was . . . something else.'

Silently I get out my phone, find my folder of photos and

show Gabrielle all the messages on the beach. She looks at them without a flicker, then nods.

'Fans.'

Something inside me clenches rebelliously. She just sounds so dismissive. To her credit, Gabrielle seems to pick up that something's amiss, because she adds, 'What did you *think* they were?'

'The messages mentioned a date,' I explain defensively. 'It was the date of a big kayak accident that happened here, years ago. We thought it might be connected.'

'Oh, I remember the accident.' Gabrielle frowns vaguely. 'But who would write messages on the beach about that?'

'Don't know,' I admit.

'That's what we couldn't crack,' explains Finn. 'Tell me, did Mavis Adler paint *Young Love* on August the eighteenth? Because that would explain a lot.'

'Not sure,' says Gabrielle, after a moment's thought. 'It was August, but I don't know what date.'

'We also thought it might be Mavis Adler doing a new art project,' I put in.

'That's more likely,' says Gabrielle, nodding. 'Except she's moved on from the beach. She does weird metal stuff. And some secret thing called *Titan*.' She turns to Finn. 'Listen. I know you want to stay anonymous, but can we tell Mavis, at least?'

'What?' Finn seems unnerved. 'But won't she tell everyone?'

'No,' Gabrielle assures him. 'She doesn't even like talking about *Young Love* any more. But I've felt so bad, all these years, lying to her. And I think she suspects it was never Patrick. I'm seeing her for coffee in a minute. Would you come?' She looks at Finn pleadingly. 'She lives close by, it won't take long. And it'll be our secret.' Gabrielle makes a gesture to include me. 'Our secret.'

Finn glances at me. 'D'you think I should?'

'Of course!'

'Really?' He makes a dubious face. 'Is it necessary? Couldn't I just leave it?'

'Finn, you're in a world-famous painting,' I say firmly. 'You have a chance to meet the artist who immortalized you. You *have* to.'

'Come too,' Finn suggests to me, but I shake my head. I'm not going to wade into Finn's big moment with Mavis Adler – it's his thing. I'll admit that Gabrielle makes me feel twitchy – for lots of reasons – but if I can't trust him to go for coffee with her and Mavis, then that says something about me.

'No. This is about you, Finn. You're a celebrity now, you know that?' I add lightly.

Finn rolls his eyes. 'That's what I'm afraid of,' he says, but he sounds good-humoured. 'OK, let's go.' He addresses Gabrielle, then glances at me. 'Catch you later?'

'Definitely. Ask Mavis what date she painted *Young Love*!' I add quickly.

'Yes.' Finn nods. 'Will do.'

I watch as they walk away, then sit down on the sand, trying to process everything. Finn is the boy in *Young Love*. He's on my tote bag. He's everywhere, all over the world. I can't quite believe it.

Then I glance at the bouquet on the sand and feel a spurt of defiance. I know it makes sense that a Mavis Adler fan wrote all the messages. But I just don't believe it. I don't *feel* it.

I get out my phone again and skim through the photos of messages, reading them here and there.

To the couple on the beach. Thank you.

To the couple on the beach. Thank you again. 18/8.

You did everything. 18/8

Maybe I'm being stubborn or deluded. But they don't feel like fan tributes to me, they feel like actual messages.

'Talk to me!' I say in frustration, waving my arms at the words on the sand. 'What is all this?'

A moment later, I hear a scuffling sound behind me and I freeze. Is someone there? Watching me? I whip my head round and hear more scuffling. Oh my God. Are they in one of the lodges?

'Who is it?' I leap to my feet. 'Who's there?'

Breathing hard, I hurry to the lodges, bursting into mine first and looking all around. But it's still and empty. I try all the lodges, look behind them, then finally peer under the deck. There's nothing.

At last I sink down on to the deck and stare out to sea. Maybe I'm losing it. Maybe I just *wanted* 'the couple on the beach' to be Finn and me.

At the thought of Finn, a soft warmth creeps over me, and I sink back on my elbows, staring up at the cloudy sky. The truth is, none of this matters. I was in Finn's arms this morning, in his bed, in his heart. *That's* all that matters.

As my phone rings, I'm actually smiling, and when I see Kirsten's name, I feel a leap of happiness. Perfect timing.

'Sorry, sorry, sorry,' she greets me in her usual vigorous way. 'I've been meaning to ring, but it's been a hellish couple of days. And nights. Ben had earache.'

'Kirsten, don't worry about me!' I say at once. 'Get some sleep!'

'Mum's snowed under,' she continues, ignoring me, 'and I said I'd keep tabs on you. Which I've failed to do. How are you? *Please* don't say you're spiralling because none of your family loves you enough to pick up the phone.'

'Of course not.' I smile. 'I'm good. It's all great. Oh, by the way, I quit my job.'

I slip this last bit of news in casually, hoping I can turn it into a small, trivial non-event. But Kirsten clearly doesn't get the memo.

'You *quit*?'

'Yes.'

'Right.' Kirsten is silent for a moment. 'OK. Well, good for you. You need a break.'

'I'll find another job. I just need, you know. A breather.'

'Yes. I do see that.' She pauses again. 'You haven't done anything else drastic while we weren't looking, have you? Cut your hair off, got a tattoo?'

'No!' I laugh. 'But . . . but I have met someone. This amazing man.' A foolish smile spreads over my face. 'Oh God, Kirsten. He's just . . . he's . . . we're . . .'

I break off, because I can't explain. How can I explain? I don't want to spoil the magic that is Finn and me by dipping into my brain to find some bunch of words that will sound lame and prosaic even as I say them.

'Right,' says Kirsten, not sounding quite as captivated as I hoped. 'Wow. Who is he?'

'It's Finn,' I say, suddenly remembering that we've discussed him. 'Finn Birchall.'

'Obnoxious Finn Birchall who made a toddler cry?' says Kirsten incredulously.

'I was wrong about that,' I explain. 'He wasn't obnoxious, he just couldn't stand the noise. He was burned out, like me.'

'Burned out, like you?' echoes Kirsten in a weird-sounding voice. 'Sasha, you said you weren't going to sleep with him by mistake. Remember?'

'I didn't sleep with him by mistake!' I say indignantly. 'We've been helping each other. And then it went further. I know it sounds sappy, but it's like we were *meant* to share the beach. He came into my life just when I needed him.'

I hear Kirsten murmur *Oh God* under her breath, and prickle. What does *Oh God* mean?

'Anything wrong with finding love?' I say defensively.

'Don't get me wrong,' says Kirsten. 'I'm all for love. But Sasha, do you really think it's a good idea to be propping up some guy with problems when you need to be looking after yourself?'

'*Propping up?*' I echo in shock. 'That's not what— Finn doesn't even talk about his stuff. He's the one helping *me*. All I know of his problems is that he was swamped, like me, and he had brief anger issues and he wanted to chainsaw a ficus plant, but he's having therapy.' I realize I'm not exactly pitching Finn in his best light. 'And he's great,' I add feebly.

'*Chainsaw a ficus plant?*' Kirsten sounds flabbergasted.

'The ficus plant is irrelevant,' I add hurriedly. 'Basically he's a kind, sensible man who got derailed. He's a management consultant. And he can surf. And he got me interested in men again. In sex,' I add. '*Finally.*'

'Well, OK,' says Kirsten. 'I hear you. Hurrah for sex. Hurrah for love. I just don't want you to get hurt. It sounds like the pair of you are pretty vulnerable. If he's having therapy and you've been signed off work . . .'

She trails off into silence and I know she's deliberately holding her tongue, being as tactful as Kirsten can be.

'So you're saying it's a bad idea,' I say, to provoke her into speech.

'I'm not. Necessarily. I'm just saying . . . be careful. What if you're two needy, broken people and you're trying to mend yourselves through hooking up with another needy, broken person instead of . . . you know, mending yourselves?'

I feel a surge of indignation. Finn and I aren't two needy, broken people!

'I am not needy,' I retort stiffly. 'Nor broken.'

'I'm just concerned, lovely! You've quit your job, you've found a new man . . . It's a lot, Sasha. You were just supposed to get some fresh air and drink some whatsit juice.'

'Noni.'

'Exactly.'

Again there's silence, as we both regroup.

Maybe Kirsten has got a point. Maybe I have slightly lost sight of why I came down here.

'I'm glad you've left your job,' she says into the silence. 'But don't go straight into a brand-new job of "making someone else better".'

'I'm not!' I try to convey this to her. 'It's the other way round! He's making *me* better.'

'Well, is that optimal either? If he's got his own problems?'

Her words draw me up short, and I feel a wave of guilt. However much I've tried to draw Finn out, he's resisted. I haven't been able to help him. I still barely know what caused his insomnia and anger. Overwork, like me, or was there something more? Something his therapist will tease out of him?

'Oh shit, I have to go,' says Kirsten, sounding distracted. 'Ben, *not* up your nose. But listen, you took this break for yourself. *Yourself*. Keep that in mind.'

'OK. I will. Thanks for calling. Oh, just one thing, quickly,' I add. 'D'you remember why I talked to the police about that kayak accident?'

'Oh, that. Sorry, I meant to text back ... Ben, give it to Mummy *now* ... It was about a fire,' Kirsten adds to me over the sound of toddler protests.

'A fire?' I stare at the phone, bewildered.

'That's all I remember. You went to the police about a fire. You saw that guy Pete burning something? I really have to go. Bye!'

A *fire*?

I put my phone away, my head spinning. A fire? What fire? I shut my eyes, picturing a bonfire on the beach, a fire in a hearth, a house on fire ... But nothing feels like a memory.

Then *boom*. My eyes pop open. I remember! Yes! The fire in the bin.

I'm breathless. It's all come back to me in a rush. I saw Pete burning something in a hidden-away yard and that's why I went to the police.

I only saw it because I'd slipped away to the newsagent to spend a pound coin that I'd found on the sand. I went right to the back of the shop, to the vending machine, and I was just choosing my gum when I glanced out of the window and saw a fire. Pete was standing in some unused yard next door, poking the fire savagely. To be fair, he often looked kind of mean, but I noticed it particularly.

Still, I thought nothing of it, bought my gum, ran back to the beach, then heard the gossip that a life jacket had failed and that's why a boy had nearly drowned.

It was only in the middle of that night that I woke up and thought, *Oh my God! Pete burned the life jacket in that bin!* I went to Mum first thing and insisted I had to go to the police with important evidence. I guess whatever I said convinced her, because she let me go along and say my piece, even though Dad was feeling unwell and we were planning to leave.

But I'd blanked it. I've blanked so many memories from that time.

Now I can see it all, though. There was a fire in the bin – I glimpsed cardboard, papers, all sorts – and Pete was poking it with a stick. When I woke up in the middle of the night all those years ago, I thought I was a top sleuth – Pete had shoved the defective life jacket in there! But I was just a thirteen-year-old girl with too much imagination. Pete couldn't have been burning the dodgy life jacket, because the gossip turned out to be wrong. The life jacket wasn't faulty. The kayak was the issue. And how do you burn a life jacket, anyway?

I feel a warm wave of shame. The whole thing was clearly nonsense. I don't remember the police laughing at me, but surely they must have done. And now I see that police visit for what it really was – Mum giving me a thing. Giving me a moment of importance. A little boost.

Anyway, at least now I know, and I might as well tell Finn. I write him a quick text:

Just remembered what I told the police about – a fire in a bin. Pete was poking it. I thought it was evidence!! Hope you're having a good time with Mavis Adler. Xx

I send it and scramble to my feet. I want to walk along the beach and think hard. Kirsten's words are still bugging me. *Needy and broken.* Am I needy and broken? Maybe I was a tad broken. But I'm fixed now. Or at least, I'm fixed-ish. I've changed. I'm sure I have. I feel stronger. Happier. Sexier.

As if to prove a point, I stride briskly along in the buffeting wind until I'm all the way at the other end of the beach, by the steep cliffs. There I stop and survey the sea, and into my mind, as ever, comes Terry's hoarse voice. *Why are you worrying about the sea? The sea sure as hell isn't worrying about you.*

The sea isn't worrying about me. It's just crashing on to the beach, over and over, totally unconcerned. I swivel around to face the cliffs, which seem to look back at me with blank, impassive expressions. They aren't worrying about me, either. I find this reassuring. And suddenly I know exactly what Wetsuit Girl meant about 'grounding'. I'm aware that I'm standing on the earth on my own two feet. Not a soul in sight. Just me.

On impulse, I rip off my trainers and socks and let my bare soles squish into the sand . . . and I feel it. I understand it. The earth is supporting me. It's holding me up. Wherever I go in life, it'll be there for me. Like these cliffs and this beach and these million-year-old pebbles.

I can't quite believe I'm saying such woo-woo stuff to myself, but it feels real and convincing and comforting.

'Hi, Dad.' The words are out of me before I know what I'm going to say. I clear my husky throat and draw breath. 'I'm here. I'm back in Rilston. I'm . . . OK. I'm OK.'

It's years since I've spoken aloud to Dad. But now, as I stand there, my feet rooted in the sand, on this beach that he loved, too, I feel tears running down my face. The earth underneath me. Dad out there for me. Both of them will always be there. Whatever else happens. Whatever rocks me or hits me or buffets me.

The wind is getting steadily colder. But with every minute that I stand there, I feel stronger. Taller. More robust. I'm not needy and broken, whatever Kirsten said. I'm mending. I'm resilient. I'm standing barefoot on a winter beach, for God's sake! I'm tougher than I thought.

Spontaneously, I take a beaming selfie of myself to send to Mum, Kirsten and Dinah later. Then I summon up the '20 steps' app and gaze at Wetsuit Girl. Her smile doesn't seem smug any more, but warm and friendly. I'm grateful to her, I realize. She's been with me the whole time, and her advice was all good. I really am a whole new Sasha. Physically, I feel in better shape. Mentally, I feel in better shape. Maybe in better shape than I've been for years.

So now I need to sort my life out. Confront it, instead of running away from it.

The thought hits me out of the blue, and I blink in shock. Am I running away? Am I dodging the big issues? I couldn't stand my life. I wanted to leave. I couldn't cope with any of it. I just wanted to blank the whole thing, get some rest and recuperate.

But now, for the first time since I've got here, I can imagine myself back in London. Tidying my flat. Finally throwing out those dead plants. Getting on top of stuff. And, most importantly, working out what my values and priorities actually are.

I want to enjoy life again, I realize. Because life is the ride and the ride is *it*. You *have* to enjoy it. I imagine myself reconnecting with all my friends. Meeting up for a drink. Maybe even buying some food and cooking supper. Doing all the things I've been putting off, that felt so impossible.

And the weird thing is, none of it feels scary any more. It feels like a challenge – but a good one. The kind that makes you feel a pleasant rush of adrenaline, not the sort that makes you want to hide in a cupboard, whimpering.

I'd like to stay here all day, thinking this through, but it's late February and my toes are practically numb. So at last I swivel to head back to the Rilston. At the very least, I decide, I'll walk all the way with bare feet, then look back at my footprints on the sand and feel momentous and maybe take a photo.

But, oh God. I can't manage that either. It's *so* bloody freezing that after about twenty strides I cave in. I bend down to put my socks and trainers back on, and as I'm standing up again, I see a distant figure coming in my direction.

Finn? No. Not Finn. But a man. A tall, skinny man with . . . I squint. Is that a hat? No, it's his hair. His wild hair.

Wild hair which seems weirdly, impossibly familiar.

That can't be . . .

That isn't . . .

No *way*. I swallow hard several times, staring in disbelief. It is. Walking towards me, like some sort of weird beach mirage, is Lev. He's dressed in a waterproof parka, jeans and black suede trainers, which are already covered in sand. And he's looking straight at me.

'Sasha Worth?' he calls as he nears me. 'I don't know if you remember me. I'm Lev Harman.'

He's introducing himself to me? The founder of Zoose is *introducing* himself to me?

'I know,' I reply, feeling unreal. 'We met when you interviewed me.'

'Quite.' He nods. 'But you've just left Zoose.'

'Yes.'

'And you sent a twelve-page memo about the company.'

'Twelve pages?' I stare at him. 'No. I just filled out the form.'

'They printed it out,' he says, pulling a sheaf of papers out of his pocket and brandishing it at me. 'Twelve pages.'

'Right.' I rub my face, which is damp with sea spray. 'Sorry. Didn't realize I had so much to say.'

'You had a lot to say.' He surveys me intently. 'And I want to hear more.'

I'm almost too bewildered to reply. Lev read my midnight rantings? And he wants to hear *more*?

'How did you know where I was?' I manage.

'You typed the hotel name into the address box. I came here to find you and the receptionist said, "Oh, she'll be down by the sea."' Lev imitates Cassidy's voice perfectly. ' "She'll be doing her beach yoga and drinking kale." Are you doing beach yoga?' He surveys me curiously. 'Am I interrupting your beach yoga?'

'No.' I smile. 'I'm not doing beach yoga.'

'Well, then, could I possibly ask for some of your time? Because I've read this piece of brutal, razor-sharp analysis.' Lev shakes the sheaf of papers and gives me a rueful look. 'And I would *really* like to talk to you.'

TWENTY-TWO

This is surreal. Life has become surreal. I'm sitting on the beach with Lev Harman, founder of Zoose, and he's asking *my* advice.

We're side by side on the sand, facing the sea, and Lev is asking me detailed questions about all the points I wrote in my feedback. He's taking notes and he has his phone on Record, and he keeps gazing at me with a screwed-up expression, as though he's trying to burrow into my mind.

'No one else says this!' he keeps exclaiming. 'No one else— Carry on. Don't stop. What else?'

His questioning is persistent but exhilarating, because he *gets* it. He's quick. He's expressive. When I describe an inefficiency, he sucks in his breath. When I mention a frustrating incident, he smacks the ground in empathy.

At first, I try not to mention Asher by name. But it's harder and harder to keep saying 'the management' or 'it was decided' or 'the powers that be'. So in the end, I just come out with it.

'It's Asher's fault,' I say bluntly, as I describe the department understaffing. 'He has terrible rows with staff. Then he hides in his office and won't recruit replacements. And then, when he emerges, he launches yet another stupid, gimmicky initiative. It's all just big talk.'

I can't believe how openly critical I'm being of Asher, and I'm half expecting to get slapped down. But *God*, it's a relief to speak the truth. Finally. To someone who gets it.

Lev winces every time I mention Asher, and I find myself wondering how Kirsten and I would manage running a company together. Probably terribly. We'd probably kill each other. In fact, we *would* kill each other. So this is a good warning.

'And he won't listen to you?' says Lev, picking up a pebble from the beach.

'Listen?' I echo incredulously. 'Asher doesn't do listening. If you complain, his henchwoman Joanne refers you to the online aspirations mood board. It's part of the joyfulness programme.'

I know I sound snarky. I've possibly moved on from 'useful, professional feedback' to 'borderline bitching'. But so what? It's true. Just remembering it all is giving me the heebie-jeebies.

Lev is silent for a few moments, staring out to sea with a strange look. Then he nods, as though he's decided something, and turns to face me.

'I'd like to apologize for your experience at Zoose, Sasha. It was . . . it is . . . a travesty. We should not have lost you.' His face crinkles with incredulity. 'Am I right, you actually ran away from the office and crashed into a brick wall?'

'Oh, that,' I say, feeling a bit mortified. 'That was no big deal . . .'

'You had to go to hospital?'

'Well, you know. It was precautionary.'

'You decided to become a *nun*, rather than work for Zoose?'

I feel a jab of embarrassment. Was every humiliating detail of my little episode noted and shared with the whole company?

'Nun was just an option I was exploring.' I try to sound casual. 'I needed a break, really.'

'But you didn't just have a break,' Lev replies. 'You quit completely. Why? Why quit?'

He gazes at me expectantly, as if he's hanging on my every word. As if he's trying to solve a puzzle. As if he's asking not as a boss, but just as a fellow human.

'I had to change things,' I say frankly. 'I'd been too afraid to. I was clinging on to the status quo, even though things were getting worse and worse. Once I took action, it was scary – but then I felt released.'

Lev nods several times, his eyes distant. And I wonder: what puzzle is he trying to solve? Is it the puzzle of himself? Of Zoose? If it's that, I can tell him at least one obvious answer. Finn realized it, too.

But maybe firing his brother is even harder for Lev than quitting my job was for me. I feel a wash of sympathy for him, because, let's face it, having Asher as your brother must be bad enough to start with.

'It can be hard to take decisive action,' I volunteer cautiously. 'Especially if it involves . . . maybe . . . a family member.'

Lev glances defensively at me and I keep a neutral expression. I'm trying to convey *safe space* and I think he gets it, because he seems to relax.

'I know Asher is . . .' He breaks off, looking despairing. 'Sub-optimal. But he's been there since the start. He's my *brother*.'

'It must be difficult,' I say, and Lev gives a weird little laugh.

'Between you and me, everything's difficult.' He stares at the horizon, exhaling slowly. 'Growing a company as fast as we have is incredible, fantastic, wonderful . . . but terrifying. You need to find more capital. Look after your existing business. Find new customers. All at once. It's relentless.'

There's a note in his voice I recognize. It reminds me of someone, only I can't place it . . . Then, with a jolt, I realize. He reminds me of me. He sounds overwhelmed.

'I think Zoose is in great shape generally,' I say. 'The concept, the profile, the sales . . . oh my God! It's a massive success story. Let's just say a couple of individuals have bent it out of shape, here and there.'

'I need to get rid of Asher.' Lev stares ahead, his face taut. 'I know it. I've known it for a while. But I don't *want* to know it.'

'If it makes you feel any better,' I venture, 'I told someone here about it, a consultant. He agreed.'

Lev is silent, and I wait, breathlessly, wondering if I've overstepped the mark.

'I don't know if that does make me feel better,' he says at last. 'But it may do later. So thank you.'

I don't have anything else to say, and Lev seems lost in thought, so we sit in silence, the sea crashing endlessly on to the sand and the gulls crying overhead. After a while, I sense Lev relaxing.

'Thank you, Sasha,' he says. 'For your time. And your wise words. We didn't speak much while you were at Zoose, and I'm sorry about that.'

'I'm not sure I had any wise words at Zoose,' I say honestly. 'I was too frazzled. But since coming here, I've had time to think. Just watching the sea . . . It gives you answers.'

'I hear you,' says Lev, his gaze on a high, cresting wave. 'It's spectacular. Is this what you've been doing every day, watching the sea?' He checks himself. 'I'm so sorry. What am I asking? It's none of my business.'

'It's fine . . .' I begin, but he shakes his head fervently.

'No, I apologize. Bad enough that I drag you away from your beach yoga, sit you down on the sand and make you talk about your least favourite company in the world. Now I'm asking intrusive questions. No wonder you left Zoose.'

His manner is so charming, I can't help smiling.

'First, Zoose is *not* my least favourite company in the world. I was very proud to work there. It just didn't . . . gel. And secondly, yes, I have been watching the sea. And walking. And all kinds of things.' A tiny smile comes to my lips before I can stop it.

Falling in love. Rediscovering sex. Standing tall on my own two feet.

A breeze catches the back of my neck and I shiver, whereupon Lev leaps up.

'You're freezing!' he exclaims. 'I'm so sorry. You've been very helpful and now I must let you get on with your day. I do have a big favour to ask, though. Would you speak to a few other directors about everything we've discussed?'

'Yes.' I nod without hesitation. 'I'd be glad to.'

'They're in Somerset at the moment, about an hour away. We're having a mini conference. Would you come there tomorrow? I'd pay you a consultancy fee and travel expenses,' he adds.

'A *consultancy* fee?' I stare at him.

'I would be consulting you,' says Lev. 'It's customary.'

'Well . . . OK.' I smile at him. 'Yes.'

'Great.' Lev smiles back. 'Thank you. I'm very grateful.'

We begin walking back towards the Rilston in companionable silence and I feel a fresh whoosh of disbelief as I think,

I'm walking along the beach with Lev. When I think of the frustration and rage I felt when I couldn't get to speak to him at the office, three floors up. And then he came all the way to Devon to find me!

As we near the Surf Shack, I see that it's open. A guy I don't recognize is on the deck, sweeping sand off it, and I realize this must be the new owner.

'Hi,' I greet him as we get near.

'Morning!' He gives me a twinkly smile. 'Want to rent a board?'

'Not right now.' I smile back. 'But maybe later. I used to learn with Terry,' I add. 'I'm Sasha and this is Lev.'

'Hello there.' He shakes our hands. 'I'm Sean. Terry's around, if you want to say hello?'

'Yes!' I say eagerly. 'I'd love to!'

'He's just gone inside. Terry!' Sean calls into the shack. 'You there?'

'Terry was my surf teacher,' I tell Lev. 'And he's the most awesome person in the world.'

'The most awesome person in the *world*?' Lev raises his eyebrows. 'OK. I have to meet him.'

'It's true,' Sean joins in, nodding. 'He taught me, too. Taught everyone. Taught us everything.' He raises his voice again. 'Terry, some friends here to see you!'

A moment later, Terry appears on the deck. He's wearing a fleece jacket and a woolly hat and there's a plaster on his chin. He looks even frailer than he did the other day. But I force myself not to react at his appearance. He's still Terry.

'Terry!' I say, stepping forward. 'It's me, Sasha. And this is Lev.'

'Of course it is!' Terry says. 'Good to see you both again!' His blue eyes dart around uncertainly. 'Now, you've both surfed before, haven't you? Because the beginner class is full today.'

'Yes, we've surfed before,' I say, nodding. Then I turn to Lev and murmur, 'He's not quite . . . Just go with it.'

'I've never surfed,' says Lev, ignoring me. He steps forward and engages Terry's gaze intently. 'I know nothing. What can you tell me, Terry? The single most important thing I should know.'

For a few moments Terry looks bewildered, and my heart wrenches. But then a sharpness returns to his eyes.

'You still don't remember, after all these lessons?' He addresses Lev tetchily. 'You haven't learned the most important thing? Are your parents paying for you to stare at the sky all day? Am I wasting my time?'

'Sorry,' says Lev humbly. 'Tell me again. I'm listening.'

Again, Terry looks momentarily caught out – but then he frowns impatiently.

'Well, look, look, look. You know it really. You all do.' He sweeps his arm as though addressing a class. 'You have to enjoy the ride. Why else are you learning to surf? The ride is *it*.'

'Enjoy the ride,' echoes Lev, and a strange half-smile spreads across his face. 'Of course. How did I forget that?'

'The ride is *it*,' says Sean, winking at us.

'The ride is *it*.' I smile back at him.

'But where are the others?' Terry's gaze drifts along the empty beach and he frowns, looking distressed. 'They're all late. Class should have begun ten minutes ago. And where's Sandra got to?' He swivels around in confusion. 'Have you seen Sandra?'

'She's fine, Terry,' says Sean quickly. 'She just had to pop out. But I'm not sure the class is happening, after all. Maybe tomorrow, mate.'

A light in Terry's face slowly dies away. He looks around the deserted beach, then nods, as though accepting something he has no control over. He looks defeated, and I feel an overpowering sadness. I don't know how aware Terry is of his situation, if he can really tell what he's lost. But right now, he looks desolate, and I want to give him back something. Anything.

'Terry, I'm here!' I exclaim impulsively. 'I'm here for class. I just need to go and change into my wetsuit. Can I still rent a board?' I add quickly to Sean.

'Sure,' says Sean, looking taken aback. 'But . . .' He glances at Terry and back at me. 'You're not serious?'

'Terry's up for teaching,' I say simply. 'And I'm up for learning. There's the sand.' I gesture. 'There's the sea. Let's do it.'

'I'm up for learning, too,' says Lev firmly. 'Can I rent a suit and a board?'

Sean looks a bit freaked out. 'OK, listen, if you're really doing this . . . this is *not* a lesson.' He glances at Terry. 'This is *not* insured. This is nothing to do with me.'

'Understood.' I nod.

'Then go for it.' Sean's face crinkles in a smile. 'Maybe I'll join in. Let me get you both boards.'

As I jog back to the lodges, I'm looking around for Finn, but I can't see him anywhere, so I send him a text and hope he'll get it in time.

Surf's up. Class is on at the Surf Shack. Terry says you're late. X

It's like going back in time. It could be the old Terry teaching us. It's unbelievable.

As he runs through the familiar warm-up routine, yelling instructions all the while; as he makes us lie down and paddle on the sand; as he gets us crouching and standing up . . . it's Terry. He's assured, he's funny, he has gimlet eyes and notices every error.

'Look, look, look,' he keeps saying to Lev. 'You're going to need to be strong. Got it?' He jabs him in the stomach, and Lev wobbles on his board. 'See? That's no good. You need to be *strong*.' His gaze drifts away down the beach. 'Now, who's this?'

I turn to see – and my heart lifts. It's Finn, in his black wetsuit, running along the sand with his board. He meets my eyes with a kind of disbelieving *What the hell?* expression, and I smile back.

'You're late!' I call.

'Sorry,' says Finn. 'Sorry, Terry.'

'Sorry is no good, young man!' Terry calls to him, exasperated. 'Sorry is no good! You're not warmed up, you've missed the basics . . .'

'I'll catch up,' says Finn quickly, then walks right up to Terry. Despite everything I've told him, I can see he's shocked at Terry's frail appearance but trying to hide it. 'How are you doing, Terry?' he says. 'I'm Finn. Finn Birchall, I don't know if you remember me—'

'You're *late*, is who you are,' says Terry crisply. 'So I wouldn't be wasting time on words if I were you.'

'Fair enough.' Finn grins. 'Glad nothing's changed.'

'The board is rigid, do you understand?' Terry slaps his board for effect. 'It's helpless. Without your skill it would get tossed about on the waves. But luckily, you all have superpowers, let's call them *surferpowers*.' He twinkles at us, knowing he's got everyone's attention. 'So use them! Your surferpower is flexibility.' He points at Finn, and I remember how he sometimes used to do this: give us 'surferpowers' before we went in the water. 'Yours is perseverance.' He points at Sean. 'And yours is vision,' he tells Lev. 'Eyes forward!'

'Eyes forward!' repeats Lev, who is standing stiffly on his board, looking totally uncomfortable in his surfing stance. 'Got it!'

'What's mine?' I can't help asking. I know it's needy, but I'm worried Terry will drift away and forget me. And I really want a surferpower.

For a moment Terry gazes at me with that blank, bewildered look, and I'm afraid I'm too late – but then he snaps back.

'Yours is love,' he says, as though it's obvious. 'Can't surf without love. Why do we get in the water in the first place? Why do we keep on trying, paddling, wiping out, picking ourselves up, going out there again?' He turns to survey the ocean. 'Because we love it.'

There's a silent beat as Terry stands there, a frail old man, surveying the ocean he's spent so much of his life in, while we all watch him. And suddenly I'm blinking hard, because I hope he realizes it's not the waves we're loving right now. It's not the waves that brought us here today. It's him.

Should I tell him? Say something?

But already he's wheeling round to us, exactly like the old Terry, and the moment's gone.

'OK, kids,' he says, and points to the ocean. 'Enough talk. Go get it.'

TWENTY-THREE

An hour later, I'm sitting with Finn in the shallows, his arm around me, our legs tangled up together. I can't stop smiling. In fact, I think I've been smiling solidly for an hour. My face will be stuck like this for ever.

'The *waves*,' I say wonderingly.

'I know.' Finn grins. 'Incredible. Thanks for texting me.'

'Oh God, of course,' I say. 'You couldn't miss Terry's special guest appearance.'

The lesson has long since finished. Sean has left the sea to get on with stuff in the Surf Shack. Terry has been collected by his friendly carer, Deirdre, and we've all clasped his hand, thanking him. Lev has had one too many wipeouts and is now getting dressed in the Surf Shack. It's just Finn and me on an empty beach again.

He leans in to kiss me, his mouth salty from the sea, and I run a hand through his surfy hair. If I could just kiss this man for ever, on this beach, I'd be OK. Why can't life just be kissing on beaches?

'What time do you have to leave for London?' I murmur.

'Not till three. So.' He meets my eyes with a glint. 'Plenty of time.'

'Maybe you could help me off with my wetsuit?' I bat my eyelashes at him. 'They're *so* difficult to manage.'

'I'd be delighted. Turn around . . .' Finn reaches for my zip and slowly pulls it down my back. 'How's that?'

'Thanks,' I say, unpeeling the top half of my wetsuit. 'That's better.'

Finn nods, then casually reaches out a hand and tugs down my swimsuit strap. 'And this is even better,' he says.

Already I'm aching for him. I'm forensically measuring the time it will take us to get from here to the lodge, rip our wetsuits off and make use of the sofa. Or the floor. Or whatever.

Except I guess I should say goodbye to Lev first. I turn to see if he's out of the Surf Shack yet, and see Sean watching us in amusement.

'Hi, Sean,' I call out, expecting Finn to take his hand out of my swimsuit. But instead he moves it to my breast.

'Stop it!' I manage, trying not to lose it as he caresses me. 'We're— Stop! People can see.'

'I want to get a room,' Finn says against my neck. 'Now. Shall we go?'

'I have to say goodbye to Lev,' I say. 'He's my old boss. He came to find me. I can't just scoot off.'

'*Fine*, have a life,' says Finn, in such deadpan, comical tones I laugh.

'You can talk! How was Mavis Adler, anyway? Was she shocked to meet you?'

'Not at all,' says Finn, finally removing his hand from under my swimsuit. 'Her exact words were, "Well, about bloody time! I always knew it wasn't Patrick. Wrong-shaped head."'

I can't help laughing. 'So she's just been going along with the lie, too.'

'Guess she didn't want to break up a marriage.' Finn shrugs.

'And what about Gabrielle?' I speak carefully, aware that I'm not entirely rational about Gabrielle, but Finn looks blank.

'What about her?'

'You didn't try to re-create your famous kiss, or anything?' I attempt a light, casual laugh.

'God, no.' Finn looks appalled, and I feel a whoosh of relief.

I need to stop being paranoid. I need to relax. The universe brought Finn to me. It wouldn't immediately reallocate him to someone else, would it?

'Anyway, I've promised to go along to the art event tomorrow night,' says Finn. 'We could go together, maybe.'

'Definitely!' I say, and I'm about to pull him in for another kiss when Lev's voice heralds us both.

'Sasha! Finn!'

I clamber to my feet to see that Lev is fully dressed in his jeans and parka, his hair damp, his cheeks still pink, and a brightness in his face which I recognize as post-surfing buzz.

'I'm off,' he says. 'See you tomorrow, Sasha. And thank you for everything. The wisdom, the surfing, the introduction to Terry . . . all of it.'

'See you tomorrow.' I nod. 'And thank *you*. For listening to what I said.'

'Of course,' says Lev gravely, and turns to Finn. 'Nice to meet you.'

'Good luck,' says Finn. 'With everything.'

We watch Lev head off over the beach, then Finn turns to me.

'I know you have many important meetings to conduct,'

he says politely. 'And I need to get in line. But now, seriously, can we go and get a room?'

By the time we've reached my lodge, Finn has unpeeled his wetsuit to the waist and I'm tugging my swimsuit down, too. I'm so desperate for him, I'm not thinking straight. We pull down the blind and barricade the door with a chair, and I'm looking around at our furniture options when Finn steps forward and cups my hips, still tightly encased in neoprene.

'What I *really* want,' he murmurs, 'is to cut this wetsuit off you. Bit by bit.'

I feel a flare of excitement inside, immediately tempered by a price tag.

'Too expensive,' I manage, my voice thick, and Finn's mouth twitches.

'Thought so. But one day.'

One day. As he pulls me closer, the phrase dances through my mind like sparkle dust. *One day my Finn will come*. But he's here, right here. My beloved Finn.

The sex is even better than last night. How can it be? Last night was perfect. But somehow it is. More prolonged, more edgy, more . . . sublime. Finn's imagination goes to places I wouldn't have guessed. In fact, I'm having to reassess him. And myself. And what sex can be.

And you know what? If the whole of the Rilston staff are lined up outside, listening to us, let them. Enjoy the show! Sell tickets! I couldn't care less.

At last, we lie on a makeshift mattress made of cushions, panting, dazed, letting the world come back into focus.

'So,' says Finn, his voice slow and low, as though all the tension has drained from him. 'The trouble with these new fancy-pants glass lodges is, where will people have sex?'

'Yes.' I nod. 'It's a design flaw. We should let the architect know.'

I nuzzle into Finn's delicious skin, breathing him in, wishing we had more time, but knowing we don't.

'I have to go,' says Finn, as though reading my mind. 'Therapy calls.'

'Of course.' I raise myself on an elbow, remembering Kirsten's words and feeling a flicker of apprehension. 'Hope it all goes well.'

'Thanks.'

'You know, if I can ever help . . . talk anything through . . .'

I keep my eyes fixed on Finn's face and watch how he closes up, turns his chin away. And for the first time, I feel a pang of actual hurt. Why won't he let me in? Why won't he let me help him?

'Thanks for the offer,' he says at last, sounding so reluctant that I feel a flare of something perilously near resentment. If we really are two vulnerable people, getting better – or whatever – then shouldn't we try getting better *together*?

'Maybe your therapist will tell you to talk to close friends,' I suggest. I have no idea if this is likely, but it's a way to prod him.

'Maybe.' Abruptly he gets to his feet and starts putting his damp swimming trunks back on. He's blinking fast and he looks quite stressed, and I suddenly feel guilty for feeling anything like resentment.

'Finn, you don't have to struggle on alone,' I say gently. 'You can tell me. Whatever's gone on.'

'I appreciate it,' he says with a nod. 'Thanks.'

My heart sinks. He sounds so formal. He could practically be dictating a work email. But if I press him, he'll just retreat more. I know it. I'm already sensing his patterns.

What's your puzzle? I think, gazing at him wistfully. But he'll tell me when he's ready, and now all I can do is be here for him.

'Meeting you has been the best thing about coming here,' I say. 'The *best* thing.'

'You too.' As he turns, his dark eyes are so warm and affectionate, I can't believe he was holding out on me a moment ago. 'Sasha, you're incredible. And I'll see you when I get back. Are you coming up to the hotel now?'

'No, I'll take my time,' I say, getting to my feet. 'You shoot off. And good luck.' I stand up and wrap my arms around him, trying to give him all the love and support he needs through physical touch. 'Good *luck*.'

'Thanks.' He kisses me one last time, then heads out of the lodge, and I sink down on the sofa, already counting down the minutes until he'll be back.

It takes me a while to pull myself together. I eat a Twix to restore my energies, then stare up at the ceiling for a bit, then wonder what to do for the rest of the day. Everything feels a bit hollow, now Finn's gone.

But at last, I wrap myself in a towel and decide I'll take a long, hot bath in my woodland-creature bathroom, which I have actually got quite fond of.

As I walk through the lobby, clutching my clothes, the phone on the desk starts ringing and I look around for someone to answer it. Cassidy is nowhere to be seen, nor are any of the other staff. So in the end, I dump my clothes on the reception desk and reach for the receiver myself.

'Hello, Rilston Hotel.' I find myself imitating Cassidy's voice and give an inward giggle.

'Oh, hello!' A breathless female voice greets me. 'I was

hoping to speak to someone about sending something to a guest. Is there a Finn Birchall staying with you?'

'Yes, he's a guest here,' I say, before wondering if I'm breaching the Data Protection Act. Oh well, too late. 'Can I help?' I add.

'Well, I was *really* hoping to send him a gift basket,' says the woman. 'I'm a colleague of his. Is there a hotel hamper or something I could order?'

I stare at the phone, agog. A colleague of Finn's? Every one of my nerve endings has pinged on to high alert. Maybe I can find out something about him. Or even *everything* about him.

But will this colleague reveal any details about him to a member of the hotel staff? No, surely not. I need to correct that misunderstanding.

'Actually, I don't work for the hotel, I'm a guest,' I clarify. 'But I'll talk to them, and I'm sure they can arrange something. Obviously, Finn's been really stressed recently, so I'm sure he'll appreciate it. I'm a friend of his,' I add casually. 'We've become quite close. Confidants, in fact. So I know a lot of . . . what went on.'

'Oh, thank goodness!' she exclaims. 'Well, I can ask you, then. Is he all right? Because we've been very worried.'

'He's fine,' I say reassuringly. 'He's on the mend. As much as he can be, after . . . what happened.'

'I'm so glad,' says the woman. 'We're all so fond of Finn. We miss him!'

My mind is feverishly taking notes. They're 'all so fond of Finn'. And they miss him. Even though he slammed his coffee cup down, punched a vending machine and threatened a ficus – despite all that, they miss him. So there's more to the story. I *knew* it.

'Has he spoken about it much?' she continues sympathetically.

'Not really,' I say honestly.

'Well, why would he?' She sighs. 'Heartbreak is always painful. And when it's a glorious, perfect couple like Finn and Olivia . . . I'm not surprised he had a delayed reaction. We could all see he was under strain for weeks.'

Hmmmrgh?

My fingers have frozen around the phone. My vision has gone a bit blurry.

Finn and Olivia? Glorious, perfect couple?

Heartbreak?

I have to speak, I realize. *Speak, Sasha.* Speak, or this conversation is over and I'll never know anything else.

'I know what you mean.' Somehow I'm forcing words out of my mouth. 'These things just don't seem real, do they?'

'Exactly!' the woman exclaims. 'We all thought they'd get married! I mean, the *chemistry* between them . . . you could just feel it! I used to say to my husband—' The woman breaks off. 'You haven't met her, have you?'

'No,' I say, my voice light and lilting. 'Remind me of her full name? I was trying to recall her surname.'

'Olivia Parham. She hasn't been down, has she?'

'Not as far as I know,' I say, and the woman sighs again.

'Oh, that's a shame. I was so hoping they would . . . you know. Patch it up. She's *so* good for him and he's always been hopelessly in love with her. Well, I'm sure you know that, if you're his confidante.'

'Absolutely.' There's a weird, rictus smile plastered on my face. 'No secrets between us.'

'She brings out the best in Finn, you know?' says the

316

woman, who is clearly wanting to chat. 'She balances him out, somehow. I mean, she can be quite direct, but he needs someone robust. The number of times I've heard her call him a workaholic. And he needed to hear it, believe me!' She breaks into laughter and I seize up still further.

Workaholic. Self-centred. Nightmare.

It all falls into place.

'Sometimes people just don't belong together,' I say, trying desperately to get some control of this conversation.

'Oh, I know that,' says the woman wistfully. 'But not Finn and Olivia. I don't know *what* went wrong, after ten years together.'

'Ten years!' Just for a moment, my composure slips. 'Ten years,' I repeat, my throat clenching up. 'Absolutely. It's baffling how a . . . a successful relationship like that could go wrong.'

'Well, as I say, I'm sure it's just a temporary little blip,' says the woman. 'We're all still expecting invites to the wedding! His assistant Mary has already bought her hat! Will I see you there, too?' She laughs, a warm, friendly laugh, and I know I should join in, but I can't, I just can't.

'Who knows?' I say shrilly. 'Should be fun, anyway. Anyway, I must go, I'm afraid, but if you give me your name, I'll get the hotel staff to call you about a hamper.'

'You're very kind!' exclaims the woman after I've scribbled down her details. 'And I'm so glad Finn's got a nice friend down there looking after him . . . Oh, I never asked. What's your name?'

I feel a spasm of panic and swallow several times, thinking how to play this.

'Don't worry about me!' I say at last, easy-breezy. 'I'm nobody. Goodbye!'

I put the phone down and stare ahead, my heart heavy with sadness, feeling everything crack around me.

No wonder he didn't talk much about his burnout. That's not why he came here. He came here after a bad breakup and that's why he assumed the same of me when he saw the ice-cream tubs in my lodge.

I suddenly remember him staring out to sea, saying, *Heartache. Burnout. Breakup. Fuckwit bosses.*

I glossed over *Heartache.* I glossed over *Breakup.* But he was telling me something. He had a broken heart.

That evening I sit on my bed, hunched over my phone, wretched. I've pieced it all together, from remembered snippets of conversation, from Google search, and most of all, from Instagram. Not his, hers. He doesn't do Instagram. He just does the odd businesslike Tweet about his consultancy. But Olivia obviously loves taking photos, loves sharing them, loves engaging with her family and friends in chatty comments . . . and why wouldn't she, with such an attractive face, such a great sense of humour, such a gilded life?

It's not gilded in a conventional sense. That's the worst of it. It's not glossy or glamorous or stage-managed. It's just warm and down to earth, with photos of her and Finn and family and dogs and barbecues and a new nephew in a onesie and cheesy Christmas sweaters under the tree and . . .

After a bit, I have to stop scrolling. I've gone back seven years of their life, gazing at every moment, even watching Olivia's sister's 'baby's first Christmas' video because it's so damned adorable. This is ridiculous. It's tragic. I'm not supposed to be doomscrolling. I've promised myself I won't. Yet with every photo I see, the doom increases. That colleague on the phone was right. Finn and Olivia are a glorious, perfect couple with a hinterland, a past, a joined-togetherness that I can only marvel at.

Then it ends. The photos dry up, bar one image of Olivia in silhouette, with a million loving comments, broken hearts and kisses from her friends, underneath. That must be when they split. Two months ago.

So they've had a blip. What kind of blip I can't imagine, except that it made Finn distraught and angry and unable to sleep. Angry at her? Angry at himself? How would I know?

But ten years. *Ten years*. It makes my heart ache. You don't give up on that in a hurry, even if you have a blip. You have the blip, the row, the moment of madness, the stand-off – and then you go back to normal. You re-commit. You realize what you're in danger of throwing away and you go and grab it again.

Finn and Olivia will grab each other again. I know it. I see their faces together – happy, connected, relaxed – and I *know* it. If he's been manifesting anything on the beach, it's that. It's her. His desolate eyes make sense. His anger at the world makes sense. It all makes sense now.

No wonder he didn't tell me. No wonder he didn't want to rewind something so painful. Now I think back, he just mirrored whatever I said. He said he was overworked, like me. Burned out, like me. He was just saying whatever would close the conversation down the quickest.

And, of course, the biggest proof of all is, he didn't want to have sex. At this thought, I close my eyes and tears seep out. No wonder he didn't want casual sex – he was still nursing a battered heart. But I guess the truth – the truth I wouldn't even admit to myself – is that I hoped it would be more than casual. It would be serious. It would be the beginning of something strong and long-lasting. The beginning of us.

319

Maybe somehow Finn realized that – and that's why he turned me down. He wasn't ready for the beginning of us, when his heart was still in turmoil over the end of him and Olivia.

I don't blame him for changing his mind. I'm *glad* he changed his mind. Oh my God, am I glad. I've found sex again, and it was incandescent, and nothing can take that away from me. But I do blame myself for seeing it as anything other than what it was: two strangers comforting each other. Two needy, broken people. Kirsten was right. I can't bear it, but she was right.

I sink my head into my hands, my face soaked with tears now, because I've been so deluded. So *stupid*. I've been trying to find all the answers in other people. First I latched on to Wetsuit Girl. Then I latched on to Finn.

At that moment, my phone buzzes and I stiffen, because it's a message from him.

Therapy was great. Intense. Finn x

I quickly type out a response and send it:

I'm so glad! Good for you! X

As my phone buzzes with his name again, I feel guilty. I've been watching his entire life with Olivia, like some sort of movie, and he has no idea. He's never told me Olivia's name; he's not tagged on Instagram. If it hadn't been for that phone call, I wouldn't have known where to look.

It's kind of surreal, that I know so much and he's oblivious. But I can't tell him what I've found out. I *won't* tell him.

If there's one thing I'm one hundred per cent resolved on, it's that.

I'll tell you about it tomorrow. Looking forward to getting back.

What will he tell me? Some edited version of his life, with no Olivia or breakup or any of it? Another tear runs down my face and I brush it away furiously as I reply:

Definitely! Can't wait to hear.

I send it and stare at my phone, feeling physically drained, my mind still turning. If Finn was ready to move on, he would have told me about Olivia. Hinted, anyway. Shared something. But he's been secret. Silent. Resolute. Can I be with a man who's still hung-up on another woman?

I let the question sit in my brain – but I already know the answer. Not now. Not with everything else. Not when I'm trying to rebuild my life.

Finn's already sent another message, and I can't stop myself opening it.

Btw I meant to tell you, I saw that fire, too. Pete was burning some stuff in a bin. In a yard, yes? I was in my cousin's house, saw it out of the window. Snap.

Hang on a minute.

I gaze for a while at the screen, grateful for the distraction. Finn saw it, too? We both saw the same random event in a hidden-away back yard? That *can't* be coincidence. In spite of everything, my heart starts thudding. Could this be linked to the messages on the beach?

Then I deflate. Even if it is, what am I going to do about it? Finn thinks the messages were written by *Young Love* fans. He's only answering to be polite.

And more crucially: why would I start up some new conversation with Finn when even thinking about him makes my heart crumple?

We were like two children on the beach, playing with our messages and mysteries. But the way I fell in love was grown-up. Grown-up hurt. Grown-up disappointment.

For a few moments, I'm consumed by a sadness that seems to tear at my insides. Then I sit up straight, wipe my face, and deliberately turn off my phone. With quick, almost urgent movements, I throw on a coat, head out of my room, down the stairs and out of the lobby.

I don't stop walking until I reach the beach. I walk straight down to the waves, then stare out at the horizon. The vast sky is inky dark, peppered with more stars than I've ever seen. The waves are washing quietly in the moonlight, as though recouping their energies for tomorrow.

And as I stand there, soaking in the magical sight, my sadness is already less sharp. I feel stronger. More resolute.

I thought I was at the beginning of something beautiful, but instead I was in the middle of another couple's blip. I just didn't know it. Well, now I need to start something else beautiful. Something that I can make beautiful, without relying on anyone else. The rest of my life.

TWENTY-FOUR

The next day, as I sit in the lobby of the White Hog Hotel in Somerset, I feel as if I've already made a start. I've just spent an hour talking to Lev, Arjun the COO and a board member called Nicole, in a special conference room they've taken for the day.

It was extraordinary. They were respectful. They were humble. They listened to everything I said. And at the end of the meeting, Lev asked me to come back and work for Zoose. That one stopped me in my tracks. Go *back*? Go back to the hell-hole of hell?

I obviously didn't hide my thoughts very well, because Lev glanced around the room then, added quickly, 'That's something you'll want to consider in your own time, Sasha. But between these four walls, Asher is . . . considering moving on. So there will be a vacancy in his position, and we thought perhaps you could fill it.'

It took me a moment to work out what he was saying.

Replace Asher? Replace the Head of Marketing? Become the boss of the department? The *boss*?

Me?

For a moment I felt light-headed. I felt exhilarated. I felt the kind of soaring ambition I thought I'd lost for ever. Then, five seconds later, the crashing reality hit me. Boss of the understaffed nightmare department that everyone wants to leave?

'Is there a budget for more staff?' I blurted out, and there was a huge laugh.

'Straight to practicalities,' said Nicole and I flushed, realizing I should have asked what the salary was. Or told them I was fielding attractive offers from all their major competitors. Well, there we go. Too bad. In my next life, I'll know all this stuff.

'Believe me, Sasha, there's a big budget for more staff.' Lev nodded. 'There has to be. Things have to be different. What do you think?'

'What do I *think*?' I said, determined to be totally honest. 'I think everything, all at once. It's a big leap. It's *massive*. It's flattering, but it's a huge job. A huge deal. And I've only just managed to switch off. So . . . I don't know. It might take me ages to decide.'

'We'll wait,' said Lev at once. 'We'll wait.' He looked at Nicole, then back at me. 'We'll wait.'

Now I'm waiting for my taxi to the train station, still a bit stupefied. Could it work, for me to go back to Zoose? Could it be part of a beautiful new life? Are the two things compatible? Voices in my head keep putting forward arguments, and I keep finding answers for them. I'm not even close to a decision yet, but I'm slowly working my way there.

The department's a nightmare. But if I were running it, maybe it wouldn't be a nightmare.

I can't go back to the way I was working. So I'd change things. Lev said it himself, things have to be different.

I'm burned out. I'm exhausted. I'm overwhelmed. But will I be for ever? Already I feel so much more energized than I did.

Am I strong enough to do the job in a healthy way? Switch off emails, take breaks, go on holiday? Yes. The emphatic thought catches me by surprise. Yes, I am. Because I have to be. My body didn't burn out for no reason. It basically told me, *Slow down, there's no alternative.*

'Your water, Madam.' A discreet waiter in a sleek grey uniform places a glass at my side.

'Thanks.' I smile at him, and he nods. This hotel is very hip, with stylish furnishings and staff who look like super-models. It's exactly the kind of place that Zoose *would* go to for a conference – and the exact opposite of the Rilston. The receptionist isn't embroidering thongs, or gossiping about the other guests, or flogging antiques. Nor could I imagine any of them playing the French horn.

To be honest, it's more fun at the Rilston, and I feel a pang of longing. I want to be back there, with Cassidy and Simon and Nikolai and Herbert. With the creaky floors and the rickety beach lodges and the waves. And Finn.

Finn.

I feel a surge of pain and shut my eyes for a moment. Then I deliberately turn my thoughts away. I can't let myself dwell. I'll see him when I get back. I know exactly what I'm going to say, I've planned it. And then . . . we'll see.

I get up to check on my taxi – then jump as I see Joanne striding into the hotel, talking loudly on the phone. Shit. *Shit.* I immediately want to run in the opposite direction – but I can't. Not this time.

She's wearing one of her relaxed luxe trouser suits and designer trainers, and is flicking back her hair.

'No, *kindness*,' she's snapping crossly at someone on her phone. 'I told you, the *kindness* project—' She breaks off and stares at me.

'Call you back.' She puts her phone away very slowly, and I can see her mind spinning.

'Sasha,' she says at last. 'What the hell are you doing here?'

For a moment, I hesitate. How much do I say? But Joanne's expression has already cleared.

'Oh my God,' she says scathingly. '*Don't* tell me you want your job back.'

'I was just . . . thinking about it,' I say truthfully.

Joanne's eyes snap in triumph.

'I knew it! I said, "She'll be back." I suppose that's why you're here.' Her disdainful gaze flicks over me. 'What were you planning to do, ambush Lev again?'

'No! Actually—'

'And what, we're all supposed to overlook the way you behaved?' Joanne cuts across me. 'You think you can just turn up and we'll put aside your unprofessional conduct? I heard you typed a load of gibberish on your exit form. I gather *my* name was mentioned several times. Were you drunk?'

'No.' I glare at her.

'Well.' I can see Joanne getting into her stride. 'If you want *any* chance of working for Zoose again, Sasha, I'm afraid we're going to have a few stipulations. I'm going to need an apology for your behaviour. I'm also going to need some evidence of your commitment to the company wellbeing philosophy,' she adds menacingly. 'I might devise a special programme for you. And *don't* expect that you can just speak to Lev whenever the mood takes you. He's a very busy and important man. He doesn't have time for—'

'Sasha!' Lev's voice interrupts us and I turn to see him hurrying into the lobby, along with Arjun. 'So glad I caught you, I thought you might have left. I just wanted to thank you again for your time. We're hugely grateful to you, aren't we, Arjun?'

'Absolutely,' says Arjun. 'Very good to meet you, Sasha.'

'And we do hope we can lure you back to Zoose,' says Lev, grasping my hand tightly. 'Whatever it takes. Whatever you need. Spending time with you has been . . .' He seems to cast around for a word. 'Profound. Yes. Profound. Ah, Joanne,' he adds, seeing her. 'You know Sasha. Sasha is the secret to our future success. If we can persuade her.'

Joanne is speechless. Her eyes are bulging. She opens her mouth, makes an indistinct sound, then closes it again.

'We know each other,' I say. 'I'd better go.'

'Well, I'll see you soon, I hope,' continues Lev, apparently oblivious to Joanne's discomfort. 'Let me know when you're back in London and we'll have lunch. And give my best regards to Finn. And of course Terry! The *meister*. You have to meet this man,' he enthuses to Arjun. 'Surfing teacher. Genius. Philosopher. We should get him to give a motivational talk. Oh, your taxi's here, Sasha. Safe travels.'

'Bye, Lev,' I say. 'And thanks for your offer. Bye, Arjun. Bye, Joanne,' I add politely.

But Joanne doesn't reply. She still seems dumbstruck. In fact, she looks a bit green. *Ha.*

I make a mental note of her expression, to cheer myself up with later. And then I make another mental note: to talk to Lev about Joanne. The prospect of her as a colleague again is nearly enough to make me turn down his offer, so we'll need to discuss that. And lots of other things, I should think. I'll start a list.

On the train, my phone lights up with Mum's name and I answer at once.

'Mum!'

'Sasha! Darling, how *are* you? Kirsten says you've left your job. Well, now, that's tremendous news. Tremendous. What a good idea. Fabulous.'

Mum sounds so ridiculously upbeat, I want to giggle. I just *know* Kirsten's given her a pep talk about not sounding negative.

'Yes, I've left.' I hesitate. 'For now.'

'Marvellous. Very good. And how's the Rilston? How's the sea view?'

'It's great,' I say, thinking of the moonlight on the waves I was gazing at last night. 'It's a magical place. I feel like I've transformed.'

'Sweetheart.' Mum's voice softens. 'I'm so glad. I've been thinking about you a lot. Thinking about us. Remembering.' She pauses. 'Maybe we should go to Rilston Bay as a family, one of these summers. All of us.'

'I'd like that.'

'Kirsten says she's found some old photos. She said they brought it all back. She wants to bring Chris and the children, rent a cottage. Carry on the tradition.'

I have an image of Ben and Coco toddling in the shallows, smooshing ice creams into their faces, maybe even having surf lessons one day . . . and feel a swell of joy.

'Yes! Let's do it.'

'So, what are your plans now? Are you staying there much longer?'

'No,' I say, after a moment's thought. 'I'm coming back soon.'

'Now, Sasha,' says Mum at once. 'Don't rush yourself. You're always a one for rushing.'

I'm a one for rushing?

'I'm not. Really. It's been great, but I need to . . . re-engage. See some friends, hang out with Kirsten, tidy my place up.'

'Well,' says Mum. 'If you're ready.'

'I'm ready.' I nod, staring out of the train window, watching fields go by. 'I've done everything I came to do.'

After we've said goodbye and rung off, I hesitate, my phone in my hand. Then, on impulse, I open the Tesco website and log into my account, barely used over the past two years. I'm going to do a shop. A proper supermarket shop. I'm going to buy *ingredients*.

I click on onions. Stock. Carrots. Turkey mince. Come on. I can do this. I can run my life.

When my basket's full, I survey it with a kind of pride. Not many people would call a Tesco online basket a thing of beauty, but right now, this is all part of my new life. Where I look after myself. Where I value myself. And it looks beautiful to me.

TWENTY-FIVE

After twenty minutes of the Mavis Adler art event, I've honed my line, which is 'Stunning, isn't it?'

To be fair, the art is stunning, in a metal girders kind of way. The pieces are strewn around the massive ballroom, looking pretty incongruous against the peeling damask wallpaper and tattered curtains. They've all got titles, but I couldn't say what any of them are supposed to mean.

But so far, I've held my own in conversations with a lady from Sotheby's, a man from some Cork Street gallery and a local journalist. It seems most art experts are happy to spout on endlessly about their own opinion. So my method is: let them do that while I get on with drinking the free champagne. And when they pause, say, 'Stunning, isn't it?'

Works a dream.

Cassidy is bustling around in a smart black dress, ordering the catering staff about, and she keeps catching my eye conspiratorially as though we're family, which makes me feel ridiculously happy. Nikolai has brought me a kale cocktail, which I've discreetly disposed of. The place is so crammed that I haven't yet spotted Mavis Adler, although I've seen Gabrielle surrounded by people wanting selfies, and Jana sitting behind a table, dispiritedly trying to sell catalogues.

'Sasha!' A voice greets me and I turn to see Keith Hardy, wearing a linen jacket and startling pink paisley cravat. 'Good to see you, young lady! Still enjoying yourself, are you?'

'Yes,' I say. 'Very much so.' There's a pause, so I add, 'Stunning, isn't it?'

'The art? Keith wrinkles his brow. 'Wouldn't know. Looks like a building site to me. But see that?' He jerks his head towards the huge draped structure on a podium. 'That's the new one.'

'Yes, I know.' I peer at the form, intrigued. It's obviously a statue, about twelve feet high, but it's hard to see what it might be.

'All the council are hoping it's a statue of *Young Love*,' Keith says confidingly. 'Bring in new visitors, boost the economy. Like a sequel. *Young Love 2*, kind of thing.'

'But it's called *Titan*,' I say dubiously.

'Could still be the lovers kissing,' says Keith, undeterred. 'Like the *Titanic*. Kate and Leo.'

'Well, maybe . . .'

'Sasha!' Another familiar voice greets me and I swivel to see Hayley and Adrian West, dressed up smartly, holding champagne flutes.

'Hi!' I say, taking in their happy, flushed faces. 'I haven't seen you around!'

'We've been . . . busy.' Hayley leans into Adrian, giggling. He nibbles her ear, whereupon she giggles some more. 'Ade!'

'Can't help it,' he says, smirking. 'Gorgeous wife like you.'

'So things are good?' I say.

'Really good,' says Hayley, and leans forward to breathe quietly into my ear. 'Thanks so much. To both of you. I don't know *what* you said to him . . .'

'Oh, it was nothing,' I say hastily. 'Just a conversation.'

'Well, it was the right conversation.' Hayley clasps my hand briefly. 'We've upgraded to the four-poster suite. Comes with butler service!'

'Really?' I'm intrigued. 'Who's the butler?'

'Nikolai. He puts on a tailcoat – keeps it on a hook in the corridor. Does his best, bless him. We haven't wanted much, though. Just a bit of room service.'

'*Do not disturb*,' says Ade, pinching Hayley's bum. 'Know what I mean?'

'Got you.' I nod. 'Loud and clear.'

'Oh, and we bought your hula hoop!' adds Hayley brightly. 'Haven't used it yet, though.'

'My what?' I say, confused.

'Your hula hoop? "Recommended by Sasha"?'

'*What?*'

'On the app.' Hayley peers at my blank face. 'The Rilston app. Don't you have the app?'

'I . . . um . . . something went wrong,' I say. 'My notifications stopped. What's "Recommended by Sasha"?'

'You don't *know*?' says Hayley incredulously. She gets out her phone, searches for something, then hands it to me, and I see a series of texts from the Rilston app.

Welcome to the Rilston Hotel health range, as recommended by our resident wellness guru Sasha Worth! Yoga mats and hula hoops are available to buy or rent at reception (limited supplies). #RecommendedbySasha

Follow Sasha's lead and do beach yoga on our glorious
sands!! Available every day, no charge.
#RecommendedbySasha

The 'Rilston' kale smoothie is now available. Created
especially for resident wellness guru Sasha Worth, it
combines health with flavour. Give it a try!
#RecommendedbySasha

Remember, Kickback Night is a vital part of your wellness
break. Half-price tequila shots at the bar tonight!!!
#RecommendedbySasha

Maybe I should be angry, but all I can do is laugh.

'I wanted to ask,' Hayley is saying now. 'Have you done an
online hula-hoop tutorial?'

Have I done an online hula-hoop tutorial?

'No,' I manage. 'Sorry.'

I guess I'm an influencer now. Maybe I could get a deal
with Club biscuits. Or White Wine, no vintage. And now I
really can't stop laughing, because it's all so ridiculous, so
Cassidy, so *Rilston*, that when I see Simon approaching me, I
almost want to give him a hug. He seems even more flus-
tered than usual. He's breathing hard, his shirt is all
skew-whiff and his hair on end, and as he gets near, I ask
anxiously, 'Simon, are you OK?'

'I have unfortunately just had to eject Mike Strangeways
the magician from the premises,' he says, looking harassed.
'It became a rather unseemly encounter—' He breaks off,
frowning as though something's puzzling him, then reaches
into his collar and slowly pulls out six colourful silk handkerchiefs, tied together.

'Very nice!' I applaud, but Simon looks stricken.

'May I assure you, that was *not* deliberate. Clearly in my recent tussle with Mike Strangeways, one of his magic props made its way into my apparel.' He holds the silk handkerchiefs fastidiously away from himself with his fingertips. 'Ms Worth, these are not the high standards we expect of ourselves at the Rilston, and I can only—'

'Don't apologize.' I cut him off, with sudden fervour. 'Please. *Don't* apologize. Simon, your hotel is wonderful. Unconventional, maybe . . . but wonderful. I've had the most amazing, transformative stay here, and if I could give you ten stars on Tripadvisor, I would.' I gaze at him earnestly. 'All the stars. *All* the stars.'

'Ms Worth!' Simon seems overcome. 'My goodness.' He rubs his face, then pulls out a fresh hanky from his pocket and blows his nose. 'Well. That is very kind of you.'

'I wish you every success. All of you.' I gesture around the faded ballroom. 'With the Skyspace Beach Studios, with the next season . . . everything.'

'You sound as though you're not planning to stay with us for much longer?' ventures Simon.

'You're right.' I smile at him. 'I think I'm coming to the end.'

'Well, I hope you enjoy this evening all the more.' He nods pleasantly and bows – then as he catches sight of something, his face tenses up. '*What* is Cassidy doing with that helium canister? Ms Worth, please excuse me . . .'

He darts off through the crowd, and I watch him fondly. I'm going to miss this place. But already, mentally, I'm checking out.

To my left, there's a slight hubbub around a grey-haired woman in a scarlet linen smock dress, and I realize this is the famous Mavis Adler. I watch for a moment as people clasp her by the hand, craning to hear every word she says, and wonder what it must be like to be her. Finn would have had a piece of that attention, if he'd only come forward—

Then, just as though thinking about him has made him appear, I hear Finn's voice, and an arrow goes through my heart.

'Sasha.'

I take a breath before I turn. He bends to kiss me and I clasp him close. I inhale the scent of him deeply, wanting to savour this *us* for ever.

I allow myself five precious seconds. Five seconds of Finn and me, in our bubble, with all the questions still unasked. But then I force myself to draw away. It's time to have the talk.

Old Sasha would have put it off. Clung to the status quo. Avoided anything challenging or hard or hurtful.

But new Sasha knows what she has to do.

'How was therapy?' I begin.

'Good.' He nods. 'Heavy duty. Kind of exhausting. How've you been? How was the meeting?'

There's so much to tell him. About my job, about Joanne, even about #RecommendedbySasha . . . But there's only one conversation I need to have right now.

'All good,' I say. 'Finn, I was wondering . . .'

'Yes?'

I take a sip of champagne, playing for time, my lips trembling. Everything depends on this.

'I never properly asked you,' I say lightly. 'Why exactly did you get so angry? What was the *source* of your stress? Was it work? Or . . . something else?'

The door is open. Wide open. If he wants to tell me now, he can.

'Work,' says Finn promptly. 'Overwork. Lack of sleep. Like you.'

'But what *led* to the overwork?' I press. 'What *led* to the lack of sleep?'

Instantly Finn looks evasive and slugs his drink.

'It was . . . a difficult situation,' he says at length. 'Things were really hard.'

Torment has come into his eyes, as though he's in a place I can't reach. That's not the look you get when you're over-worked. It's the look you get when your heart is twisted up by love. He's twisted up, I can tell. He's not mended, not healed, and not nearly ready to find love with anyone else.

'What kind of difficult situation?' I force myself to ask, and Finn starts as though he was completely lost in thought for a moment.

'Well. Like yours, I guess. Having to take on the work of other staff, because of . . .' He trails off vaguely and my heart shrivels. He's just mirroring what I said.

'Did you speak to your manager about it?' I ask, and Finn's eyes swivel.

'Not really. Should have done, I guess.'

'But that was the main issue?' I persist. 'Understaffing at work? Or . . .?'

A kind of desperation has come to Finn's face. 'It was . . . I don't know. Things were difficult.'

I gaze at him silently. If my eyes could talk, they'd be say-ing, *Finn, you can't hide from me. You're keeping her a secret. You're keeping it all a secret. You're not ready to move on.*

'Where are the drinks?' adds Finn, looking around as though he has a burning need to escape, and I feel a wave of compassion for him. Because here's the thing. I never actu-ally asked him, 'Are you in love with someone else?' My bad.

Maybe next time I ask the universe for a man, I'll know better.

I have two options. I can reveal. I can demand to know. I can tear down this tender friendship we have, for the sake of . . . what?

Or I can act with dignity.

'So, I was thinking,' I say. 'We need to be careful.'

'Careful?' Finn looks confused.

'We've both been burned out. We've both been through bad times. We both need to sort our lives. And this has been so great.' I gesture from him to me. '*So* great.' I sound for all the world like a kind, confident woman letting a man down lightly. 'But, Finn, we can't be each other's sticking plaster.'

'Sticking plaster?' He looks aghast. 'That's not . . . I don't see you as . . .'

'I know. But maybe this isn't . . .' I swallow. 'Maybe this isn't such a good idea. After all.'

I lapse into silence and see the emotions pass through his eyes – shock as he understands, followed by resistance, acceptance, sadness. Each one makes me want to cry out, 'Only joking!' But I stay motionless, resolute, the strong one.

'Right,' says Finn at last, his voice heavy. 'I mean, I get what you're saying.'

'You should focus on your therapy.'

And your heart. And your shattered relationship with the love of your life.

'I guess.' He nods. 'I just thought . . . we were having a good time.'

'We were. It was amazing.' Tears are pricking my eyes. '*Amazing.*'

'Sasha, are you OK?' His eyes are searching my face anxiously, as though for answers. 'Was it . . . us . . . a mistake?'

Yes, because I'm spoilt for anyone else, for ever.

'Of course not. It was . . .' I shake my head. 'Sublime.'

'That's how I feel, too.' He grasps my forearms. 'Sasha, I respect what you're saying. I do. There are issues. But do we have to be so hasty? Could we talk?'

I gaze up into his perplexed face, seeing the tension etched in every fine line. There's an unhappiness there that I never detected before. A big, private unhappiness that I can't soothe.

'Look after yourself, Finn,' I whisper, feeling my throat constrict.

For a few tense moments he just stares at me desperately, as though casting around for the way to make this not happen. Then, with a sigh, he gives up.

'Look after yourself, too.' He releases my arms and runs a tender hand down my cheek. 'Let's both look after ourselves, OK?'

'OK.' I nod, my face stiff with a not-real smile. 'It's a deal. I'll manifest it. *Finn's wellness.* I'll write it on a piece of paper and keep it in my pocket and the universe will grant it.'

'I'll do the same.' His face contorts itself into the same kind of miserable, effortful smile as mine. 'I'll write *Sasha's wellness* on mine.'

'It's bound to work.' I force a light tone. 'Manifestation is on the "20 steps" app, after all.'

'The app never lies,' affirms Finn.

Somehow we're edging back into a safe place, where our emotions are tucked away, where we can joke and make eye contact and my heart doesn't feel shredded.

'Do you want another drink?' says Finn. 'I'll get us both another one.'

He turns away, as though he needs a breather to pull

338

himself together, and I exhale. There. Done. Band-Aid ripped off.

Skin raw.

Heart a mess.

But it'll heal. *I'll* heal. Let's look at what I have to be grateful for. I have my Tesco order and I have my job offer and I have my beautiful life to make . . . Plants to throw away . . . I must buy Coco a birthday present . . .

My thoughts break off as I see Terry's daughter Tessa hovering a couple of metres away.

'Hi,' I say, and gesture around. 'Stunning, isn't it?'

I wait for her to make some remark in return, but she just keeps on gazing at me from behind her curls, in that imploring way she has.

'I hope you didn't mind,' she says at last, her voice low and anxious.

'*Mind?*' I echo, baffled. 'Mind what?'

'I know it was a bit strange, only I *couldn't* just come up and . . .' She looks warily around, then lowers her voice. 'Dad wouldn't let us talk about it. Ever. Even years later.'

'Tessa . . .' I stare at her. I'm getting the weirdest feeling. My head is prickling. Everything's coming together in my mind. Tessa takes a step forward, her big-eyed gaze still on me, biting her lip nervously.

'But then I saw your names.' She seems consumed by some emotion. 'You were back in Rilston. Well, I couldn't do nothing.'

'Tessa . . .' I swallow several times. 'Did you write the messages on the beach?'

'Of course.'

'Right.' I try to stay calm, even though I feel a bit overwhelmed. 'I see. It was you.'

'Of course it was me. I thought you knew.'

She seems quite matter-of-fact. But at the same time, she's got such a twitchy manner, I feel as though she might skitter away at any moment. I need to tread carefully.

'You wrote, *To the couple on the beach. Thank you*,' I clarify. 'Was that addressed to . . . both of us?'

'You and Finn,' she nods. 'Joint.'

I'm feeling an almighty surge of exhilaration. I was right! It wasn't a Mavis Adler fan. It was a series of messages to Finn and me, exactly as we first suspected, and there's only one small question remaining.

'But, Tessa . . . *why*?'

'*Why?*' She seems perplexed. 'Well . . . because of what you did. Because you saved Dad.'

'We saved Terry?' I stare at her, bewildered. 'What do you mean?'

'You told the police what you saw,' she says simply. 'Both of you came forward, told the same story. Honest-sounding kids, no reason to lie. It changed their minds. Sasha Worth and Finn Birchall.' She pauses, with a reminiscent smile. 'Sandra's best friend was in the police and told her your names, though she shouldn't have. Sandra always wanted to find you, say thank you, but you weren't here the next year.'

'Neither of us have been back for twenty years,' I say slowly, then look up as Finn approaches.

'Finn, let me introduce our sand fairy,' I say, and watch in satisfaction as his jaw sags. 'It *was* to do with the accident, after all. We changed the police's minds, apparently. You and me!'

'Changed the police's minds?' Finn looks thunderstruck.

'They thought it was Dad's faulty kayak at first,' Tessa explains. 'Pete tried to stitch him up, good and proper.'

'But I still don't get how we helped,' I say. 'I went to the police with some ridiculous story about a life jacket, when it wasn't even the life jacket that was faulty. How could that have changed their minds?'

'The life jacket wasn't the point,' says Tessa. 'The *fire* was the point. You both saw Pete poking a fire, and that got them thinking.'

'So what did Pete do, exactly?' asks Finn. 'Do you know?'

'Pretty much,' says Tessa. 'First of all, during the accident everyone was on the beach, looking out to sea, trying to help. No one was minding the Surf Shack. So Pete slipped in and stole Dad's log book, records, old packaging even, anything he could think of. Went and burned the lot. Because he knew Dad's records were meticulous, and he needed them not to be available. Then he went to the police and spun his story. You know how Dad and Pete sometimes helped each other out, lent each other boards and equipment? Pete had loaned the kayak to James Reynolds, but he swore blind it was from Dad's stock. Said Dad had vouched for its safety. Got in there quick. Tried to pin it all on him.'

'Ridiculous,' says Finn shortly. 'Terry's equipment was never anything other than immaculate.'

'Yes, but he couldn't *prove* it,' says Tessa. 'Because the record book had disappeared. And Pete could be pretty convincing when he wanted to be. The gossip was already starting on the beach, doesn't take long.' She draws a deep breath. 'Anyway. Then two kids told the police how they'd seen Pete burning stuff in a bin. You two.'

I have a flashback to that moment. Idly looking out of the shop window. Catching sight of Pete's taut face as he poked at what must have been Terry's rental book in the flames.

'He *was* getting rid of evidence,' I say, suddenly feeling thirteen years old again. 'I *knew* it.'

'Was Pete prosecuted?' says Finn curiously.

'Never got that far.' Tessa replies, shaking her head. 'Once the police started asking the right questions, his assistant Ryan freaked out and blabbed the lot. Pete got a rap on the knuckles and a visit from Health and Safety. But he lost business. No one in town would recommend him. The gossip was out there. He closed down. Left Rilston Bay.' She pauses. 'If you two hadn't spoken up, that might have been Dad. He might have lost the Surf Shack. Twenty years more teaching he had, because of two children. You two.'

Finn is silent, and I feel a bit speechless myself. My mind roams back over the messages on the sand, and I find myself wanting to ask questions.

'How did you know we were here?'

'Cassidy sent over the names of two guests at the Rilston who wanted to visit the caves. Sasha Worth and Finn Birchall. I couldn't believe it!'

'But why didn't you just come up to us?'

'Dad hated us talking about the accident,' says Tessa, her face turning red. 'We had to forget it ever happened. I didn't want to start a conversation in public. It just seemed easier to thank you silently. Secretly. I thought you'd understand straight away. But then I heard you talking at the caves and I realized you hadn't made the connection, so the next time I added the date.'

'But you wrote "To the couple on the beach",' I say, still flummoxed. 'You didn't know us. Why did you think we were a couple?'

'I saw you arguing,' says Tessa, looking surprised. 'Shouting at each other on the beach. You sounded like a couple.

And I thought, "Oh, the children who saved Dad fell in love."
It felt right.' She pauses, her brow wrinkling. '*Aren't* you a couple?'

I can't look at Finn. My eyes feel a bit hot, and I'm wondering if I'll need to make an excuse and leave, when a fruity voice behind me booms, 'Tessa, what did you just say? The children who saved Terry? What children?'

I swing round to see Mavis Adler looking avidly from me to Finn to Tessa. She has a whisky glass in her hand, her fingers are covered in traces of clay and she smells of tobacco.

'Hello, Ms Adler,' I say quickly. 'Congratulations on your exhibition, it's stunning.'

'What children?' demands Mavis Adler, ignoring me.

'These children!' Tessa gestures from me to Finn. 'Only they're grown-up now.'

'Well, I know *one* of them,' says Mavis, giving Finn an almighty wink.

'And this is Sasha,' Finn says, hastily gesturing at me.

'They're the ones who pointed the police in the right direction after the kayak accident,' Tessa says. 'If it hadn't been for them, Dad might have lost everything. I was just saying thank you.'

'My goodness!' Mavis grabs first my hand, then Finn's. 'I remember that incident well! And as an old friend of Terry, I'm absolutely delighted—'

'Ladies and gentlemen!' Jana's voice interrupts us and we all turn our heads to see her on the small stage. 'Welcome to the launch of *Figures*, a new collection by Mavis Adler.' A round of applause breaks out and Mavis Adler shifts uncomfortably.

'Lot of nonsense,' she mutters. 'Anyone got any more whisky?'

'In a few minutes, Mavis will be participating in a Q and A session. But first, we'd like to welcome her on stage. Mavis?' Jana scans the ballroom, then spots her and beckons vigorously. 'Please put your hands together for one of the finest artists working in the UK today, Mavis Adler!'

The crowd parts as Mavis makes her way to the stage, stomps up the three steps, then stands surveying the room, her feet planted wide apart.

'Well, thank you for coming,' she says briskly. 'And I hope my pieces speak to you in some way. But if my art is about anything, it's about community. *Our* community.'

'Community,' echoes Jana reverentially. 'Of course, this is one of the central concepts of *Figures*, and underpins so much of your work. Mavis, could you expand on that idea for us a little?'

'Yes, I could,' says Mavis. 'Forget *Figures* for a moment. There's another story in this room tonight and I think you need to hear it. Is anyone here a friend of Terry Connolly?'

There's a surprised murmur, then laughter as people begin putting up their hands, all around the room.

'Who's Terry Connolly?' I hear the lady from Sotheby's saying to the Cork Street gallery guy, who starts googling on his phone.

'Terry means a lot to many of us here,' says Mavis emphatically. 'He means a lot to this community and we love him. Well, some of you may remember an event that happened on the beach, twenty years ago.' She pauses, until the entire ballroom is silent. 'There was an attempt to smear Terry, and it might have been successful, if it hadn't been for two children who told the police what they saw. Twenty years later, those children are here tonight. Finn, Sasha . . .' She gestures at us and slowly the faces begin to turn. 'As you know, Terry doesn't have it easy any more. I'm not sure he'd be able to thank you himself. So from all of us, from the friends of Terry in this room, thank you.'

She brings her hands together, but the ripple of applause has already begun. Keith is clapping, Simon is clapping, Herbert cheers hoarsely, and before long the whole ballroom is alive with stamping. I feel hands grasping mine and shaking them. A voice murmurs 'Well done!' in my ear and now, to my disbelief, we're being ushered up to the stage.

'This is *insane*,' Finn mutters in my ear.

'This isn't for us,' I say. 'This is for Terry.'

Tessa has come on to the little stage with us, and to my surprise, she steps to the front, pushes her hair off her face and surveys the audience.

'I don't much like speaking up,' she says in trembling tones. 'But sometimes you have to. By speaking up when they did, Finn and Sasha gave my dad twenty years of teaching surfing on Rilston Bay that he might have lost. For my dad, as some of you know, teaching surfing is life. Was life,' she amends, then draws breath. 'So they gave him his life.'

The applause rises to a roar, and I glance at Finn, feeling a bit overwhelmed. Mavis lifts her hands and gradually the crowd quietens.

'To celebrate this special moment,' she says dramatically, 'I would like to change the programme of events. I now ask Finn and Sasha to do me the great honour of unveiling my new work, *Titan*. In this new piece, I depict the vulnerability and beauty of humanity in all its rawness, all its power, all its nakedness.'

At the word *nakedness* I sense the crowd perk up with interest. Maybe Keith's right. Maybe it's a naked kissing couple!

Naked Young Lovers 2. That would bring in the tourists, all right.

Jana, looking a bit miffed at the change in arrangements, shows Finn and me where the rope is to unveil the artwork. We take hold of it together, then glance at Mavis.

'I am delighted to present my most ambitious, significant work to date,' she announces to the audience. 'I give you *Titan*.'

Together, Finn and I pull on the rope, and gradually the drapery over the massive structure falls to the ground, revealing . . .

Oh my *God*.

It's Herbert. It's a massive twelve-foot statue of Herbert, totally naked, made from some rough grey-white clay. Fully anatomical. *Fully*.

There's a muffled squeak from the audience, which sounds like Cassidy, and a couple of startled shouts, and now some laughter, and finally the clapping starts. Herbert is standing, looking totally composed, a mysterious little smile on his face, while Simon looks as if he might keel over in horror at any moment.

Sensing that our role is over, Finn and I make our way back down from the stage and are immediately surrounded by people, all asking questions. Meanwhile, Cassidy has elbowed her way over to us and is busily fielding all the enquiries like some sort of publicist.

'They're staying at the Rilston with us . . . Yes, they used to come here as children . . . Did you know Sasha is our resident wellness guru?'

'I thought they were a couple,' I hear Tessa telling someone else, over the hubbub. 'So I wrote them a message on the sand: "To the couple on the beach".'

'They *are* a couple!' Cassidy wheels round, overhearing. 'They're definitely a couple.' Her eyes twinkle. 'I've seen them at it.'

'Are you?' says Tessa, glancing at me uncertainly. 'I thought . . .'

'Aren't you?' Cassidy stares at us, her face gradually falling in dismay. 'Oh, you two! No! Don't do this to me, guys. *Aren't* you?'

The clamour of the room seems to die away as I look at Finn's warm face.

'We're not a couple,' I say softly to him. 'Friends, though.'

'Friends always.' He takes my hand and kisses my fingertips. 'Always.'

TWENTY-SIX

It's Finn who helps me carry all my stuff down to the station, after I've said my fond goodbyes to Simon, Herbert, Nikolai, and been hugged about twenty times by Cassidy.

The two of us stand on the platform, occasional spatters of rain hitting us on the head, and we don't say much. Occasionally one of us will send the other a wary little smile as though to say, *Are we still good?* And the other will return it. *Of course we are.*

'Never did get to the watercolour kit,' I say, after one of the silences becomes too unbearable. 'I was going to paint Rilston Bay. Become the next Mavis Adler.'

'Always save something for next time,' replies Finn. 'How many steps did you get through in the end?'

'Oh, at least twenty-five.' I smile ironically at him. 'Can't you tell? I'm transformed. I'm a whole new me!'

'I think you are,' he says seriously. 'You're transformed from the person I first met.'

I flash back to the way I was when I first encountered Finn.

Exhausted, defensive, binging on chocolate and wine. He's right: I am a different person now. More assertive. Stronger. Calmer. Fitter.

Then I remember the angry sociopath I thought I heard in the dunes and look up at the balanced, wise, kind guy in front of me.

'Same,' I say. 'You're a whole new you.'

'I'd better be,' says Finn with a wry smile. 'The old me is unemployable.'

The sound of the approaching train comes faintly through the air, and I feel such dread I'm almost giddy.

'So!' I muster every acting power I possess to sound cheerful. 'Train's on time.'

'It's pretty reliable.' He nods.

'Yes, it's a good service.'

We're into platitudes, because where else can we go?

'Finn . . .' I meet his eyes, and just for a moment his guard drops and I see it in his face, too. A kind of loss. And bewilderment that this is happening.

He couldn't love me – I'm convinced of this to my bones. He couldn't share his anguish, his loss, or anything of his heart. He closed himself off – and he's still closed off, because his heart is reserved for someone else.

So I closed myself off, too – because something I've learned, these last few weeks, is self-preservation. I couldn't let myself get hurt. Not now, not after everything that's happened. I've been hurt enough by life; I'm still mending.

'Finn . . . thank you.' I reach out to touch his fingertips, the safest level of connection. 'Thank you.'

'Sasha . . .' His eyes crinkle. 'Thank *you*. Without you, I never would have known the joy of noni juice.'

'Oh, you *didn't* try the noni juice!' I burst into shocked laughter. 'Please tell me you didn't.'

'I got Nikolai to bring me a glass yesterday. It is *vile*. It is *unspeakable*.' He shudders. 'Recommended by Sasha, huh?'

'Sorry!' I can't stop giggling. 'I should have warned you.'

The train is already pulling into the station. Thirty more seconds.

'Well, good luck. I'll be manifesting for you.' I pull a piece of paper out of my pocket and show him. '*Finn's wellness*, see?'

'Snap.' He produces one from his own jeans pocket and I see *Sasha's wellness* written on a sheet of Rilston notepaper.

The train doors are opening. We shove all my clobber on to the train and then I force myself to step on, too, leaving Finn on the platform. Ten more seconds.

'Bye.' Tears are gathering in my eyes as I turn to face him. 'Bye. It's been . . . Bye.'

'Bye.' He nods, then draws breath as though to add something. But the train doors are closing, and I feel panic. Wait. *Wait*. I had more to say.

But then, maybe I didn't.

I don't sit down. I stand at the door, my eyes fixed on Finn's face as he gazes back at me through the rain. I'm trying to memorize him, absorb every pixel of his image, internalize him. Until the train is round the bend and I'm staring at a bank of weeds.

For a while, I don't move. Then at last I make my way to a seat and sit, staring ahead. I feel kind of blank. Like a void.

I know this is good. New life. New start. I just have to wait for it to start *feeling* good.

After a minute or two my phone bleeps, and I feel an

almighty pang of hope as I pull it out of my pocket with scrabbling fingers. *Finn?*

No. Kirsten.

I'll need to wean myself off those pangs of hope. It's fine. I'll manage it.

I open the text from Kirsten and read her message.

Hi, was looking through old photos of Rilston Bay and found this. Is this Finn Birchall?!

I open the photo, my heart thumping, and find myself staring at Kirsten and me in matching pink gingham bikinis, which I'd forgotten about. I look about eight years old, which makes Kirsten eleven. We're holding spades and sitting in a sand hole and I'm making one of my trademark funny faces. Mum's sitting beside us in her swimsuit, which means Dad must have taken the photo. Her face is light and carefree as she smiles up at him. The Mum we had before we lost Dad. She never quite came back in the same way.

And behind us, several feet away, is a boy in red swimming trunks. He has dark hair and he's holding a fishing net and he's looking off into the middle distance. Even at the age of eleven, he has distinctive eyebrows, lowered in a frown. He shows no sign of having noticed me or Kirsten, and we're oblivious to him.

I can't help smiling, because he's so *totally* Finn, even then. But I also have a tightness in my throat as I survey the scene, because we all look so blithe. None of us knew what was coming our way, back then.

As the train gathers speed, I gaze and gaze at the image. At the holiday-happy faces. At the beach that I've come to love again so dearly. At this snapshot of everyone that I cherish in the world. Then, at last, I put it away.

Maybe I'll show Finn this photo one day, over drinks or something. Maybe I'll be detached enough to see it as a novelty. Maybe I'll have got my heart back from him.

Maybe.

TWENTY-SEVEN

Six months later

I'm not saying it's *easy*, running the marketing department. It's super-busy. It's complicated. Every day is a heart-thumping mix of strategy and fire-fighting and diplomacy. Oh, and emails. The emails haven't magically disappeared.

The difference is, now I have ownership. I have agency. I hadn't realized how stressful it was, sitting at that old desk of mine, seething and brooding and worrying, waiting to be told what was possible, what could happen, what couldn't happen.

Now, I don't wait. I make things happen.

I have slightly more respect for Asher than I did, since learning how many facets there are to this role: how many demands, how many problems. But also slightly less respect, because what the hell was he *thinking*? (From 'Asher's video diary' which I stumbled on a few weeks ago, he was just thinking, *I'm Asher, I'm cool, look at me.*)

I'm constantly unpicking problems that Asher made, which is a pain, but each time I feel fresh satisfaction, because I'm remaking the department how I want it. And hopefully how Lev wants it. It took me a long time to decide I wanted this role, and I had a few long, honest chats with Lev along the way. He's now admitted that he was so wary of conflict with Asher that he backed away from marketing completely while his brother was running it. No wonder we felt abandoned. But now things are different. Lev shows an interest. He asks me constantly, 'Are we spending enough? Do we have enough staff? You need to tell me.' And we get on really, *really* well. I've even been to his house and had dinner with him and his boyfriend.

I'm often tired, but *good* tired. Not drained. Not ground down. Not burned out. I sometimes glance out of the window at the convent opposite and ... let's say I'm quite relieved I'm here, not there. Sister Agnes knew what she was about. I belong in the workplace, as long as the work is healthy. And I'm being proactive to keep it that way. I'm even managing to switch off my emails in the evening.

OK, not *every* evening. But most evenings.

I'm on my way to see Lev right now, to give him some promotional coffee-cup samples. And as I travel up to his floor, I have a flashback to my stand-off with Ruby. My confrontation with Joanne. Bolting down the stairwell, banging my head . . . I can't believe any of it happened.

In just a few months, so much has changed. Ruby has gone. Joanne has gone. The whole set-up feels different. There are staff here now who've never even *heard* of the joyfulness programme. We've long since axed that. The aspirations mood board is still up on the staff portal, but it's become a place for people to pitch ideas for evenings out to the social secretary.

I reckon the more you label something 'joyful', the more you suck the joy out of it. Whereas the karaoke night we had last week truly *was* joyful.

Instead of the joyfulness programme, we now have new rules about emails out of office. We have boundaries. We have realistic expectations of staff. The other day, I noticed our new assistant, Josh, looking beleaguered when I asked him to do something quite small and I just *knew* he was feeling overwhelmed. At once I reassigned the task and scheduled a casual coffee meeting to talk about his workload, making sure to say how pleased we all were with his contribution and gently enquiring about what he found challenging. It turned out he was overthinking quite a lot and had completely misunderstood one hurried request thrown at him. No wonder he felt like the job was massive. After we'd ironed that out, we chatted about his hobbies, he told me about his passion for cycling and seemed a lot happier as he left.

I hope I'm watching out for my staff. I *hope* I am. And by watching out for them, I'm watching out for myself, too. I have energy. And optimism. My flat isn't immaculate, but it has a sense of order now and I have a new yucca, which is flourishing. It's amazing how much easier it is to look after a plant when you're looking after yourself.

As I emerge on to Lev's floor, his new assistant Shireen smiles at me and waves me straight in.

'OK,' Lev says, as soon as I enter, from his customary position, which is cross-legged on his coffee table. 'So I watched *Traingang*.'

Zoose is considering sponsoring a TV drama series about some characters who commute together, and last night I sent Lev the pilot episode to check out.

'Views?' I say cautiously, because I can tell something's brewing.

'None of it makes sense!' he erupts. 'The guy who suddenly got violent. Why? And the thing with the horse was just *stupid*. Now, if I were the screenwriter . . .'

I can see his eyes drift off in a way that I've come to recognize. Lev has a very fertile imagination and is constantly full of ideas for the strategic development of Zoose. Unfortunately he's also full of ideas about other things, like how newspapers have gone wrong, or what font the government should use in its official missives, or random bits of new code, which he sends to the team at 2 a.m. And now, how to rewrite a TV series.

I can see where Asher gets his randomness from now: it's a family trait. Only, Asher didn't have the genius of Lev. Lev is the creative engine of Zoose, and he really *is* a genius, but he needs managing if you're going to work closely with him. I've learned to rein him in and keep him on topic, whilst still keeping an ear out for the flashes of brilliance which keep us all employed.

'Lev, you're not a screenwriter,' I say patiently. 'You run a travel app.'

'I know,' he says almost regretfully, and I know that given half a chance he would now take the rest of the day off to go and write a pilot episode to his own liking.

'It gets better,' I say. 'And it's a great demographic for us.'

'Hmm.' Lev still looks moody. 'I just object to *crapness*.'

'Try that new crime thing on Sky,' I suggest. 'The one set in Amsterdam. I've seen a couple of episodes. It's good.'

I watch box sets now. I can enjoy them and even talk about them. Sometimes, for old times' sake, I get out *Legally Blonde*, but it's more to smile at and say, *Thanks for being there when I needed you.*

Now I put the sample coffee cups on Lev's desk and say, 'Look at these when you have a moment. But I'm afraid I've got to shoot off. You know today's—'

'Yes!' says Lev, coming out of his trance. 'Of course I know! Red-letter day.' He looks at his watch. 'In fact, what are you still doing here? You must go and catch your train! I'll see you there.'

'You're really coming?' I say incredulously.

'I've told you I'm coming!' says Lev, sounding a bit offended. 'I wouldn't miss this!' He pauses, then adds, 'Will Finn be there?'

My stomach gives a painful churn. It's been churning pretty much solidly ever since I woke up this morning and thought, *It's today*.

But my smile stays steady. I'm good at keeping a steady smile.

'Yes,' I say. 'Finn'll be there.'

I haven't seen Finn since that day I left Rilston Bay. We've talked a bit via text and email, and we've kept it friendly, but very much focused on arrangements for today. So I know that he's well and back at work. He's even sleeping eight hours a night, these days. But that's all I know.

He hasn't mentioned Olivia. And the trouble is, I'm not supposed to know about Olivia. So that's been a bit of a gap in our communications. Both of us have studiously avoided the whole area of love, sex, dating, any of it.

I've stalked him online a bit, because I'm only human. But he doesn't do social media, and Olivia has made her Instagram account private, and so there hasn't been a lot to see. I'm only guessing that behind Olivia's private Instagram gate there's been a joyful reunion. Because I *did* see a photo of Finn and Olivia on her sister's Instagram page, arm-in-arm, smiling for the camera at some garden party. (I instantly closed it down.) And Finn has said he's 'bringing someone' today. 'Bringing someone' were his exact words.

So maybe today's the day I get to meet her. It's fine. I can deal with it. Maybe I won't even find him attractive any more. So. All good.

As I head out of the office, I pause and look upwards. Even at 10 a.m., the sky is blue and hazy, promising a gorgeous summer's day. Perfect. I head into Pret and smile at the girl behind the counter.

'A cappuccino, please. That's all.'

I haven't had a halloumi wrap since I've been back. I can't even look at them any more. Instead I've invested in a slow cooker and have learned to enjoy chopping an onion again. I swap recipes with Mum and Kirsten and my Tupperware lunch box is my new best friend. Who would have thought? Not me. I do still pop into Pret for the odd coffee and snack; sometimes even lunch. But not every single meal.

Nor have I ever seen the Pret guy again, which is a relief. Probably for both of us.

As the coffee machine roars and hisses, I turn around and survey the street through the glass front of the shop. I watch the buses, the people, the pigeons even, all busily going about their day in the sunshine. And I feel a kind of wave of love for it all. OK, there's noise, fumes, bits of litter gusting along in the summer breeze. But even so, London doesn't look like a world of stress to me any more. It looks like a place of endeavour, of human connection, of chances.

I'm enjoying life, I think as I take my coffee. I'm enjoying the ride. And that's all you can ask.

TWENTY-EIGHT

I see the first surfboards at Paddington. Two guys in their twenties are carrying them along the concourse, chatting and grinning and clearly in high spirits. At first I'm not sure if they're with us – but then I overhear one say 'Terry' and I know.

I don't recognize either of them – but that's no surprise. I've been in touch with a lot of people, these last few weeks, mostly through my new Facebook page, and the account has mushroomed.

'Hi,' I say, approaching the taller guy, who stops in surprise. 'I'm Sasha Worth.'

'You're Sasha!' His face creases in delight and he shakes my hand warmly. 'Great to meet you! I'm Sam.'

'Dan,' chimes in his friend. 'We're so stoked. This is an awesome idea.'

'Awesome,' Sam echoes. 'We always talk about Terry. When I heard about the reunion I was like, dude, we *have* to do this.'

'I haven't been back to Rilston Bay for years,' chimes in Dan. 'This is like . . . awesome.'

On the platform is another guy with a surfboard, talking to a group of five girls – and as I approach, I realize I recognize one of them, even though it's been over twenty years. She has red hair in a bob. I remember when it was in a long pigtail down her back.

'Kate,' I say, hurrying up. 'Oh my God, Kate! We were in Terry's lessons together!'

'Sasha!' She pulls me in for a hug. 'When I got the email, I thought, is that the same Sasha?'

'Same Sasha!' I nod, beaming.

'It's so good to see you again! And you had a sister, Kirsten?'

'She'll be there. She's driving down with her kids.'

'*Kids!*' Kate pantomimes shock.

'I know, right?'

We're quite a group now, and I can hear someone saying, 'So what's the plan, exactly?'

'Hi!' I address everyone, feeling like a teacher. 'Thank you so much for coming. I'm Sasha, and I just heard someone asking what's the plan. Well, I'm about to send out an itinerary and various requests for help, so keep checking your phones. But the main thing to know is, when we get to Rilston, head for the beach.'

'How many people are coming, altogether?' asks Kate.

'Well.' I hesitate, because the truth is, I'm not sure. 'Let's see.'

By the time two more groups have joined us, we're commandeering a whole carriage of the train. And as more and more surfboards bob past the window, I start to wonder just how many people are on their way to Rilston Bay.

At Reading, more surfboards appear. People are standing in the corridors, high-fiving each other, calling to one another and drinking beers.

As we pass through Taunton, a harassed ticket inspector comes up to me and says, 'I hear you're in charge of the surfing group? In future, should you wish to stage such an event, please could you book it in?'

'Sorry,' I say apologetically. 'I honestly didn't know it would be so big.'

And it gets bigger. The train from Campion Sands is one big party, and as we arrive at Rilston Bay, a massive cheer goes through the shuttle train. Cassidy is waiting for us on the platform, holding up an umbrella – she volunteered to act as a steward – and as she sees me through the streaming crowd, her face lights up.

'Oh my *God*, Sasha!' she exclaims, coming forward to give me a hug. 'This is nuts! Everyone's come! The hotel's full, all the guest houses are full, the beach is full . . . All the tourists here for *Young Love* are like, what the hell?'

'It's quite something,' I say, watching the throng trooping down the hill towards the beach.

'It's brilliant. *You're* brilliant. The way you had the idea, the way you've got everyone together . . . It's amazing. Everyone's saying so. Simon, Herbert, Finn . . .'

'Finn?' The word pops out before I can stop it and I curse myself. I wasn't going to react to his name. I was going to be cool. But look at me, jumping like a rabbit.

'Yeah, he's already here, helping set up.' Cassidy nods. 'He's . . . Oh, there he is.' She points over my shoulder.

Shit. I'm not ready.

Yes I am. Come on, Sasha. Chin up.

I turn and feel my stomach tingle as I see him coming

towards us across the station platform. He's tanned, his hair is blowing in the wind and his shades are glinting in the sunshine.

So much for *Maybe I won't even find him attractive any more.*

'Hi, Sasha.' He hesitates, then bends to kiss me lightly on the cheek.

'Hi, Finn,' I manage.

'This is quite something!' He spreads his arms out, taking in the mêlée.

'I know. Thanks for helping.'

'Of course. Waves look good today, so that's one thing.'

'Thank *God,*' I say with feeling. 'Because I didn't have a back-up plan.'

There's silence, during which time Cassidy looks avidly from my face to Finn's, then back again.

'Well,' says Finn at last. 'There's a lot to do, and you'll want to check in. I'll be on the beach if you need me.'

He heads off and I silently breathe out. There. That was the hardest bit, and it's done.

'Now, I've put you in the Presidential Suite,' says Cassidy as I pick up my case.

'The Presidential Suite!'

'We've just renamed it, actually, Simon's idea. It was Room Forty-two, before. Of course, another time, you can have a Skyspace Beach Studio, only there's been some snag with planning, so don't hold your breath.' She rolls her eyes. 'They haven't even knocked down the old ones.'

'Oh dear,' I say, even though I'm quite glad the dear old lodges haven't been bulldozed quite yet.

'Oh, and I've bought you a new hairdryer,' she adds, giving me a nudge. 'Just for you. Got it at TK Maxx.'

'Cassidy.' I give her an impulsive hug. 'Thank you!'

'Superking bed,' she adds, waggling an eyebrow at me. 'Just saying . . .'

'Good to know. So . . . is Finn staying at the Rilston, too?' I can't help asking, even though I wasn't supposed to be showing an interest.

'Hasn't he told you?' Cassidy sounds astonished. 'Don't you two talk?'

'We do. But it hasn't come up.'

In all our correspondence recently, I haven't dared to ask Finn what he was doing about accommodation tonight. Just in case he said something like *My girlfriend Olivia has found an Airbnb for us. Oh, have I mentioned Olivia?*

So I just haven't gone there, and nor has he. We've just focused on practicalities.

'Well, yes, he is,' says Cassidy. 'Same floor as you.' She gazes at me, looking a bit crestfallen. 'Sure you don't want to be put in the same room?'

'No. Thanks.'

'We thought you two would get back together.' She shakes her head, looking doleful. 'We really did. You made such a great couple. I guess you're a not-couple again, now.'

'Yes,' I say tightly, then nod towards the beach. 'Well. We should get going.'

Cassidy sighs, but doesn't push it any further, and we begin walking down the hill together, like old friends.

'Oh, you'll like this,' she says chattily. 'We've got a couple staying with us, *Young Love* fans, wanted Mavis Adler to marry them on the beach. They went to an event and pestered her, and in the end she goes, "Sorry, I only do divorces." '

I laugh, grateful for the distraction from Finn-related thoughts.

'They were so gutted, poor loves,' Cassidy continues. 'So I

said, "Ask Gabrielle, I bet she'll do it." Well, she jumped at it! She's getting qualified online. It'll be the new big thing, you'll see, *Young Love* marriages on the beach.' She pauses and surveys the hordes of people gathering on the beach, in shorts, wetsuits and swimwear, clutching surfboards and high-fiving one another. 'Mind you, this looks like an even bigger thing.' She stares incredulously for a few more moments, then turns to give me a friendly push on the shoulder. 'Sasha Worth! What have you started?'

TWENTY-NINE

The next two hours are a blur of organization. Finn and I are totally engrossed, working as a team, instructing groups of willing helpers and turning the beach into a party arena. The council have been great. They put bollards up this morning, saving a massive stretch of the beach just for us. They wouldn't have done that for just anyone – but then, this isn't just anyone.

There's a stage for Terry, because everyone will want to see him. There's bunting everywhere. There's a sound system and some tents for shade and lots of water stations and a huge cocktail tent run by Feels of Rilston, which is a new addition to the town and claims to be a 'drinks and vibes' venue.

Chef Leslie is masterminding the food, Cassidy is bossing all the hired staff and Simon has already told me how mortified and devastated he is that we couldn't host the entire thing in the Rilston ballroom, which is out of action due to a recent flood.

'Simon,' I said, looking around the thronging beach. 'Are you kidding? This wouldn't *fit* in the Rilston ballroom.'

Because so many people have come. *So* many. Every time I look around, I'm blown away. When I first had the idea for today, I'm not sure what I expected – but it wasn't this. It wasn't these hundreds of people. There are former pupils of Terry here of all ages. From teenagers who maybe had a lesson a couple of years ago, through to the middle-aged and elderly, who learned with him forty years ago. All here, all eager to help, all thrilled that we tracked them down.

It took a while. We started with the names of all the pupils that I remembered, that Finn remembered, that Tessa remembered, that people around town remembered. Every time we got a new name, we pinged off an invitation and said, *Please spread the word, do you know anyone else, can you get the message out?*

And it got out. Far and wide. The beach is a happy, buzzing crowd of hundreds of people with one thing connecting them. No – one person.

It's not a surprise event *per se*. Tessa's been telling Terry about it for days, trying to prepare him. But it probably will still come as a surprise. To him.

'Sasha!' Mum's voice greets me and I wheel round, my heart lifting. There she is, with Kirsten, Chris and the children in their off-road double buggy, all in matching shortie wetsuits.

'Those dinky wetsuits!' I exclaim, after I've hugged everyone. 'They're *adorable*!'

'Couldn't resist.' Kirsten grins.

'Mum, are you going to surf?' I look at her wetsuit in astonishment. 'You never used to.'

'I'll give it a go!' she says cheerfully. 'Pam's here, she's going to mind the children. She doesn't want to surf, she wants to do wild swimming later. Says it's very good for—'

'The menopause,' Kirsten and I both chime in, and start laughing.

'He's here.' Finn's voice crackles in my earpiece and I start. It's on.

'Terry's here,' I say to Mum and Kirsten. 'I've got to go. See you later!'

'Good luck!' says Kirsten. 'And well *done*, Sasha.' Then she adds lightly, 'Is Finn here?'

'Yup.' I meet her eye – then look away. 'Yup, he is.'

Kirsten and I have had lots of long chats about Finn, so she's followed me through my rollercoaster of feelings. For about two months after I got back to London, I was convinced I'd done the right thing, ending things. Because how could I be with a man who was so heartbroken over another woman? If he couldn't even *tell* me about her, he was definitely not over her. And Kirsten was right, we were both still a bit fragile.

Then I woke up one morning, feeling like I'd made a terrible mistake. I should text him and say so! Ask him out on a date, even! We could be back together within the week! I hesitated for a few days, plucking up courage, getting my hair cut, painting my toenails.

Then I saw that picture of Finn and Olivia on Instagram, arm-in-arm, happy, radiant.

Then I went on eleven online dates in about a week. I even started a bit of a fling with a guy called Marc. It lasted until he told me his 'plans for the future' and it turned out they involved settling down with a girl 'a bit like me'. Not me, obviously, a girl a *bit* like me. I didn't have the heart to ask which bit.

There hasn't been anyone since him. But there's been work

and friends and cooking and my new yoga class and seeing my family more. There's been life.

Now I push my way through the crowd towards the stage, where Finn is standing, together with a tall, bearded guy I don't recognize.

'Sasha.' Finn's face crinkles in a warm smile that makes my heart tug. 'Meet my colleague, Dave. Demon surfer.'

'Welcome to Rilston Bay!' I say, feeling an instant, ridiculous flare of hope. 'I'm so glad you could come! So, Finn . . .' I try to sound casual. 'You said you were bringing someone. Did you mean Dave?'

'No,' says Finn, after a pause, and his eyes move away from mine evasively. 'I meant . . . someone else.'

Right. Got it.

'Right!' I say, bright and breezy. 'Got it! Someone else. Of course. Well, anyway, Dave, welcome!'

Finn is still avoiding my eye, and I feel a pang of grief because this only means one thing. Olivia. And I guess up until now I was wondering . . . hoping, even . . .

Anyway.

'Looking forward to it.' Dave slaps his board. 'I hear we're all having a lesson first.'

'If the teacher's up for it.' I grin, suddenly spotting Tessa and Sean escorting Terry towards the stage, like two celebrity minders. 'Terry! It's Sasha! Welcome! How are you?'

Terry is wearing board shorts and a bright-red T-shirt, his skin tanned and wrinkled on his skinny frame. His hair has been cropped short and his eyes are looking uncertainly around the crowd – adults and children in wetsuits and swimsuits, all holding boards, all beginning to turn towards the stage.

'That's Terry!' I hear a voice say.

'It's him!' chimes in another.

'Look, it's Terry!'

The message starts spreading through the throng and the faces turn and the surfers start to press forward.

'I think we should begin,' says Sean. 'Or Terry will be mobbed. He's pretty much Beyoncé right now. All right, Terry?' he adds encouragingly.

'Who are all these people?' Terry looks confused and a little fractious. 'Did they book?'

'That's your four o'clock class, mate,' says Sean. 'Big turn-out today. *Big* turnout,' he adds to me, looking impressed. 'They've hired every board in the town and Campion Sands and up the coast, most likely.' He pauses, running his eyes over the crowd. 'Can any of them surf?'

'Don't know.' I laugh. 'But they can all learn.'

'True.' He turns to Terry. 'You ready, squire? You've got an audience waiting for you. Wanting a lesson.'

For a moment Terry is silent as he surveys the waiting crowd, his eyes flickering in confusion. And I feel myself tense up, wondering if he's going to be overwhelmed, if this was a bad idea.

'Why are there so many people?' he says at last, in familiar, tetchy tones. 'It's twelve to a class, Sandra will tell you that. Twelve!'

'I know,' says Sean reassuringly. 'But this is like an extra class. We thought we'd squeeze in a few more.'

Terry nods, as though making sense of this, then frowns again. 'But how will they all *hear* me?'

'We thought of that,' says Finn, quickly fitting a microphone to Terry's collar. 'See? Testing, one-two, one-two,' he says into it, and his voice booms through the speakers on the beach. 'All yours, Terry.' He nods at the stage.

After a moment's hesitation, Terry walks up on to it. And

the cheering begins, a colossal roar of appreciation, up and down the beach. Everyone is clapping, whooping, stamping. Now the cheering turns to a chant: 'Ter-ry! Ter-ry!' and Terry gazes back, looking perplexed, a slender old man with spindly legs and white hair and the love of all these people on the beach.

'Well,' he says at last, as the noise dies away. '*Well.*' He pauses, and there's a breathless hush in the crowd. 'There are too many of you, for a start.' There's a ripple of laughter, and Terry looks still more confused. 'Have they surfed before?' he asks Sean, who nods.

'They've surfed before.'

'Right,' says Terry, sounding more sure of himself. 'Well, in that case . . .' He steps forward, looking at the faces, the boards, the sea, as though sinking back into a world he'd lost. 'In that case, here's what I need to tell you,' he says, his voice gaining strength. 'You won't like it. But you'd better listen.'

There's silence on the beach. I can see Cassidy in a neon-pink bikini top and board shorts, Simon in a blue shortie wetsuit, surprisingly muscled, and Herbert looking like a black daddy-long-legs . . . I can see Mum . . . Kirsten . . . Gabrielle, waving at me . . . and, oh my God, there's Lev, in a sleek steel-grey wetsuit. When did *he* get here? I glance at Finn, and he winks back. Then we both turn to gaze at Terry, along with everyone else.

'You *think* you can surf,' Terry continues at last. 'Oh, you all want to rush ahead, catch the hugest waves, show off to your friends . . . But that's not what it's about, don't you see?' He looks around the avid faces. 'It's not about showing off. It's about you and the sea. You and the ride. The ride is *it.*'

'What's the ride?' chimes in Sean, leaning into Terry's microphone, his eyes twinkling at the audience.

'The ride is *it*!'

The mammoth shout from the crowd echoes round the beach as if we're at a rock festival, and I feel shivers. I turn to Terry, wanting to see if he has any appreciation of the reach he has, the power he has, the effect he's had on so many people. He blinks, his vague gaze travelling over the eager faces, and I hope above anything that the sight is sinking in. That it will warm him and cheer him for the rest of his life.

'You've been listening!' he says at last, and there's a huge laugh. 'Well. This is encouraging. I might make surfers of you yet. The ride is *it*.' He nods. 'So. Remember that. And now, let's begin our warm-ups.'

It's quite a sight. Several hundred people, all lined up on the beach, all following Terry's warm-up exercises. New people keep joining in at the edges, holidaymakers and passers-by and children holding lollies, until it seems that the whole endless stretch of sand is one big class, with Terry calling out instructions from the stage.

As everyone starts practising getting up on their boards, Terry looks tetchy again.

'I can't correct them all,' he says to Sean. 'I can't get round them all.'

'Leave it to me, mate,' Sean assures him. 'I'll have a word with a few of them.'

And he roams around the crowd, greeting people and high-fiving and constantly glancing back up at Terry with a thumbs-up.

Soon after that, it becomes apparent that Terry is flagging in energy, and Sean leaps back on to the stage, taking a hand-held microphone from Finn.

'Surfers,' he greets the crowd. 'I'm Sean Knowles, the new owner of the Surf Shack, trying to follow in the footsteps of the giant, Terry Connolly!' Again the cheers ring out over the beach, and I exchange smiles with Finn.

I'm finally breathing out, I realize. I'm relaxing. My plan worked. Terry has given one last, epic surf lesson.

'There are lots of thank-yous to give,' says Sean. 'And I'm sure there'll be a speech or two later on. But for now, one very special person needs special thanks, for pulling this all together. Sasha Worth, get on stage!'

The roar from the beach almost deafens me as I step on to the stage, and I feel my eyes welling. I'll never forget this moment, looking out to the blue horizon, with a sea of joyous people in front of me. The love on this beach feels as real as the salt in the air.

'I'm so thrilled you could all be here,' I say into the microphone. 'Thank you all for coming. This is so much bigger than I ever thought it would be, and that's down to Terry. As Sean says, there'll be speeches later, but now I just want to thank one other person, who did a huge amount of work putting this on.' I glance at him. 'Finn Birchall.'

Finn makes a show of reluctance, then comes on to stage, grinning, and nods at the deafening applause which greets him. 'I have only one thing to say,' he deadpans into the microphone. 'Seize that wave.' Another roar goes up, and Finn laughs. 'Over to Terry.'

We make way for Terry, and he stands silently for a moment as the hubbub dies to a respectful hush. His eyes look momentarily bewildered as he surveys the crowd – then snap into focus.

'Well, what are you all still doing here?' he says sharply, his familiar, hoarse voice travelling across the sands. 'You won't catch a wave by standing on the beach! Enough talk.' He points to the sea. 'Go get it.'

THIRTY

There are so many surfers that the sea soon becomes ridiculously crowded. But after a while, only the hardcore surfers are still out there and the others are paddling or sitting on the beach, drinking beers, catching up.

I surf for a bit, then come in, get changed into shorts and check up on the food. There's a smell of charcoal in the air and the barbecues are already churning out burgers. There are picnic rugs everywhere on the sand and someone's playing guitar. Keith Hardy is doing some kind of Mr Poppit set with his puppet to an audience of children, and he gives me a cheery wave, which I return while walking firmly straight past.

I collect a 'Rilston' cocktail from the drinks tent, reassuring Nikolai that I don't need an extra kale shot in it, then take it on to the beach and sip it, watching Ben dig blissfully in the sand.

'We need to come here *every* year,' I say to Kirsten.

'Oh, I'm ahead of you,' she says. 'Already booked the

cottage for next summer. And Pam wants to bring her meno-pause lot. Dunk them in the sea, sort out their hot flushes.' I catch Kirsten's eye and we both start giggling helplessly. 'So,' she adds as we come to a pause. 'Finn. What's that situation?'

'Bringing his girlfriend.'

'Huh.' She removes a tangled piece of seaweed from Ben's fingers. 'Well. You're not short of hot surfing types here.' She surveys the beach, which, to be fair, is full of athletic guys. 'Are you *sure* this wasn't just you organizing yourself a speed-dating event?'

'Busted.' I grin, and she nods.

'Nicely done. No one would suspect.'

She has a point. There are loads of eligible men here, all strapping and cheerful and charming. But I can't seem to focus on any of them. I start conversations with a few guys about random topics . . . but I'm constantly aware of Finn's presence. He doesn't seem to be with his girlfriend, but maybe she's here and I just can't spot her, or maybe she's at the hotel changing into her super-hot bikini, or maybe she hasn't arrived yet. Anyway. No big deal.

The afternoon slowly drifts into evening, and the party settles into a relaxed vibe. I chat to as many people as I can, including Gabrielle and Mavis and Lev, who says every five minutes that he has to leave, then shakes some-one else's hand. Terry says a final goodbye at the microphone and the responding cheer sounds as though it's reaching right round town. A few speeches are made and some songs are sung. Now, as the sun drops lower in the sky, there are fires appearing here and there on the beach. Three guitars are playing and a few people are dancing.

At last, the children start getting cranky, and Kirsten loads up the double buggy.

'See you tomorrow, OK?' She kisses me. 'Wild swimming at dawn? Kale for breakfast? Meditating?'

'All three.'

'*Excellent*.' She grins.

'I'll come, too,' says Mum to Kirsten. 'Help you put them to bed. Well done, Sasha. It's been a wonderful day. Dad would have been so proud.' She gives one of her little wistful smiles. 'I was just thinking of that pub he loved, the White Hart. Do you think it still exists?'

'It does,' I say. 'Let's go there tomorrow and toast Dad.'

'Yes,' says Kirsten softly. 'Nice idea.'

They move off, and I'm just wondering whether Lev's still here when I hear a voice saying, '. . . she was held up by some train situation. Finn's gone to collect her from the station.'

Something inside me freezes. I look round to see who spoke – and it's Finn's colleague, Dave.

Finn's gone to collect her from the station.

A slow pounding begins in my chest. *Olivia.* She was held up, but now she's here. Finn's gone to get her, and soon he'll be back on the beach with her. Maybe walking around, arm-in-arm, maybe dancing, maybe sitting in the shallows, with their legs tangled up.

And suddenly I know that I can't be here to see that. I just can't. She'll be too glorious, and they'll be too radiantly happy and my heart won't survive.

I thought my heart would survive, but hearts put on brave faces, it turns out. And now I know, without any doubt, that I need to leave.

'So!' I say brightly, randomly, to anyone who will listen. 'I need to go, it's been fab . . .'

'Go?' says Cassidy, overhearing. 'Party's just starting! Have a noni juice, get in the mood!' She swigs her cocktail, then puts her head on one side and surveys me. Drunkenly, I realize. 'Oh, Sasha.' She plonks a hand on one of my shoulders. 'Lovely Sash. Gorgeous, lovely Sash.'

'Yes?' I can't help smiling.

'Tell me. Tell your Auntie Cassidy.' She leans closer. 'Why aren't you together with Finny-Finn-Finn? No one can understand it, *no one*. Me, Herbert, Mavis, the girls in the tea shop . . .'

'Have you been talking about it?' I begin, shocked – then remember who I'm addressing. 'Of course you have. Look . . .' I exhale, trying to keep hold of my steady smile. 'I'm fairly sure Finn's with someone else. So.'

'Someone else?' echoes Cassidy, looking affronted. 'Are you kidding me? *Someone else?*'

'Well . . . isn't he?' I say uncertainly. 'Didn't he book his room for himself and someone called Olivia?'

'*Olivia?*' she retorts, as though Olivia is the most repulsive name she's ever heard of. 'O-liv-ia? Nope. Never heard of her.'

'But he's picking her up from the station. Someone,' I correct myself. 'He's picking up someone from the station. A "her".'

'A "her".' Cassidy narrows her eyes as though making calculations. 'A "her". OK, we need intel. I'm asking Herbert. He'll know.'

'*Herbert?*' I echo dubiously, but Cassidy is already hauling me across the sand to where Herbert is sitting in a deck chair, down by the waves, smoking a cigar.

'Herbert!' she says breathlessly as we arrive. 'Who's Finn picking up at the station? And it better not be someone called O-liv-ia.'

Herbert blows out a cloud of smoke and seems to consider this. 'He booked a room for a lady,' he declares at last. 'Separate room. She's called Margaret Langdale.'

'Margaret Langdale?' Cassidy stares at him. 'Room Sixteen, non-smoker? That was booked by *Finn*? You need to tell me these things, Herbert!' She swings round. 'Well, there we are. Separate rooms. That's who he's gone to get. His separate-rooms friend, Margaret Langdale.'

I can't quite reply. I can't even move. My heart is squeezing with the worst emotion in the world, hope. It *kills* you. For six months I've been telling myself that Finn is with Olivia, and I have to make peace with it. Six months. You'd think the 'making peace with it' would have stuck.

But it's instantly fallen away, as if there was never any glue. And now, instead, hope is jumping around me, saying, *Maybe, just maybe . . .*

'He's here,' says Cassidy in my ear, making me jump. 'Behind you. Just arrived back. On his own.'

Slowly, feeling unreal, I turn around. And there he is, walking up to me, a tall figure in his sea-green T-shirt, a streak of sand on one leg, his eyes glowing in the light of a nearby fire.

The nearer he gets, the more I want him. I want him so badly, I can't think about anything else. My mind is consumed. My body is consumed. I've been avoiding Finn all afternoon for fear of *exactly* this kind of one-on-one encounter. Instinctively I back away, but after two steps I've reached the sea. A wave washes my ankle and I find myself taking a step back towards him.

'Hi.' My voice catches in my throat and I try again. 'Hi.'

'Hi.' He meets my gaze, steady and relaxed. 'We haven't really talked. How are you?'

'Really well.' I nod. 'You?'

'Really well, too.' He smiles. 'Job's good. Haven't shouted at anyone recently, so that's a bonus.'

'Have you slammed down a coffee cup, causing spillage and damage to papers?' I can't help teasing him, even though I'd planned to be formal and reserved today.

'No spillage, nor damage to papers.' His eyes crinkle. 'Losing my touch. Whereas *you*, I hear from Lev, are running the show.'

'Hardly.' I roll my eyes, although it's quite a thrill to hear that.

'He likes you.' Finn raises his eyebrows. 'A lot.'

'Well, I like him.' I pause, watching a foamy wave run on to the beach and away again. 'How's . . . therapy going?'

'Good, thanks. I still go, we still talk about stuff.' Finn frowns, rubbing the back of his neck, as though pondering something, then looks directly at me. 'We've talked about you.'

'*Me?*' I'm staggered.

'Yes. And I wanted to say, Sasha, I understand now.' He gazes at me earnestly. 'You were smart. You were *smart* to say it wasn't the right time. We were both in weird places. I wasn't ready for . . .' He shakes his head. 'I guess neither of us was. Burnout. It's a bitch.'

The sounds of chatter and music and seagulls all fade away from my head as I gaze back at Finn, trying to process what he's just said.

'Wait,' I manage at last. 'Did you think that I ended things just because we were both burned out?'

'Yes.' Finn seems nonplussed, his eyes scanning my face as though he's missing something. 'Of course. That was the reason. What else?'

'Because of Olivia!' I explode. 'Olivia! O-liv-ia!'

'*Olivia?*' Now it's Finn's turn to look staggered. 'But that was ages ago. We'd finished before I even met you!'

'I know, but you didn't *tell* me about her! You didn't mention her. I thought you were heartbroken! You didn't admit you were getting over a breakup, you said it was all about work.'

'It *was* all about work.' Finn stares at me. 'I was overworked. I told you that. Why would you think it wasn't?'

'Because you would never open up about it!' All my feelings are pouring out. 'I told you all about Zoose. You didn't share anything! I thought you must be using work as a smokescreen.'

'Right,' says Finn, after a long pause. 'Right. Right. I see. Yes.'

He lapses into silence. Is that all he's giving me?

'Yes, *what*?' I prompt him. 'Is there any more to this?'

For an agonizing few moments there's silence. Finn's brow is rumpled in his familiar brooding frown and I'm holding my breath. I'm trying to be patient but feeling my tension mount, because if he can't open up, even now . . .

'OK.' Finn breathes out and I start. 'Here goes. The reason I didn't tell you more about my work issues is that I couldn't. There was . . . a situation.' His face becomes bleak. 'A close colleague of mine became ill. A good friend. She didn't want anyone to know while she was getting treatment, so I said I'd help her out. I was covering a lot for her. Doing a lot of work at night. Too much. Existing on coffee, basically. And no one else knew.' His face twists at the memory. 'It was a suboptimal plan, for me to take everything on. As it turned out.'

'Is she . . .?' I begin the question hesitantly.

'Fine.' He nods. 'Thanks. The treatment was successful. And eventually, when I went back to work, the whole thing

379

came out. My friend went public. She said it was a relief, actually. But I guess when I was down here I was still trying to keep it all under wraps.' He gives a short laugh. 'I was so bloody stupid. Who were you going to tell?'

My head is spinning. He was helping a friend. He was keeping her secret. He was genuinely overworked. It *wasn't* the breakup. I'm seeing everything differently.

'Finn, I'm sorry,' I say tentatively. 'That must have been . . .'

'It was tough for everyone.' 'But it's over. It's all good.'

He gives me a cautious smile, and I feel as if he expects me to smile back. As if every question I had has been answered. But they haven't. And if I've learned anything during the last six months, it's don't let the little things fester. Not at work. Not in love. Not in life.

'So, who did you meet at the station just now?' I try to sound light. 'You told me you were bringing someone, and you looked weird, as if you were trying to hide something. Also, I've seen you with Olivia on Instagram, arm-in-arm at a garden party,' I add, abandoning any attempt to be cool.

Let's just chuck all of it out there. Every worry, every paranoia, every admission that I've been stalking him.

'I saw Olivia at a friend's thing,' says Finn, looking perplexed. 'We're trying to be friendly. If someone took a photo, I don't remember.'

'Right,' I say, feeling myself relax a bit. 'OK. And who did you just meet at the station?'

A flush comes to Finn's face.

'Actually . . .' he says, looking embarrassed. 'Actually, that's my mum. She was delayed, otherwise she would have been here for the surfing. I thought you might like to meet her. But then I thought, "That's a dumb idea."'

His mum. His *mum*?

I almost want to laugh at how wrong I was. How I've conjured up problems that weren't there. How I've imagined the wrong story, all the way along.

Maybe, just maybe, there's a different story? A story which begins here? Finn's eyes are fixed on mine and I feel the tingles begin inside me, the delicious buzz I remember, the ache.

'Are you with anyone else?' I say, needing to be sure, one hundred per cent sure, and he shakes his head.

'You?'

'No.'

'I'm not burned out any more,' says Finn, as though he needs to be sure, too. 'Are you?'

'No. I feel good. Healthy. All fine.'

There's a silent beat, and I feel the tension building in me as I consider what we're both saying. Where we might be heading.

'I've been thinking about you this whole time,' Finn says, his voice grave. 'This *whole* time.'

'Me too.' I swallow hard. 'I never stopped. Every day. Every night.'

Slowly Finn reaches into his back pocket and pulls out a crumpled, worn piece of paper, on which is written a single word. *Sasha.*

'I didn't just want your wellness,' he says, his face as frank as I've ever seen it. 'I wanted you. *You*. In my life. With me. So I wrote this and I put it in my pocket and . . . I hoped.'

He hands me the paper and I gaze at it, my eyes hot. Then, wordlessly, I reach into my own pocket and drag out the tattered piece of paper I've been carrying around for six months. It just reads *Finn*. As I give it to him, I see the spark of surprise, a new hope dawning on his face. Have we been going through the exact same emotions, all this time? Manifesting each other, miles apart?

Oh my God. Did it *work*?

'I hoped, too. Even when I thought I mustn't hope, because it was impossible . . . I still hoped. It was agony.'

'Hope's a bitch,' says Finn, and I make a strange attempt at a laugh.

'I thought burnout was a bitch.'

'Burnout's a picnic compared to hope. Unless your hopes come true.' He takes a step forward, his face questioning. 'Doesn't happen very often.'

His hair is ruffling in the sea breeze, his dark eyes are fixed on mine, and I'm feeling a magnetic pull towards him. I'm feeling the rest of my life stream away, unimportant, irrelevant. All that matters right now is this man and me and what we can make with each other.

'We need to talk,' says Finn, after what seems like an endless pause. 'We need to go somewhere private, Sasha. We need to talk properly . . .'

I glance automatically along the beach – then double-take. Wait – *what*?

This can't be real. But . . . it is.

'Finn, look,' I gulp. 'We don't need to go anywhere. Look.'

Finn follows my gaze and blinks in shock. While we've been standing here by the waves, the beach has emptied around us. It was full of people and activity and noise, but now there's almost no one left. The sand stretches both ways, pristine and clear. What's happened? Where are all the *people*?

As I peer around in bewilderment, I see Cassidy talking quietly to a remaining group of surfers. They listen for a moment, then nod and move off. What did she say to them? Meanwhile, Herbert is addressing a group of picnickers, who glance at us, then start to gather their things up. And Simon is doing the same on the other side, shepherding a group of children away.

'This area is now reserved.' The breeze carries his voice towards us. 'Private event happening, please move along.'

Nikolai is talking to another group, I see, with many earnest gesticulations. As he finishes, they get to their feet and troop away, some looking back at us, some smiling. I look around for Cassidy, then spot her, a good way down the shoreline. She waves merrily, blowing me a kiss and plonking a bollard down firmly.

It's like a kind of magic. It's a vanishing act. Gradually, discreetly, everyone has disappeared. It's the height of summer, the height of the season, the busiest time for Rilston. But right now, it's just Finn and me on an empty beach again. Like we always were.

The waves are washing in, and the summer evening sun is glittering on the water, and the man I love is standing in front of me. Sometimes you have to take your moments. See them for the treasure they are.

'I want to make this work,' says Finn at last, his face grave.

'I want to make it work, too.' I swallow. 'I really do.'

'OK.' He nods, and his eyes crinkle in the way that makes my heart flip. 'Well, then . . .'

He glances at the sea and suddenly I know what he's going to say. Because I know him. It was never casual between us. Even when we were fighting; even when we refused to share the beach. It was always intimate. As though we already sensed what we might become.

'Well, then,' he resumes. 'Could we walk along the waves while I tell you why I fell in love with you in the first place?'

I take a moment. I take a breath. *Enjoy the ride.*

Then I look at Finn and I know my face is shining, because I can feel the sunlight in me.

'Yes,' I say. 'Please.'

Finn puts out an arm and I take it and we begin to move, our feet splashing in the water, his voice deep, sincere, already mesmerizing me. The waves keep washing, the gulls keep crying and we keep walking.

ACKNOWLEDGEMENTS

Almighty thanks to the team of heroes who helped me with this book in so many ways. Frankie Gray, Whitney Frick, Araminta Whitley, Kim Witherspoon, Marina de Pass . . . I am unendingly grateful. And most of all to my valiant team-mate and husband, Henry Wickham.

Sophie Kinsella is an internationally bestselling writer. She is the author of many number one bestsellers, including the hugely popular Shopaholic series. She has also written seven bestselling novels as Madeleine Wickham and several books for children. She lives in the UK with her husband and family.

Visit her website at www.sophiekinsella.co.uk and find her on Facebook at www.facebook.com/SophieKinsellaOfficial. You can also follow her on X @KinsellaSophie and Instagram @sophiekinsellawriter.

The Party Crasher

**'This family may be broken. It may be shattered.
But it's my broken, shattered family.'**

Effie's still not over her parents splitting up a year ago and
her dad and his awful new girlfriend are posting PDA photos
everywhere. Now they're selling the family home and
holding a 'house-cooling' party, but Effie hasn't been invited.

Then she remembers her precious Russian dolls, safely
tucked away up a chimney, and has no choice but to go back
for them. She'll just creep in, grab the dolls and leave.
No one will know she was ever there.

But as she secretly clambers around dusty attics, hides
under tables and tries (and fails) to avoid bumping into
her ex-boyfriend, she discovers unexpected truths about
her family – and even about herself…

Out now in paperback, ebook and audio

My (not so) Perfect Life

'As long as I can remember, I've wanted out of Somerset. I've wanted London. I never had boy bands on my bedroom wall, I had the Tube map.'

Katie Brenner has the perfect life: a ~~tiny~~ flat in London, a glamorous ~~admin~~ job, and a super-cool ~~staged~~ Instagram feed.

Fake it till you make it, right?

Then her London life comes crashing down when her boss, Demeter, sacks her and she has to move home to help her dad with his new glamping business.

So when Demeter and her family book in for a holiday, Katie sees her chance to get revenge on the woman who ruined her dreams. But does Demeter – the woman who has everything – actually have such an idyllic life herself? Maybe they have more in common than it seems.

And what's wrong with not-so-perfect, anyway?

Out now in paperback, ebook and audio

Love Your Life

'Love is the ineffable, mysterious connection that happens between two humans when they connect, and they feel it . . . and they just know.'

Ava is sick of online dating. She's always trusted her own instincts over an algorithm, anyway, and she wants a break from it all. So she signs up to a semi-silent, anonymous writing retreat in glorious Italy.

Then she meets a handsome stranger . . . All she knows is that he's funny, he's kind and – she soon learns – he's great in bed. He's equally smitten, and they pledge their love without even knowing each other's real names.

But when they return home, reality hits. They're both driven mad by each other's weird quirks and, as disaster follows disaster, it seems that while they love each other, they just can't love each other's lives.

Can they overcome their differences to find one life, together?

Out now in paperback, ebook and audio

WIN A JET2HOLIDAY
PLUS £200 OF BOOKS!

Jet2holidays
Package holidays you can trust

We've teamed up with our friends at Jet2holidays to give you the chance to win your dream holiday to a choice of six amazing destinations! Plus, you could also win £200 worth of books to enjoy on your holiday!

You'll get the full Jet2holidays package, for up to two adults and two children* with VIP service from start to finish. The prize will include return Jet2.com flights from one of twelve UK airports, 22kg baggage per person, overseas transfers, and a choice of accommodation:

- Iberostar Creta Panorama and Mare, Crete
- Evenia Zoraida Garden, Costa de Almeria
- La Blanche Island, Bodrum
- Cerro Mar Atlantic Apartments, the Algarve
- Fuerteventura Princess, Fuerteventura
- DoubleTree by Hilton Malta, Malta

To be in with a chance of winning enter now at:

www.jet2holidays.com/penguin

Closing date 31/07/2024